PENGUIN BOOKS

THE ACCIDENT

Dexter Masters was editor (with the physicist Katharine Way) of *One World or None: A Report to the Public,* written by a number of the scientists most intimately involved with the early atomic project—Einstein, Szilard, Oppenheimer, Bethe, Wigner, and Urey among them. Before that he was a staff member of M.I.T's Radiation Laboratory. He was one of the founders of the nonprofit Consumers Union, first editor of its magazine (*Consumer Reports*), and for some years its director. Born and brought up in Springfield, Illinois, he graduated from Choate and the University of Chicago. He has been married twice: to Christina Malman, an artist for *The New Yorker;* and, after her death, to Joan Brady, then dancing with the New York City Ballet. He lives in England with her and their son, Alexander, a student at King's College London.

THE
ACCIDENT

Dexter Masters

PENGUIN BOOKS

PENGUIN BOOKS

Viking Penguin Inc., 40 West 23rd Street, New York, New York 10010, U.S.A.
Penguin Books Ltd, Harmondsworth, Middlesex, England
Penguin Books Australia Ltd, Ringwood, Victoria, Australia
Penguin Books Canada Limited, 2801 John Street, Markham, Ontario, Canada L3R 1B4
Penguin Books (N.Z.) Ltd, 182–190 Wairau Road, Auckland 10, New Zealand

First published by Alfred A. Knopf, Inc., 1955
Published with a Foreword by Milton Mayer by Alfred A. Knopf, Inc., 1965
This edition with a new Foreword and revisions by the Author first published
in Penguin Books 1985

Published simultaneously in Canada

LIBRARY OF CONGRESS CATALOGING IN PUBLICATION DATA
Masters, Dexter.
The accident.
Reprint. Originally published: New York: Knopf, 1955.
I. Title.
PS3525.A8298A64   1985   813'.54   85-3482
ISBN 0 14 00.7776 6

Grateful acknowledgment is made to Holt, Rinehart and Winston, Inc., for
permission to reprint the poem "Fire and Ice," from *New Hampshire,* by Robert Frost.
Copyright 1923 by Henry Holt and Company, Inc. Copyright 1951 by Robert Frost.

A portion of Chapter 6, Part 2, appeared originally in *The New Yorker* in different form.

Printed in the United States of America by
R. R. Donnelley & Sons Company, Harrisonburg, Virginia
Set in Garamond

To the memory of

LOUIS SLOTIN

*and an unknown number of others**

*Earlier editions of *The Accident* were dedicated "To Louis Slotin and more than one hundred thousand others." One hundred thousand was as close as anyone could come in those days to an approximation of the dead of Hiroshima and Nagasaki. Since then, estimates of deaths from the bombings themselves have had to be revised steadily upwards; many people have died and continue to die in Japan from delayed effects of the bombings; and many in other parts of the world have died from effects of the drift of radiation in bomb tests. About all anyone can say for certain is that the number of atomic casualties to date is probably in excess of a quarter of a million, will never be known precisely, and continues to grow.

FOREWORD

Early in 1955, just before *The Accident* first appeared in print, a producer in Los Angeles optioned movie rights to the book. He hadn't made a movie for several years (*The Accident* was to be his comeback), and he didn't have enough money on his own to make the film he had in mind. But this was David O. Selznick, who had made *Gone With the Wind, The Third Man,* and a number of other successful films, and he had no doubts that he would raise what he needed.

He employed me to write the screenplay, and we worked on it together for about three months. Then one day Selznick told me the project was off. There was nothing unusual in that; movie projects are dropped all the time. What was unusual was the explanation.

"They won't give me an export license," he told me. "I can't raise the money without an export license."

The explanation didn't mean anything special to me at the time. But not long after that I wrote a play of *The Accident*. An acting school in New York tried a scene from it as a class exercise, and I went to watch. There I heard an actor refer to my novel as "banned."

"What do you mean?" I asked him. "Who banned it?"

"The State Department wouldn't give Selznick an export license. Everyone in Hollywood knew what that meant," he said. "The government banned it."

In the thirty years since—and indeed in all the forty years since the bombs were dropped—not many novels about the bomb have been published; it is almost as though novelists have largely banned such work at the source. There have been nonfiction works by the dozens, some of them (leading off with John Hersey's notable *Hiroshima*) as compelling as any novel. But not many novels, even as the bomb has come to hang more and more heavily over all of us.

I wondered about this without resolving my wonderings until a first-rate novelist, E.L. Doctorow, provided an explanation in the form of a Commencement Address delivered at Sarah Lawrence College on July 4th, 1983. "What is unsettling about the writing of fiction now," he told the students, "is that the story of any individual may not be able to sustain an implication for the collective fate. If that is so, it is a serious setback to people in my trade. There is a loss of consequence, and the very assumption that makes fiction possible, the moral immensity of the single soul, is under derisive question because of the Bomb."

Doctorow's theory is impressive. Still, as Louis Saxl says in my novel, questions are the important things, more important than answers; and novelists have contrived to work at their trade in the face of other large questions. Does the bomb silence novelists more than the Nazi Holocaust, one of the very few other destroyers of assumptions on a comparable scale? One possible answer is that in fact it does. It seems possible that writers in general have become so preoccupied with bomb answers—what answers are there with that other Holocaust?—that they have given up on bomb questions.

An important part of *The Accident* is about the beginnings of the work out of which the bomb came. For that reason, since it is easier to understand something when you watch it grow than when you look at it fully formed, I think my book probably served to some extent an all-around usefulness when it first appeared, which may explain why it has been published over the years in a dozen foreign editions (in languages spoken on both sides of the Iron Curtain). But that cannot explain this new edition, coming out thirty years after the first edition and forty years after the destruction of Hiroshima and Nagasaki.

I think *The Accident* is being brought out now for a new audience because the individual whose story it tells not only sustains but enlarges on an implication for the collective fate. More importantly than it is a novel about the work that brought the bomb to birth, *The Accident* is a novel about a single soul in its confrontation with the bomb. In the years during which it was written—1948–1954, the same years in which McCarthyism and the Cold War were breaking out and the novel's substance proved unsettling enough to bring down a government ban—this early tale of the atomic age did seem almost incidental to the collective fate; too many events were questioning too derisively the moral immensity of single souls.

But now, when our accidents have come to suggest the quality of design, the answers we seek (if there are to be any) depend more than ever on our questions, and the questions seem to me more than ever just such questions as Louis Saxl asked while pondering what he and his fellow scientists had done at Los Alamos:

"If I am not for myself, who will be? But if I am for myself alone, what do I amount to?"

Those are the words of Hillel, a Babylonian who wrote at about the time of the birth of Christ, and the way they ring as they strike on a single human soul carries, these two thousand years later, the profoundest implications for the collective fate. The first question forces itself on us more than ever in the times we have come to. And the second leads us probably to the only answer left us if we are to find our way out.

Furthermore, though it was doubtless phrased differently in whatever memo the State Department issued in banning *The Accident,* this is at heart the question that caused the ban—a question as dangerous now as it was two thousand years ago, and far more urgent.

As Milton Mayer wrote in his foreword to the last edition of *The Accident,* "No man who makes or throws the bomb we want made or thrown is more of a killer than the rest of us, or more of a penitent. We are all Saxls." And the simple fact is that all of us now confront his fate. It may be that we can avoid his fate, but the fate insists on being confronted.

Dexter Masters
Totnes, Devon, England

NOTE

In the years since I started to write *The Accident* I have received support from many people, including the book's first publisher, Alfred Knopf, and first editor, Harold Strauss, both now dead. They made it possible for me to continue work on the book at a time when I had barely begun it, and I want to note my special indebtedness to them. In the same spirit I want to thank Al Hart and Richard Magat for their drive to restore the book to print.

Beyond this, I should like to express my deepest gratitude to three friends of particular importance to me and to this work: Philip Morrison, Christina Malman, and— over twenty-five years, in ways beyond any counting (and in private celebration)—my wife, Joan Brady.

*"If I am not for myself, who will
be? But if I am for myself alone,
what do I amount to?"*—Hillel

CONTENTS

PART 1

Tuesday: a glow in the canyon

1

Going out of Santa Fe along the road that leads north, you climb steadily for two or three miles along the spine of hills, around curves carved from the sides of them, and thus out onto a flat plateau. There, although you have been climbing and were seven thousand feet up to begin with, you suddenly find yourself on the floor of a valley.

On either side of this valley road stunted tree-shrubs, baked in summer, bleak in winter, stretch for fifteen miles or more to a mountain range. It is all brown out to the gray and silver and timber shades of the mountains, but there's a cast of green in the shrubs and the ground too, an infinitely pale cast, as though the living green of a dozen trees had been tapped and drained to color a hundred square miles. At sunset the valley road reaches up to spots and sweeps and splashes of all colors, but sunsets are brief moments in the long days here, where time and the land alike seem to be waiting, and an Indian away from the road may sit motionless from noon until nightfall. The Indians who live in this valley are seldom seen from the road, or their towns either, baked and brown in the brown baked earth. From the road it is a landscape without people, or except for road runners, much of any life at all.

So it is for some miles going north.

The mountain ranges run quite parallel to each other, the road runs straight between them, and it grows on you that you are grooved and channeled, so to speak. Then, looking west, you see that the Jemez Mountains have reached up to their highest point and, looking east to the Sangre de Christo range, you see Truchas Peak, the highest in all New Mexico; and at just this point a smaller road breaks out of the channel to the west. It crosses the Rio Grande, which is usually so slight a stream along here that you have scarcely paid any attention to it, and starts off across the valley to the mountains.

For all that signs of life in the landscape are small and quiet and indirect, this land has been used for a very long time. Santa Fe became a seat of government before the Pilgrims landed at Plymouth Rock, in the very year in which Henry Hudson first pushed up the river since named for him, at just about the time that Galileo began those observations that gave shape to modern science. But Santa Fe is still much younger than the pueblos here and there along the Rio Grande, some of which are visible in panorama for a moment from the road steadily rising up from the valley. Then the road is caught and twisted by the open ends of ancient canyons reaching down from the mountains; the empty foreground of twenty miles past fills suddenly with eruptions and swellings of the mesas that are taking form; and abruptly a blanket of trees, tall green pines, is thrown over the canyons and the swellings. The prospect softens, the air cools, smells sharpen.

It can be seen as the road comes up over the edge of one of the mesas that there are five here, splayed out from the mountain mass like the fingers of a hand waiting, like the outstretched hand of an idol, for a sacrifice. The road runs along the mesa, and there was once a time when you could have continued on into the mountains, or could have stopped to meditate on the immutability of things here in the shimmering quiet. Now, after a mile or so, there is a gate, and beyond the gate a city; the mountains cannot be reached from here, and unless your business here is the business of the city, you must turn around and go elsewhere.

2

A decade means nothing in the life of the usual city, but the city on the mesa, whose existence among the ruins of the Pueblo country was discovered with great excitement about that long ago, is not now to be recognized from what it was then. Few knew it then; those who did were not random visitors but people who had come, by secret ways, from various parts of the world to live behind the city's walls for a time; many of them left after performing tasks that they had come expressly to perform within the city; and of these a number have not gone back. But others have; they have returned, sometimes after long trips on transoceanic planes or liners, to take the road out from Santa Fe between the mountain ranges, across the Rio Grande, and up onto the mesa. And it is said that none of them has failed to comment on the remarkable changes that the city has undergone, even those who have only stood silently at night in the center of town looking down long streets that had not been there before, lined with houses and buildings that are all new.

Most of what was there in 1945, the year in which the Second World War ended and the existence of Los Alamos

became known, is still there: the barrack residences, even
the big, wooden laboratory buildings. The hospital is still
the same, a long, two-story, simply constructed barracks
painted white, in the center of things now as then. The
difference is in the enormous expansion that has taken
place, swallowing up the tight little community, as compact
as a pueblo, of a few years ago.

Los Alamos has become a city of about fourteen thousand people and it will not get much bigger, for it has
spread onto all five fingers of the outstretched hand. It
contains filling stations, supermarkets, shiny shops that sell
summer furniture and dinnerware, handsome schools and
playing fields, a community center, sidewalks and lawns of
real grass instead of the mud or dust that once was everywhere, a golf course, banks, split-level houses, and a bridge
connecting new buildings on one mesa with more new
buildings on another. People pass each other in the streets
and on the walks without recognizing each other, a thing
that was not possible before the city's discovery at the end
of the Second World War. For Los Alamos then was only
two years removed from the very first guarded sounds of
its construction and the first influx of its inhabitants, coming in along the single road from the great research centers,
east and west, where the ceremonies necessary to the city's
birth had been conducted.

In the Indian ceremonies that have been performed
around here for centuries, and are still performed in pueblos down from the mesas, there is a transmuting moment,
lost to those who do not know to watch for it, when the
priest says the word that brings in the magic. Ceremonies
may go on for some time before this word is said, and may
be very colorful, but they are all prologue and preparation.
Then the priest says the word and from that point on
everything is potent, has meaning, is to be respected and
feared.

It is very much like this, as the philosopher Comte noted,
with the development of man's great concepts: they pro-

ceed from the theological or fictitious stage to the metaphysical or abstract (when the word is often formulated) and finally to the scientific or positive (when the word is said). And it was like this with the work whose potency Los Alamos was built to secure. The ceremonies had been going on for years, in inquiring minds the world around. In the abstractions of Danes and Germans, Englishmen, Poles, Austrians, Hungarians, Swedes, Italians, Dutchmen, Frenchmen, Americans and Russians, the word had been formulated. And then, while the scientists danced with excitement in their laboratories like priests at a fiesta and circled the fires of their oscilloscopes all through many nights on end, the word was said: fission. The magic was brought in, everything was potent, and the construction of the city began.

In the spaces between the outstretched mesas the land dips down into washes or canyons or arroyos, some of them several hundred feet deep, all of them filled with grains and particles of the lava rock that flowed here long ago, all of them dark and quiet under the trees. Even in the early days of the city it was seen by the planners that, although the canyons were not possible as places for people to live, they made excellent sites for some of the more delicate types of work. The central mesa had been selected for the city because of its remoteness; for the most delicate work a further remoteness, from the city itself, was needed.

A road left over from earlier days, when the isolation of the country was an attraction only to campers and lovers and contemplative people of one sort and another, leads down from the rim of the central mesa through the trees to the floor of one of the canyons, to an area not too rocky and not too rough. Here, while the city was being built up above, a clearing was made, and in the clearing a building was constructed of concrete blocks and wood, about forty feet in one direction and fifty in the other; on one side a small porch led to the only door. The building gave

no clue to its function and was notable to the eye only for
being almost certainly the first building in this location
since the beginning of the world. If any others had been
here even their ruins had vanished. The builders overcame
all difficulties; over an improved road the first trucks brought
in construction materials and then came trucks with desks
and cabinets, laboratory tables, and carefully packed loads
of gauged and metered equipment. A short time after this,
military cars going back and forth along the road were a
common sight, although there was no one to see it except
the occupants of the cars.

Into the clearing, every morning, the cars came from
the canyon road, three or four within the space of a few
minutes. Drivers and passengers got out and walked on
through the door. Often they brought their lunches and
did not emerge until late afternoon. Often they came back
at night, and lights shone through the windows along one
side of the building until ten or eleven, sometimes until
one or two in the morning, not infrequently all through
the night. Sometimes the door opened and a man stepped
onto the porch or walked out into the clearing, to stand
for a few minutes, looking off into the trees, smoking a
cigarette or a pipe, or talking idly to one or another of the
soldiers who were always by the door, day or night, in the
beginning.

It was quiet at the bottom of the canyon, after the building was put there as before; no particular noise accompanied the work that went on inside. On some of the winter
days, when the trees stood cold in the sifting snow, the
canyon walls echoed slightly to the rasp of metal, and from
time to time a blurred, mechanical clicking sound rose to
a nervous pitch, fell to a muttering, rose, fell, and stopped.
In other seasons the foliage of the trees and the chattering
of the birds flying in and out muffled even the routine
sounds of the men's voices, of typewriters, of the door
opening and closing.

In the spring, with the middle of May, brilliant green

leaves shook and trembled on the gray trunks of the aspens, and at the edges of the clearing blue columbine and mountain flowers bloomed where wind or the birds had carried seeds.

From the beginning of the silent, secret work in this building there was no letup, until one Tuesday afternoon in May following the end of the Second World War.

3

On that afternoon, at about four-thirty, Dr Charles Pederson stood in the doctors' conference room of the Los Alamos hospital. The conference room was at the eastern end of the long frame building; it had two windows through which Dr Pederson could see, forty miles away across the valley of the Rio Grande, the triangular shape of Truchas Peak, and the snow line, which had receded sharply with the thaws of spring, and the saddle between Truchas and its slightly smaller twin peak to the south. He could see himself, toiling up the slope from the saddle, a lone and intrepid figure on an elemental stage. From the moment that he had made his climb to stand on the top of Truchas nine days before, Dr Pederson had been agitated with feelings, even with thoughts, too personal to be communicated, too remote from the small body of his convictions (which had always served him well enough) to be tamed and tethered by any one of them.

He had always been able to handle such feelings in the past, or, better yet, had not been especially conscious of them. The dutiful son of a secure family in a tight Eastern suburb, Charley Pederson had been aimed like an arrow at the medical profession; his mother had pulled the bowstring, his father had greased the bow, Charley had worked manfully, and here he was, aged twenty-eight, with a Captain's commission, with the sure conviction that a year or so with history would make a valued contribution

to his career, and with his mind now all confused by im-
ponderables that he had always been able to group, label,
and set aside as proper fare for college boys, suitable ac-
companiment to an evening of beer-drinking, nothing to
take seriously. But the enormity of standing on top of
Truchas, alone in the sky, the wind at his feet—no one
had prepared him for that.

He did not hear the nurse come into the room.

"Back to work, *mon capitaine*. Herzog is outside."

"Again? You'd think he runs the place. What's he so
fussed up about? It's not as though there's a war on."

"Dear Dr Pederson," the nurse said, cocking her head
to one side, folding her hands before her, "I've heard you
say that before. You are—how you say—*un innocent*. Bombs
are made here. It makes some people uneasy, always excepting doctors. There, there."

Dr Pederson began to walk back and forth, in a way that
Dr Septimus Steel of his medical school had walked back
and forth. Betsy Pilcher thought of Herzog, not so pomp-
ous, in her opinion, as the strutting doctor, but probably
not uneasy about anything except his own prerogatives.
She walked to the window, swaying her hips slightly.

"I suppose I have to talk to him," Pederson said.

Betsy Pilcher played with the cord of the window shade,
waiting. She stared at Truchas, which she had never climbed
and had no wish to climb. But Truchas was casting spells
today, or possibly Charley Pederson had left some of his
worries floating by the window. At all events Betsy felt a
sudden gloom; she would stay in her room tonight instead
of going to the movies or the Service Club.

"I think I know how to fix him too, this time," said
Charley, still walking back and forth in the manner of Dr
Septimus Steel.

The mountain sheep are sweeter but the valley sheep
are fatter, I therefore deem it meeter to feed upon the
latter, Betsy said to herself. The thought began with Truchas, without a doubt, but it ended with Staff Sergeant

Robert Chavez, who had taught her these old and sonorous words, and much besides, and who would have taken her to the movies or to the Service Club tonight if he had not been shipped to Bikini for those bomb tests. (If he wants me to go get Herzog he can ask me, I'm no mind reader.) If Robert had been there just then, she would have had some things to say to him.

"This is all going on too long," she would have said. ("I am newly back from the Isles of the Pacific—I am dirty, thirsty, hungry—let's go to the Service Club.")

"The Army and the bombs, testing new bombs and all, it's no way to live." ("Mine eyes have seen wondrous sights out there but none to compare with you—let's go to a movie.")

"People are edgy, it's no way to live, everybody's edgy." ("You're edgy—aren't you glad to see me back?—let's go out to the Valle Grande and lie upon the grasses.")

She pressed forward against the window, kissed him and straightened his tie, and then they went to the Service Club, while she snapped the cord of the window shade.

"Tell him to come on in, will you?" Charley said.

"But of course," Betsy replied, and she walked out of the room. Pederson looked at her swaying hips irritably; but the irritation passed with Betsy, and he resumed his pacing.

"I'll fix him," said Charley. He chuckled. Then he ran his hand over his face, for in fact he was more nervous than amused, and embarrassed too, because he had nothing really to be nervous about. Not so far as Herzog was concerned, Herzog being after all no more than a man. A mountain is different, which is to say (Charley said) that a man is different when the man is yourself. He was impressed by his perception, and he thought with brief contempt of Betsy Pilcher, a know-nothing and a bitch, although the word she used had startled him with its accuracy: uneasy, or possibly edgy, a little edgy.

The truth of the matter was that he had no experience

in dealing with these fireballs like Herzog. (?) thought
Charley. Well, then, the real truth of the matter was that
Dr Pederson was not a figure crucial to the functioning of
this gated city; he knew little of the workings of the secret
buildings, was not even allowed in most of them, and besides had been here less than a year, which meant that he
was forever excluded from the private world of those who
had come to settle the city and to pioneer in its great work.
Whereas Herzog— Surely this explained his edginess?

"I am most sorry to bother you, doctor," said Herzog,
coming into the room, "but our patient says he hurts. Don't
you think, perhaps—?"

Herzog's voice was gentle and polite, and his manner
infinitely respectful. He was a small man, and his suit hung
and sagged with the weight of numerous pencils, pens, and
paper in various forms and covers. He stood quietly just
inside the door, his head a little to one side, and, in one
hand, what seemed to be a jar of preserves.

"Oh, Mr Herzog," Dr Pederson said (he had learned
that most of the many Europeans here—all of whom were
doctors of one thing or another—preferred to be called
Mr; as for the "Oh," he had not meant to say "Oh," he
had meant to say "Ah," but he had not yet mastered this).

"It would really be much better to take him to that
hospital—Bruns Hospital?—in Santa Fe. I think it would.
He does not seem to be getting better fast."

"Now, Mr Herzog. He's got a perfectly simple broken
leg. It's been set, it's mending nicely."

"I do not want to lose him from his job a day longer
than has to be. It is very important."

At any rate, Herzog's voice made it seem important. He
spoke with a dogged enunciation of each syllable, and he
looked steadily at Pederson. From the door, where she
had been standing, Betsy Pilcher spoke.

"So why's it so important? The war's over."

Herzog twisted around until he could see Betsy over
his shoulder. He glanced at her obliquely, smiled, and then
turned back to Pederson.

"There is always a degree of urgency here. It would not harm to have the Santa Fe hospital make an examination?"

"Mr Herzog—" Charley began, but his voice broke on the "zog"; he's nervous, thought Betsy, looking at him with more interest than usual.

"Mr Herzog—" he also started to pace again—"There's a great deal I don't know about your work. But, you know, it's occurred to me sometimes that a fresh, outside viewpoint—maybe just because of that—well, I'd really like to go over with you sometime and see if—well—"

He came to a stop facing Herzog; he spread his hands a little and widened his eyes inquiringly. Well, what do you know, Betsy's expression said for her. Herzog looked at Charley for a moment, then turned his head so that he could see through the window.

"All of us are a little tightened up, aren't we?" he said at last. "I suppose it is the tests. I think there is no danger in them—to the personnel, that is—possibly some political unwisdom, right now, in such a demonstration. However, here and there a little work goes on which offers some hope for other uses, peacetime uses. It is neither war nor bomb tests that Mr Matousek delays. You might say a small sector of peace. So? A little edgy, all of us. I leave him in your hands, yes. You are quite right. Betsy, will you give these to Mr Matousek? I forgot."

He handed Betsy the preserves, and left. After a quick look at Dr Pederson, Betsy followed. Pederson wandered over to the window again, and again stared through it.

Very few people have been on a mountaintop, except such mountaintops as have roads built up to them and refreshment stands en route; fewer still have made the trip alone, for those who climb to a mountaintop usually want or even need company to corroborate their impressions. A lone individual on a mountaintop is most likely to be a prophet, and it is significant that Moses and Zarathustra and indeed most prophets retired either to mountaintops or, what is not so different, deserts. If one is not a prophet when he goes up to a mountaintop, one is very apt to become a prophet, at least for a while, and this was the case with Dr Pederson.

Mr Herzog will quit bothering us, he said to himself, but the thought moved to one side as his eyes and mind fastened on his remembered self at the top of Truchas, the wind at his feet, his feet in snow, and before him the spread of the remarkable land of the mesas and the mountains and the canyons, the polished sky, the quiet pueblos, and the overhanging past.

For a few minutes on the mountaintop he had faced the other direction, east, where the land stretched as far as he could see in endless plains. He was struck by the notion that standing there he was like someone who had scaled a wall, and was peeking over it, and really should be calling down to the plains below to tell people there what was going on in the canyons and on the mesa. He had entertained the notion long enough to visualize what he should say: "They've got their fingers on the controls of eternity down there."

So nine days later there was this very fanciful notion (and the romantic phrase) knocking around in his head, making him feel like a schoolboy or a poet or at least like something other than the practical person he was. And then, after he'd looked around for a while up there on Truchas, eaten a sandwich, thrown a few stones, and listened to the unbelievably thin sound of his own voice in some experimental shouts, he had remembered this thing that one of the scientists was supposed to have said just before the explosion of the first bomb, the test bomb, at Alamogordo. He had not heard about it until after that explosion—until after the explosions at Hiroshima and Nagasaki, for that matter; it had upset him every one of the times he had thought about it since; but on the mountaintop, what an absolutely fantastic thing to think!

"I should estimate," this scientist was supposed to have said, "that there is one chance in ten nothing will happen with the bomb, and one chance in a hundred that it will ignite the atmosphere." The scientist was named Baillie, and Baillie was a very eminent man, a Nobel Prize winner among other things.

Charley had come to Los Alamos in the middle of the three-week period between Alamogordo and Hiroshima. He knew no one when he came, and in the high tension of that time about the only ones he saw except in passing were the "Monday patients." These were the minor and varied casualties of the weekend camping trips, fishing trips, rock-gathering expeditions, pueblo-inspecting excursions, mountain climbs, and other such concentrated activities with which the population of Los Alamos—most of whom came from the built-up parts of the country—relieved the stresses of bad housing, water shortages, the frustrations of secrecy, the weight of the moral justifications of bomb-making, and other unnaturalnesses of life on the mesa. He met them over bruises and bandages, hearing stories of tumbles and unseen nails, and not much else. The manu-factured product of Los Alamos was not discussable socially in the summer of 1945, although everyone in the city knew that big things were going on, and most of them knew more or less what. No one said anything about them to the new doctor, and he did not know how to ask.

About a week after the end of the war a young physicist named Louis Saxl had come in to see him. Saxl was going to fly out to the shattered Japanese cities to appraise the bomb damage —"what's visible, anyway," he said to Ped-erson with a wry smile. Pederson gave him shots, treated an infected finger, and tried out some cautious questions. After a few days Saxl invited the doctor to come around to his room for a drink. It was Saxl who had mentioned, over the drink, what Baillie had said.

"But he didn't mean that, did he?" Pederson said, stop-ping his glass mid-air. "I mean, he didn't really mean it?"

"I suppose he did," Saxl said. "Yes, he meant it, Baillie being Baillie."

"Well, but Jesus!" said Pederson, who seldom swore.

"You'd go ahead and explode a bomb that might blow up the world?"

Pederson knew that Saxl had delivered the test bomb to Alamogordo; he had asked him about that, and Saxl had made a rather funny story of his answer. He had escorted the parts of the bomb down to the test site somewhat like a mother and somewhat like a bank messenger, and had actually received a written receipt for them from an Army Colonel, just as if the bomb had been some quite ordinary parcel. Pederson asked if he could see the receipt and Saxl showed it to him. Dr Pederson had come to like Louis Saxl in a few days. But his feelings just then, as he waited for what Saxl would say next, were a springboard for anything.

"There were three possibilities, remember," Saxl said finally, "and I guess the only good one was that it wouldn't work at all. Some thought that's what would happen, but I don't think Baillie. What ten to one means to Baillie is something that, in the light of what's known, is extremely unlikely. And what a hundred to one means is a miracle, or something like that, or even more. Baillie didn't think the bomb might blow up the world, but I guess you can say he didn't exclude the possibility. I didn't either."

Pederson was appalled.

"But suppose you didn't know enough? Couldn't you have forgotten some little thing? Made a miscalculation? Couldn't that have happened?"

"Yes, it could have; there was about one chance in a hundred that could have happened too. I think Baillie— he's not the only one, of course—I think he'd say there's one chance in a hundred of anything happening you might name."

"Please look," Saxl had said a little later. "We—I—came into this at the wrong end. We are misunderstanding each other, and for bad reasons." They were certainly misunderstanding each other; they had been talking, or rather Saxl had been talking, about quantum theory and the uncertainty principle, with references to the statistical nature

of the modern physical sciences; and Pederson was—it was
harder to put a finger on what he was talking about, but
the last words he had used were "irresponsibility of self-
appointed intellectual tyrannies." He had not said them;
he had muttered them, partly because he was not used to
putting together so many words like that and partly because
he had begun to lose his grip on what they were talking
about at all.

"Charley, look," Saxl went on, "suppose you're standing
some place and somebody fires a thirteen-inch shell at you.
It comes toward you, several thousand feet a second, headed
right at you. If you don't move, the consequences are
almost certainly predictable. But it just might pass through
you and produce no effect at all. There is a certain definite
chance that this will happen—very small, but definite.
Therefore you cannot exclude it. But to mention it is not
to—well, it's simply to pay a kind of tribute to possibility."

Pederson had pondered this, and it had made him feel
better. And then, in a flare of irritation, he had demanded
to know why Baillie had said one in a hundred.

"Couldn't he have said one in a million?"

"He was talking to physicists. If he'd been talking to
someone else, he might have—or would have said what
one in a hundred means to him."

"Everybody's not a physicist, how's everybody to know?"

"He didn't say it to everyone, he said it to physicists."

It had turned out to be a reasonable point, at last, as
made by a new friend who talked earnestly, without airs,
and made a drink from time to time. If absolutes had
disappeared under the inquiries of science, why then the
only rational procedure, the only procedure consistent with
man's development, was to follow where the probabilities
led.

"But the science ended at Chicago, in 1942," Pederson
remembered Saxl saying later, shortly before the evening
ended. "There's been no science to speak of out here, we
manufacture a product here. What it has to do with man's

development I don't know. Anyway, I can't say. At least
I won't. And where the probabilities of this lead—that's
something else, something for social scientists, politicians,
philosophers, citizens, but not us physicists except as we're
those too. Charley, there was a science and there is a bomb.
There was peace and there has been a war. There were
scientists and there is and has been a great big national
project, like an army. Are we talking about the same things?"

But on the mountaintop, possibly because the atmosphere was everything there, Baillie's words had echoed
louder than Saxl's explanation, and one was one, Pederson
decided, whether in a hundred or a billion. A question
that he couldn't ask of anyone settled on Charley Pederson
like a dream, like a fog, like an obdurate clinker in his eye.
What meaning did life have if its obliteration could be
contemplated as one possibility in anything?

After a while the question took a different form. Didn't
people have a responsibility to life itself, if not to other
people, not to go this far? He walked back and forth, ate
another sandwich, threw more stones, and stared for a long
time directly at the mesa of Los Alamos forty miles away,
for it was a kind of extra underlying bother to him that all
the enormous work being done on the mesa was not even
a point in the haze of distance, was not to be seen or
suspected or sensed, was nothing. From where he stood,
the whole mesa, which he knew to be full of people he
knew, to be covered with buildings, and alive with the
sounds of drills and generators and automobiles and calling
children, was small and deserted, testifying by not so much
as a glint from the declining sun that men down there had
their fingers on the controls of eternity—and if the phrase
was romantic and could not, of course, be mentioned, still
it seemed to say what he meant.

As he looked he thought of the young man who, in a
small building in one of the canyons, just a day or two
after this conversation with Saxl, had pushed one of the
controls too far, and twenty days later had died from doing

so. He could not move his eyes slightly enough to change their focus from the mesa to, say, the canyon in which stood the building where the young man had worked and where his friend Saxl worked too. Two or three miles intervened, a fifteen-minute ride by car along the turning road—but nothing from the mountain or the eyes on the mountain. It was all nothing from the eyes on the mountain.

He came down from the mountain, but his mood had come with him. He was so abstracted that some of his friends noticed it, one or two of his patients even, and, of course, Betsy Pilcher, who had plugged him up with nonsense.

"You feeling nervous, irritable, run down?" she asked him.

"I am feeling perfectly OK," he said.

"You're acting two or three of those things," she said. "I feel sort of the same way myself. I'll be glad when we get past Tuesday the twenty-first."

"Why? What's that?"

"Well, Nolan, you remember, the accident that killed him was Tuesday the twenty-first of August. This month's the first one since."

"The first what? What are you talking about?"

"The first Tuesday the twenty-first since Tuesday the twenty-first of August."

"Well, so what?" he demanded, beginning to see, refusing to admit it, staring at her with exasperation.

"So nothing. I'll be glad when it's past, that's all."

"You're out of your head. Are you really that superstitious? Are you really like that?"

"Don't give me that out-of-your-head stuff. I'm not the only one."

On the afternoon of Tuesday the twenty-first of May this knowledge hovered in Pederson's mind, suspended beside the thought that Mr Herzog would bother him no more. The hospital was quiet. From the walk that ran past

the window a young woman, the mother of a child from
whose feet Pederson had extracted four thorns the day
before, waved to him. And Pederson nodded back, re-
flecting that from the peak of Truchas nothing had happened. The calendar on the wall embarrassed him, and he
avoided it. The clock on the wall said forty minutes past
four, and it occurred to him that he was waiting: for the
clock to say five, when he would leave; for Betsy's nonsense
to die in him; for something to happen. He remembered
all those people waiting in his mind beyond the mountain
wall, filling the plains with puzzlement, while he peeked
over, searching the distant mesa for a meaning, but finding
nothing, seeing nothing, unable even to separate the mesa
from a canyon where, five miles away and nine months ago
(to the day), someone had pushed the controls just slightly
too far. Oh, troubled mind!

4

The soldier is sitting on the porch of the building in the
canyon, tilted back in his chair beside the door, alternately
reading a comic book and watching a mountain cardinal
flicking among the branches of the trees that ring the clearing. The bird flashes past him, banks and lifts, and disap-
pears.

"Veda, don't look!" he reads. "That got them, all right!
What happened? We knocked out their gravity equilibrator
with our astral ray! Your father will be safe now, Veda,
and the garden people of Bucephalon will be free again.
Oh, if only the space marauders would stay away! But will
they?"

The soldier lets the book fall in his lap. He looks out
into the clearing, and now that the bird is gone he looks
among the flowers, his glance moving among them, flicking
like the bird from one patch to another. He knows what
he wants to look at, but he approaches it slowly and in a

roundabout way, as before. He does not know the name of the strange flower near the edge of the clearing a little way out from the porch, but he has come to know the flower, and as his eyes reach it he shifts in his chair and alerts his senses to the possibility of someone coming out of the building to catch him unaware. He notices now the blurred, mechanical, clicking sound, rising almost imperceptibly from moment to moment as he listens. He cannot hear it without restiveness, for he knows enough about what goes on inside to know that the sound is a measurement of dangers, bad dangers, and all the worse because he doesn't know just what they are. But the sound is reassuring too, for while it goes on no one will come out of the building, and so he gives himself over to looking at the flower.

It is the enormously large pollen-covered organ sticking straight out from the center of the flower that he stares at. He has stared at it secretly many times in the several days since one of the men who works in the building pointed it out to him and asked him if it didn't make him want to go to Santa Fe. And not understanding, not having seen anything the like of this before, for it is a western flower and a mountain flower, the soldier had taken so long to catch on that when he did he had to feel uncomfortable for the time it took as well as for what he learned. Even staring at it secretly, even now, it makes him feel uncomfortable, but excited too. He has a plan that the next time he goes to Santa Fe he might pick this flower and take it in with him to give to the girl he sees there, as a joke, because she is not a girl he will ever marry.

What the dangers are that the sound measures he has never been told, has had to guess at from the accident that happened here before he came, and concerning this he knows less than he would usually like to know, but more than he wants to know at other times, of which the present is one. He knows, specifically and for a fact, because a fellow who knew Nolan told him, that if Nolan had lived he would never have been able to have a kid, and for that matter wouldn't have been any good, kid or no kid. So whatever happens when something goes wrong, if something goes wrong, it hits where it hurts and must be a terrible thing that he has not been able to bring himself to ask about. An officer, a very strict military disciplinarian, had given it as his opinion that Nolan deserved no better than he got, because he had violated very important rules in being down in the building alone and wasn't supposed to be performing the experiment at all. But, looking at the flower, the soldier feels sorry for this poor Nolan and wonders what really does go on inside, where now, he senses, the clicking sound has become a rasp, high and steady, and louder—it occurs to him so sharply that he forgets the flower and straightens in his chair—than he has ever heard it in the three months that he has been coming down here to sit by the door.

The sound frightens him, for what can happen for sure, even though the walls are thick? He gets up from the chair and stands away from the door, at the edge of the small porch.

He is standing there, listening, waiting for something, as a voice comes up out of the rasping sound and mounts above it, a cry—"Louieeeeeee!" And out of the shrill, trailing stretch of the cry blooms a crash, sudden, sharp, brief, breaking off at once under silence rolling from the building like a wave.

The soldier's flesh is pimply; he is half crouching, his head drawn in, his shoulders hunched, his hands between his legs pressed tight, a shield himself against himself, for in the building all is quiet, the walls stand, the porch is clear, and the flowers that edge the clearing gently sway in a normal breeze. Yet something is very wrong; the soldier knows it; it is only that the danger was not here where the protection, the ridiculous protection, was.

So he runs forward, his training swelling up within him, and pulls open wide the door. All seven of the men he knows to be in the big, cluttered room are standing there, all whole; his eyes take them in, his mind records them, and relief touches him like a fairy's wand in a picture book. But none of them moves, no one turns to look at him, each stands motionless as though he has a part to play in a game of Living Statues. Six of them, rooted here and there about the room, are looking at the seventh, Louis Saxl, the one in charge.

Saxl is standing farthest from the door, although still some feet back from the main table, with a rubble of scientific things on it, under gauges and meters, at the far end of the room. He is standing with his head down and his hands before him, one over the other, and he looks not unlike a teacher who has been speaking to a class and has stopped for a moment to reflect on a complicated point. No one moves, and the soldier's flesh goes pimply again, worse than before. It seems to him that the room itself is trembling, and the air seems filled with a slow sighing, which his ears tell him is the heavy breathing of the men standing, and his own too, but it seems a sigh.

There is finally a movement. Saxl turns. He looks from one man to another, and at the soldier, with an expression that seems more contemplative than anything else. He turns away from the table and takes a step forward, and then stops. He says: "I'll give Charley Pederson a call," and he looks around again at the men.

Several of the men offer to make this call, but Saxl says he will make it. He walks across the room to where the phone is; he still holds his hands a little in front of him and out from his body, and he talks on the way to the telephone, looking from one man to another.

"I'll get him to send the ambulance down. There's no point to the risk of driving up ourselves. Nausea's the thing right away. Most of you were far enough away, I think, but maybe a couple of us. I remember—nausea can come fairly fast sometimes. We'll probably all feel fine, but we might as well get a ride, don't you think?"

"Dr Pederson at the hospital, please," he says into the phone.

And turning again to the men in the room, he continues:

"We all moved back after it went critical. It'd be a good thing to know where each of us was standing. Try to recall it, will you? Make a note of any obstructions between you and the pile. You were pretty much behind me, weren't you, Tim?"

One of the men nods. The soldier looks from Saxl to the man and back again to Saxl.

"Charley?" Saxl says into the phone. "Hello, Charley? This is Louis Saxl. Charley, we've had an accident down here—radiation. No melting or anything, but it was intense, all right. Yes—a blue glow."

The soldier stands by the door, not knowing what to do. The telephone talk does not last long, and after it Saxl and the others spend several minutes talking together, walking back and forth, and then some of them begin to chalk in rough squares or circles or even the crude outlines of feet at various points on the floor away from the main table. No one goes very close to it. The soldier asks if he can do anything, but one of them says no, there is nothing to do, except to stay outside and make sure no one comes in to disturb anything.

"I'm going to get Dave Thiel to come down," Saxl says, turning from where he is standing. "You know him, don't you?" he says to the soldier, and the soldier nods.

"He can come down and reconstruct things," Saxl continues, walking away and speaking to no one in particular. "He can get the record off the controls."

The soldier sees that Saxl has moved up a little toward the table. His head is lifted and he seems to be looking from one meter to another in the bank of meters above the table. He picks up a small metal block from a pile of blocks on a smaller table and turns it over slowly several times, looking at it carefully. The soldier notices that some of the other men have stopped what they were doing to

watch Saxl. He puts the block down, again studies the
patterned faces of the meters, then lifts his hands slightly
and looks down at them. He is doing this when the sound
of the ambulance, a low and distant sound that breaks with
the shifting of gears and continues on a higher pitch, comes
to all of them in the room.

The soldier is desperate to know what happened and,
even more, what is going to happen, but he does not know
how to ask, and besides he can tell that this is not the time
to ask. Still, he cannot stop himself as the men file out of
the room, onto the porch, and down to the clearing into
which the ambulance is just now coming. He touches the
arm of the last man, makes a kind of gesture, and starts to
frame some words, but the question mark of his curiosity
is stamped all over him, and the man addresses that before
the words are said.

"Why, I can't tell you, I don't know, except he lost
control." The man looks at the soldier with some surprise.
"I don't know why."

PART 2

Wednesday: of the mind and heart, but not the hands

1

From the mesa the lights that play on Truchas at dawn are lavender and blue, and gold sifts onto the plain between the mesa and the peak before the peak is brightened. From the mesa the peak is inexpressibly remote and lovely in the early morning light. It is cold, in May as it will be in July, at dawn on the mesa, and the town itself has the special enchantment that many towns have before the people who live in them are up and around.

The main street of Los Alamos runs east and west along the mesa, and as the sun comes up to surmount Truchas it makes long shadows of street lights and signposts and of any figures that happen to be abroad. At a little before seven o'clock on the morning after the accident in the canyon building, just as the rays of the sun were pouring across Truchas, David Thiel came out of the hospital, out onto the pavement of the street, for the paths along the side were muddy from spring rains, and turned to walk along it, leading a gigantic shadow into the sun.

He raised the collar of his jacket, which was wrinkled and stained, and hunched his shoulders to raise it higher. He walked with his head held forward, because it was easier to walk with his lameness this way, and bent down against the cold. From behind or from the side he made a very slight and delicate figure and his head was hardly noticeable. He was thinking to himself about a line from a writer, a Russian writer, he thought; the line was:

"All prayers come to this: 'Dear Lord, please make two and two not equal four.' "

From time to time he lifted his head, and then you could see how well formed it was; the expression on his face was intense, with his thought, with the cold, and with the stamp of the night he had spent. From the front he was an impressive figure, leading the long shadow.

One of David Thiel's legs was shorter than the other, and was twisted too. His heavy cane was an imposing thing, massive out of proportion to the man, and it glistened in the sun as though it had been oiled. He made intricate use of this stick, of his good leg, and of his crippled leg to proceed in a way that seemed to leave the upper part of his body relatively motionless, as though it had resigned itself to the effort that walking called for. There was no one else on the street, and no one else to be seen anyplace on the mesa.

"Dear Lord," David said, half aloud. Some old Russian writer, he said to himself, but he couldn't remember which one.

He came to a narrow cross-street, not much more than a lane, but paved; it led between two rows of houses, and David turned and went down it; shadows from the houses in the eastern row alternated with bands of sunlight from the spaces in between, and the figure of the small, laboring

walker faded and brightened across them. At the eighth
house he turned, without looking up and as sharply as
though he had been suspended on a wire; he went to the
door and knocked. There was a nameplate just to the right
of the door, a brass plate with polished letters that read:
"Col. Cornelius Hough." David traced the letters with the
tip of his cane; after a minute or so, he rapped on the door
several times with the cane's head. Interior noises followed: shufflings, shiftings, and voices laced with sleep.
The door opened and Colonel Hough stood there, quite
trim and soldierly even at this hour, even in his dressing
gown.

"David," he said, and his voice saying this one word was
sympathetic and paternal and only slightly reproachful. All
in this one word and in his expression the Colonel was
saying: "You shouldn't have stayed at the hospital all night,"
and "You shouldn't be here so early," and "You shouldn't
be in the mood I can see you're in," and "Still, I understand,
I think."

"Come in, Dave. Has anything happened?" he said as
he turned, stopping his turning to say it.

"No," said David, "everything proceeds according to
plan."

The Colonel walked on back into the house, David followed, and the Colonel called to his wife. She called down
that it was a terrible thing that had happened to Louis Saxl
and the others. Her voice was agreeable and she asked no
questions, for she had been married to Colonel Hough
thirteen years and most of this time she had spent at one
Army post or another.

"Well, no change," the Colonel said. "That's good, isn't
it?"

David shrugged his shoulders.

"His hands?" the Colonel said. "Are they bad?"

"What time did you leave the hospital?"

"Why, it must have been eleven or so; ten-thirty, I guess
it was."

"They put his hands in ice a little after that," David said. "The left one's about the size of a cantaloupe. They won't save his hands."

"I see," the Colonel said. He walked around the room, taking occasional quick looks at David, who stood in the middle of the room tracing a figure on the Indian rug with his cane. The Colonel's wife had bought the rug at one of the pueblos soon after she and her husband had come to this post.

"Would it be possible, by doing that, by amputating the hands—" The Colonel started, and then after a pause continued: "With gangrene and things like that, if they amputate in time they stop it from spreading. Is that a possibility?" The Colonel paused again, and after a moment continued again. "Confine the mistake to the part that made it."

"No," David said, "not with this."

"I see," the Colonel said once more.

"Did you ever read the report on the medical effects of the bombings in Japan?" David asked. "Louis was supposed to have gone out with the group that made that report, but he stayed with Nolan. Same experiment, same effects, only worse this time. Did you ever read that report?"

"I remember. Yes, I read it; well, not in detail, I guess."

"You brasshats never read anything in detail. But you know what happens well enough. Seven men dosed up with radiation and you solace yourself with silly questions."

"What about the other six?" the Colonel asked after a little pause.

"They'll live," David said.

"That was an heroic thing Louis did," said the Colonel. David looked at him. "What was heroic?"

"Why, knocking the pile apart. Stopping the reaction with his hands, you know."

"Neil, quit this silly talk. What do you do if someone hands you a hot brick? You drop it. Is this heroic? It's a reflex."

"Yes, but still—"

"You've never seen the experiment. The damage was done in microseconds. It was done, and that was that. Neil, I want somebody's assurance from the military side that this experiment won't be done again this way."

"I don't make those decisions, David."

"You have a voice in them."

"Yes, I have a voice in them, but a lot of you scientists have just as much—more, probably."

"Yes, and a lot of us scientists have been arguing since the end of the war to put it under remote control. This is still an Army post."

"Like no other I ever saw," the Colonel said with some fervor. "David, will you please sit down?"

They sat. From the kitchen came sounds of the Colonel's wife.

"David," the Colonel said. "From the very beginning this project has had two heads. I'll bet you never heard the story about General Meacham and our friend Cardo. Cardo never talks—particularly so's I can understand him. And the General never talked much about this one. Anyway, back in '43 the General told Cardo he wanted such and such a piece of equipment in operation by such and such a date. Cardo said it might be possible, said he'd keep the General informed. Brother! This burned the General up. He said, 'Cardo, this is a military undertaking, I'm the officer in charge here, I expect results, and your reputation might suffer if I don't get them!' Well, Cardo, with a Nobel Prize and all, he just looked at the General and shook his head slowly. Like this. Just moved his head back and forth. Then he said: 'Not my reputation, General. Mine won't be made or unmade here. Yours might suffer, though.'"

"No, I never heard it," David said. He chuckled nominally. "Puts you stuffy bastards in your place." His face tightened as he looked down at the Indian rug.

"In those days," the Colonel went on, turning his head to look toward the kitchen, "the idea was to teach you fancy boys some spit-and-polish. But we gave up trying to run prima donnas like we do soldiers a long time ago, and I never could understand why you keep on beefing about the military mind. Live and let live. We got the job done, one way or the other. Anyway, Dave, you know what I do here. I'm partly in charge, but I'm a glorified housekeeper. I'll have you shot at sunrise if you quote me, except it's no secret and except I can't have you shot."

He bent forward a little to see the expression on David's downturned face, and saw that his run of talk had not succeeded.

"No," David said, in a voice so low, to begin with, that the Colonel had to lean forward to catch the words. "But you prove what I mean. We beef about the military mind, because the military mind, even yours, subordinates people to routines, and refers decisions elsewhere, and makes an art of buckpassing. It hasn't any interest in what is, or might be, but only in what has been, and only in what's been officially sanctioned out of that. It's not only always fighting the last war, as some of you admit, but it's always thinking in terms of the future war. You're paid to defend us, but you're not paid to make it necessary to defend us, which is what your thinking leads to. Nine months since the end of the war, and this is still an Army post, still making bombs, and in Washington the military mind is beating its brains out to make sure it keeps control of what us scientists, meaning us engineers and machinists, have put together out here. There's a little time gap now, it's possible somebody might put a peace together, and the military mind has devised as its contribution the test of new bombs at Bikini—a demonstration that is essentially political and a hell of a contribution to keeping the peace! So an obsolete experiment has been allowed to take a sacrifice, while you talk about let's live and let live. Confine the mistake to the part that made it. I heard what you said. So poor Nolan serves a final purpose. His hands slipped, he dropped a screwdriver, to be specific. Ergo, Louis must have dropped a screwdriver too. I ran through that experiment last night, as soon as the stuff cooled down. I talked to Louis about it, I got the charts, I talked to everyone who was down there. Nobody's hand slipped. My God, he'd run that experiment sixty-three times, this was the sixty-fourth. He was supposed to go out to Bikini today. I went to the store with him yesterday to help him buy some water fins to take along. This was supposed to be his last run-through of that goddamned, out-of-date, meaningless business, which never should have been set up the way it was and should have been changed over at least nine months ago. God damn it, why wasn't it? Because you all passed the buck, none of you makes those decisions, but they come through the Army! Well, why weren't they made? Why? Do you know why?"

The Colonel had stiffened noticeably during this. He was not looking at David as David finished talking, and for quite a while neither of them said anything. From just beyond the door to the kitchen came a soft rattle of cups and saucers.

"It's my impression Saxl himself didn't argue too strongly for mechanizing that experiment," the Colonel said finally. "We had some meetings, you know, and I heard him say several times—"

"You heard him say he'd go on doing it because he could," David interrupted coldly. "You also heard him say it made no sense for anyone else to do it that way. I suppose you know why he was doing it yesterday. He was going through it with Tim Haeber. Haeber takes over while Louis goes to Bikini—was to go. And so? Well, we all try to win the war, each in his own way. What war? Why, the war civilization cannot stand up under, if I may quote General Meacham from the Sunday papers."

"David, you've been at it all night," the Colonel said, getting up. "A very bad thing has happened. I understand how you feel. I'm sorry, sorry as can be. But we won't help anything by talking this way. It certainly needs discussion, but—Lorraine!"

The door opened at once and the Colonel's wife came

in, dressed in a faded housecoat, her hair in curlers. She bore a tray with the coffee things on it. She looked at David with compassion and poured coffee for all of them, while murmuring sympathetic words and suppressing curiosities.

So they sipped and said what there was to say, which was less than it might have been because David now offered very little. He put his cup down half full and sat with his head propped on his cane, cocking his head this way or that occasionally to trace with his eye the geometry of the rug's pattern.

"Well, we'll just hope," the Colonel's wife said, "hope and pray. They do wonderful things nowadays."

Louis did not want his parents to be notified of the accident, David told them; he had said he wanted to wait, he had said there was no point in getting them all alarmed.

"Is this possible?" he said, eyeing the Colonel. "Or is there an Army regulation against it?"

"We'll have to notify all the families concerned," the Colonel said. But he would, of course, talk to the doctors before doing anything; nobody would be unnecessarily alarmed.

"David," the Colonel said, "do you know what he thinks himself?"

"No."

"He hasn't said anything to you?"

"Not about what he thinks."

"The poor boy," said the Colonel's wife.

"David," the Colonel said, "if there wasn't a slip somewhere, what did happen? You said you ran it through last night."

"Well, a slip, yes," David said, "but not of the hands. The mind or the heart, maybe, but not the hands."

"The mind—"

"It's a very delicate experiment. It requires very sure control."

"Yes," said the Colonel, "I know it does, I've heard about that. But that's just what—"

"Well, if you knew about it, why did you let it go on?" David half shouted. He struggled to get to his feet, and stood facing the Colonel, leaning on his cane. "Look, I thank you for the coffee, and I'm sorry to rout you out so early in the morning. I wanted to ask you a question, Neil. What are you going to say about this business?"

"Why, I'll talk to the doctors before we do anything."

"I don't mean that. What are you going to tell a reporter if he calls out here?"

"Oh, I don't think the papers will call."

"Something you said last night, something in the way you said something—you're planning to deny there's been an accident? There's been a serious accident, no matter what happens. What are you going to say?"

"There's a security angle to this, you know. There's also a question of public morale."

"You *are* planning to deny it, aren't you?"

"It's not a matter of denying anything, God damn it, Dave. I just plain don't know yet what we can say, or whether. Personally, I must say I don't see much point in a big splash in the papers. 'Seven injured at Bomb Laboratory'—stuff like that. Particularly with radiation involved. That scares people."

David was moving toward the door.

"The point is seven *were* injured at bomb laboratory," he was saying, "and one of them maybe more than injured. You Army guys slap a security angle on everything that embarrasses you. The Army's embarrassment is not quite so important as what happened though, and that it not happen any more." He reached the door, opened it, and walked through it without stopping. "There's going to be a story—one way or another. Good-by."

The Colonel's wife came to the open door and stood beside her husband. Together they watched the small figure move down the walk to the street again.

"You shouldn't let him get away with that kind of talk. I'd have slapped his face," she said, and then she was petulant. "Why do you let them talk to you that way, and you're supposed to be in charge of the Post, partly anyway. They all think they're so special, even that cripple. You let them walk all over you."

The Colonel turned away from the door. He sat on the sofa where David had been sitting, stretched his legs out before him, and contemplated them. "I wouldn't so much mind a newspaper story on the heroism angle. Mistakes do happen, but that heroism angle makes it a different story." He lifted one of his legs slowly, bent it, straightened it out, and lowered it slowly to the floor again.

"A different kind of story," he said.

2

Towns are settled and people go to them for the most varied and astonishing reasons. Louis Saxl's great-grand-father, who had come out of Germany not long after Carl Schurz, had gone, of course, to New York, where for some time he made, or failed to make, a living as a music teacher. After the Civil War many people he knew, even including some who had succeeded in making livings, fell in with the great move westward, and he came to spend much of his plentiful time talking to friends who were leaving.

One evening, listening with respect but not with great interest to a statement of mission by a young man who was going to take a pulpit in Philadelphia, he learned that in all the sweep of the nation between the big coastal cities there were no more than five rabbis who spoke English. He went so far as to consult a map, whereon, to begin with, he sought out the locations of the cities in which the English-speaking rabbis were. One of these cities was Quincy, a place he had never heard of, in the state of Illinois, about which he knew nothing except that the great Lincoln had come from there. Pondering the map, he made the discovery that the fortieth parallel and the ninetieth meridian crossed at a point not far from Quincy, and he noticed that many of the nation's greatest cities fell within a few degrees one way or the other of these two lines. Nothing he had heard and nothing he felt seemed so reasonable to him as the notion that their juncture must be marked by destiny; and besides, this notion was his own.

There was no town where the two lines crossed (and more than a century later there still is none); but a collection of houses and stores called Georgetown, a little mass in the void of the fields, was trying to become a town not far from the juncture. Mordecai Saxl took his wife there; the day after he arrived he found out from a local surveyor exactly where the lines crossed, and then he walked to the spot, which turned out to be seven miles away. This pleased him because seven was a good number. He arrived poor, and he got no richer, but he probably did as well in this place as he would have done in another. In the course of time Mordecai and his wife died; they left a son named Abraham to carry on the family's name and improve its fortunes, and each of these things he did.

No one can say for sure why the Pueblo Indians came to make a town on the mesa of Los Alamos or why they came to leave it; the ruins found there bear no testimony on either point, except that both events took place so long ago that they belong to a realm of things that cannot very well be conceived of as ever having had the capacity to be different than they were. Or they have to be approached so broadly that the minor variables of life, which might once have explained much and which attach themselves endlessly to explanations of the events of last week or a year ago, cannot be invoked and so are ignored, and finally are buried under references to the law of necessity, which states that these things happened because they did.

Perhaps, in fact, an ancient Pueblo sage, made aware of certain new developments in the war-making potential of his tribe, recalled that in his youth he had once ridden north along the Rio Grande to test the hunting. And perhaps he had come out upon a mesa so isolated, so advantageous to the private development of tribal achievements, that, having thought of this, he at once led the warriors back to the mesa, there to set up a secret camp, which flourished for a while before going to ruin under forces now forgotten.

The formal histories of the atomic project simply state that at the appropriate time in the great undertaking an appropriate site was selected, the selection being dictated by considerations to insure the utmost secrecy. This is to say little more than that the bomb was made at Los Alamos because it was. But the law of necessity does not need to be invoked for an event so recent as the establishment of a town in 1943.

In the latter months of 1942, in fact, a young theoretical physicist, aware that a chain reaction in the fission of uranium was about to be achieved, and further aware that a supremely secret site was being sought at which the new scientific advance could be translated into the technical triumph of a weapon, recalled the mesa of Los Alamos, a place near which he had spent many happy days as a boy, riding horseback, camping, fishing, hunting. It occurred to him that characteristics that had made the mesa a place of glory to his childhood, its remoteness and its isolation, recommended it for the projected work, and he proposed it to the military authorities, and took several generals out to look at it, and they concurred. That is how the Army post known as Site Y, or the Los Alamos Scientific Laboratory, or "the Hill," or "the Magic Mountain," or by other names, came to be set up among the ruins of an ancient people's camp.

"You know," one can imagine the physicist telling the generals, "there's a place where I used to camp out as a boy—" and at once a chink opens in the massive impenetrability of the two-billion-dollar project, through which fancy can discern, among the stern, implacable figures she has already conceived, the generals warming slightly beneath their uniforms, their eyes turning in on evocations of moments safe from prying eyes on riverbanks, or even in niches below the cellar stairs, and speaking or thinking for a moment not of bombs but of boyhood. The secret times of that time are the most secret of all, the most everlastingly private, the safest in retrospect, the most like unto the prime secrecy of the womb; and hence the physicist's proposal must have given an almost sentimental sanction to the choice of the mesa of Los Alamos for the secret gestation of the atomic bomb.

Indeed there had to be something like this, so formidable were the obstacles that the mesa imposed on the ones who went there.

Like the Indian sky town of Acoma farther south, or like a moated castle of the Middle Ages, the mesa of Los Alamos was all but inaccessible. The single road that led up to it, a narrow and winding mountain road, intended for the horse and barely usable by the automobile, was well-nigh impassable to the big trucks that began to creep along it early in 1943. The trucks brought spectrographs, X-ray diffraction machines, Wilson cloud chambers, and tons of other equipment from New Jersey; two Van de Graaff generators from Wisconsin; all the massive and delicate parts and pieces of a cyclotron from Massachusetts; the very special elements of a Cockcroft-Walton high-voltage device from Illinois; and a thousand other things, including waxes and lacquers, flasks and acids and solvents, rubber sheets, and battery clips, from dozens of other places. Nothing of the sort was there and nothing of the sort was even near.

The trucks maneuvered these things up the road with great difficulty, and the trucks also brought great loads of nuts and bolts (round and hexagonal), screws (brass and stainless), and saws and hammers and lumber, for nothing of this sort was there either. Houses had to be built for the people who would do the work in the laboratories, which also had to be built, for there was nothing there, nothing at all beyond a few structures that had served as

a small ranch school for boys. There was no power plant,
no machine shop, and too little water.

The people had to be brought, under instructions that
gave away no secrets, not knowing what they would find
when they got to where they did not know, from New
York and California, from England and Canada and other
places. Many, who were not able to discern the magnitude
of the goal through the wrappings of the secrecy, would
not come. And some who discerned fled in dismay from
the primitivism of the site, where, they were sure, the goal
would never be reached.

All of these were of faint heart, and wrong besides.

It is a measure of the magnificence of the effort on the
mesa that the difficulties were all overcome. But it was the
almost holy deference to secrecy that made it necessary to
overcome them, and that was a measure of something else.
This something else was woven with the magnificence into
the fabric of the town's life; it threaded the words that
were said beside high-vacuum pumps in the laboratories
and the words that were said under bridge lamps in the
newly built homes and rooms at night. What it was can no
longer be felt or sensed in the life of the city, and what it
had been was half forgotten even in the spring of 1946,
for by then it had raveled out to edginess, to many forms
of edginess.

But in the beginning . . .

In the beginning Mr Herzog, the most patient and the
most polite of men, stood waiting for the arrival of the
truck that would bring him the can of Glyptal without
which he could not join a length of glass tubing to a metal
collar. Until he could do that, he could not proceed with
the measurements he was making, and on his measurements a hundred others waited. He stood quietly by a
Coca-Cola cooler in the corner of his laboratory, and his
mind turned on one thought: what was Max Ottoberger
doing? Although Ottoberger had stopped seeing him more

than a year before he had had to leave Germany, they had been for several years before that close friends and colleagues. Presuming on this fact, Herzog had written Ottoberger from England, in the late thirties, asking if he would not intercede with the Nazis on behalf of an elderly Jewish physicist who, from all the signs, had disappeared into a concentration camp. Herzog had received no answer to his letter, which did not necessarily mean one thing more than another, but from that time he had thought no more of the days of friendship with Ottoberger and had thought increasingly of Ottoberger's capacities and bents as one of the world's best physicists and as one of the few such left in Germany.

Now, in the constructive debris of this fantastic burgeoning on the mesa, Herzog eyed the Coca-Cola cooler, wondered what Ottoberger was eyeing and thinking and doing, and waited for the Glyptal. An hour and a half after he had been told the truck would arrive, a soldier attached to his laboratory came to tell him that the truck had just come in but that the Glyptal was not on it. With the soldier, Herzog walked a quarter of a mile to the unloading station; several Army officers, soldiers, mechanics and people from the stockrooms were there, and so were two or three of the physicists and chemists. There was no Glyptal. Among the crates and boxes containing many other things, there was, however, a new and shining Coca-Cola cooler.

Herzog looked at it and began to shake. He stood in one spot and, as the others stopped talking and turned to look at him, his head and his arms and his legs shook. They shook for nearly a minute.

"Will you go to hell—please?" Herzog said then. His face ashen, he turned and walked away toward his laboratory. The phrase became famous. Truck-drivers battling their trucks up the rickety mountain road sometimes called it out to each other, although Herzog's colleagues never said it in his presence.

In the beginning there was fear. Most of all, the settlers of Los Alamos feared what they did not know. Forty years before, their mission on the mesa could not have been dreamed of; five years before, it had only been dreamed of; nobody had ever undertaken anything remotely like what they came to do; they were by no means sure it could be done. There was thus a fear of failure, and their failure (they feared) might mean the loss of the war and the beginning of barbarity.

But the fear of success was no less a fear, for they were—precisely what were they preparing? They were preparing an instrument so horrible in its power to maim and destroy that its use, which would be the crown of their efforts, could not easily be separated from barbarity. It was necessary to fear that the enemy was working to the same end, for their fear that the enemy might reach it first could solace that other fear about the barbarity of the instrument. But their work had led them into industrial involvements that would clearly overtax the bombed and strained resources of the enemy; consequently, if what they were doing was the way to the solution, the enemy was much less to be feared.

The naggingest fear of all thereupon took over: that the enemy might somehow contrive a simple and wholly unforeseen solution. And because there was so much they did not know when they came to the mesa, there was reason, as well as the solacing need, to fear this.

So the scientists—to whom secrecy is a noxious thing, the bane of work, of inquiry, of truth, of results—embraced the secrecy that they deplored, finding in the cluttering extremes of it not only a concealment but perhaps a cloak for the tormenting doubts of the enormous thing they were about; a margin for their errors; a kind of hope among the fears. And if they were going to stop their science (for the work on the bomb made mechanics of all of them) and put their researches aside (for who could say how long?), perhaps a remote mesa was the best place for that.

From the beginning of 1943 the physicists and chemists, and the engineers and technicians, moved into Los Alamos without a letup. They came to do the work of the city; and the Army, officers and soldiers of all ranks and many skills, came with them to administer the city. Others, doctors, teachers, construction workers, maintenance men, nurses, personnel directors, cooks and firemen, came to service the city. They all moved away from wherever they had been, and took the trip to Santa Fe, moving on at once into the remarkable land of the mesas and the mountains, the polished skies, the overhanging past, and the new fears.

The mesa was what it was; the water ran out, was carted in, ran short, and was carted in; the road broke down, was repaired, broke down, and was rebuilt; walks that were paths turned to mud in the rains; and until the spring of 1946, by which time six thousand people lived on the mesa, there were thirteen bathtubs in all of Los Alamos. But the tension of achievement took over everything, subordinated everything, at last. And the end of the war ended the extremes of the secrecy, many of the stresses, and all of the fears but one.

There were several answers to the question—what have we wrought?—and one of the answers was to leave the mesa. In the months following the end of the war, although the administrators and servicers of the city continued to increase, the scientists who had worked to the city's single purpose left by the hundreds. They left for many reasons, and not all who left because they had no other answer to that question told why it was they left. Many of those who stayed lived now with agonies of indecision or with a kind of troubled apathy, as though they were animals in a long-fenced pasture from which the fences had just been removed. For these the difficult question grew daily more difficult; in wartime it had penetrated all but the most ecstatic of patriotisms and the most rigid of realisms to set up a resonance in some protesting center of the spirit; each had been able to justify his wartime dedication in his own way, more or less satisfactorily; but the wartime justifica-

tions did not work so well, and for some not at all, without
the war.

In the spring of 1946 Los Alamos was edgy with the
residue of many fears, and with preparations for the tests
of new bombs in the lagoon of the coral island of Bikini;
and with the twists and turns of the great legislative battle
in Washington to perpetuate, or to end, the military control
of the universal atom; and with echoes of this battle and
reports in the papers, and speeches before Elks Clubs and
the United Nations, which seemed to mean that very many
people did not know at all what they had wrought, or even
that there was a question.

"The three conditions of scientific work are the feeling
that one ought not to leave his path, the belief that work
is not all intellectual but moral as well, and the feeling of
human solidarity." So wrote the Nobel Laureate Szent-
Gyorgyi two years before the fission of the atom was discovered. In the spring of 1946 all three of these conditions
were lacking at Los Alamos for the scientists who had left
their science to take on the building of the bomb, who
were having trouble with their beliefs in their work, and
whose feelings of human solidarity were the source of the
trouble.

In the spring of 1946, at just this time, the snows on
Truchas Peak fell back, the spring flowers unfolded along
the trails and paths around the mesa, three hundred new
bathtubs were installed in the town's houses, and the lovely,
peaceful evenings, growing longer, were a joy. On weekends the paths and trails were full of walkers and riders,
campers were out in the mountains, rock-collectors were
down among the rocks, and many of the residents of the
town were talking to the Indians in their pueblos, buying
rugs and bowls. Still, taking one thing with another, there
was not only an edginess, there were many kinds of edginess, the residue of fears passed by and the mirror of
one that would not leave.

3

From the Colonel's house David Thiel went back along the streets by which he had come. Hardly more than an hour had passed since he had moved through them alone; a few lights for the night still burned in the bright day. But now from their houses west and north and east on the mesa, people were walking in to the center of the city, and through it to the southern side, where, behind a tall steel fence, topped with barbed wire and punctuated with guarded gates, lay the Technical Area. A jumble of buildings, of many heights and all shapes, sprawled behind the fence; and through spaces between them, beyond the canyon that the buildings rimmed, several low, long buildings could be seen on the next mesa. The land did not rise much again beyond that; it stretched flat along the foot of the mountains, sloping off to the south, past Santa Fe, into the low desertland of Alamogordo nearly two hundred miles directly below.

There was traffic in the streets now, jeeps, military cars, trucks and ordinary cars, but most of the walkers went along ignoring them, avoiding the muddy paths, as David did. Most of those on the streets knew each other, and some proceeded in pairs or in little groups; but largely they went by themselves, each at his own pace, signalizing friendship with a movement of his arm, a dip of his head, or a word or two. It was apparent that most of them had heard of the happening of the night before; they had on their faces, as they looked at David, a shading of melancholy that bore delicate reference to the fact that they knew. Some quickened their steps or moved across the street to speak to him.

Halfway along the main street from the Colonel's house to the hospital, David went up a walk leading to a small frame building. He took a piece of paper from his inside coat pocket; then, reading it, he groped briefly for the

doorknob. Inside, a counter bisected the building's one
room. A woman in uniform, talking into a telephone, stood
back among the typewriters and desks that made a kind
of office of the space behind the counter. A younger woman
in a brightly colored dress was leaning over a magazine at
one end of the counter. She looked up as David approached. Her face was long and bony, a pure American
Gothic face, and her skin, pocked from some old illness,
had the earth-tint of a half- or quarter-breed Indian.

"Hello," he said, somewhat timidly, holding out toward
her the draft of his telegram.

In her eyes was an expression of insolent appraisal—
odd in that face and curious in that place at that hour—
and a faint smile played at the corners of her mouth. She
took the paper from him without speaking, and at once
began to check off the words with little taps of the pencil
she held; but she stopped almost as soon as she had started
and returned her naked glance to his face.

"It's been a long time, David," she said in a low voice,
almost a whisper.

"Yes," he said, and she resumed her counting, while
David, staring at the pencil, read the words upside down.

When she had finished she looked up at him again.
"Bad?" she said.

He nodded. They transacted the details and David went
out of the building.

Very shortly after this Colonel Hough came in. He smiled
at the woman in the brightly colored dress, who was leaning
over her magazine again, and spoke to the woman in uniform, who came forward.

"I am Colonel—"

"Oh, I know," the woman said, smiling at him. "Colonel
Hough. I'm Sergeant Myra Quick."

"Several people were hurt here yesterday," the Colonel
said.

"I know, I heard about it last night."

"What did you hear?"

"It was a kind of explosion, wasn't it? They got burned or something."

"No. Both of you," he said, turning to include the other woman, who looked up from her magazine. "There wasn't anything like an explosion. There was just an accident in some of the work, one of the men's hands slipped and he did get burned. They're all in the hospital, they're all getting fine care."

The Colonel paused; the two women looked at him.

"The point is," he continued, "if anyone brings in a telegram mentioning it, don't send it right away. There'll be an order on this. I just happened to be going by, thought I could save a little time."

"We've got a wire from someone already," the Sergeant said. "David Thiel was in just a minute ago. She took it. It was just—"

"Is that so?" the Colonel interrupted. "Well, don't send it yet. I'll let you know."

Again the Colonel paused, and the two women stood silently watching him.

"The one who made the mistake did a very brave thing," he said finally. "He protected the others."

It seemed that he wanted to say something else, but he didn't. Abruptly he turned and left the building.

The woman in the bright-colored dress looked at the Sergeant with contempt.

"Why did you tell him?" she said.

4

Many little towns don't have hospitals at all, maintaining their seriously sick in their own homes or referring them to the nearest city. And there the hospitals are often well away from the center of the city. If you have no occasion to go to a hospital it is quite possible to live in many cities, year in, year out, without ever seeing one. But in Los

Alamos in 1946 the hospital, which looked somewhat like the community center of a small New England town, stood at the very center of things and served somewhat, on its outside at least, the function of a community center. Although most of the buildings of Los Alamos were painted barracks green or cold gray, the hospital was painted white. It fronted on the main street; paths and walks crossed and curved through an open space, a kind of barren park, between it and the street. A hundred yards down a slope from the back of the building was a pond, a nearly round body of water. It, like the hospital itself, has been surrounded and swallowed up in recent years. Once it was a gathering place for the children of the town, a rink for skaters, a hole for swimmers, a place for playing.

In the open space in front of the hospital were half a dozen crude benches. On these, and on the stoop before the hospital entrance, people often sat at noon; and, although there were regulations to the contrary, the friends of patients on the first floor of the building drew the benches up and, standing on them, talked through the windows. The maternity cases usually were put in the rooms with these accessible windows, and in the evenings sometimes three or four young men at once, sometimes for an hour at a stretch, talked through the windows to their wives. Los Alamos was a young town, and the hospital served mainly the medical events of the young.

On the morning after the accident in the canyon, Dr Herman Romach slowed down as he passed the open space on his way to the Technical Area, and finally stopped altogether. He put his briefcase down on the ground against his legs, lit a cigarette, and gazed at the hospital. Mr George Ulanov observed him from the other side of the street and, crossing over, joined him.

"Saxl's room is at that corner on the second floor," Ulanov said. "There," and he pointed. "What have you heard?" Ulanov emphasized the "you" ever so slightly.

Romach shrugged his shoulders. "I heard he got it worse

than Nolan did last summer, but then I don't consider my source infallible. Besides, Louis is much healthier than Nolan was. Nolan's heart wasn't too good, and he was fat— fatter than he should have been anyway. Did you know about his heart? Things like that can be important."

"Why, I suppose they can," Ulanov said, continuing to look at the hospital. "But I'm not sure of what order of importance they are."

"Well, it might not mean anything," Romach said, "and then again you can see how it might just be the margin. It's certainly something on the good side."

"It is if it means anything," Ulanov said. "Did you know I had that same room a couple of months ago? When I broke my toe out skiing with Saxl as a matter of fact. I got well in that room very quickly. It's a good sign, don't you think?"

"Oh, for Christ's sake," said Romach.

"You should be carrying a bland broth you made yourself and just wanted to bring over for the poor boy. There will be a period during which everything will be distorted and elaborated into meanings it doesn't have, and this will be to salve ourselves, not him."

"So what are the meanings things should have?" Romach asked, in a loud angry voice, turning to face Ulanov. "I didn't know you were an authority on radiation sickness. I didn't know anybody was."

"No?" Ulanov said. "Saxl is, for one. At least he's an authority on the case of Nolan. He sat with him like a mother for most of those twenty days it took him to die. And at the very least he knows more than you, who will infect others with well-meaning nonsense, and this will be earnestly passed on to him in well-meaning calls to the sickroom—for him to see through, and brood about in the hours without visitors." Ulanov looked up at the corner of the room again, and then again said: "The hours without visitors."

Three men stopped in the street a little distance away.

"Any news?" one of them called.

"What have you been doing to Romach?" said another. "He looks mad."

"People seem not to understand—days it will take to establish level of neutron radiation," the third said, walking toward Romach and Ulanov. "Gamma radiation—not too difficult. But neutron radiation—very different matter. Is it not so, Ulanov?"

Two more men came over to join the little group. A man walking by himself came in from the opposite direction.

"There is a time for this, and a time for that," Ulanov said to Romach.

Romach was a big, solid figure, and he stood with his feet firmly planted, his briefcase still against one leg, and his arms folded across his chest; he did look angry, but not as though he were angry at anyone. And in fact he was more puzzled than angry; he could not understand Ulanov, and wasn't it obvious that Ulanov had simply chosen to misunderstand him?

"—necessary to speak carefully to a sick person, of course, and absolutely to one who has had an experience with his sickness," Romach was saying. "But it's true nonetheless that things like a good heart or a bad one—I was saying that Nolan had a bad heart, or, well, a record of some trouble with it anyway. Did you know that?" And he looked around the group in general.

"What I want to know," one of them said, "is how it happened. My God, if it could happen to Saxl it could happen to anyone."

Ulanov was talking earnestly to the man who was worried about the neutron radiation, a stocky Pole whose name was Peplow.

"—not at all like the Japanese explosions," he was saying. "The sequence of nuclear reactions is the same, of course, but this assembly produced only ionizing radiation—no heat, no explosion. Also, they were close to the origin. Several thousand feet of air filtered the radiation from the bombs, but these guys got theirs through hardly any air and only that lousy little excuse for shielding down there. Much higher neutron-to-gamma ratio. More beta rays. If Saxl's hands were actually touching the assembly, he could lose them just from the beta rays."

"If it could happen to Saxl it could happen to anyone," said the man who had said this before.

A very young man, not more than twenty-two or twenty-three, with stringy blond hair and pale blue eyes, spoke up, trying to interrupt.

"Please," he said.

"That is a funny thing about the dates," one of the others said. "Tuesday the twenty-first again, and out of all the times they've done it."

"Please," said the young man, "perhaps Mr Ulanov and you were not talking about the same things."

"What's that about the dates?" Ulanov said.

Only two of the eight men gathered here had heard about the curious coincidence of the dates. Several of them smiled, one pursed his lips, and the others, except for Ulanov, listened without expression. Ulanov began to walk back and forth in short steps.

"Why, isn't that remarkable?" he murmured. "Really quite remarkable."

"Nonetheless," Romach was saying to the young man, "he says I spread nonsense because I say the health of the heart is a cause for hope."

"Third day, two and one," Ulanov said. "This is certainly very interesting. Three, two, one, *shunya*."

"Is true enough about high ratio of neutrons in this situation," Peplow was explaining to one of the others, "but how was neutron dosage distributed? For example, how much of dosage goes into these men's bones, where induced radioactivity of the phosphorus intensifies effects on adjacent tissues. This is very interesting, and very difficult."

"Are you superstitious, Ulanov?" one of the men said, smiling at him.

"Naturally," Ulanov said, "who isn't? But it's a most unusual sequence, even once. Twice, you must either ignore it or dislike it. Three, two, one, zero, *shunya,* nothing." He spread his hands and made a grimace. "I cannot like it."

"This *shunya,* what—"

"Mr Ulanov is just going back to first sources," the very young man interrupted. "*Shunya* is the Indian word for zero, which the Indians invented. But, Mr Ulanov, aren't you consulting your fears too much, particularly such an exotic one?"

"Unquestionably," Ulanov said, "but what can you do with a thing like this? It is simply so beautifully pat and simple, it is there, and it will not go away. I apologize to Romach, however. Romach, I apologize. I am even a bigger fool than you."

"As a physicist," one of the men said, "I can take you both with toleration. Mathematicians like Ulanov always run to mysticism. Think of Ramanujan writing down those beautiful formulae—and when he couldn't supply the proofs, he said a goddess inspired him with the formulae in his dreams. What do you say to that, Romach? As for you, you're just quarrelsome and conservative. That's because chemists are impressed by how much they know. Us physicists know how little it is."

The polished air, warming quickly from the sun, vibrated in the open space with reflections and opinions, although from the peak of Truchas nothing was happening and from across the street or from the corner nothing could be heard. From even twenty feet away the voices were scarcely more than murmurs, for, after Romach's one outburst, all of the men talked quietly. From a block away, where Betsy Pilcher first noticed the group, they seemed to be standing both silently and motionlessly, like cows in a pasture, Betsy thought, growing angry at the sight.

She walked faster; I will show them, she said to herself, that some people have better things to do than stand and stare. She tightened her face, which was slack and loose after the brief sleep she had had. At two o'clock in the morning the cold slap of the night wind, the enormous street, and the indifferent stars had bent her thoughts down and into blackness. And it was not better in the warming day, on the street with people.

She had taken a Benzedrine tablet and had drunk three cups of coffee; she had let cold water from her shower run over her; but the consequence of these measures, together with her thoughts, was that she hated everyone she saw. No one knew what she knew, and no one felt as she felt, and everywhere were enemies. She made no effort to mask her tightly drawn face, and what she thought was in it.

But the men were not motionless, not standing quite like cows, she saw as she came closer. She checked off their faces in one quick look and discovered that they were not all gaping at her. More than she saw, she sensed the small movements, the restlessness, and the slightly strained stances, which betrayed feelings not meant to be shown and embarrassment over the failure. She sensed also that one of them, and then another, was about to speak to her; and she proceeded steadily past them. Like other nurses, Betsy had learned to chart—toward the end of dealing with or of absenting herself so she would not have to deal with—the coursings of emotion that might lead to intractableness in the friends and relatives of patients. What she felt now, as she went on up to the stoop, was no more than a climate favorable to that, which is to say that instead of the morbidity she had set her face against she had discovered a concern that might have touched her. But still no one knew what she knew and no one felt as she did, and she cursed the men silently for the trouble they might eventually be.

As for the men, they could not, in the wake of Betsy's passing, pick up again the threads of their talk; Betsy had ignored them, but Betsy, or the meaning of Betsy, could not be ignored. The physicist, who had been speaking so urbanely when she had come upon them, turned abruptly and walked off. The three who had arrived together reassembled themselves out of the gathering and together they moved away. But others were coming into the open space. As this group disbanded, another was forming.

5

When David Thiel came along the street from the telegraph office a few minutes later, Ulanov had gone, the second group had broken up, and a third had formed across the street from the hospital. The half-dozen men in this gathering were intent on their talk and did not notice David, who paid no attention to them until he was halfway across the open space. One of the men broke away from the group and ran across, calling David as he ran.

"Any luck?" said David, half turning but still continuing on toward the hospital.

"Yes and no, or rather no and yes," the man said. He seemed to want to stop and talk, but David continued on and he continued too, walking half sideways. "That motor you thought about is no good—somebody took the brushes out of it. But my kid's got a little one, twentieth horsepower you know."

"We could find another."

"He won't miss it. Also I got hold of Dombrowski at the cyclotron shop. I'm seeing him later. They'll be glad to—Dave! Goddamnit! Wait a minute, will you? What's the word this morning?"

David had started up the three steps to the little porch before the hospital entrance. He stopped on the middle one.

"I haven't heard anything, not since last night. There won't be much to go on for a while."

"What do you think now?"

David started up the steps again. He said something in answer to the question, but the sound of his cane against the boards buried it. At the top of the steps, he half turned. Across the street he saw Colonel Hough just joining the group of men; he looked at them for a moment before he spoke again.

"You know," he said, "you might take one of those hospital trays on wheels that slide over the bed—you could build the machine right on that. You'd save time. Anyway, it's a thought. Have you figured out how you're going to work it?"

"We'll manage, Dave. You look like the wrath of God. Why don't you go home and get some sleep?"

David nodded, then turned and went on into the hospital.

Across the street, Colonel Hough watched him disappear before continuing with what he had been saying.

"Well, I thought he might have stopped to talk with you. I had a word with him this morning. He got no sleep, none at all. Of course, Louis is his closest friend."

"That was a very tricky experiment, I often wondered—" one of the men began.

"Soldiers take chances," the Colonel's wife had said to him, "soldiers know they have to take chances. Is it different with scientists? Don't they have to take chances too?"

"Yes," the Colonel said now, "it was that kind of experiment. I never saw it, but we'd had discussions about it. One thing was that Louis had done it so many times—"

"Do you know exactly what went wrong?" someone broke in. "I must say it's hard to avoid the thought that if it could happen to him it could happen to anyone."

The Colonel did not know these men well. Most of them were engineers and machinists from the electronics laboratory and the machine shop, and three or four of them were new at Los Alamos; that is, they had come since the end of the war. As a rule the Colonel got along rather better with such men as these than he did with the physicists and chemists and mathematicians; he could tell more clearly what they were thinking, and what they were thinking was more apt to be what he was thinking, or could think about if he tried. But he found himself looking at them with a sort of uneasiness. There was so much these new ones didn't know about, and could never know about, from the war years, from the great exciting times, the secret times. You punk! he said to himself, looking into the face of the young man who had asked him what went wrong.

"I don't know yet," he said, and the men continued to look at him.

He had stopped to make a point of something to them, but all this looking had driven it out of his mind—although it was not precisely out, only shadowed by something else, the sudden recollection of a scene from a book of Koestler's his wife had read to him in bed some time before. The Nazis had put the hero on a table, had taken off all his clothes and pinned him there, and one of them then moved slowly toward him, toward his penis, with a lighted cigar. And the hero, perfectly helpless, could only look at the Nazi, who looked steadily at him while moving closer and closer. But in the end something in the look prevailed, the mute appeal reached the man beneath the Nazi, and the cigar was withdrawn before it burned. But who was appealing to whom?

"I don't know yet," he repeated. "But Louis did a very brave thing, I know that," he went on, remembering. "You heard how he knocked the assembly apart with his hands? The others can thank him for that."

"I've been thinking about that," one of the men said. "I wonder if there's time in such a situation to act bravely. Please understand me. I admire Saxl greatly, and from all I've heard he's very competent with his hands. As an engineer, I can appreciate that; they're not all." There were some murmurs of agreement. "But it was a very small fraction of a second, and the brain must act on impulses that take—"

"You can say it was instinctive," the Colonel broke in sharply, "but the instinct of a brave man then. I've seen it in soldiers."

The Colonel looked across at the hospital. He asked the men if they would mind saying nothing about the accident for the time being to anyone outside Los Alamos, and explained the importance of official notifications, with a word on security and public morale. He left them abruptly and walked on.

"I wonder if the instincts are susceptible to moral evaluations," one of them said.

"Did you see what Truman said yesterday?" another asked. "He said the atom bomb destroyed nationalism and started a new and unprecedented age of the soul."

"I say, look over there," said a clipped British voice.

"Forward to Bikini and the age of the soul," said a dry voice. Several of the men laughed.

"The trouble with the Colonel is he just can't visualize a millionth of a second," the engineer said. "It's very hard to visualize."

"Look over there, I say."

At the end of the hospital there was a door to the cellar, and a small truck stood close to it. Two men were lifting down a barrel of cracked ice; the ice glistened in the sun and pieces of it shone from the ground where they had fallen.

"It's for his hands, I guess," one of the men said. "They must have run out."

At the window of Louis Saxl's room the slats of the venetian blind flipped; behind them, for a moment, Betsy Pilcher was visible, looking out into the open space. There was no one in it; everyone had gone. Later in the morning some shoppers stopped by there to stare at the hospital, to tell what they had heard, to listen to what others had heard, and to see if, by putting the two together, they could know more than they did. Later in the afternoon, as the Jemez Mountains to the west of Los Alamos began to show against the sun, children came walking, running, and skipping along the street, across the open space, down to the pool to play for a while before dinner. As the shadows of the mountains reached across the mesa, lights went on; an unshielded globe on a tall pole burned brightly near the pool, and the yellow glow of it reached the hospital, growing stronger in the gathering darkness against the windows there. The noises of the children playing at the pool sounded for a while, and then, with the last of the light, the children went, walking and running and skipping away.

6

When he turned his head to the right, Louis could look through a window that faced the area in front of the hospital. Even if he shifted himself up as much as the troughs that trapped his hands permitted, he could not see down into the open space, whence, from time to time during the day, he had heard the murmur of voices. If the slats of the blind slanted in, he could see the tops of some trees. If they slanted out, and at just the right angle, the angle to which Betsy had adjusted them earlier in the day, the walk on the far side of the street ran along the windowsill. In the intervals between the regular taking of blood samples, two injections of penicillin, a blood transfusion, numerous refreshenings of the ice in the troughs, several talks with David Thiel, one with Colonel Hough, and many with the doctors, not to mention times out for the bedpan and more for various examinations—in the intervals Louis had walked a number of his friends along the windowsill, moving his head slightly up or slightly down to keep their feet aligned.

But he had not turned his head or shifted his body to look through the window for some time. The ice in the

troughs that trapped his hands failed to trap the pain that
was moving up into his arms; soon, he thought, it would
be necessary to mention this. Meanwhile, it was more comfortable to lie straight and look through, or at, the window
directly beyond the end of his bed. The slats of the blind
at this window overlapped, and he could see nothing there
except a yellow glow growing on the blind as the daylight
faded. But he knew the light that cast the glow, and in his
mind's eye he could see the pool by which it stood, and
the children playing there; he could hear them calling, one
to another.

He lay quietly. They had given him a sedative, but he
did not feel sleepy. He felt exhaustion, but he also felt
apprehension, and he felt each feeling through the other,
and he did not feel sleepy. Nothing they had so far done
was new, except for the ice. They had done all of these
things with Nolan, except that Nolan had not had ice.

The yellow glow penetrated the slats of the blind as
though it were trying to reach into the room and enfold
him. Both of the windows in his room were closed, but
he could feel that the night chill had come into the air,
and he got some comfort from looking at the glow of light,
growing warmer, reaching in. He closed his eyes, opened
them, and closed them again. It did not make much difference; he could feel the glow, and even see it, equally
well either way.

Watching the glow, listening to the children, it seemed
to him that he could remember the sounds and the sight
from somewhere else, and years away, but he was too tired
to think just where and when. His mind slipped on, and
shaped some words. *Some say the world will end in fire, some
say in ice; from what I've tasted of desire, I hold with those
who favor fire*—He could not remember further. He turned
these words in his head, watching the glow, listening to
the children.

It would be darker in the canyon than it was up here
on the mesa; making allowances for that (and putting the

words out of mind), he estimated from the quality of day-light coming through the window at his right that the accident had happened something more than twenty-four hours before. He would have to ask Betsy where his watch was. He tried to remember how many times he had been nauseated; four, he decided. That was not good. But he had no temperature to speak of, or he had had none half an hour or so before (although that really meant nothing this early, not really). As for his blood count—they had not told him what they were learning from the steady procession of samples, and he had not yet asked. He would have to ask Betsy to hang his watch up so he could read it from where he lay.

"Ice," he said aloud, "is also great and would suffice." He spoke softly, almost in a whisper. David will know the words between, he said to himself. But at once he decided he could not ask this; the gap in his memory annoyed him, but his interest in the poem would be thought morbid. He moved his left hand slightly in the trough and the pain in his arm increased. It was, moreover, an excellent poem. He would get David to bring him his anthology, and he would get Betsy to read it to him.

After a while he had the impression that the door to his room opened. He did not want to turn his head to see, and yet he could see quite clearly the expression of infinite solicitude at the open door, and even noticed, with some amusement, how it changed to a smile of embracing cheerfulness, appropriate to airline hostesses and nurses. Because he saw what he could not see, he concluded he must be dreaming, which bothered him because he had intended to stay awake. And yet he could not be dreaming because at just this moment it came to him distinctly that the sounds of the children playing outside had stopped. It seemed to him that the quality of the silence was such as to suggest that the children had not gone away but had simply stopped their sounds, possibly to listen to something. Then he heard a high, shrill voice calling: "Harry! Harry! Nine o'clock,

Harry! Do you hear?" The voice came out of the middle
of the yellow glow of light, which had come right into his
room and was enfolding him.

He could distinguish Betsy standing beside his bed. She
was holding a jar of preserves toward him, and she was
saying: "I have a gift for thee. Did you nap any?"

He heard himself say, "How are the others?"

And Betsy went on: "Crowds of people all night and all
day. What are they trying to do? Did you nap any?"

But more clearly, louder than before, he heard the voice
calling: "Harry! Harry! Nine o'clock, Harry! Do you hear
me?"

He tried to reach out for the jar of preserves, but a
terrible pain in his left arm stopped him. Betsy drew back
as though pulled along a rail; her smile faded, the shape
of her wavered, and he saw that she was about to speak.
But she was still a great distance away, and it was not yet
nine o'clock, despite Harry's mother. He knew that when
she did speak, her words would end in a happening he
desperately did not want. But he might possibly avoid this,
if he were to stay very still and say nothing.

"Nine o'clock, Harry!"

Then, although he was not looking, he saw her coming
toward him again, still with the jar of preserves. He could
tell from the expression on her face that something was
up.

"Do you remember that night you found grandpa?" she
said. "I never should have let you do it—a perfectly terrible
experience for a boy."

Oh, mother, it was long ago, it was all right.

Evenings like this.

On such evenings the big, square, boxlike houses, with
meaningless cupolas and ungainly porches rimmed by bushes
and shrubs, joined the trees to make soft and singular
patterns in the dark of Longfellow Avenue. The trees stood
evenly spaced in even rows on either side of the street.
But some reached out and almost touched above the pave-

ment, and all of them spread back across the sidewalks and made canopies above the lawns, and through the heavy upper foliage shone the lights of random upstairs windows.

On evenings like this the porches of the houses held people who sat on swings that creaked slightly, and who smoked cigarettes or cigars that made small, moving points of light in the dark. Sometimes the sitters called across to the porch next door, and regularly they turned their eyes to the center of the street, where the children played on a narrow grassy strip that was called the boulevard.

The street lights stood along this strip, two to a block, and in the yellow circles they made after dark the children gathered to stand and stare, pick at each other, back away, sit down, get up, and play games in which they would run beyond the yellow circles to hide, be found, and come screaming back. The sound of the children playing was the loudest sound in the evening along Longfellow Avenue, and the yellow circles of the street lights held almost all the movement. From the porches the observant eyes looked out. At nine o'clock or thereabouts there came the first call: "Harry! Nine o'clock, Harry! Do you hear?" And the games began to end, and one by one the children all went straggling home. Finally the porches emptied and the downstairs lights went out, and after a while the upstairs lights, and by midnight there were only the empty yellow circles from the street lights, and no movement at all.

The boulevard was a playground for very young children mostly; after they got to be twelve or so they had to give up the games, because the only games that could be played there between the porches were games like red light and tap-the-icebox. But some of the older ones went out to the boulevard after supper occasionally. They leaned against the street lights or sat on the curbing of the grassy strip and talked, or laughed at the children, or caught them and held them when they came running past to hide. Skip Seago, who lived a block away on Holmes, came around once in a while even when he was fifteen years old. Louis was only eleven then and Skip was his hero; aware of this, Skip spoke to him and didn't tease him much. More than this is seldom found to span the enormous distance that separates the orbit of childhood and the orbit of adolescence. But this evening the orbits shifted and actually came together, touching across the distance. (Oh, mother, do not come tonight.)

On this evening his mother stepped down from their porch and walked across the street to the boulevard. He saw her coming over and wondered, because it was not yet time to go in and besides none of the mothers ever walked across; they only called. She came up and he said it wasn't time. She said it was getting close to time and she wanted to walk around to Grandfather Saxl's house to see how he was getting along; she had a jar of preserves to take; she wanted him to go with her.

A few months before this, Grandfather Saxl had felt a swelling in his chest and had suddenly been drenched with sweat; with the sweat had come a wild fluttering within him, and when the fluttering had gone away and the doctor had left, Grandfather Saxl had changed from a vigorous man of sixty-seven into a preoccupied old person.

He had lived alone for a number of years, and even after the attack he continued to live alone. He could and did move around, take care of himself, putter in the back yard, where there was a little garden with a grape arbor, and even take short walks. Louis's mother went over every day, sometimes twice, taking things to eat, and books and magazines. Usually she stayed for an hour or so while they talked of the past, and of the family. She installed a phone beside his bed and in the evenings she called him. But this evening there had been no answer. She had sat by the phone for a moment tapping a pencil against the little table. ("Your father had driven over to Springfield and I knew he wouldn't be back for an hour or more; still—") She did not want to ask any of the neighbors; not yet, she thought, remembering fleetingly how tall and handsome Abraham

Saxl had looked only a few months before, with his thick white hair that looked thick no longer.

Grandfather Abraham Saxl lived around the corner on the next street, in a house with an ungainly porch rimmed by shrubs and bushes. His bedroom was on the second floor behind a rounded window that looked out across the roof of the porch; they could see the light in it as they went around the corner and they could see that the window was half open. They could even see the large framed engraving of ducks in flight that hung on the wall above the bed, but from the sidewalk they could not see the bed, or could see only the pointed posts of it against the wall under the engraving.

"I suppose he's just dozed off," she said after they started. Not until they had gone around the corner did Louis sense the worry in her. "I wish your father were back," she said then, and as they walked toward the house looking at the window Louis began to feel the worry in himself. Halfway from the corner to the house she put an arm across his shoulders. "Grandpa will be sixty-eight this fall," she said, "he oughtn't to be living alone like that, not well and all." After another few steps she said: "He was the handsomest thing, you don't remember. He wore white linen suits and people turned in the streets to look at him."

There was a street light almost in front of the house, with the lamp painted black on the inner side so it would not shine in the windows. The house next door was dark and the porches for several houses around were deserted. In the quiet his mother called softly, "Father, are you awake? . . . Grandpa?" They waited, and then went up on the porch and she rang the bell. It sounded loud in the house and they stood there listening. She rang it again. "I don't know why he always keeps them locked," she said, trying the door; it was locked.

"Can you climb up on this porch roof?"

"Sure."

"I've told you not to often enough, but—oh, dear." She

took hold of him. "Now listen," she said, "you climb up there—and do be careful, darling—try the window that goes into the hall. It may be open, but if it isn't, go through the window in grandpa's room. Go right through the room. Don't stop to say anything or look at anything, and come right down and let me in. Can you do that?"

"Sure," he said. As he had done many times before, playing, he shinnied up the porch pillar to the overhang, took hold of it, and swung himself up on the roof.

"Come right downstairs," she called.

The window to the hall, he knew, was stuck fast; he didn't even look at it. And first of all he just glanced quickly by the window to his grandfather's room, letting his eyes not quite stop to see inside the room but getting a kind of feel of it, the whiteness of the bedclothes and the sense of his grandfather lying there, particularly his head against the whiteness of the pillow. Even in this very quick not-quite-look he saw his grandfather's eyes looking out at him, and as he walked across the flat roof to the window he was looking straight across the room into his grandfather's eyes. He had to push the window up only a little way to get through, and as he went through he looked all the time, not taking his eyes from the eyes that looked at him from the bed.

Inside the window as he straightened up he stood uncertainly, still looking at his grandfather; he noticed that his grandfather's lips were moving although he could not hear the words. And he noticed that his grandfather was lying half doubled up at the upper end of the bed, as though he had been pushed there and almost as though he were being held there even now. His head was moving too, forward a little and then back, then forward again and then back. The old man lay there doubled up and the boy stood there and they looked at each other, and no word was spoken. The boy looked away in embarrassment, but the embarrassment gave way to fear, and he looked back again, into the eyes of the old man, seeking the source of the fear, fearful to leave it. Still he stood there; he had simply forgotten to move, and it did not occur to him to move even when he heard his mother's voice, calling something from below and outside. He remembered better than his mother thought how his grandfather had looked in his white suits. And he remembered how he and his father and mother and his sister came over to his grandfather's house sometimes—and, "Who knows One?" his grandfather had asked, sitting beside the table and looking down at him with eyes staring—"Who knows One?" he had said, sitting quietly and expectantly beside the table. "I know One—One Lord of the Universe." "Who knows Two?"

And suddenly he turned his eyes away and ran across the room, into the hall, and down the stairs, to the front door, and opened it, and ran up against his mother, clinging to her, shivering.

It had been all right later. Posted on the curb of the boulevard to watch for his father, he had won first the attention and then the whole interest of Skip Seago. As the other children went home to their beds, understanding nothing, he felt like a courier who has run a long distance and is given audience by the prince. Bars were let down while the prince, respectful of youth's valor, moved over and invited him to sit. His mother had cried over him, and the doctor, after he had come, had called him a brave boy. But Skip understood the real and great importance of what had happened.

"I know a couple of kids who've seen dead people," Skip said, "but you're the only one's seen someone dying. If he dies."

"He'll die, I guess."

"Well, you can't be sure until he actually does though. The second attack doesn't necessarily kill you. The third kills you, like going down the third time swimming always kills you. Of course the second attack can kill you. I don't know if it counts if he doesn't die tonight though."

"Yes, but if he dies from this attack, he was dying even

if he doesn't actually die tonight, wasn't he? Even if he dies tomorrow or even the day after?"

Skip thought about this, tugging gently at a tuft of grass beside him, while from the porches came the sound of swings creaking slightly.

"I guess so," he said graciously after a while. "Anyway we'll have to see. You know, soldiers on battlefields see people dying all the time. I bet they get used to it. Or race drivers, those little midget race drivers, they see themselves get killed plenty. Do you suppose you'd get used to it if you saw people dying all the time?"

"I bet no one gets used to it."

"Oh, I don't know. How scared were you, really?"

"Well, I was really sort of scared."

"Tell me again how he looked there, lying on the bed."

Grandfather Saxl hadn't died that night. He recovered enough to move about, although not enough to resume his puttering in the garden. Instead he learned to cultivate within himself the dry but nourishing fruits that grow only on the slopes of death. A housekeeper was installed and the front porch was rearranged so that he could live on it during warm afternoons and watch the events of the street. Quite often in the days that followed this second attack he noticed Louis and the older boy together on the street in front of his house. He couldn't even place the older boy, but he waved to them from the porch and several times they came up to see him. Although they only stood there, saying almost nothing and looking at each other, the way children do, he enjoyed the fact of these little visits. He felt very happy to see Jew and Gentile, eleven and fifteen, together, and happy that they would stop their playing long enough to come up and see an old man, and a sick old man at that.

("He was very fond of you, son. There was much of himself in you. He thought—" "I know. We used to talk— when I used to go there—" But mother, not tonight— not—)

They were heirs of the age of wonders, he and Skip, and their difference in years became a detail lost among the wonders—automobiles, airplanes, radios, construction kits of innumerable parts and pieces. It would never have occurred to Skip that here was a fit companion except in the presence of wonders, but fitness meant love for these, which could be assumed, and comprehension, which proved itself.

And then to his horror Louis found that he was growing bored with the wonders. He lay awake defending his established ways against the heretical encroachment. But from the moment he was consciously aware of the weakness in himself he could not entirely down the nagging notion that he had nothing more to learn from putting pieces together. He would have died rather than confess it; Skip knew more than he did and so plainly there was more to be learned. If so, grim voices within him said, you just aren't interested in learning. But I am, he cried back, it's only, it's only—

He continued to be sent home by Skip's mother, working her way through carpentry and metal work and wires, and in the end it was not his defection but Skip's; the noncommunicable discoveries of life intervened and Skip grew distant. It happened very suddenly, and for a week or so he doggedly went to the Seago house to tinker alone with the radio, sometimes seeing Skip go in or out and sometimes not. Then Skip told him it wouldn't be necessary for him to come around any more. It was plain that he had transgressed in some way or had been found inadequate, and the bright and shining hours were lost in the hurt. He did not even notice the quiet relaxation of his defenses against his heresy.

And he was hardly aware how often, as time went on, he came to go to his grandfather's house, not now for little visits, to stand and stare, but for hours at a time on the floor with the books of which Grandfather Saxl had more than anyone. He called questions to his grandfather, and tried thoughts on him; together they tried to understand how there could be such a thing as the square root of minus one, which he came across in a book one day. His grandfather made a password of it.

"Say there, what's the square root of minus one, boy?" he would call from the porch as Louis came up the walk.

"I'll have to read up on that," Louis would say.

The parents of the neighborhood thought him exemplary, and some indeed kept track of his comings and goings with something akin to worry.

"It doesn't seem right for a boy to spend so much time with an old man, even his grandfather."

"Even sick and all. A boy ought to play."

"Of course Jewish families are very close."

On the days he did not go to his grandfather's house he played mostly with Chuck Braley, across the street, who had a big barn behind his house. Here they made pushmobiles, for the barn was full of boxes and old bicycle wheels and a thousand things; and if he had grown bored with the wonders, he had not grown bored with things that could be designed to patterns of his own. In the barn the boys who came and went made pushmobiles, and learned to smoke, and talked of girls.

But not all of him went there, on afternoons after school, on evenings after dinner. As the parents noted his visits to his grandfather, Chuck noticed his absences from the barn, and his withholding when he was there. Because he had a grandfather who might die at any time he was granted a certain caste by Chuck; because he was a Jew he was allowed and even required to show differences. But Chuck, he knew, arrived at approximately the same conclusions the parents had reached.

Still, by the time he had moved far enough out of the world of the barn and the boulevard for the fact to be noted, he had moved far enough into the world of his grandfather's books to be unconcerned with the noting. The core of this world, the sun and the fulcrum of it, was a set of the Eleventh Edition of the *Encyclopaedia Britannica* that had lain undisturbed in his grandfather's house for years. The index was missing and so was the volume LOR—MEC, but this left twenty-seven worlds beyond boredom, beyond doubts, and indeed, beyond understanding. Lacking the index, he followed cross-references wherever they led, losing himself in subdivisions and side-alleys: Huyghens, Air Pump, and the Problem of Three Bodies (which see, which see, which see). Full of yearnings but empty of aims, he came eventually to dazzle himself with visions of himself as a scientist of a kind not defined, confronting and leveling mountains of uncertainties to reach truths not specified.

And on an evening (like this) he found that there was a harbor for his hopes, and was touched with glory. He found it in a lone volume of Thomas Huxley's *Selected Works*, the survivor of a set that his grandfather had bought in 1895 when he had been looking everywhere for knowledge and had been impressed by the encomiums that the death of the great English biologist had brought forth. Lying on the floor of the front hall of his grandfather's house, just beyond the door where he and his mother had once stood listening to the sound of the bell in the house, Louis read what Huxley had to say from a great yet conceivable height:

"In the course of his work the physical philosopher, sometimes intentionally, more often unintentionally, lights upon something that proves to be of practical value. For the moment science is the Diana of all the craftsmen. But even while the cries of jubilation resound and this flotsam and jetsam of the tide of investigation is being turned into the wages of workmen and the wealth of capitalists, the crest of the wave of scientific investigation is far away on its course over the illimitable ocean of the unknown."

Oh, this is where I'll go, Louis cried within himself. He read the words again, and they turned and rose in his mind, gleaming before him. He kicked himself over on his back and looked up at the light in the dusty yellow shell hanging from the ceiling above him. Far away on the illimitable ocean of the unknown, he whispered, and saw visions of beacon lights in churning waves, the lights turning slowly, cutting sharp paths along the jagged line of the waves, swinging closer and closer suddenly to bathe him there on a wave's crest in their brilliance.

Oh, no! *Oh, no!*

"Did you nap any?" Betsy was saying; and then, after a little pause, leaning closer: "Louis? Oh, Louis, let me—"

In the pit of his stomach he could feel the waves tightening and mounting for the break. There was nothing he could do; he could not speak, least of all could he speak. The tightening and the mounting went on and on; and then broke and filled him with the stuff that came pouring out of his mouth, over his pajamas and the bedclothes, wave after wave of it. He saw Betsy's hands moving about before him. He saw also, although he did not comprehend at once what it was, one of his own hands—splotchy in red and white, a great blister between two fingers, dripping water. It was lifted somewhat above the bedclothes as though it were not to be touched by what was there. It hung against the yellow glow on the blind, and as he looked at it he pushed back involuntarily against the bars of the bed. He tried to speak to Betsy, but, although he could feel his lips moving, there were no words. Staring at his hand, retching dryly now, he lay half doubled up at the top of the bed, as though he had been pushed there.

7

Throughout the evening of the first day after the accident, Betsy Pilcher sat in Louis Saxl's room, anticipating wants and needs, attending to them, and, finally, yielding him to sleep. The terrible vomiting with which the afternoon had ended, Betsy decided, might have been a helpful purge; the body must have rid itself of some unknown noxious

things. At a little after ten o'clock she went quietly out of
Louis's room and walked with slow steps down the corridor, looking in at one room and another. All of the rooms
were dark, but voices spoke to her from three of them,
asking about Louis. She could tell them honestly that he
was feeling much better, that he was resting very well. She
took the starched rustle of her uniform down the stairway,
and the floor was left to silence.

At the landing halfway down, Betsy turned and looked
back at the dimly lit corridor she had just left; it was only
a glance, part of the pattern of habit. Vomiting, she was
thinking—standing like a grace taken form in the dark,
the small light from above toning her intent face—was
sometimes a good thing. This stood to reason and was a
part of nature's way. If vomiting was a symptom to be
watched for and noted with forebodings in this serious
sickness, still it might also be to some extent a corrective
of the condition it reflected. Moreover, doctors were known
to dramatize or simplify, and to pigeonhole unduly. Everything had turned to the better after that last siege; his
apprehension had dropped away, even the pain in his left
arm had seemed to diminish, a relief had seemed to enter
him.

At eight o'clock, an hour after the siege had passed, his
respiration was normal, his pulse and blood pressure were
normal and his temperature less than a degree above normal; at nine thirty they were the same. They had talked
about some of his friends and some of hers; he had made
jokes with her; and he had fallen off to sleep as the sedatives took hold.

A door opened below and a murmur of voices sharpened
and bunched into words. Betsy turned her head and looked
down, but still she stood on the landing. Some of the
doctors, she knew, had been meeting in the conference
room; she would wait for them to go.

Of the workings of radiation sickness Betsy did not
know much. She had been new at the hospital at the time

of the first accident, nine months before. She had not really read the report on it that Dr Pederson had shown her three or four times. She had only glanced at the endless documents, folders, and photographs constituting the medical findings from numerous surveys of the Hiroshima and Nagasaki areas. She was not in the least a squeamish person; there was little, indeed, in all the muck and dirty work of her profession to which she could not assign some kind of value. But she knew not what to get hold of, or where to look for meanings, in the mysteries of radiation sickness.

It did not bother her that she had had no more experience with it than with leprosy or the king's evil; it bothered her that this sickness was more comprehensible to physicists and chemists than to doctors and nurses, and seemed truly comprehensible to no one. It bothered her that, even so, Dr Pederson was considered something of an expert beyond his years and training because he had sat in attendance on Nolan. Most of all, it bothered her that there was nothing she could think to do about this sickness—except to hold to the possible hopeful significance of vomit.

"The Japanese made no such tests."

Betsy, looking down, still saw no one in the lower hall. But these words came to her clearly from just around the turn in the wall at the foot of the stairway; they came in the soft, noninsistent voice of Dr Morgenstern. Betsy withdrew herself a little. She saw Dr Morgenstern appear from just beyond the wall, but at once he turned and went back out of sight. He was a very tall man, four or five inches over six feet, and all of the visible parts of him were large and bony; her mind reported, automatically as it often did when she caught a glimpse of him, the clinical description of his nude figure that Staff Sergeant Robert Chavez, who had seen him in a shower, had once given her.

She watched as Dr Morgenstern came into view again, followed by Mr Herzog and a small, dapper man whom Betsy had never seen before. The dapper man was talking.

He had some papers in his hand and he swung them back and forth as he spoke.

"It's an irritating little point. I've read of similar findings in laboratory animals, I know I have, though I can't think where. It doesn't mean anything, I know that too—irritating point all the same."

Betsy shifted her eyes from this man, whose words meant nothing to her, to Dr Morgenstern; he was the doctor in direct charge of the hospital. He looked down his nose at the one who had spoken, moved his fingers, and said nothing.

The three men had come to a stop at the very foot of the stairs. Dr Morgenstern looked back along the corridor.

"Coming?" he said.

There was a flurry of sound from the conference room, coughs, a shuffling of feet, the tap of a cane. A voice boomed up, and a softer voice urged it to quiet. There was a texture of noises, of rustling papers and rustling clothes, of someone blowing his nose, of shiftings and movements, and the texture was heavy, of the sort that Betsy identified with men, with many men. It sounds like dozens, she said to herself; who? for just what?

"The capture cross-section of sodium is, however, just that much greater than the cross-section of phosphorus," Mr Herzog was saying in his quiet voice.

Betsy had turned her head meaninglessly toward the wall, toward the still invisible source of the sounds. As Herzog spoke she looked back and saw him prod his unseen listener.

"Do you know any biologic factors to account for this great disparity in the case of Saxl?"

David Thiel came into sight in the corridor. He was walking very slowly, barely using his cane, holding a pamphlet or a journal before him; he was reading aloud, too quietly for Betsy to make out any words, to two men. One was Novali, a young doctor at the hospital; the other was unknown to her. They were listening intently and were matching their steps to David's. Two more men appeared; she did not know either of them. Then she saw Edward Wisla's portly figure; she knew him, all right, everyone at Los Alamos knew him; people all over knew him, if only from his pictures in the papers. But only three or four days ago he had left for Washington—to "tell Congress about the atom, and incidentally about the Army"; so Louis Saxl himself had told her, this evening, only an hour or so ago.

She stared down at Wisla, and the unexpectedness of his presence there joined with the unfamiliarity of the other men to alert her senses. Another unknown appeared. All of these men followed each other across the space framed by the stair opening, passing into and out of Betsy's sight, moving toward the door of the hospital, fifty feet along the corridor. Pederson came up, still in his laboratory coat.

She heard him say good-night to someone around the turn of the wall, and then she heard another voice.

"Yes, good-night." There was a pause. "You know, we'd better aspirate some marrow in the morning." And another pause. "Good-night."

The man who said this, when he came into sight, was struggling with his overcoat. He turned his head, searching for the sleeve, holding his arm up awkwardly. He found the sleeve and straightened himself, looking across his shoulder and then up the stairway as he did so; from where she stood at the edge of the landing Betsy saw the flicker of surprise that crossed his face.

He seemed about to say something to her, but turned instead and started down the corridor. Then he turned back, crossing to the foot of the stairs.

"Were you just coming down?" he said.

Betsy nodded her head.

"From where—who?"

"Mr Saxl's room."

The man looked down at his feet, and up again at Betsy.

"You are Miss Pilcher?"

Again Betsy nodded. The man continued to look at her.

"Well—why don't you come down?" he said after a moment, smiling a little. He backed away from the stairs, as though to make room for her, and she started down them slowly.

"Is everything all right?"

"Quite all right," she said. She wondered why she answered him so, for the words reflected neither her hopes nor her fears; they were suitable for a relative, but she knew well enough that this one was a doctor. He was even more, however, a part of a procession, a disturbing procession that she didn't like. She came to a stop on the last step.

"Dr Morgenstern asked me to come here. I came from Berkeley—late—or maybe I'd have seen you before. My name is Berrain. I'm consulting. May I see the patient?"

"Now?" said Betsy, stiffening.

"Yes, now. Will you take me up?"

"He's sleeping, he just got to sleep. He wasn't to be disturbed at all." Dr Morgenstern himself had emphasized this.

"Well, I won't wake him. I just want to have a look at him."

Betsy came down from the last step. She found this phrasing offensive, and she gazed at Berrain coldly; she noticed that he had a wart just above the bridge of his nose; she fixed her eyes on that.

"Mr Saxl is not to be 'looked at' tonight. I can't take you up. If Dr Morgenstern asked you here, I suggest you see Dr Morgenstern."

"You'd be surprised how many nurses forget their orders though," Berrain said at once. "I'm glad you're a good nurse. They said you were. Good nursing's one of the few things we know helps for sure in a case like this. Did you bathe him this evening?"

"Yes, just lightly, about an hour ago."

"I understand he's very sunburned—tanned, that is. But

there's a demarcation? He wore something, I suppose. Could you notice any erythema on the lower abdomen? That is, did you?"

"Well, you know, I didn't really look, I mean I didn't notice," Betsy said, somewhat self-conscious despite herself. "I didn't see anything, but he may have— I mean, I think he thought there was a little reddening."

"You think he thought?"

"Well, I mean, he did say something, more to himself— what I mean is—"

"So? Yes, well," Berrain said, after a pause. "So how is he? Feeling pretty good?"

"Oh, really so much better all evening. He vomited badly about six o'clock. But since then—it's been just as if—" She took half a step toward Berrain.

"As if it cleaned out some of the trouble," Berrain said. "Yes, well, some of the trouble ended with it, didn't it? How many times was that? Five or six, I think I heard. I've been looking at some of that vomit. Quite a mess. No nausea since, huh?"

"None at all. He was fine all evening. Isn't it just possible—?"

Berrain moved his head around, up and down and from side to side. The hair receded on his head, and his face, which was large and fleshy, had an exposed look. His mouth drooped a little at the sides. Betsy had addressed her question and herself to the intentness that she had seen there a moment before, but it was not there anymore.

"You must be pretty tired," he said. "I shouldn't add to your burdens. I'll see you tomorrow."

He said good-night to her and started down the corridor again. But he had not gone three feet before he spoke once more, over his shoulder, without turning his head.

"About that vomiting, it may have helped. We don't any of us know too much, except that good nursing's very important. The vomiting may have helped—quite possible."

Betsy watched him enter the small vestibule that led to

the door, and, as he disappeared, suddenly she thought of
her walk home from the hospital in the cold morning of
the night before, and of how then, or even earlier, Dr
Morgenstern, or somebody, must have been making the
urgent calls that had brought Berrain from California, Wisla
from Washington, and all the others from their own places.
From the low rise of her small and cherished hope she saw
the ominous, complex reality that grew out of this heavy
gathering, but she could not move to it. Her head seemed
big for her shoulders; she looked at her wristwatch and
smoothed her skirt. She did feel tired. She saw the door
of the conference room open, and watched, without moving, as Pederson came out into the corridor. He had on
his hat and coat.

"I was just going up to look for you," he said. "Anything
wrong?" he added quickly, stopping twenty feet away.

"No. Everything's been fine."

"What was his temperature?"

"Ninety-nine point four at nine-thirty, just before he
went to sleep. No change since eight o'clock."

Pederson walked toward her. He asked her several questions and fingered a loose button on his coat. Under one
arm he had three or four brown filing folders, fat with
papers and journals; she recognized the gray cover of the
medical report on Nolan's case. Pederson seemed nervous,
even excited. He asked what she thought he should have
asked, although he was plainly anxious to be on his way,
and very soon he was. It had not occurred to her to ask
him about the meaning of the gathering whose break-up
she had witnessed; she had, in fact, accepted its meaning,
or the overriding meaning, whatever other meanings there
might be; there was no question in her mind that the details
she fed Pederson were intended for, and would be duly
scrutinized by, the whole gathering; and besides, in the
space of ten minutes she had moved quietly into place
among all the others. It was she, not Berrain or Pederson,
who finally brought up the end of the procession as she

walked out of the hospital a little later, working the collar of her coat around her neck, shivering in advance against the cold walk home.

But none of this was in her conscious thoughts. She was really very tired, and her conscious thoughts were already laying themselves down, one by one, for sleep—although it did occur to her as she neared her room that Pederson had not, in fact, asked all she thought he should have, for he had said nothing about the reddening of Louis Saxl's abdomen (and if Louis had mentioned it and Berrain had mentioned it, Pederson, of course, should have mentioned it too).

She wasn't sure of the precise significance of this reddening of the abdomen, except that it was plainly one more item in the lengthening list of complexities and oddities and unknowns that went to make up what she was now beginning to think of under the card-index title of "acute radiation syndrome." She had already half-filed away this reddening of the abdomen, along with much else, under the subheading of "What Can One Be Sure of Anyway with a Sickness Like This?" But then it struck her with sudden force—how stupid she was! how insensitive could she be!—that of course the reddening there, down in that area, had a perfectly obvious and elemental meaning.

"Oh, the poor worried boy!" she said, almost aloud.

But though the thought was sad, it was not the saddest thought possible; and therefore—possibly?—the saddest thought was somewhat stayed by this attention to the other. For would one worry, would a man worry about his manhood, if he despaired of his life? She felt herself to be in the presence of a question that was rooted in mysteries, although at the same time, at this precise moment, the figure that fancy and Staff Sergeant Robert Chavez had distilled for her out of the gross reality of Dr Morgenstern stood obscenely on the rim of her mind. But this figure shamed and embarrassed her now, and before it she fled from the halfway thought.

Is he going to die?

Her mind framed the words, but they did not take hold. Because she was very tired, and the night was cold, and sleep and warmth were just ahead of her, and because she knew she could not trust her answer—and again she told herself: who knows anything for sure?, and accepted it for what it meant—she fled from this too.

Her heels tapped louder, and her breath came faster, and she hunched her collar higher, and the air was colder, and the last few steps to her room she ran.

PART 3

Thursday: the illimitable ocean of the unknown

1

In the dim light of the day just forming, everything is indistinct and some things are illusions. The trees have no color; they are all one, and are motionless. In the thin air a voice carries a long way and the sound of a mountain lion may be either that or the bounce of a dislodged stone. Half an hour before, the guard house that blocks the main road to Los Alamos was an island in the night; its lights glowed warmly and were visible even from the valley road nearly ten miles distant. In another half-hour the lights will be out, and the guard house will stand forth for the unpretentious little hutment that it is, built of wood that has warped early. But now it is a bastion, tight and dominant in the empty scene. It stands a mile or so out from the edge of town and a mile or so in from the edge of the mesa where the road comes up. In this moment of dawn its lights press against the day moving across from Truchas, and are cold as metal. The heavy wire fence that runs off the mesa north and south from the guard house gapes beside it to make an entrance to the town, but the gape is as substantial as the fence in the general grayness.

This fence runs for many miles to enclose completely the town and even the buildings out in the canyons. It is not a very formidable fence, but it is sufficient to prevent nuisances and annoyances from the idly curious, the local ranchers, and the unlikely tourist away from his roads. More important than the fence are the postings that distinguish it clearly from other fences of this area: "Peligro— Propriedad del Gobierno" and "No Trespassing—Government Property." More important than these are the armed guards, who ride along the fence on horseback, look out over it from machine-gun installations at a number of commanding sites, and man the guard houses, of which the one here on the main road is the most important among half a dozen.

At the heart of the city, where the work is done, is a very formidable fence, fifteen feet high; not an inch of that one is out of range of the machine guns and the observation towers; an untoward move in its vicinity can cause sirens to blow, bullets to spray, and soldiers to run according to efficient plans. Nothing of the sort has happened, any more than the anti-aircraft guns in properly concealed clearings have been fired. For this, one may thank the almost ritualistic pattern of security measures that began with the selection of the mesa and continued on into all the conventional impedimenta of countersigned passes, sealed orders, forbidden movements, secret codes, censored mail, planned deceptions, false information for the local populace, and—even after the end of the war—general surveillance of everyone leaving or entering the city.

Here at this guard house on the main road, during the night just ending, each of the forty to fifty cars that have passed through the gates has first stopped while one of the guards on duty has verified the pass (countersigned) of each of its occupants; usually the guard has smiled and said a few words, for most of the occupants have been known to him. Six big trucks have rolled up, their brakes shushing, and have stood with engines softly roaring while their drivers declared themselves, were noted, and waved on. The Director of the Division of Theoretical Physics, a resident of the town for three years, forgot his pass and had to drive himself, his wife, and two friends back to get it; the guards apologized, there was some grumbling, but everyone knew it had to be done. At three o'clock in the morning the telephone in the guard house rang; it was Colonel Hough, saying that one Dr Jacob Briggle had landed at Albuquerque on a flight from Chicago and would be driving up in a military car, and was to be admitted; a special pass to accomplish this arrived at the guard house by jeep thirty minutes later.

In the morning the Security Office will receive a brief report on these events of the night. It will note, before it files, the theoretical physicist's forgetfulness; it will have checked already Dr Briggle's movements; it can learn from the guards, if it wishes to, even such details as that the horn on Dr Klaus Fuchs's car stuck as he was returning from Santa Fe, and one of the guards helped him to unstick it.

But in this moment of dawn the area around the gateway to Los Alamos seems deserted. No one is visible in the guard house, whose door stands open; no one is around the military jeep, which stands a few feet inside the fence. The lights touch no one, and the silence—save for a barely perceptible throbbing sound, hardly more than a vibration in the air, from the direction of the town—is complete. The birds are not yet awake; there is no wind.

The moment passes with six explosions. Two make rather muffled, thudding sounds, one sends a spinning crack across the mesa, and the last three are high, thin, and sharp, as though they pose a querulous question. The sounds come from some miles away, to the north. They die off, and again it is silent.

But it is possible now to make out two figures, standing by the side of the road just beyond the arc of lights from the guard house. They are facing the shrubs and trees that begin a little way back from the road. The thin beam of a flashlight suddenly streams out from them, moves slowly back and forth, holds steady at a certain point, and then suddenly goes out.

"I can't rightly say it was a mountain lion the other time either," one of them says. "Can't say for certain I ever heard a mountain lion. But it was a mean noise, meaner than this one. I had my gun out. Right over by that tree yonder."

"So let's get back. Leave the mountain lions to the mountains." This voice is irritable.

The flashlight goes on again; its beam runs along the road, intersects the arc of the guard house lights, and loses itself there. The figures start walking; the beam bobs for a few feet and again goes out.

"Nothing to be scared of," the first voice says. "They don't come up on the roads, not around the lights anyway. The explosions probably scared her away."

"Maybe it was a dog or a deer, or a rock even. They make funny noises sometimes, falling."

The lights sharpen the figures in front; they walk in toward the guard house like actors moving downstage; they are soldiers, and each of them has a revolver at his side. One of them is swinging the flashlight at the end of a leather strap; the other, walking a step or two behind, is munching a sandwich; he is wearing cloth gloves, and crumbs from the sandwich stick to the material.

"There was a guy home got killed by a rock once," the sandwich-eater says.

They walk on as before. They come up to the guard house, just outside the door, and there the soldier in front stops and turns.

"Well, so what happened?"

"You left the door open, for one thing," says a voice inside the hut.

"He got killed, like I said."

"I know you said it. How, for Christ's sake?"

"By this rock."

"Will you shut the goddamn door, in or out?"

The one room of the guard house is very plain. Three unshaded light bulbs illuminate it. Coats, hats, and a variety of odds and ends hang from nails in the walls, covering a small part of the clippings and pictures and mimeographed notices that overlap each other around the room. A soldier is lying on the floor beside a desk; his head almost touches the kerosene stove, which stands against one wall. He is playing cards with himself, and he does not look up as the other soldiers come in. But they bang the door and he grunts.

The soldier with the flashlight is glaring at his companion, who eats and looks down at the card-player.

"The rock bit him, maybe?"

"Bit who?" the card-player asks.

"The rock rolled, like we was talking about. He pushed his little kid out from the way of it."

"Who?" the card-player demands.

"Fellow back home," Sandwich says. "He pushed his little kid away, but he got killed. This big rock rolled over him."

"I've heard about cases like that," the card-player observes. He still has not looked up; he is playing from the pack to seven rows of cards aligned in front of him, and he moves his eyes from one row to another as he turns up each card. The soldier with the flashlight has taken a stand beside the card-player and is swinging the flashlight slowly in a circle over his head. The other soldier still stands just inside the door, watching; he has not removed his gloves, and from time to time he licks a crumb from them.

"If I only get the six of diamonds, I'll go out," the card-player says. "You hear about cases like that every once in a while," he continues. "Sometimes they both get killed. There isn't anything you can do about it. It's like with a bullet, if your number's on it. Will you quit swinging that goddamn flashlight?"

"I don't know about that," Flashlight says; he raises the instrument a few inches but continues to dangle it over the player's head. "If you don't go running in front of rocks and bullets you don't get hit. Sometimes you maybe ain't got a choice. Otherwise—"

"Sure," Sandwich says, "if it's your little kid, you ain't got a choice. I don't know about this number business though. One guy may be faster than another. Accidents happen, they just plain happen."

"Who's to say they're accidents?" The card-player raises his head. "Who's to say they could of turned out different? You can tell us all about these things?"

"I don't know whether he can, but I can tell you about some of these things," Flashlight says. "I guess some other guys can tell you about some other things. But you take, for instance, coal mines, where guys used to get killed by the thousands every year, and not because their numbers were up. Put in some inspectors, pass some safety laws, keep the union strong and your eyes open —and, by Jesus, they don't get killed as much, not by a damned sight. I can tell you about that."

"They still get killed though," says the card-player. "I got no objection to taking precautions. That still leaves plenty of times when the precautions don't do you any good. You think people run their lives, but they don't."

"As for that guy," Flashlight says, "he could of been faster or he could of been slower. In either case things might of turned out different. Also, he could of just yelled. Why didn't he just yell? He had a choice."

"He did," says Sandwich. "He yelled all the way, but his kid didn't pay him no attention."

"Somewhere along the line he had a choice."

"You can say so afterward."

"I'll break your head, so help me, if you don't put that flashlight up," the card-player grumbles. But it is not really more than a fly to him; he is only annoyed and the soldier with the flashlight continues to dangle it.

"You find out a whole lot of things afterwards," he says. "But who's to say you couldn't of found them out before if you'd thought to."

"Truck's coming," Sandwich says.

All three of them turn their heads toward the faint growl that reaches them from some point beyond the edge of the mesa.

"Do you guys know what you think you're arguing about?" Sandwich asks.

"Mysterious forces," says Flashlight. "It's no argument. Some people like to get their answers without asking no questions."

He lets his flashlight tap the card-player lightly on the head, and then he walks over to a window and looks out. It is quite light by now.

"It's probably one of them from the Quartermaster up at Denver," Sandwich says. "Three more tons of frozen boneless beef. No fresh meat in three weeks. Who won the war?"

"But about that fellow and his kid," Flashlight says. "What was the situation with this rock? Couldn't someone of known it'd roll? You got to know things like that. Maybe somebody was blasting, like at a quarry close by. Huh? Maybe he was plain negligent, letting his kid play there. Maybe it wasn't just an accident."

"Accidents just happen. You don't have to get fancy about it. They just happen, sometimes."

"Nine times out of ten it comes down to who they happen to. There must of been other guys with kids in your town. Why—"

"It comes down to who's where the accident happens. It might of been other guys, but it was this one. Lichty. That was his name."

The card-player is pulling himself up from the floor; he struggles up until he is squatting on his haunches, looking down at his cards with disgust.

Sandwich, watching him, reaches into the pocket of a field coat hanging on the wall beside him. He brings forth a paper sack, and from this takes a sandwich to replace the one he has just finished. He turns to the door and opens it.

"Some guys," the card-player says, lifting himself to his feet, "get so hopped up asking questions they never see an answer even if it hits them in the face."

The truck's growl has become a roar, and the truck itself is now in sight on the road. It is a big Army trailer truck, coming up slowly, with spits and sighs from its air brakes. It rolls to a stop just before the gate, and all three of the soldiers from the guard house walk out beside it. There are three soldiers in the truck too, sitting high in the cab. Papers are produced and examined; the soldiers in the truck are tired and bored and do not say much. But after the driver has started the truck moving again, he stops it and, leaning out of the cab window, calls back.

"Say, what happened up here? Heard some guys got killed in an explosion."

The soldiers on the ground look at each other.

"You hear stuff all the time," says the card-player. "Nobody got killed I know of."

"There was an explosion, I heard. Six or seven guys killed."

"We got explosions all the time, for Christ's sake—half a dozen this morning already."

"I heard them. I don't mean those kind. This one I heard about killed some guys. An accident."

The soldiers from the guard house shrug their shoulders and protest that they know nothing of this at all. The driver of the truck pulls in his head and the truck moves on again, along the road into the town.

"Somebody said no talkee," the driver remarks.

At the guard house the card-player says, "Those bastards was just trying to pump us. We'd of heard if anyone got killed."

"It'd be a funny thing," Sandwich says, "if a lot of guys got killed right here and those characters from Denver know about it before we do."

"They didn't get killed, you damned fool," Flashlight shouts at him. "You said yourself you saw them in the ambulance."

"Well, it must of been them. I don't know them. It must of been them."

"They could of died since," the card-player says. He looks with bright, interested eyes from one to the other of his companions.

In the truck the driver leans across the wheel. One of the men is dozing. The truck rolls quietly along the straight, smooth road, past the first of the town's buildings, small, two-family houses fronted by identical yards enclosed by identical low white fences. The soldier next to the driver lets his eyes inspect the houses, each in turn, and listens after a fashion to what the driver is saying.

"—but if Einstein's for it, I'm for it too. I never heard a mean thing about him. Two hundred thousand bucks they're trying to raise for public education about atom bombs. I sent five so's I'd feel better than I do, but I guess I still don't. The little guy don't know what he's up against. Educate the public! Make us all see what we got hold of! Oh, little Jesus, my oh my! What've we got hold of? Power of the universe, biggest fucking thing since fire. That's what the scientists say. World's best bomb. That's what the military says. Hell, two hundred thousand bucks won't do the military out of the world's best bomb."

"I never send money for stuff like that. It's a waste."

"I read where one of those scientists says they ought to take the bomb around the world in a road show, kind of. Have an atomic explosion outside big cities and invite people to have a look. That'd scare their pants off, this

guy says. But it wouldn't. Half wouldn't show up and
the other half'd run around punching each other. 'Boy
oh boy, look what we got hold of!' That's what they'd
say."

"I never could see what they invented it for if they're
so hot against it. They do a lot of talking now."

"I don't know as they set out to invent a bomb. Anyhow,
I get the idea they're mostly against the military having all
the say. That way you'll only get bombs. How was they to
talk before, for Christ's sake? You don't talk like that on
Army time."

The truck is passing a campsite for trailers. There must
be two hundred of them, arranged roughly in rows, clean
and polished and ready to gleam in the sun that will soon
surmount Truchas. Flowers in homemade boxes are set
against the streamlined trailer windows. Beyond the trailers the road branches; the main part of it goes straight on
into the center of town; the white end of the hospital can
be seen three or four blocks off. The branch leads away
to the left, to the south, toward a mass of cement-block
buildings, Quonset huts, and standing trucks. The driver
straightens, gripping the wheel for the turn.

"Like those guys killed in this accident here. This is
where it happened, but there ain't going to be any public
educating here if the Army can help it. I'd be real curious
about it if I didn't know the Army."

At the guard house the three soldiers are finally sure
that the men could not have been killed; certainly they
would have known of this.

"Even if they die now," the card-player says, "that's a
different thing from being killed right in the accident. There's
more than just this accident, anyway, there's all that's been
happening since, like these doctors coming in."

"They didn't know about that," Flashlight points out.
"You wouldn't have doctors coming in now if they got
killed then."

The sun appears; the trees move in the morning breeze;

the birds are speaking; and the talk at the guard house goes on.

Five young men drive up in an old Army passenger car.

"Quite some thunder this morning," says Flashlight.

One of the men in the car smiles wanly, as at an old joke.

"But no rain."

The soldiers look after them as they drive through, and on into the town. The car is pulling a small two-wheeled metal cart behind it. This cart, the soldiers know, holds measuring instruments of one kind and another. They have seen it, and others like it, hundreds of times—and have heard a thousand explosions between the goings and comings of the carts.

The scientists returning are quiet, as they usually are. For what they have been measuring their eyes are poor judges and their ears no good at all. The instruments in the cart, when they are opened and read in half an hour or so, will provide some answers and pose some questions, from which much talk will start. This afternoon there will be meetings; tonight there may be work in the machine shop; tomorrow there will be more explosions.

At the bend in the road, where the frozen boneless beef turned off, the passenger car starts to turn, slows, then swings back onto the main road again. It moves ahead through the town, moves slowly past the hospital, and takes the turn to the left, to the Technical Area just beyond.

At the guard house Dr Jacob Briggle has arrived.

"Briggle," he is saying to Sandwich.

"Jacob Briggle," Sandwich says, looking at the paper in his hand. He still has on his gloves and there are still come crumbs on them.

"Yes, Jacob Briggle."

"M.D."

"M.D., yes," the doctor says in a tired voice.

"They didn't get killed, did they, in that accident?"

The driver and the other two soldiers turn to look at

Sandwich, and the doctor stretches his neck and runs a finger under his collar.

"Is this a part of the routine for getting through this goddamned gate?"

"Are we clear?" the driver asks.

All three of the soldiers nod.

"No, nobody was killed," the doctor says, in the same tired voice. The car goes ahead fast.

The first bus from Santa Fe is waddling up over the crest of the mesa. This can go straight through, for the soldier driving the bus has checked the passes of the civilian workers who are his load. But the bus stops when it gets to the gate, and the driver opens his window and leans out.

"Saw a mountain lion back there!"

Several of the passengers nod agreement. One indicates with his hands that it was a big one.

"Just over the rise. Did you see it?"

The soldiers on the ground are looking at each other again.

"Well, take care," the driver calls down. He grins, waves his hand, and gives his attention again to the bus, which pulls forward slowly.

There are about fifty people on this bus—mechanics, carpenters, store clerks, filling-station attendants, and others. From a seat beside a window at the back the young woman from the telegraph office looks out at the guard house soldiers as the bus moves past them. Several hundred more of the town's maintenance population will be along on other buses that have already left Santa Fe or soon will. Still more will drive up in their own cars. Some will come from Espanola, the little Spanish town fifteen miles or so off to the northeast. A few, domestic workers mostly and mostly Indians and Mexicans and Spaniards, will come up from the ranches and pueblos that lie between the mesa and the river, and some of these will come by foot, over ancient trails. The sun is brilliant. Every object in the landscape is sharp.

2

Even from three or four blocks away the grinding of the trailer truck's gears at the turn-off reached the hospital; the sound rippled along the building walls and moved the windows to tiny buzzes. It reached in under the half-open window of Louis Saxl's room, and within the room it lifted one veil of sleep from the sleeper. Vaguely he heard the passenger car with the slightly rattling cart. The residue of drugs from the night before thickened his perceptions; it seemed to him, and yet he was not sure, that another car followed this one, or that this one went by twice. The pricking of the uncertainty, so slight a thing, became a step for wakefulness. And yet a moment passed during which, from the threshold to which the step had taken him, he looked backward, or down, like a person going in one direction who pauses to peer in another at some small event—a boy running, two boys talking, cars passing—irrelevant to his progress and hence no obstacle, but a claim on his attentions if they are not wholly fixed. Aware of his room, of his bed, of himself in general, and most aware that a part of himself was trapped in some circumstance to which, in another moment, he would have to give his whole attention—he lingered still, isolating from the shadows of his visions the night before this casual cap to them, this way of waking—

"Did you hear about Ives Coleman?"

—nothing more.

They were walking along the sidewalk that led to the high school. Dr Coleman's car passed; it was an old car and it rattled slightly.

There was something quite important in this, for Chuck was walking half sideways, the better to watch his reaction. Pointed one way, proceeding another, he waited for Louis to answer. He was only a year younger than Louis and he was almost Louis's height, but he danced along, intent and awkward, as though he were no more than ten or eleven instead of fourteen.

"No, what about?"

"Hah, wait'll you hear. Didn't you hear, really?"

"I didn't hear anything."

"About his father, what he said, he said Ives could have his choice."

"Choice of what?"

"Didn't you hear, really? I heard about it yesterday."

"Well, what? What're you talking about?"

"College or a car," said the dancing boy triumphantly. "Ives can go to college or have a car, any car he wants. His father said so. He can take his choice. Didn't you really hear?"

"Did he really say that?" Louis looked at his friend in astonishment. "That sounds screwy. How do you know he said that?"

"It is not screwy. Everybody knows it except you. Anyway, that's what he said. What would you take if you was him?"

"College," said Louis, thinking of that but thinking also of Ives and Ives's father and this strange choice.

"College! Well, maybe, but I mean if you took the car, what kind?"

"But I wouldn't take the car. That's crazy, Chuck."

"Says you. I bet Ives does though. I bet he isn't the only one would either. Anyway, if you *did*. What car would you take? Just supposing?"

Louis refused to pick a car, and Chuck picked several, chafing at his perversity. They walked a block in silence.

"I'll tell you what that choice is," Louis said then. "These cars and stuff are just flotsam and jetsam of the tide of scientific investigation—" he looked quickly at his friend out of the corner of his eye— "But at college you're on the crest of the wave—" he paused, but he didn't turn his head at all— "far away on its course over the illimitable ocean of the unknown."

"Oh, brother!"

"That's true though. It sounds that way because it's out of a book, but it's true though."

"You and Old Fatty Oliver."

"Oliver's OK."

The other boy started his sideways hopping again, looking at Louis with a mocking expression.

"Old Fatty Oliver thinks you're OK too. Old Fatty Oliver said you're real bright. I know something else Old Fatty Oliver said too. Oh, those great big beautiful eyes!"

Louis reached out an arm and pushed the boy backward.

"Don't push me."

"Well, don't say that."

"Take it easy who you're pushing."

They walked nearly two blocks more in silence, and this brought them within sight of the school campus on the far side of the street. They could see boys and girls going up the walks and several little groups standing on the lawn; they could tell from the look of things that the first bell hadn't rung yet. Suddenly Chuck was running ahead.

"See you later," he called back.

Chuck ran down the sidewalk until he was nearly across from the school, and then he cut across the street and up to the lawn, up to a little group of four or five boys. Louis slowed down, looking hard to make out just who was in the group. Abruptly he turned and crossed the street; shielded by the houses that ran right up to the school lawn, he could walk any way he wanted to. He extracted one book from the three under his arm so he could swing it around, or whack his leg with it, or balance it on his head. He dawdled along until he heard the first bell. By this time the lawn was in view again, but all the groups had broken up, and he didn't see anyone he recognized especially. He ran across the lawn, tossing the book like a football.

Louis turned in his bed, or tried to turn. Something held him, and it was to this, it occurred to him (but not strongly), that his attention should be going. His eyes opened, and the slight rattle of the cart with the measuring instruments in it and the distant din of the passengers getting out of the Santa Fe bus two blocks away were already fading, though he could still feel the book in his hand. His eyes closed again to a white slit, through which he saw that Betsy had hung his watch where he could see it, at the foot of the bed, where now he noticed not the time but, with some embarrassment, the massive figure of Miss Oliver, walking ponderously toward him. She was speaking, and her fingers touched the strung pieces of coral or amber or imitation pearl (or jade) that she always wore, moving among them in a way suggestive at once of the abstraction of a mother and the passion of a girl.

"Sometimes I wonder if people really know what science is about. You'll know a little, I hope, and that's a consolation."

It was really difficult to tell where, between being asleep and being awake, he was. He smiled at the words, remembering them from long ago but not able to remember from one instant to the next whether he was actually hearing them now. Then he closed his eyes altogether and it was as though Miss Oliver had been real and he had shut her out, as though he were looking into a pitch-black room that might contain anything. But something was not right about the feel of the book in his hand; and a thing he had seen, at the foot of the bed (but not the watch) or perhaps at the side, was not right; his lazy review of a small incident, well remembered, was not going as it should.

Miss Oliver's hair was copper and silken and coiled with care.

"You'll know a little, I hope, and that's a consolation. At least you'll know better than to think a man just says, well, I guess it's time we invented the blast furnace, so I'll

just discover one of nature's secrets—presto! My heavens, why do people have such thoughts? It says it the right way in the Bible. Some of you ought to remember, I should think—"

Everyone liked Miss Oliver; even the pupils who only stared as she talked to them, even the ones who called her Old Fatty Oliver behind her back, even the parents who from time to time started moves to replace her with a man who would direct science teaching along vocational lines and maybe coach basketball on the side. The parents who had once compressed science into a textbook like a faded flower had come to see it as a bloom once you got it out of the textbooks and called it engineering. And it was widely held that a woman had no business with this. Miss Oliver, it was known, had become a science teacher out of tribute to Marie Curie; she was taken on, it was understood, because she had been the least expensive of three candidates. Both events had happened many years before.

"—in the book of Job, Job says: 'Speak to the earth and it shall teach thee.' That's what the great ones did. That's what Lavoisier was doing when he first did this experiment you're doing right now. He was trying to find out what happens when fire burns, and if anyone could make use of what he found out—well, let them. As for him, he was trying to find out what happens when fire burns. Heavens! Isn't that enough?"

Miss Oliver liked to walk among her students, none of them older than eighteen, mostly boys but some girls too, and think to herself how any one of them, even the ones who would have forgotten everything before the sound of the bell, was closer to a truth of nature in this moment, sitting at the single laboratory table, burning tin to make the oxide, than any scientist who had lived up to the Revolutionary War. She wanted them to know that this little experiment, or one much like it, had made a revolution in the minds of men.

"Where would we all be if it weren't for these men who

just wanted to know? No blast furnaces, I can tell you that. What a lot of strange notions people used to have about fire, not so awfully long ago, except I suppose it seems like forever to you. Most of them came from the Middle Ages and before, from the alchemists and the practical men, the metal-makers. Practical men! It took a scientist who just wanted to find out about fire to set things straight."

She walked up and down the room talking not so much to her pupils as into the air, so the boys and girls would breathe it in and not be able to escape the truths she so much wanted them to know. She had responded early to the long linked sweep of science, and, having glimpsed the whole, she hadn't bothered with the parts.

"For centuries people just guessed about those things, fire and combustion. There's been lots of guessing in science, let me tell you, not all of it very good. But if you're going to speak to nature the important thing's to speak. Sometimes half a guess gets half an answer. There was a man who lived a long time before Lavoisier, he almost figured it out. I can't think of his name now, he died young. I must tell you something Isaac Newton said, he said, 'I could see so far because I stood on the shoulders of giants.' You should remember that. The great ones were helped by others all the time."

As reverent toward the word as a mystic and as impatient of detail, Miss Oliver marched her pupils past whole rooms full of stored knowledge and brought them out to vistas too great for them to grasp. Louis watched her walking up and down, speaking to the air, fingering the coral (or the jade) of her necklace. Suddenly she looked at him sitting sideways on his stool at the laboratory table.

"You see what I'm getting at, don't you, Louis? Say it in your own words, won't you? Tell us what this means."

"Well," he mumbled finally, "these discoveries, like you said, they—I mean lots of people share—what you said."

"Oh, children, children, remember some of these things that great men did, not for anything except to find out!

These experiments, why, they're questions people asked, and what they found are the answers we live by, they're just that. Speak to the earth. There's a lovely poem by Tennyson:

> *Flower in the crannied wall,*
> *I hold you here in my hand,*
> *If I could know what you are, all in all,*
> *I think I should understand*
> *I think—*

Oh, dear, I never can remember how it goes. Do any of you know?"

No one did, or at least no one said.

The bell rang and the classroom started to empty. Louis went up to her, opened his mouth, shut it, stood there, and then spoke rapidly.

"I read that poem you were saying and I was thinking about what you said, but there's something in the poem I don't—I mean, he says, Tennyson says, you hold the flower and if you could know—but that's not the point. The flower's not going to tell you, you've got to find out, don't you?"

Miss Oliver laughed. "Well, yes, you do, but there's never been any lack of questions. They're, oh, so many things we still don't know, things we're trying to find out. You know some of those things."

"Yes, I know, but what I mean is different. I mean, aren't all the answers to everything just there—all around, waiting? Isn't the important thing knowing the questions to ask?"

"Why, yes, I suppose you could put it that way." But she was puzzled. "You have to know what's gone before though, I think—you know, earlier answers to earlier questions, if you're going to know what you're after. Don't you?"

"Yes, I know," Louis said again. "But you're telling us how real discoveries don't just come from getting a lot of

facts together, even if you have to do that too. But then
you have to interpret them, and then you have to get to
the right next question. I mean you have to ask a question,
or you have to make an experiment, whichever, that jumps
ahead, sort of. The poem says it backwards. It's the questions that are the important things, not the answers. It's
the questions. Don't you see?"

They stood for a moment, with this halting, half-shrewd,
wholly exalted statement of the scientist's mission hanging
between them, and then Louis murmured some words and
ran out of the room—

If I forget thee, oh Miss Oliver, he murmured now.

—into Chuck and the others on the lawn and the jokes.

At the foot of the bed the watch: "Grandpa wanted you
to have this, son. It tells good time, even now."

And on the window ledge, the one overlooking the pond
where the children played, someone had put a flower in a
pot.

"He goes up and has these little private talks with her
all the time. He waits till everyone's gone and goes up and
has these little talks."

"Oh, those great big beautiful eyes!"

He kicked his legs straight out (and got rid of the covers
more easily than he had expected; soon, if he could work
the hospital gown up, he perhaps could see what he had
to see). He pushed himself forward into a hard dive at
Chuck, who jumped, and hopping and jumping made a
wide curve out over the lawn.

"She said he had pretty eyelashes! Ask him what she
said about his eyelashes! That's what she said."

On the quiet lawn the faces were quiet, and the lunches
uneaten; as when a dog lies dead the dogs come running
for miles to sniff; on the quiet lawn Miss Oliver stood
sunning herself massively, not looking.

"Jew eyes!"

The watch ticks and the flower stirs.

On the quiet lawn, he walked slowly, loudly saying:

"I don't care what Old Fatty Oliver says. What Old Fatty Oliver says makes no difference to me," his face reddening, his whole body reddening.

"Jew eyes!"

The watch ticks and the sleeper moves his legs and his whole body, the better to see. At the edge of the lawn the boy turns, and his eyes are burning hot. The watch ticks and the questions are like flowers. But the eyes stay, bright as the ceaselessly questioning eyes of laboratory animals, searching for choices among their instincts.

The reddening is of the uniform deep red color of the erythema of the abdomen that came to Nolan beginning about the third day (not inconsistent with a radiation dosage of the size computed) and did not ever go away; "the cutaneous reaction of the torso in this case presented some interesting features."

> *If I forget thee, oh Jerusalem,*
> *Let my right hand forget her cunning*
> *Let my tongue cleave . . .*

The sleeper moves and the gown creeps up. The eyes open, and the watch on the end of the bed and the flower on the window ledge fill them.

From down the street two blocks away the distant din of the passengers leaving the Santa Fe bus is dying away.

The watch says that it is not quite seven; the flower is white and it sleeps; the bedclothes have been pushed down to the end of the bed; the gown has been pushed up far enough so the legs show, but not far enough.

3

For some little time after he awoke fully, Louis lay quite motionless on the bed, his bare legs drawn up, the gown crumpled in a heap over his middle. His body moved only with his breathing, which was heavy from the exertions he had been making; his recollection of these was not clear; he had been too deep down in the lode of sleep that had figured his waking.

He tried to raise his head, to peer over the folds of the hospital gown. But they were too high, the gown would have to be worked back; he slid his body down the bed and then slid it back; the gown shifted and moved, but ended up almost as it had been. He would get to that in a minute; in a minute he could do it, for his mind had measured a gain. He did not this morning feel tired as he had felt tired yesterday—bone-tired and jangle-weary, his mother sometimes said. The influence of the drugs was in him but he could isolate that; a cup of coffee would dispel it. The bare thought of a cup of coffee yesterday would have sickened him. He turned his attention to the two troughs, extending out from either side of the bed, that held the lower parts of his arms.

The trough to his left was covered heavily with towels; they made a bulky, ugly mound in which his arm disappeared up to the elbow, and he could see nothing even of the structure that had this part of him within it. There was ice beneath the towels and around his arm, he knew, although he could not feel it; all he could feel was a pain that came back from what seemed a very great distance. Not for several moments did he remember that the ice that now covered half his arm had last night covered only his hand.

He drew one leg up against his body as much as he could; the thigh pressed against his abdomen, but he could see nothing this way; the question was, would the gown fall higher up when he moved his leg back? It did not; the stiff material followed his leg, coming to rest, in peaks and folds, lower than before.

His right arm entered its trough at a point just above his wrist; his forearm rested on a padding of towels and his hand within the trough rested on more towels laid over the ice; but no towels covered the hand. Lying in its own cold bed, this hand seemed a separate thing, and a re-straining strap across his forearm near the end of the trough served to make the separation manifest.

He studied his hand for perhaps a minute before making any attempt to move it; it was tightly swollen, and the swelling extended along his arm several inches beyond the strap. The skin here was of a pale bluish cast; there were no blisters or any other signs of injury. Louis tried a very small twisting movement of his arm; it moved as it should have, but he felt nothing from his hand; the fingers did not respond at all.

Like the trough on his left, the trough on his right pro-jected out from the bed at approximately a forty-five-degree angle. From what he could see beneath the towels, there was a rubber sheet to hold the ice and a wooden frame to hold the sheet. The movements of his arm made a swishing sound; he guessed that the trough might hold twenty to twenty-five pounds of ice, and he judged from the sound that possibly a quarter of it had melted.

He leaned toward the trough a little to see what it rested on, but the side of the bed and more towels obscured his view. He studied his hand, remembering as he did a doctor in his home town, who had written a death certificate for an arm that a local carpenter had lost to a circular saw; the man had made a small coffin for his arm and his whole family attended its burial in the family plot.

"If thine eye offend thee," Louis said, half aloud.

Once more he turned his attention to his body. He made a sudden spasmodic arching of his back, pressing heavily on the muscles of his neck, driving down with his legs to lift his buttocks clear from the sheet, and, in this position, wriggled and twisted to free his abdomen from the cursed gown, which moved easily with him but moved back not an inch. He relaxed his muscles and fell back upon the bed, breathing heavily, but at once arched his back again, wriggled down the bed as he had before, pressing hard against the sheets, then pulled his body back up to begin

all over again. He kept his eyes on the gown across his
abdomen; it twisted and moved now forward and now back;
once he thought he saw the tan line on one leg, running
from just below his crotch diagonally out to the midpoint
of his hip. But at the next moment the gown covered it,
if indeed he had even seen it.

His breathing was labored and he felt sweat on his chest.
He varied his movements around his basic pattern, swinging his body out first to one side then to the other; he
cursed his shorts, which had been swimming shorts cut
very trimly; and he cursed the stiff and unyielding gown.
After what seemed a very long time he softened and quieted on the bed. There were tears in his eyes and he cursed
whatever came into his mind. "God damn it, God damn
it, God damn it"—over and over to himself, in a whisper,
and finally aloud.

The sweat he had worked up chilled him; his legs were
cold; he was cold all over, except for his hands, which lay
in ice without sensation. The pain in his left arm had its
origin somewhere off to the side of the bed, in the air for
all he could tell, and entered his arm at an indeterminate
point, not sharply but in a throb that was a little less here
than there and finally ceased to be.

But it is unimportant, Louis thought—one pain more
or less. Burns, blisters, bruises, breaks—how many painful
things begin with *b,* he went on, blows and beatings too;
and beta rays. Also bombs. But bombs were too complex
for the simplicity of the thought, and he jumped back to
the beginning of it: pain, one more or less, is not of any
consequence. This was true enough, because the pain was
a detail; the hand, presumably somewhere down underneath the soggy mound of towels, was more important.
And yet, he thought, the hand is a detail too; what is one
hand more or less? He waited a moment for some internal
censor to correct this thought, but nothing happened. His
eyes moved to his right hand; it is unimportant, he said to
himself, it is not so important. He turned his arm and the

hand turned; he turned his arm back and the hand turned back.

The important thing is—and then he stopped, simply because he was not sure. He did not know how to phrase the important thing, and, in fact, he could not bring his mind to focus on precisely what it was that he wanted to state.

The watch at the end of the bed said eleven or twelve minutes after seven; he seemed to remember having looked at it when it said a few minutes before seven, but that could not have been so recently; perhaps he remembered it from last night; perhaps the watch had stopped, for who would have wound it? Who will wind it, he thought.

Am I going to die?

He formed these words in his mind distinctly, deliberately, with at least half a notion that he might take the important thing by surprise. But they produced no very great impression on him. They posed a question that did not seem to involve him personally; and they did not bring his thoughts to focus. The words floated on his mind, then drifted off, unanswered, hardly asked, only allowed to pass through.

When they had passed he discovered that his thoughts were again, or still, with his hands. And then, quite suddenly, he shivered violently; his bare legs erupted in goose-pimples; his heart pounded. He closed his eyes, felt racked by his heart's pounding, and in the dark behind his eyes seemed to see himself shouting, insisting: "No! No! They are important! They are all important!" What he meant to include in this he was not sure; it was not an exact thought, in any event, but a feeling. And it, with the pounding and the shivering and the goose-pimples, in time came to an end too.

Again he contemplated the hospital gown. He drew both legs up, spread them, and moved them back and forth separately; but he did this without much energy. The fact is, he thought, the words of an old joke coming into his

mind, I don't reckon there's any way to get there from
here.

He could move his body up and down the bed a little,
but not enough; his legs brought the gown to within a few
inches of where he wanted it, but all the motions he could
devise would not budge it across those few inches. How
like an animal one became with one's hands immobilized;
what a fine example, he thought, of the absolute importance of the opposable thumb and forefinger.

His eyes turned again to his visible hand, and his mind
moved on to the ape, which, when the bananas were lifted
out of reach, learned to pick up a stick and knock them
down. How like a stick my arm looks, he was thinking;
and my hand, how like a knob or burl. What kept him
from making the connection that the ape had made was
the restraining strap, which had been put there by a doctor
or a nurse (although he did not remember it being done)
and was therefore a part of the law of the room, promul-
gated by others, deserving of respect.

There was another thing too, and this was, so to speak,
a feeling for the fitness of instruments, a feeling, in this
instance, that his hand was quite useless because it could
not provide the delicacy of movement that was the virtue
and the beauty and the utility of the human hand. Thinking
of a hand that could so easily lift the gown away from his
abdomen, he could think only of a healthy hand, which
would lift it with an opposable thumb and forefinger. The
clock ticked off five minutes more before his disciplines
began to weaken in the face of a situation too simple for
them.

"I'm a son of a bitch," he whispered.

He moved his arms up to try the tightness of the strap,
and found it, as it looked to be, tight enough only to keep
him from pulling or jerking his arm over in sleep. Even
with the swelling of his hand he could withdraw it, working
gently and carefully; and so he did.

As he lifted his arm, bringing it across the bed, it per-

formed very much the movement it had performed just
before the counters began their crazy jangling at the laboratory table two days before; the position of his arm and
hand, for a moment, was the position they held at the
moment he had released the last small block of fissionable
material, seeing, in that very instant, the faint blue glow
that had disappeared under his hammering thrusts at the
structure even before his brain had completed its recording
of what the glow meant.

This unwitting reconstruction his brain recorded now,
but his arm paused hardly perceptibly; then it moved down,
and the stiff and massy hand came to rest below the hospital
gown on the bare skin of his leg, which it could not feel
but which felt its weight and coldness as the gown moved.

4

Dr Pederson had one room in a bleak two-story structure
given over to the housing of single men. This dormitory,
dark green and jerry-built, had been one of the first to
arise on the mesa after the Army's bulldozers moved in
early in 1943. Although it sagged in the middle and tem-
porariness oozed from every nail hole, it had still what
might be described as a sufficient look; and the view from
any of its windows was magnificent. In the spring of 1946
the dormitory housed sixty-eight men, most of whom were
minor members (that is, they had published few papers)
of the highest orders (that is, they were physicists and
chemists) of the hierarchy of the town.

The one window in Dr Pederson's room looked west
toward the Jemez Mountains, which he had stared at rap-
turously mornings and evenings during the first weeks of
his tenancy; which had, for that period of time, compen-
sated for his distaste at not having a bathroom of his own;
and which he had memorialized in several letters to his
parents back east, never failing to touch on the morbid

irony of the setting that this ancient, lovely range provided
for the making of bombs. Since those early days, however,
his interest had been much more in the foreground of his
view. This encompassed a number of things, most notably—across the handsomest sweep of lawn in Los Alamos,
a green stretch of a hundred yards or more—the Lodge
and its terrace.

A two-story log structure, the Lodge was, along with
the lawn, the most impressive inheritance from the boys'
school that had existed quietly here for twenty years before
the young physicist, following his memories of the beauty
of the spot, led the Generals out to calculate its utility. A
recreation center and dining hall for the boys, the Lodge
had been left very much as it was to serve the scientists
and the military men in the same ways. A wide flagstone
terrace had been laid across the entire front. And on this,
at mealtimes and at odd hours in between, whenever the
weather allowed, which was very often now that spring had
come, those of the town's citizens who had the social assurance (the Lodge's airs were those of an officers' club)
gathered for food, drinks, and gossip. Distinguished visitors were put up in the dozen or so well-furnished rooms
that occupied the second floor.

Dr Pederson had come to enjoy very much his view of
the Lodge and its terrace; he could see who was meeting
and sitting with whom, and when the striped umbrellas
were opened over the tables in the morning he was often
pleasantly reminded of the country club at his home town
in Massachusetts, where he had gone to his first dances.

On this morning Charley Pederson woke late. It was
after eight-thirty. He had stayed up until nearly four
o'clock, reading. He had made some notes, and had reached
a conviction, the essence of which was that he alone, of
the doctors assembled to attend Louis Saxl (and, of course,
the others), had not condemned his patient in advance.
The meeting of the doctors in the hospital the night before
had begun by shocking him and had gone on to make him

feel hopeless. But what he woke with was a degree of anger.

The bathroom was fifty feet down the hall; he dispensed with a shower, and with washing too. As he dressed he reviewed in his mind what he had been able to extract, from his night's reading and reflection, to support the cause for hope. There was not much; but there were at least a few things that had yet to be answered.

"If you put them all together—" he said angrily to his mirror.

And who knows anything for sure? he thought as he looked out his window.

On the terrace of the Lodge were three people. One of them was sitting alone, a newspaper before him. This was Edward Wisla; his portly figure and his stiff posture were at once recognizable, even as he sat.

At the other end of the terrace a young man was at a table with a young woman. Pederson did not know the woman—she had on a yellow jacket that shone across the lawn, and she was leaning forward on her elbows looking at the man. His name was Sydney Weigert; he was a physicist whom Pederson knew no better than, as a doctor, he knew everyone at Los Alamos. He barely glanced at Sydney and the woman. His gaze rested on Wisla, and his anger mounted.

"Just really what does a scientist, except one like Louis—but you, for instance," he said to himself, "an important, practically automatic brain, and a great man, all right, I have no doubt—but what do you know about the meaning of loyalty or hope, or friendship even, because you're Louis's friend, or so you're supposed to be? Do you know anything about anything like that? The mathematical sciences don't tell you anything like that. There aren't any words like that in your kind of science. Your friend, what about your friend? Well, so you shrug your shoulders and there's that frosty smile, and 'I fear not,' you say, 'I fear not.'"

On the terrace Wisla turned a page of his newspaper and at the window of his room Pederson watched.

Then he gathered up his reading. He stood for a moment staring at the top document, a thin reprint from a medical journal bearing the title, "Effect of Total-Body Radiation Dosage on Distribution of Radio Sodium in Rats." In a page of this Pederson had found a hope, which he had tried out at the meeting in the doctors' conference room, and concerning which Wisla had said his "I fear nots." Pederson only looked at the title now and went on out of his room. He would go at once to the hospital, he decided; he could get some coffee there if he wanted it, and he wanted nothing more; he would decide as he crossed the lawn whether or not to stop and say a word to Wisla, and what word.

On the terrace Wisla belched loudly, looked about him impassively, and turned a page of his newspaper. At the other end of the terrace the woman with Weigert turned her head to stare at Wisla.

"Is that a great one?" she asked Weigert. She was smiling as she turned back to face him, half from amusement, half from love.

"That would be Wisla," Weigert said, smiling too, and for the same reasons. "That's the one and only Wisla. Can't you tell him from his pictures?"

She stole another look.

"No, I guess not. I don't think so. I'm not sure I remember his pictures."

"Well, you know who he is. He's not around here much any more. He's making big experiments in Washington now."

The woman nodded to show she sensed the meaning of this.

"Anyway," Weigert went on, "no matter how many pictures, the way to see Wisla is as I saw him once, unforgettable. The British Mission had a party—the ones from England here all through the project—and they gave some good parties, one after the Alamogordo shot especially, to celebrate it. That was some party. But at this one I'm telling about last winter, Wisla had a big red woolen scarf of some sort wrapped around his head when he was leaving, and then another scarf around his neck, and God knows how many sweaters and coats too. He had all these things on and he bulged out in one great big bulge and then in various little bulges, and he looked like—well, I just don't know what he looked like. Unforgettable. He's an Austrian."

"I don't think he looks like a scientist."

"Oh, Sarah, for God's sake, what's a scientist look like? You know better than to say things like that. That sounds like a crummy magazine."

"You're afraid I'll say something to embarrass you. Nobody's listening, Sydney. I think you look like a scientist."

From a door in the Lodge beyond Wisla's table Dr Berrain came forth. He inhaled very deeply, stood looking at Truchas, and then, noticing Wisla, walked across to him.

"Why you spend your time in a hellhole like Washington when you could be out here in this glorious country is more than I can understand," Berrain said. "I was in Washington for a while during the war. Awful."

Wisla nodded. He scarcely looked at Berrain, but he put his paper aside as Berrain sat down, and he pulled his coffee cup an inch toward him. Sitting erect, he moved his eyes this way and that, as though assessing the locale in the light of Berrain's tribute. He looked straight at Weigert, who immediately stopped talking.

"It's the asshole of creation, is it not so?" Wisla said suddenly. "However, the enemy is there."

"The enemy?"

"Ignorance, this unconcern—apathy—and then suspicion. The instrument of these is the Army. They all have their headquarters in Washington."

Berrain smiled and shook his head.

"Oh, no, Mr Wisla. Those things have no headquarters. Branch offices, maybe, in Washington as elsewhere."

A waiter came over to the table and Berrain ordered breakfast.

"Of course, when you come down to it," Weigert was saying, his eyes on Wisla, "he's a lobbyist now really, not really a physicist any more. But he did wonderful things. Some of the very first experiments that confirmed fission. He was one of the key ones, all through this project, he was one of the key ones. He could have got a Nobel for the work he did on scattering from crystals—well, it was the kind of work you get a Nobel for. Of course that was years ago and in another place, the place the Nazis drove him out of. So he's been doing all these other things."

"But how is the battle going?" Berrain asked Wisla.

Wisla shrugged his shoulders. "I have been thinking of two men named May. Even this minute I was thinking of them both. The paper mentions both, one in jail and one in the Congress. You know this Alan Nunn May? Ten years for giving nuclear information to the Russians. What he could give I do not know, nothing of much importance—what is important, the industry big enough to make bombs, nobody can give. So he is in jail and the scientific workers of Britain—doubtless many here and other places too—they protest the sentence. I do not blame them. This Alan May—I know him, he was never here, but at Chicago and other places—he is of course a breaker of his trust. His motivations are interesting—great idealism, the hopes for peace among nations, beliefs in the scientific meanings of his work. All very dangerous, most dangerous in a strong man and a terrible bother in a weak one. Of course he had to go to jail—but of course the sentence is protested."

Berrain was leaning back in his chair, his thumbs in the pockets of his vest. He was looking not at Wisla, but at the figure of Pederson, all the way across the lawn beyond the terrace. Berrain squinted his eyes a little.

"To thine own self be true," he said then, still watching Pederson, "and it follows as the day the night, thou canst not then be false to any man."

Wisla gave a loud, short laugh.

"OK! OK!" he said. "Is it so always? But if it isn't, what is? Yes. This other May, one Andrew, in the Congress, had a law to give us all to the Army. His motivations are interesting too—suspicion, such a very bad understanding, and then that apathy. If you cannot concern yourself about the consequences, you hand the concern over. If you do not understand, but even more if you do not want to understand, then you begin to fear. A suspicious one prepares for his fears. Make more bombs, put the Army in charge, and then—bam! hey? Why should not this May be in jail as much as the other? Perhaps more so."

"This May is called a Representative," Berrain said, studying Wisla with some amusement. "He represents."

Pederson was walking slowly across the lawn, and again Berrain turned his head to look at him.

"There was a bill to turn the whole atomic-energy business over to the Army," Weigert was saying. "Wisla and some others just moved into Washington and started buttonholing Congressmen and making speeches. They've beat the bill too. But you know, still and all, a scientist's place is with his science. Wisla was the same before the war. He spent half his time beating the drums to get the government to see the importance of fission. If it hadn't been for Wisla and a few others like him, Europeans mostly, there wouldn't have been a project. So first he gets us all turned over to the Army and then he gets the Army turned out. I don't disagree, but these are the triumphs of a lobbyist."

"A representative is intended to represent," said Wisla. "He can misrepresent as well. The point is specious."

"Very possibly," Berrain said. As he watched, Pederson came to a stop on the lawn, still a hundred feet or so away. "But, you know, I wish you'd tell me something about Louis Saxl," Berrain went on. He took two dollar bills from his pocket and put them on the table. "Why don't we get on to the hospital—you're coming, aren't you?—and will you tell me a little about Saxl? I've heard about him, but I never met him."

"To be sure," Wisla said, pushing his chair back. "We're

all in the hands of the doctors sooner or later, is it not
so?" Disentangling himself from the table and chairs, Wisla
straightened. Turning his head first one way and then the
other in a slow and rather majestic movement, he noticed
Pederson on the lawn. He bowed slightly.

"But what shall I tell you about Louis Saxl?" he said to
Berrain. "He had the capacity to be surprised, a very un-
common capacity. And we have lost him to the enemy.
What shall I tell you?"

Walking slowly, the two men went along the edge of
the terrace toward the hospital.

At the time of Nolan's death nine months before and for
some time after it, Charley Pederson had been able to
remember, in extenuation of the sadness for the young
man's dying, that Nolan had made a very foolish mistake
down in the canyon that night, performing an experiment
that he had never performed before and should not have
been performing, in direct violation of the rules, and as a
joke. It had been Nolan's notion, or so some had said, to
rig the equipment in the laboratory, to predetermine the
experiment, so to speak, thus to insure that when Louis
Saxl ran it off the next day it would give a result known
in advance to Nolan. The men who worked in the building
in the canyon sometimes made bets on what certain readings would be; everyone put in a dollar or so and made a
guess; Nolan stood to make six or seven dollars, although
the important thing, of course, had been the joke.

More than he remembered the sadness, Pederson, and
others too, remembered these circumstances. And as time
passed Pederson had come to turn his memories of Nolan
still less to the sadness and more to the part he had taken
in the treatment of the first and only "domestic" casualty
of the Los Alamos project. Like the Hiroshimans, who
were said to have developed a kind of pride in the dis-
tinction that had come to their city, Pederson had been
able to withdraw from the sadness into a small pride that

he was mentioned in the medical report on this historic case.

Still, his pride had no core to it and it was of no service to him now. He stood irresolutely on the lawn, his anger taken by despair, looking after Wisla and Berrain as they moved along the edge of the terrace in the bright sun, against the gaily colored awnings. Quite without pride, simply as a matter of fact, he knew that none of the doctors brought in to attend Louis Saxl knew more of any practical utility for the present need than he knew himself—even the eminent Berrain, the very sight of whom had the effect of making him stiffen mentally with respect. There was nothing really that Berrain could say; and what could he say to Berrain? For he did not really expect Berrain or any of the others to say anything, knowing that there was nothing for them to say; what he expected he expected of himself. In the orderly arrangement of his knowledge there was a disorder that came from his feelings, and this allowed and even compelled him to root among the things he knew, viewing them from this angle and from that, seeking a forgotten piece or a relationship not yet noticed.

Standing on the lawn, his books and papers under his arm, held back and urged forward by the shiftings of his thoughts, Charley Pederson watched as the two men moved beyond the terrace, still walking very slowly. Once or twice Berrain looked back, with small half-turns of his head. But Pederson could see that Wisla was talking steadily, and for the most part Berrain was paying close attention to him.

Sydney Weigert, to whom Wisla had bowed in passing, had caught some of his words, enough to know that the radiation accident was under discussion. Rather defensively, with a private irritation even, he recorded to himself the fact that he felt very badly about this accident. And yet it was impossible, sitting here, a stone's throw from the seven men who lay over there in beds because of it, and almost under Louis Saxl's window, simply to record his feeling without comment. A decent respect at least—

and yet a decent respect was owed Sarah too, here not yet twelve hours, and himself as well; she had looked so plain good to see, getting off the bus at Santa Fe. Now, or in an hour, they would go to the stable and get the horses he had ordered, and ride off to a private place in the mountains, for a picnic, for total immersion in themselves, and for raptures that were becoming more specific every minute.

He noticed that Pederson was moving on the lawn. If Pederson should come close enough to speak and be spoken to, she would say, of course, "Who is he?" and if this happened he would tell her about the accident. It could be argued certainly that to speak of it would upset her for no purpose, even though she knew none of the men involved and nothing of the circumstances. Besides, she was fresh from Albion, Michigan, and this must all be very strange to her, and hence her emphasis and dependence on him would be double.

He had thought of this already, thinking of the raptures. But now he thought of it again, thinking of the accident, and of how in a sense to tell her about it would be to take away not only the pleasure that shone on her face as her jacket shone in the sun, but the prop and reliance of himself, because he would recede from her in the telling, and of course she from him, and the day from both of them. And it wouldn't do anyone any good at all; it wouldn't help matters.

But if Pederson came close enough, he said again to himself, he would tell her. He would let chance decide it. He squirmed in his chair, and noticed that Sarah was looking at him with an expression that was just moving from the look of happiness that had been on her face to the beginning of another expression, possibly of concern or puzzlement. But he smiled at her to reassure her and noticed, without any change of expression on his own face, that David Thiel had appeared at the very corner of his eye, out on the lawn some distance beyond Pederson. He heard Thiel call to Pederson and saw Pederson turn and walk away to join him.

5

"This is the real crossroads of the town, right out here," Betsy Pilcher was saying. She had the blinds at the front window in Louis's room adjusted for maximum vision, and she stood before them, looking out, twisting the cord this way and that with her hand. "The roads don't cross here, but the people certainly do. I can tell you about everybody, right from here."

She looked back over her shoulder at Louis and he smiled at her. All was neat on and around the bed. An hour before he had been struggling vainly to push the gown back over him, rubbing his hand without effect over the caught folds (for if the opposable thumb and forefinger were not necessary to disclose reality, they apparently were needed to conceal it). Their eyes had met, hers struck with concern, his almost vacant, and had turned together to stare at his nakedness, as at something that held no meaning for either a man or a woman but only for a chart. She had pulled the gown at once over the red flesh between the lines of tan, lifted his hand away, and, in a succession of movements, all of which seemed to be variants of the same one, she had tended to everything else, putting the bed in order, replenishing the ice, brushing his teeth, watering the flower. His temperature was down three-tenths of a degree. It was a very good sign, Betsy was sure; for she did know, she had read or heard, that bad radiation dosages were marked by a slow, inexorable rise in temperature. Not much could be drawn from it, Louis thought, remembering that the slow, inexorable rise of Nolan's temperature had been marked by ups and downs.

Nothing was said of the erythema; Dr Morgenstern had been in and had a look at it, and had rubbed his nose.

"Would you say the cutaneous reaction of the torso in this case presents some interesting features?" Louis asked him.

"You got a little burn there," Dr Morgenstern said, looking down at Louis, pursing his lips, then looking at Louis more intently.

A photographer had been in; he had fumbled with his camera and bulbs, and had steadfastly avoided looking at Louis's face. He had taken pictures of both hands and a picture of the abdomen, and for the latter purpose a small hand towel was draped over Louis's genitals. His eyes and Betsy's had met again over this small preparation, and this time Louis blushed.

He had half a cup of coffee and some food, received some codeine for the pain in his arm, and gave more blood to Dr Novali for the counts—of the lymphocytes, the neutrophils, the monocytes, the red blood cells, the platelets, and the rest.

"So tell me," he said to Betsy.

"The great Wisla approaches, just below," she said. Of Berrain, who was with him, she did not know what to say, and so said nothing.

"And Dr Pederson is standing out there on the lawn like he's lost. Perhaps he is, since he ought to be here by now."

"He's got a lot of things with him, I suppose."

"Things?"

"Books and journals and so forth."

"He's got something under his arm. Yes, I suppose— It looks like what I saw him with last night."

She looked at Louis curiously; his expression was placid, almost dreamy; the top of his bed had been cranked up and he lay with his head inclined toward her and the window. The word peaceable came to her mind, and it seemed to her a shame that doctors and scientists would be trooping in and out of the room as they had done the day before, involving Louis in endless discussion, making it impossible for him to rest. She turned to the window again.

"I can't see who it is on the terrace. Someone with a strange girl—not from here, I mean. I know who's with her, except that I can't remember his name. There's your friend David Thiel coming across the lawn. He's a real nice person. I like him."

Someone had left the window open in the rain, Louis was thinking, possibly Ulanov, who had had this room for a day or two when he broke his toe and was the sort of person not necessarily to leave a window open in the rain but to get up and open it if it were closed. In the glowing light the streaks and lines on the slats of the blind resembled, if he squinted his eyes a little, a series of atomic or molecular spectra—or, to be precise, photographs of spectra, since the color was not analyzed.

He ran his tongue over the gold cap that Dr Coleman, an old-fashioned dentist, had put over the second molar of his lower right jaw after killing the nerve many years before. Subsequent dentists had deplored Dr Coleman's dentistry, but at least an extraction had been avoided and the abcesses so frequently predicted by brisker practitioners had never developed. The part of his tongue against the tooth was sore, or was beginning to be sore. He sighed, more mentally than physically; the gold cap that had saved him the pain of an extraction as a child was obviously going to cause some pain now. If the neutron dosage had been high enough—and then he stopped this thought. Given the neutron dosage, he continued, whatever it was exactly, the induced radioactivity of this gold cap was going to be enough to burn possibly quite a little hole of its own in his tongue. He would have to mention it, later. It was not a good sign.

But if the streaked slats of the window blind brought spectra to mind, he now asked himself, where did Betsy fit in the picture? The way she was standing, against the blind at one end of it, the spectra seemed to be radiating from her body. One might entitle this composition, he thought, "Figure with Line Spectrum of an Incandescent Gas." Helium, he thought; she is roughly of the nature of yellow but her yellow is not so intense as helium's. Also, her nose is too bony, and her face too thin.

The difference between Theresa and all others who glowed yellow—yellow was Theresa's color too—was the difference between sodium vapor and helium gas. Theresa's yellow was the complex yellow, the dual yellow of the luminous vapor, wholly indistinguishable from the simple, single yellow of the incandescent gas to the eye un-aided and unlearned, but very different through the prism, very different when you really saw it.

But there were several things of which, by private de-cree, he was not going to think, among them Theresa, from whom at all events there might be a wire today and, to-morrow, perhaps a letter.

I, Louis Saxl, he said to himself, will this day think not of the future beyond two days from now, and no more of the past beyond two days ago, and of the present I will think selectively.

I will compile an Index Librorum and will amend and modify it as I see fit and will not publish it even to myself, for I will know what is on it and what is not. Do I dare to think a thought?

"Did you hear?" Betsy said. "Did you hear Mr Thiel calling Dr Pederson just then? It sounded so clear."

Louis's eyes moved to the watch at the end of the bed, to the flower on the window ledge, and back to Betsy, who had turned to look at him. He moved his right arm slightly and heard the sound of ice water in the trough.

"Your friend David's got such a nice face. There's so much life in it, you can see it even from here."

Books and journals, books and journals, he repeated to himself. Everybody will be reading something, mostly about mice and dogs because there isn't very much about us humans, he thought; and the usefulness of all the reports on the casualties and survivors in Japan is not much since there were so many variables in estimating the radiation and most of them died or lived on their own, the doctors

being killed and the nurses being killed and the hospital
beds destroyed. Out of seventeen hundred and fifty nurses
in Hiroshima, more than sixteen hundred killed or injured.
Out of eight hundred and fifty medical students in Nagasaki, six hundred killed outright. Out of forty-seven hospitals, three left usable. Do I remember right? he asked
himself. Out of two hundred doctors in Hiroshima, twenty
left to work. But this is not the writing that will be read
now, he reflected. These specifics are not right for now
and might as well be written on the other side of the moon,
for they cast no usable light. Yet what a dreadful light they
cast and is anything else worth reading? But everyone here
will be reading Marshak's paper about the effects of
X-rays and neutrons on mouse lymphoma chromosomes
in different stages of the nuclear cycle and whose-was-it
on the effects of low temperatures on the roentgen irra-
diation reaction of skin in humans.

Everybody will be reading something, except Novali and
his laboratory technicians, who will be making notes to be
read, constituting the clinical laboratory findings in seven
cases of acute radiation syndrome.

And including much hematology and many examinations of scrapings from the epidermis and the contents and
breakdowns of all the voidings and dischargings of seven
bodies, together with sperm counts, to say nothing of many,
many considerations and reconsiderations of the calculated
radiation doses in terms of the observed biologic response
of the patients, expressed as roentgens, reps, rems, gram
roentgens, or megagram roentgens.

The important thing about reading a chart is to read no
more than is there. The important thing about reading how
six hundred out of eight hundred and fifty medical students
were killed in a city of secondary importance bombed without warning is to read more than is there. The important
thing about a chart—I read Nolan's charts for twenty days,
but after eight or nine days I read them differently than
before, read them in terms of what they would show at

the end, for instance the temperature, just how high would it go? and the white count, just how low? But it is hard to read a chart right, I suppose I would read my own the same way, and whoever will be reading mine—

The thing I remember about Nolan is not the charts but the night he wet the bed and, lying in the ulcerated skin and the pain and all the mess he was becoming, was embarrassed most by that. And the night he turned to me, the skin gone from his arms, gone from his belly, and the hair gone from the left side of his head, the expression gone from his eyes, about the fifteenth or sixteenth day— turned and said with his tongue thickened and some of the flesh gone from it, said: "I was playing it for a joke, Louis, I meant it for a joke." After two or three minutes he said: "Honest."

"Honest," Louis said aloud.

"Honest?" Betsy said, turning again to look at him and moving away from the window. "You mean about David Thiel? You think I'm being patronizing, don't you? Really I'm not. Everyone I know likes him. They think just the same as me, as I."

"No, I didn't mean that," Louis said.

He urged her to look out the window again to see if she couldn't tell who was on the terrace. What did the man on the terrace look like?

"Well, he's got a crew haircut. Typical longhair. I know his name, it'll come to me. They're dressed up for riding. He's going to show his girl the beauties of the West."

My advice to you is to take the road west into the Valle Grande for about eight miles, Louis said to himself, and then take the little road that turns off there to the south, and go down it for another six or seven miles. It's rough, but it's a pretty road and it will bring you out at the foot of St Peter's dome, where it's nice to lie in the sun with your girl.

Theresa, he said, did you get the wire?

"Weigert," Betsy said. "That's his name. Sydney Weigert."

6

"We could have some more coffee if you'd like some," Sydney was saying, "and then we can go down and get the horses. Or shall we go down now?"

"Whichever you want to do, Sydney."

"Well, what do you want?" he asked her, but his eyes skipped to Pederson and Thiel, walking very slowly across the lawn. Involuntarily he glanced up at the window to Louis Saxl's room.

"Oh, Sydney, you decide."

He raised his arm to attract the attention of the waiter, who was clearing off the table at which Wisla and Berrain had been sitting. "Let's have some more coffee," he said.

Pederson, barely moving from step to step, was doing the talking. David Thiel had his stick under one arm and his hands clasped behind his back.

"I'd forgotten. You left the day after it happened. That's when you went to Japan, I remember now."

"Louis was supposed to go," David said. "I took his place."

"I remember now. It was because of Nolan he called it off. That's a funny thing, I hadn't thought of that."

"Of what?" David asked.

"How it happened to Nolan the day before he's supposed to go to Japan and then to himself the day before he's supposed to go to Bikini."

"Well, don't think of it," David said. "Think of medicines."

"What I was getting at was that if you'd seen Nolan from day to day you'd have noticed the difference. There isn't much I can tell you, with what you saw in Japan and then in general you know— But I did watch Nolan from the first, and he was really sicker than a dog clear through the second day with nausea and prostration. He couldn't lift his little finger. But Louis was sitting up last night, feeling pretty good. Louis got through the first phase in about a day. That's a good sign, Dave, it can only be a good sign."

David turned his head up quickly and turned it back, seeming almost to duck away. He said nothing. They continued their slow walk.

"And aside from being a good sign in its own right," Pederson went on, "it might mean the way he was standing protected his abdomen." He said the last of these words with a rising inflection, which turned them into a delicate question.

"We'll just have to wait and see," David said quickly. "It's not possible to reconstruct things that precisely. I can't tell you any more than I did yesterday. No one can."

"No," Pederson said, sighing. "Anyway, I'm positive he couldn't have got it in the belly anything like Nolan did. The pictures don't show how bad it was when the skin started to macerate. The belly's the breach to watch, all right. You know, after I got home last night the first thing I read was an evaluation of some of Berrain's work with rabbits. I'm glad he's here, he knows his stuff. Anyway, he found they could take nearly twice as much total radiation if their abdomens weren't involved."

"When did Nolan's skin—" David began.

"Start to macerate? About the—"

"No, when did the erythema first show?"

"The third day," Pederson said. "That's what did it for Nolan, I think, the heavy burst in the abdomen. And I'm just sure—well, as you say, we'll have to wait."

They walked on in silence for a few steps, and then Pederson continued.

"There's no comparison between them physically. Nolan's health wasn't too good. He had that heart conditon, he was overweight by about fifteen pounds, and some other things. Louis's health is perfect. He's a wonderful specimen, weight just about right or better, not a trace of anything wrong anywhere."

Pederson shook his head. He shifted his books and journals from one arm to the other, dropped one in the process, picked it up, and went on.

"I know as well as you do that this probably doesn't mean a thing. Still, it might give him an edge, I wouldn't make more of it. There are some other things though."

"There was too much confusion in Japan," David said. "Nobody ever got to know much about most of the people who died there. There's enough we don't know about the ones who lived."

He looked up at Pederson again.

"What are the other things?"

"There's one thing you can tell me, tell all of us, that'll answer everything, I suppose," Pederson said. "You're computing the probable dosage, and if it turns out just enormous— I know you haven't got the answer yet. I suppose you may not ever figure it exactly. But I imagine you've got a pretty good idea."

David said nothing.

"Haven't you?"

"It's full of complications. Don't underestimate our ignorance."

"I'm not sure I want to hear it. I know it's high enough. I know some of the complications too. Such as the radioactivity of the blood sodium. If you're basing the neutron dosage on that, I don't see how you can be sure of your results."

David extracted his stick from under his arm and began to walk a little faster.

"I heard your point about that last night," he said. "I wish you wouldn't let it worry you."

"Yes, I know, nobody's impressed, but no one says why. Herzog seemed to think something of it anyway. Here's a fact, so the physicists say—blood sodium will show ninety times the radiosensitivity of blood phosphorus—and then Louis's blood sodium shows five times, less than six anyway, and you all say it doesn't mean anything. If one so-called fact can be that much off, maybe some others can. Isn't there that at least?"

"There is not that at least," David said sharply. He lifted his stick and made some circles in the air with it. "Charley, stop trying to be a physicist. The relation of phosphorus neutron capture to sodium neutron capture is of some interest to anyone trying to compute the dosage, but it's not decisive even there. Nobody told you why he wasn't impressed because it doesn't make any difference to getting Louis through this, which is your concern. Quit wasting time."

"I've got to know what I'm dealing with," Pederson said doggedly.

"You said a minute ago you weren't sure you wanted to hear what you're dealing with," David said, and his voice was patient again. "But you're certainly dealing with a jungle subject, and you're going out of your way to get lost, poking around looking for reasons to hope instead of ways to treat. The ways to treat are what's needed. Have you found anything? What are those other things you mentioned?"

Pederson came to a full stop, swinging around to face David.

"Dave, I can't say anything more until you tell me whatever you can tell me. Is there any reason to hope?"

From the terrace Sydney was watching them and Sarah was sitting silently, turning her coffee cup around and around. Berrain and Wisla were just disappearing through the hospital door. At the window of Louis's room the white of Betsy's uniform was still visible behind the open slats of the blind. A few men were walking one way or another in the streets, but most of them were at work and their wives were not yet out for their shopping. The air was getting quite hot. Two small boys came along on scooters.

"Hi, Charley!" one of them called.

Pederson waved absently and continued to look at David.

"No," David said, "there's no reason to hope. No reason. You said to begin with you had some thoughts that might help. Are you going to withdraw them now? There may be reasons to be patient. You've mentioned some. Won't that do? When hope breaks, let patience hold. Won't that do?"

"Dave—" Pederson began.

But David had moved ahead. He was walking fast and strenuously, hunched over, bent forward. Pederson ran forward and caught him in the street.

"Dave!" he demanded.

"If you can think of any way to make two and two not equal four, concentrate on that," David said, muttering the words.

"What did you say?"

"I don't like your questions, they're the wrong questions," David replied crossly. He turned his head away from Pederson, looking down the street toward the center of town. The clerk from the telegraph office was standing down there, a hundred yards or so away at one side of the street and just back from it; she had on the same brightly colored dress she had worn the day before. David turned his head again almost at once, too soon to have noticed that she was walking toward them. Pederson, first puzzled and then hurt, noticed nothing.

"The trouble with us is you're trying to think my way and I'm trying to think yours," David said. "If Louis dies it will be because he got a lethal dose, which the physicists will compute, and if he lives it may be because the doctors thought of something."

They looked at each other in silence for a moment, and then again they moved toward the hospital, slowly as before.

"I don't know yet how much radiation was involved," David said. "I know roughly—so does Louis, I imagine, so do some others—and of course it was high. Does it help to say that? How high? you want to know. Meaning does it leave any reason to hope? or—what's the alterna-

tive?—shall we all give up and go home? Our ignorance
is a reason to hope, and I shouldn't have said there was
no reason. That's one. What's a lethal dose of total-body
ionizing radiation? Six hundred roentgen equivalents, it
says in all the literature—all since the beginning of this
year. Before that it didn't say. You know, I sat in on a
meeting trying to determine the lethal radiation level, just
to bring some order out of chaos. The range of estimates
ran from four hundred to two thousand roentgen equivalents. Everybody made a guess, and this was after Hiroshima and Nagasaki. We're still guessing. That six-hundred
figure came out of such a meeting and was somebody's
guess, maybe somebody with a train to catch and no great
reverence for the sanctity of numbers. One of the difficulties is that most of what we know comes from mice and
dogs and rabbits. The results are not perfectly applicable
to humans. They get you into oversimplifications and
guesswork. I trust this difficulty will be preserved.

"Did I ever tell you about Professor Tanaki? He's a
Japanese physicist, a small, dignified man. I met him at
MacArthur's headquarters in Tokyo—he came there to
show his reports on the radiation casualties at Hiroshima.
After he discussed them he spoke about how he'd gone
to school at the University of California years before, how
he'd done some experimental X-ray work there on rats. I
didn't tell you about him? But let me tell you what he said,
when he finished talking about his work. 'I did those experiments years ago,' he said—his voice was very precise,
and soft—'only on a few rats, of course. But you Americans, you are wonderful, you have made the human experiment.' He paused just before 'human.' 'You have made
the—human experiment,' he said."

"May I speak to you?"

David turned. The clerk from the telegraph office was
standing right beside him; she looked only at David and
she said nothing more.

"Of course," said David, leaning forward slightly on his
stick.

She turned away at once. She walked some eight or nine steps back toward the street and stood facing it. Pederson started to say something, but David was already walking back to where she stood.

"Your wire could not be sent," she said as soon as he reached her. "Do you know?"

"No, I didn't know."

"An order is against it."

"An order from whom?"

"Colonel— that Colonel. I will send it from Santa Fe if you want me to."

David said nothing. He had been looking into the clerk's face, and now he looked down at the ground.

"Do you want me to?"

"I don't want you to get into trouble," David said, and he continued to look down.

"There is no trouble. I will send it from Santa Fe."

"Yes, but there might someday be trouble," said David, looking up at her. "Still—you could say I asked you to send it. Or told you to. Will you say I told you to send it?"

"Who do I say this to?"

"To anyone who might ask about it. Later, I mean."

"But nobody—" she began, and then, after quite a long pause, she smiled at David. "I will say you told me."

She turned and walked away.

"Thank you," David called after her.

She said something over her shoulder, but he couldn't make it out. For a moment he stood watching her; then he went back to where Pederson was standing, and they moved on.

"Is she a friend of yours?" Pederson asked.

"I—yes, she is."

"I've heard a lot about her."

"Really? Is she well known?"

"She is to the GI's. They all know her pretty well," Pederson said primly.

David, peering up at him, smiled; he felt a small and

quiet exhilaration, as one might savor a private victory or some achievement of a friend, and he withdrew into this sufficiently to dissuade Pederson from saying anything more. They walked in silence to the foot of the stoop before the hospital door.

"But our experiment—it was not a good experiment, even ironically," David said abruptly. "Even in Professor Tanaki's horrible irony, it wasn't a good experiment. We killed a hundred thousand humans, maybe more, and their doctors as well. They died in the rubble, untended most of them, and we still know most of what we know from rats and rabbits."

Shocked, Pederson said nothing. "Do you know why so many doctors are here?" David went on, mounting the stoop briskly. "Berrain, Kahn, Jerome Woodyall, and the rest of them? What a footnote to Professor Tanaki's theme! Well, why? Do you know what galvanizes the Army into private planes and urgent phone calls—come quick and time and money no object? Seven aren't worth a hundred thousand. Not any seven. Except as they provide the first completely observed and measured cases of acute radiation syndrome in history—nicely graduated too, from intense to negligible exposure. Nolan died in confusion. The checks and controls weren't working when he dropped his miserable screwdriver, nobody was looking, and what we learned was by guess and by God. And the Japanese—nobody who knew what happened was anywhere around."

At the top of the stoop David whacked the screen door with his cane, and turned on Pederson.

"But what a full set of curves and charts and graphs we'll get from Louis! How greatly we'll enrich the literature! How attentive the Army is to every need and detail—now!"

It was too much for Pederson. The bitterness was not lost on him, nor the irony either, but he could not partake of them. If he had been listening to someone other than David, the bitterness might have driven him on to annoyance. Because it was David he simply withdrew his interest, much as one might overlook an unworthy act when it is done by a friend who is not properly represented by it. The end of David's speech Pederson hardly heard. One following the other, they went inside.

On the terrace Sydney Weigert was leaning forward on the table, his arms folded before him, his head slightly bent down. He was talking steadily to Sarah, who, sitting straight up, her hands in her lap, was listening carefully; her eyes strayed every few seconds to the hospital across the street, to the door and the windows. At the window of the room that had been pointed out to her the white of a uniform was still visible. Then, even as she looked, it disappeared.

7

Along the street from the center of the town came Colonel Hough, walking smartly; from the door of the cafeteria building, nearly a block in back of him, Ulanov and a small, black-haired woman emerged. Ulanov surveyed the street and saw the Colonel.

"Hey, Hough!" he yelled.

The Colonel stopped.

Ulanov leaned over and kissed the woman, ran his hand down the side of her leg and kissed her again, said something at which she laughed, then turned and sprinted up the street to where the Colonel stood, watching him without approval.

"It'd be useful all around to have you in uniform," said the Colonel.

"Arrange it," Ulanov panted. "I could use—" he breathed deeply—"the basic training. And for the rest—" another breath—"it would be an excellent way to get off this project, along with the rest of the uniforms."

"I hate to think where we'd be—"

"Please don't then. I want to complain about a stove."

"You have complained about a stove."

"Look, General," Ulanov said, taking Hough by the arm and pulling him along. "You cannot know how our stove smells up the place. You refer me to the Housing Office, which fails to know too. Nonetheless it delivers yesterday another, alleged to be an improvement. This other sits overnight outside our door. This morning it was to be hooked up, the Housing agents promised so. But this morning the Housing agents come and take away the new one! Orders, they said! Our house still stinks. My wife and I still must go to the cafeteria. Now, God damn it to hell— what now? *Ce n'est pas la guerre! Was ist?* Uniforms?"

"You should go to the Lodge," the Colonel said. "A pleasant place on a nice morning. Go back to the Housing Office. My apologies to Mrs Ulanov, but the problem isn't insoluble. My God—"

"Sure, sure," Ulanov said. He relaxed his hold on the Colonel. "Now another thing, different. I met a Congressman last night."

"Did you?" Hough said with some surprise. "That Representative, the one from—?"

"He's staying at the Lodge. Just arrived yesterday."

"That's the one. Jesus! Where?"

"I met this distinguished character at midnight in a vacuum. But truly! I met him at Herman Romach's house. He was there for dinner."

"They're friends?"

"Well, this person used to be a tax lawyer for wicked corporations, and Romach's a corporation man himself— took leave from Lowe & Waterson to join the project. He'll go back too. They met somehow, before the war. Anyway, really, do you know him?"

"I'm seeing him today. He's a committee chairman. I hope to God—"

"He says the Lodge is better than any motel he's come across, except one. He liked one in California better."

The Colonel said nothing.

"He says the nation is proud of our work, and considering what it cost, he says, it damn well ought to be. He says it could have been done for less, but he's not necessarily kicking, he says."

"I'm glad to hear that."

"He thinks Alan Nunn May ought to be shot."

"Alan Nunn May was a goddamned fool, and I thank God he never got out to Los Alamos. I also thank God he's England's problem, not ours. So I suppose you set the Congressman straight on everything. I suppose—"

"He too thanks God. He thanks God for giving us the secret—I set him straight on that, I told him nobody gave it to us. I told him we've had to work for it ever since us Poles got the track of it fifty years ago—and he says—"

"Oh, God!"

"—he says well anyway the Russians won't get it for another fifty years. He says the Russians haven't got the know-how. He says it might be necessary to have perhaps some preventive war, a little sort of one, perhaps drop a few bombs on them, show them what's what, but not necessarily, and he says not to get him wrong. He says many wonderful things, and he is *not* an important man."

"He could bring down a Congressional investigation on our heads if the idea occurs to him, and I wouldn't be surprised if it does after listening to you. What's the point of getting a committee chairman all worked up? He's only here for a day."

"I didn't work him up, old friend. He listened to a broadcast on our radio station last night. A respected scientist member of the community told why the Bikini bomb tests were a bad idea—a threatening, asinine idea, I believe he said, and so forth—and Congressman What's-his-name took off from that. I got there late."

"I should have listened. He'll want to talk about that, I suppose."

"But if this is where the power is, then, believe me, we

are all lost," Ulanov said. "Believe me, I know this kind of person. I did not meet him just last night. Some even live here, and I knew them elsewhere, including in Poland and England—people who ask questions only when they've decided on the answers. They live backwards and know no place to go except where they've been—or where their tribal ancestors were. This is a fault in men like faults in rock, and once there was tolerance enough for it, sometimes just barely. But what is the critical amount of this unreality now? How much can we tolerate before it blows up in our faces and puts our eyes out—Congressman What's-his-name's as well as mine? and yours?"

"This is quite a lot of effect for an unimportant man to have," the Colonel said wryly.

"Is true," Ulanov agreed. "So let us not let him have such effects. Let us talk to his voters and maybe they will vote him out. Have you sent a dollar to Einstein's committee? But you might at least quit quaking before frauds like this."

The Colonel patted Ulanov on the back.

"I'll send a dollar to Einstein's committee. Nice to have known you."

He turned away from Ulanov toward the hospital.

"Just a minute, Lieutenant. The most important thing is now to be said."

"I want to get to the hospital, Ulanov," the Colonel said impatiently, but he stopped. "What is it? Can you just say it?"

"This Congressman wants to investigate Louis Saxl."

"He what?"

"He wants to investigate Saxl because Saxl was in the Spanish war. He doesn't necessarily think Saxl should be shot right away, but he finds this disturbing."

Colonel Hough took three steps back to Ulanov.

"But I knew about that. The Security Office knows about it. He's been cleared three times over. Is this a joke?"

"Not to the Congressman. The Congressman has not cleared him. You said—"

"I mean, are you telling this straight?"

"Yes," said Ulanov, speaking with great simplicity. "The Congressman was perfectly serious. I came late because I was at the hospital. He asked me about things, quite solicitously. I told him something about Saxl because—I suppose because Saxl is worth telling about. I mentioned Spain, and the Congressman went up like a rocket. 'Fought for the Communists?' he said. 'Good God, how long's he been on this project?' And Romach—Romach's thickheaded, but he has no malice—Romach said: 'He's one of those who is the project.' Well, the Congressman wants to talk to people, including you—and Louis."

"Talk to Louis?" said the Colonel in a thin voice. "But doesn't he know the shape he's in? You told him, didn't you? I'm sure the doctors—I'm sure he'd understand."

The Colonel did not go on. After a moment Ulanov shrugged his shoulders, and then he laughed.

"As you say, he is an important man. You know, I must confess—though I recognized him, there was something not right in the picture. It may be his importance. I'd forgotten to look for it."

They continued to look at each other.

"Well," Ulanov said finally, "you have your meeting. Two meetings. After the doctors, the Congressman. Fine, fine. I suppose you know Louis isn't so good this morning?"

"No." The Colonel frowned and looked sharply at Ulanov. "That's not so. I called. They told me he was feeling much better."

"Well," said Ulanov pleasantly, "one of us must have heard wrong. I must go. I hope everything turns out well." And he walked away.

The Colonel gazed up at the hospital windows, frowned automatically at a box someone had left under one of the first-floor windows, and wriggled his shoulders to straighten his jacket. Ulanov, he was thinking, and people like Ulanov— the fancy foreigners, he sometimes called them, although they were not always foreigners—whatever their common denominator, such people cast spells on him, he had to admit it. And this time everything was complicated by the fact that the civilian director of the project was away in Washington on the Bikini bomb-test business, and so he must think on his own.

As to this crazy notion of investigating, the Congressman simply could not comprehend the situation, and no wonder, with Ulanov to tell it to him. No one started investigating a man who might be dying. But quite aside from this, mightn't it have occurred to Ulanov to point out that the Spanish business (he wouldn't defend it, of course) had been looked into years before? Ulanov had probably fought the war all over again with the Congressman—which could have got the Congressman so worked up that he really might start an investigation.

But of what? the Colonel asked himself.

Simply on the premise that any part of a project into which so much of the taxpayer's money had gone might be fair game for Congressional scrutiny, the Colonel, in common with all others in positions of any authority, had thought often of the possibility of investigations. These thoughts had been largely nominal in the first years of the project; they had become acute in the months and weeks before the test explosion at Alamagordo; and they had all but evaporated in that moment's blinding crown to all the effort, all the worry, and all the money. Some of the scientists had danced for joy on the sands of lower New Mexico that cold July morning; among the military men the general reaction was one of plain relief.

But the real problem was that the story of the accident was out of hand, or was on its way to being so. If this Congressman knew about it, it could no longer be kept on the reservation. The Congressman himself was to blame for this, just by showing up now of all times; the Colonel would do what he could when he talked to the Congressman; he would explain the importance of official notifications; he would say a few words about security and public morale. And he would get a story ready.

8

By nine o'clock or a little later, on this Thursday morning two days after the accident, nearly everyone concerned with it had put in an appearance at the doctors' conference room in the hospital; and all of them had heard the news about the burn on Louis Saxl's abdomen. Dr Morgenstern told the first arrivals. Dr Berrain mentioned it to Pederson; he asked if Pederson did not agree that it was a good idea to keep the abdomen covered with ice bags.

"There is no pain there yet," Berrain said, speaking conversationally to his young colleague. "But aside from that, I was thinking we might be able to hold back somewhat the circulation of the cell debris. Mild chilling, not below sixty degrees Farenheit or thereabouts. Don't you think?"

Pederson's round, bland face showed the shock the news had been to him. But Berrain took him beyond it well enough, and Pederson started off to make sure that the ice bags were being properly applied.

"May I join you?" said Dr Briggle, who, still haggard from his night's journey and a one-hour nap, was standing close by.

"Of course. Have you been upstairs yet?"

Dr Briggle was known for work he had done with certain dyes that had proved effective, when used on experimental animals, at preventing the small, oozing hemorrhages characteristic of the late stages of severe radiation sickness. This work was recent; it had reached no usable result at the time of Nolan's accident and had not been available, of course, to the Japanese. No one had made a decision that Dr Briggle would try his dyes on Louis Saxl if the necessity should arise. He had simply been called to Los Alamos.

"I saw three or four of the less sick patients a few minutes ago, not Saxl," Briggle said.

"Well," Pederson began; but then he didn't know what he wanted to say.

The news of the burn stayed on everyone's mind.

Doctors came and went between the conference room and the rooms of the patients and Dr Novali's laboratory. Two of them did not examine the patients or even see them; these two, hematologists summoned from Chicago the day before, found themselves an empty room near the laboratory and moved into it with piles of literature and books and notebooks, emerging from time to time to study some of the numerous charts on wooden boards that hung from the walls or lay on the tables in the laboratory. They peered at slides with blood samples fixed on them, or sucked at pipettes, or checked counts of diluted blood in hemocytometer chambers. They worked with hardly a word, discussed things for a while, smoked cigarettes, and discussed them over again.

"I think I'll have a word with someone—Berrain, I guess—about the staining technique Novali's been using."

"It's standard."

"Yes, for a crude picture. But really he shouldn't use Wright's stain except for run-of-the-mill stuff. This calls for Giemsa."

"Well, so far as Saxl's concerned I don't think it's going to make a hell of a lot of difference. The changes are so gross you can practically hear them."

"I understand he's the guy who put together the first bomb. Do you know him? Ever met him?"

"No. Don't know any of them."

"Someone told me he sat through that other case out here last year. That'd give you something to think about, hey?"

"If I were Saxl, I guess I'd be thinking about that burn on the belly right now. If it shows up this fast, I hate to think what we're going to be seeing in a day or so."

So the blood men talked; today's burn would be to-morrow's new fall in the monocytes and the reticulocytes, would show up in floods of swollen and pallid cells, in toxic granulation of the neutrophils, and in all the other uncon-trollable, steadily accumulating wreckage of the fine bal-ance of the blood elements. As a reflection of the subatomic storm that had lashed Louis for a tiny fraction of a second, the burn was ominous but not conclusive.

On the landing of the stairway, where Betsy had watched the procession leaving the night before, three doctors held a small caucus. Louis's blood pressure had shown a no-ticeable fall when it had been taken early in the morning of the first day after the accident, had stayed about the same during the day, but had shown a partial return when the last reading was taken on Wednesday evening. One of the three doctors had just been trying to take it again.

"But I can't do it," he was saying. "I can't inflate the cuff. It's just too damned painful on either arm."

"You know, we used to get readings from the finger tips. Well, hell, that's a bright thought. I forgot about his hands."

"Let's skip it," the first one said. "I can't see why we have to keep track of initial alarm reaction from here on out. If we don't know, we don't know."

But they also agreed that it was too bad not to have the readings for the record of what was obviously going to be a most important case.

Dr Morgenstern was off somewhere for half an hour or so. When he returned everyone was in the middle of some-thing, and to tell the truth most of the doctors had not noticed that he had been away.

"I myself know at least eleven distinct theories of the etiology of radiation sickness," one doctor, standing in the corridor, was saying to a colleague. "And I suppose there's a little something to all of them. Well, this might tell us something." He was holding a large needle.

"Sternal pucture?" Morgenstern said, looking at the needle.

"Yes," said the colleague. "It should have been done yesterday."

"He felt so badly," Morgenstern said.

A gracious man, Dr Morgenstern felt that his position as the doctor in charge of the hospital imposed on him some of the obligations of a host, and so he wandered about the corridors, peeked into rooms, and occasionally had a word or two with one of the other doctors. But it did not happen, for an hour or more, that he encountered Dr Berrain. This morning Berrain had spent some time with all seven of the radiation cases, examining each of them. He went over blood samples, studied specimens of urine and feces, looked at charts of blood-clotting times, and himself called a doctor in Salt Lake City to discuss with him the advisability of trying an exchange transfusion. After deciding to withhold that for the time being, Berrain went to Saxl's room and stood in on the administration of a pint and a half of blood, a hundred thousand units of penicillin, and twenty milligrams of thiamin chloride. He also arranged for a drip injection of glucose in saline for that afternoon. He stood by the window watching while the doctor with the large needle stuck it into Louis's breast-bone and drew off a sample of the marrow. With Betsy and Dr Pederson helping, he examined Louis's hands. He said little during all this, and he left the room as a young physicist came in with a Geiger counter to make check counts of the radioactivity of several parts of Louis's body.

None of these actions, nor any of the many others taken this morning, would have any known or measurable effects on the progress of the radiation sickness itself. All of them were perfectly justified for one reason or another, and each of them would find its place in the growing records; in any event, they kept everyone busy. Through the morning a degree of excitement came in to infect all the doctors, the nurses, the technicians, and the patients as well, including even Mr Matousek with his broken leg down on the first floor. It failed to reach only Wisla and David Thiel, who spent the morning largely by themselves, in a cubbyhole next to the conference room, filling sheets of paper with computations designed to help establish the precise quantity of neutrons that had entered seven bodies, what proportion had been fast as opposed to slow, what had entered directly and what had come from scatterings off the floor and walls of the canyon room, what might have penetrated beyond the superficial tissues to reach the bones, and what might have induced further radioactivity in the cells of the bodies, and approximately how much.

Dr Berrain came to the door of the cubbyhole where Wisla and David were working and stood there a moment looking in at them. He shrugged his shoulders, smiled ruefully, even a little cynically, took off his glasses, and rubbed his hand over his forehead. David turned a pencil in his hand and looked at him. Wisla glanced up, and then went on making notes on a sheet of paper.

"Those computations are beyond me," Berrain said. "I could ask a hundred questions." He leaned against the door. "I imagine you are much less lost in my field."

"How long before you'll know the answer?" David asked.

"Another two or three days, I'd guess. It's a guess."

There was a pause; Wisla went on writing.

"May I ask you the same thing?"

"Same answer, more or less."

Berrain nodded his head.

"A few days to define the cause, a few days to define the effects," he said finally. "Nature balances things out."

"This is all somewhat too elegant," Wisla said, looking up. "In two or three days we shall know whether he got the biologic equivalent of perhaps five hundred roentgens of hard gamma rays or perhaps six or seven hundred, or even more, and some details of varying importances. In short, we know something right now, such as that he did not receive only three hundred. Is it so different with you?"

"Yes," said Berrain, pulling himself away from the door. "It's different with me. But I didn't know you knew this much. You didn't say so last night."

"We didn't know this much last night. That burn tells us something. But we don't know it now either," David said.

"We do not know it to be proven to the exclusion of all else," Wisla remarked. "It has been established as probable."

"But not certain."

"There is one possibility against it. This is a very unlikely possibility."

"It is still a possibility."

"To be sure," Wisla said. "There is one chance in a hundred it is correct." And he returned to his writing.

"A little better than that," David murmured. He was tapping his pencil nervously, but suddenly he put it down and smiled up at Berrain.

"The shielding around the critical assembly used in this experiment is very inadequate," he explained. "Partly because of the way the shielding is put together, the radiation flux around the assembly was mixed. Certain parts of the body would have been in high-intensity areas and the rest in the shadow cast—"

"Stop there," Berrain said, throwing up his hands. "I am half a biologist but not at all a physicist. I can always tell what I am with words like 'flux.' What do I think of? This time, watery diarrhea. But I can't tell you anything in the face of seven hundred roentgens, except that as half a biologist I can tell you he will then die. If it's four hundred, say, maybe we can preserve the fluid balance—maybe. In a couple of days I will see if the white blood cells begin to disappear. Then I will know for sure—unless you tell me first."

"I would not wish to be premature," Wisla said, looking up at Berrain. "The year I came to this country that's what they were calling people who were going off to that war in Spain—premature anti-fascists. Is it not a remarkable phrase? Well, no prematureness. There is this possibility Thiel speaks of."

"Everyone reassures everyone," said Berrain, and again he smiled. "We will do what we can. I am going to propose that four of the cases be discharged from the hospital today, and possibly one in another two or three days. It looks like they were far back enough, or shielded enough. That one standing just behind Saxl—Haeber—should stay for a while. As for Saxl—"

Berrain paused; he reached into his pocket and withdrew a chain with two or three keys, which he began to dangle.

"He will have to lose his hands," Berrain went on. "We are amputating them by refrigeration, as of course he knows. He knows so much, much too much. I do hope his ego is strong."

"Aren't those Louis's car keys?" David asked.

"He gave them to me."

Dr Morgenstern, Dr Pederson and Dr Novali came walking along the hall; a few steps behind was Colonel Hough. They stopped at the door of the cubbyhole, but nobody said anything. Berrain continued to dangle the keys, which clinked faintly against each other. Dr Novali finally spoke.

"I was just showing Julian here—" he indicated Dr Morgenstern—"what we found from that bone marrow we aspirated. No clumps, nary a one."

"Yes, well, any cells?"

"Not enough to do a differential count, doctor. Some fat globules, debris and stuff. Degenerating cells, yes, we saw those."

"Maybe you should aspirate another sample."

"Well, we did, doctor. This here, what I'm telling you, is after two punctures. We figured we ought to try another."

"Unfortunately," Dr Morgenstern began, and the heads

turned toward him. "Unfortunately, no marrow samples were taken from Mr Nolan. I believe only one sample is known to have been taken among the Japanese—that is, this early. There is not much for direct comparison."

He broke off, peering over his glasses at Dr Berrain.

"Yes," said Dr Berrain. "I'm sorry to hear it. I want to go over the slides."

"Please look," Pederson broke in. His voice was so intense that Colonel Hough looked at him sharply, and David, out of sight of Pederson within the cubbyhole but well within range of his voice, lowered his eyes.

"The marrow tissue, of course, everyone knows how radio-sensitive it is," Pederson said, speaking quite fast. "But this doesn't prove anything, really it doesn't. This tissue regenerates so fast, even while cell destruction is going on. And there are cases too, I've been reading some, in animals, but among the Japanese too, some late samples in survivors were very bad, but they survived. Even as an index to the dose—I know that's what you're thinking of, but Dr Berrain, look, there's an extra factor here, really very important, and you can't measure it. I mean the bone tissue scatters the particles much more. I'm sure you know, of course you know, but I mean to say had you thought about that?"

And he went on speaking, mentioning the energy buildup that you were bound to get in the bone because of its density, which meant—

Berrain still held the key chain in his hand, though now it hung motionless; he pursed his lips, checking off Pederson's points, even though the confusion that underlay them was perfectly clear: this extra factor was true enough for soft X-rays, but unfortunately they were not dealing with soft X-rays, they were dealing with neutrons. Would the calcium and phosphorus of the bone scatter neutrons into the soft tissues of the marrow? Not appreciably. Was the deteriorated state of the marrow, assuming Morgenstern and Novali had made no mistakes, a reasonably direct

consequence of the radiation dose? Reasonably enough.
Was he, in fact, thinking of the state of the marrow as an
index to the dose? Not particularly, since he already had
indices enough and had confirmed them from what Wisla
and Thiel had and had not said. Was an error like this to
be expected from a man with at least some experience in
radiation sickness? Well, who could say? Here it was, at
all events. So what do we do now? Why, we correct the
error. And then? And then we take our fevered colleague
out to lunch and try to persuade him that our patient needs
a good doctor more than a good friend. So we soothe each
other, but who will reassure the patient?

Pederson came to a stop and seemed about to cry. What
a hell of a sickness this is! Berrain sighed within himself.
In an immeasurable fraction of a second a man is exposed
to a blast of energy that, when it is more than enough to
kill him, is yet less than a hundred-thousandth of the energy spent by his whole body in the normal metabolism
of one day—a blast that affects directly no more than one
molecule out of ten million in a cell of average size? And
then? And then we wait for the untouchable processes of
breakdown to spread silently and secretly, remote from
any feeling of the patient, save for the burn, to total en-
gulfment of the whole being, heralded in its time by that
sudden sharp and awful fading of the white blood cells
away. There is not another sickness like it. It is going to
be a tough few days. So what shall I say? he asked himself
again. For if my young colleague's feelings are good and
must be preserved, so must the rest of us. God damn it,
is there any reason why Morgenstern could not—?

Dr Morgenstern, bending over Pederson and clasping
and unclasping his hands, was already explaining. Mr Wisla,
half risen from his chair in the little room, was explaining
too. And before Berrain could say anything—or, more
accurately, before he did—Pederson turned to Novali, and
the two of them detached themselves from the group and
walked on toward the conference room just beyond.

Berrain thrust the key chain into his coat pocket and, facing Dr Morgenstern, said what it had been on his mind to say, strongly enough for his words to be general.

"Well, I'd like to have a look at the slides, as I say. But from what you tell me, and from what I've been able to see for myself, I think we ought to give that pathologist in St. Louis a call—Beale. I think—well, to be blunt about it, I think we ought to get him out here, just to have him here in case. Much as with Briggle."

"To tell the truth, I did call him. Yes," Dr Morgenstern said, "in fact, I called him this morning, an hour or two ago."

"I—well, I see," Berrain said. "Well, I didn't know that. Do you think he'd be agreeable to coming out?"

"Oh, yes, yes, entirely so. The fact is, I asked him. To tell the truth, he should be on his way now." Dr Morgenstern pulled his watch from his pocket and studied it for a moment. "Oh, yes," he continued. "Why, I should say he'd be getting here by the end of the day." He looked at Berrain anxiously. "It seemed simplest just to get it done," he said. "Colonel Hough here has kindly agreed to pick him up."

"No trouble," said Colonel Hough.

Berrain nodded his head to the left, and then to the right, and pursed his lips again. He half turned to look at the two physicists at the desk in the cubbyhole; Wisla was writing again, David was looking out, turning his pencil still, and with the faintest suggestion of a smile on his face. Barrain suddenly laughed.

"I was telling Mr Wisla at breakfast that stupidity had no headquarters," he said, speaking to them all. "Perhaps it has—here," he tapped his head. "Well, so be it," he said. "The abdomen is bad news, and the marrow is more. The simplest thing, as Dr Morgenstern says, is to get it done."

And as he spoke he reached into his pocket and pulled out the key chain again.

"Did he say anything?" David asked.

"He said I ought to be able to use a car while I'm here. He said to use it as long as I liked. His sister drove it out only a month or so ago for him to use, he said—an old family car. He said I could give you the keys when I'm through."

The keys clinked and no one spoke.

"I'm not entirely sure what was in his mind," Berrain went on then. "Maybe he doesn't really know what he knows. Even the least illusioned persons develop some refinement of the facts—sometimes—though develop isn't right. Cushion maybe—cushion the facts—put them on ice like we've put his hands. You know, he makes me think of that character in *War and Peace*—Rostov, wasn't it?— when he lay there wounded and the French coming at him, and he said, 'Why are they coming at me? To kill me? Me—of whom everyone is so fond?' Remember? I was thinking when I talked to Louis that there's something like that—something rather childlike, in an old-fashioned way, about him. Maybe he's just absorbed in himself—dying can make a person very self-absorbed. Still—"

Berrain jangled the keys sharply, put them back in his pocket, and continued more crisply.

"He also said he'd like to wait one more day before letting his family know. He asked me whether you'd heard anything from a friend of his—you'd wired her, he said. I can't recommend that we wait another day to call his family, but that's not up to me. At any rate, I was glad to hear him say it. I'm afraid he's wrong, and that's good—whatever he knows it's too much. Dr Morgenstern, I was going to ask young Pederson to have lunch with me. Might we all three have it?"

And Berrain and Morgenstern went down the hall to the conference room, leaving Colonel Hough alone in the hall, where David joined him. For five minutes they talked quietly. Wisla came out, glanced at them as though he had never seen either before, and left the hospital. Some of the doctors walked by. The steam whistle in the Technical

Area, which was blown to start and stop each workday and to punctuate it for lunch, filled the air with its brief and wheezing sound.

"No," David said finally, "no, I'm not calling you a liar. I believe you're going to say something, and I don't trust what you're going to say. If you can hedge it, you'll hedge it. If you could avoid it altogether, you'd do that. For some reason I don't get, you've decided it's safe or advisable to go ahead, but your aim isn't any different than it was. It's to tell as little as possible as inconspicuously as possible— SOP. All right, if what you put out is the travesty I think it will be, I'm going into Albuquerque and sit down with every wire service in town and tell them what did happen."

"Don't do anything foolish, Dave," said the Colonel seriously.

"And if they want to do some investigating, they'll know what to investigate. I don't intend to do anything foolish," he added, "and I don't intend to see it done either. What a word to use! Don't you know what happened here?"

9

The sound of the noon whistle thinned out, dying off across the canyons. The doors of the three schools on the mesa were banged open, and the children came running out. Their fathers streamed from the many buildings of the Technical Area, through the high and guarded gates, and from the workshops and the offices around. The cafeterias filled, and on the terrace of the Lodge, among the tables under the bright umbrellas, the noon shift of waiters passed back and forth. Sydney and Sarah were not there; they had taken their horses and gone riding into the Valle Grande, and the road had proved too rough. They were lying now wrapped around each other under the shelter of a tremulous aspen, in whose branches birds chippered to make the only sound in the world; as it turned out, she had taken the news of the accident very well.

Berrain, Morgenstern and Pederson left the hospital and walked across to the Lodge for lunch; three of the other doctors joined them. They sat inside, at a big round table in the big dining hall which, because the weather was so nice, was otherwise deserted. Two or three of them ordered cocktails. The talk was desultory. The Medical Society of the State of New York had just issued a statement forecasting wider medical uses of atomic-energy techniques; they talked about this briefly. One of the doctors had noticed that in his paper this item had been flanked by a story entitled "Milestone in Push-Button-War Tests," telling how a Navy V-2 rocket had climbed almost seventy-five miles in the air, and by another story reporting that the Committee on International Peace of the Society for the Psychological Study of Social Issues was worried by the mental state of the nation that atomic problems had induced. Some of them laughed and some shook their heads.

"Did you read about the Eastman Report?"

Stories about this had been on front pages all over the country only the day before; studies by the Eastman Kodak Company had disclosed that radioactive particles had, within a few days following the first atomic explosion at Alamogordo, covered an area equal in size to the subcontinent of Australia; film put into containers made from midwestern strawboard had been fogged by the radioactivity of the straw. They had all read about it; some of them shook their heads again.

"Some day—" one of them began, "some day they may actually get around to using this stuff for power and such. Better than bombs, but it's mean stuff—they'd better be careful—they'd better work everything out very carefully."

One of the doctors remembered, thinking of that first test explosion, how some people who hadn't been supposed to know about it, except a scientist friend of his had—well, that was all too complicated—anyway, some of them gathered very early that morning on Sawyer's Ridge, a ski slope back in the Jemez Mountains, to watch for what was going to happen nearly two hundred miles south in the desert proving-ground. They waited for an hour or more, he said, in the dark and cold, and some of them had just about given up expecting anything—or were thinking that something terrible might have happened—when, a few minutes after five, they saw the distant flash and then, a long time later, heard the long, slow rumble, quite faint really but almost more awesome than the flash, considering how far away the source was.

And then toward the end of the day, he said, the ones who had gone down with the bomb started showing up; they'd driven, some of them in jeeps all the way, and they were filthy, and completely bushed, most of them, except they were full of excitement too. But of course the wraps were still on; they didn't know whether anyone up here even knew about it—that is, people in general, guys like me, he said. They hadn't talked to anybody but themselves.

"Well, you know," he went on, and he gave a short, nervous laugh, because he had just discovered that his recital had fixed the table's attention, and he was not used to this. "I was in the cafeteria about six or so, I guess it was, and about two carloads of them came in, six or seven of them. They looked like tramps. Saxl was one of them, David Thiel was another. I remember they got just inside the door and stopped there and looked around. They were all standing together, these six or eight, but, you know, real close together, like half a dozen guys going into a tough bar. They didn't know how to act, not knowing who knew what, I guess. Anyway, after a couple of seconds there was a yell from someone in the middle of the room, and then some more, and all of a sudden the goddamnedest hullabaloo. You could hear dishes drop and people were running over. Saxl and Thiel were covered with people— and all these voices going at it—excitement and relief, and God knows what all pouring out."

He dropped his eyes to the table and started rearranging the silver in front of him. The doctors were halfway through

lunch before anyone mentioned the radiation cases; thereafter they talked of nothing else.

Pederson, sitting between Morgenstern and Berrain, did
not contribute much, and before the lunch was over he
excused himself; he wanted to get back to the hospital.
Berrain watched him leave, as he had watched him approach across the lawn several hours before.

As they were finishing their coffee and paying their
checks, Colonel Hough came into the room. He stopped
some feet away from the table, motioned to Morgenstern,
and waited impatiently, looking this way and that, as the
doctor got up and came over to where he stood. He began
to speak, in a low voice, as soon as Morgenstern reached
him.

He was having lunch on the terrace with a Congressman
who was passing through Los Alamos on a quick visit. The
Congressman had got it into his head that Louis Saxl was
a security risk—this was just what the Congressman had
said and the Colonel knew very well where he'd got the
notion, namely, from some of that prime fool Ulanov's
overheated guff—and now he was demanding that he be
allowed into the sickroom to ask Louis some questions.
The Congressman, Colonel Hough said, standing almost
on tiptoe to get closer to Morgenstern's ear, was getting
loud and people on the terrace were beginning to look at
them. He couldn't seem to get him off the subject or even
postpone it to a better time and place. What, in the name
of God, could Morgenstern do about this?

"Coming from a doctor—" Hough finished.

Morgenstern listened with his head cocked and his eyes
on a deer's head hanging over the dining hall's big fireplace.

"I should think—well, of course he can't see him. I
should think though—can't you just tell him so? Did you
tell him how sick Saxl is?"

"I told him," said Hough, "yes, I told him that." But a
doctor, he added, could tell him much better.

"Did he say why it is so urgent to see a man so sick?"

"Why don't you just see him?" Hough asked plaintively. "Why don't you just tell him it's medically impossible?"

"All right," said Morgenstern. "Where is he?"

The doctors had been talking about the possible influence of extensive chilling on body temperatures when Morgenstern left the table; he had been much interested in the subject; it had occurred to him that Louis's temperature, so anxiously and hopefully watched by Pederson and indeed by all of them, might have been held down by the ice packs. But when he got back from seeing Hough, they were discussing Haeber, who had been just behind Louis at the time of the accident; the barrier of Louis's body had certainly saved him; he had received, in fact, a very interesting dose—just enough to give him the typical symptoms of the acute radiation syndrome in quite a pure form, without burns, without too much risk of serious infection or serious aftermath.

"Although we'll have to keep tabs on him for a while," one of the doctors was saying. "I'd expect we might find something a little special in the blood picture three or four years from now."

Morgenstern said nothing of what Hough had told him. The doctors left the Lodge and walked back to the hospital; by the time they got there Morgenstern had succeeded in getting the discussion back on the subject of body chilling and body temperature.

From the terrace, Colonel Hough pointed out the doctors to the Congressman.

"He's a fine doctor and you'll find him a very reasonable man too," the Colonel said. "If it's possible at all, I'm sure he'll be glad to arrange it. You know how doctors are—like ship Captains, the whole law in their own bailiwicks. And of course it's a medical matter, entirely a medical matter."

"If I may say so, Colonel," the Congressman said, "it is also a matter of the national interest and security."

But he said this calmly enough, and Colonel Hough's embarrassment was no longer acute.

"Oh, I certainly agree with that," he said.

At two o'clock that afternoon, as scheduled, a drip injection of glucose was inserted into Louis's ankle. He continued to feel quite well, except that the pain in his left arm was incompletely controlled by the refrigeration. He was given morphine, and shortly afterward fell into a peaceful sleep, during which several photographs were taken and two Geiger readings were made. He slept through most of the afternoon and awoke feeling hungry; the pain in his left arm had ceased to bother him.

He was not disturbed either by the visit of the Congressman and Colonel Hough to the hospital about three o'clock. The Congressman and the Colonel met Dr Morgenstern, who was accompanied by Berrain and Wisla, in the conference room. They talked for a few minutes, after which the Congressman walked out swinging his shoulders, and speaking not to the doctors and the physicists but to Colonel Hough.

"Look here, Colonel, I'm a representative of the people of the United States of America, and I'm taking no runarounds from you. You knew that's what they'd say. But this isn't the end of it."

David Thiel spent half an hour or so during the early part of the afternoon in the cyclotron machine shop looking at the reading machine that was being made for Louis; half a dozen people had had a hand in it. It would be clamped to the end of Louis's bed; it had a long arm that would hold a book in front of his eyes, and a foot pedal operated by a motor that drove a linkage that would turn the book's pages one by one. Dombrowski himself, one of the best machinists around, had worked on it, and the machine was just about ready.

After this, David went down to the laboratory in the canyon. There were two soldiers at the door, both new since the accident. The soldier who drove David down stayed outside to talk with them; there was no one inside. The night after the accident David had reassembled the critical assembly that Louis had knocked apart. Since then

many people had been in the room, checking and cali-
brating the monitoring and counting devices that were part
of the room's equipment, measuring distances and sighting
angles from the assembly to the footprints that had been
chalked in immediately after the accident and from these
to all the scattering surfaces in the room. With such findings
David and Wisla and the others could proceed to the dosage estimates. Or to a fair approximation of the doses—
the radiations had been so intense and so complex in their
interactions that no one would ever know them precisely.

For a few minutes David sat on a stool just inside the
door. He could hear the drone of the soldiers' voices outside, but there wasn't a sound in the room itself; sunlight
sifted through the row of windows on one side of the room,
catching an edge of the table on which the critical assembly
stood.

The table was no more than a simple framework, un-
dressed and crude in appearance; its legs and bracings supported a metal top, and on this, in the center, a number
of grayish bricks of a smooth metallic material had been
arranged to make a cube-shaped pile. The pile presented
no face, no handle, no entrance; its sides, broken only by
lines demarcating the edges of the bricks, were smooth
and identical. Over the rest of the table top a variety of
objects were scattered; two large open notebooks, a tum-
bler full of black and red pencils, several ordinary tools—
pliers, screwdrivers, a small hammer. Half a dozen small
blocks of a brownish metallic material lay at one end, and
an empty soft-drink bottle stood near them. From the concrete wall just beyond, the patterned faces of several dials
and gauges looked out across all this; from the wall too, a
small superstructure extended, and hanging from it, reaching down almost to the center of the top of the neat, cube-
shaped pile, was a thin wire. It hung free, but it was motionless.

David got up from his stool after a while and walked
across to the table, moving carefully to avoid areas where

the residual radioactivity was still fairly strong, and then, for half an hour, he studied the notebooks. When he finished, he looked among the small brown blocks on the table, picked one up, and moved it around in his hand. It was about an inch and a half wide and about half an inch thick; but it was in reality two pieces, for part of it was a plug or core that fitted smoothly into the other part. David pushed the core in and out, ran his fingers over the block with the core in it and with it out, hefted it both ways, tossed it, held it and moved it with his eyes closed, and finally put it down.

Some time after he left the laboratory he stopped at Louis's room. Except for the dormitory maid, no one had been in the room for nearly three days. A spray of columbine, probably picked during the last weekend, drooped on Louis's desk just under the closed window; the air of the room was flat and dead. The water fins that Louis had bought for the Bikini trip were on the desk. David knew this room as well as any at Los Alamos, including his own. It was in one of the log buildings left over from the boys' school, and was therefore bigger and more comfortable than most, and for that reason many parties had been held in it. They'd had a party here—when?—only four nights before? David shook his head. He reached out to touch the columbine, dislodged a small spider that had spun a web from the flower to the desk, and watched as the spider scurried away. It seemed hardly possible that they had been having a party here so recently. Theresa had sung two songs; a sad refrain from one still ran in his head:

> *Down in the valley, valley so low,*
> *Hang your head over, hear the wind blow.*

And then Ulanov had run back to his house and got a banjo and they played a whole string of songs. Theresa sat on the desk most of the evening and Louis sat beside her and the party went on for hours; nothing much happened; so long ago.

One thing happened though, after they came to the end of their songs. Charley Pederson, who'd been rather quiet all evening, suddenly began talking about that Eastman report. He was upset over something Ulanov said to him that David hadn't heard.

"—yes, well, what's so great about that? Suppose they really do get to using this stuff for power and so forth, really use it—what about that Eastman report? What about building piles all over. If one bomb test can do all that, who's to say—?"

Half the men at the party were up at once to call out that Pederson was all mixed up. In the hubbub of clarification that followed David heard Theresa's voice.

"I read that Einstein says it's dangerous to do anything—maybe after what you've all done you should try not doing anything for a while."

David saw Louis look at Theresa quizzically and saw her look away. They've been having an argument, he thought. He smiled at both of them and then he urged Ulanov into telling a funny story, and so the party had ended.

PART 4

Thursday evening: there's a brightness in all the rooms

1

Toward the end of Thursday afternoon a dull military plane touched ground, rolled across the small Santa Fe airfield, swung back, and came to a stop near a waiting military car. Two officers, a Colonel and a Lieutenant, walked forward from the car. For a moment there was only the soft sound of the idling motors, then these were cut off, and a ground man moved up with a dismounting stair. A door opened and a soldier came out, followed at once by a civilian, a plain man in a rumpled brown suit, who carried a large brown bag in one hand. The soldier and the civilian stepped down the stair and the civilian walked to the car, the officers falling in with him. Beside the car they stopped briefly and there was some conversation, a few questions and answers. Then they all got in and the car headed straight down the field to a gate near the end.

The soldier had stopped to talk with the ground man; they both watched the car drive away.

"A chicken Colonel and a private car to meet him," said the ground man. "Who's he?"

"Well, I don't know, excepting he's a doctor," the soldier said. "Didn't say a word."

"Where from?"

"St. Louis."

"Didn't say a word in all that time?"

"No, he didn't say a word in all that time, like I just told you. He snored pretty good though."

"That's Colonel Hough from the Hill. He's not a bad guy. I met him once."

"What hill?"

"Where they made the bomb. Los Alamos. Everybody calls it the Hill."

"Well, he didn't say anything about it," the soldier said. "This isn't much of a field," he added.

"Planes like yours shouldn't ought to use this field. It wasn't meant for those kind of planes. You should've gone to Albuquerque."

"They said to come straight here."

At the entrance to the sprawling, pink-clay, fancy-simple hotel in the center of Santa Fe the car stopped and the civilian got out. A bellboy came for his bag, but the man shook his head. Colonel Hough spoke to him from the car, and he listened with his head half turned away, his eyes looking through the bright corridor that ran from the hotel's entrance back to the big lobby, on the far side of which, visible even from the street, was the hotel's barroom.

"Well, so we'll leave you here for the time being," Colonel Hough was saying. "I'm sorry about this arrangement, but you know—"

"Yes," said the man, "only keep me posted. And Dr Pederson, be sure he calls right away. I'll be here, in my room or the bar, one place or the other. Let me know."

He walked inside and gave his name to the clerk, a young
girl in a peasant blouse and a bright print skirt.

"Oh, yes, sir," she said, "your room is ready. Will you
be staying with us a while, Dr Beale?"

"Don't know. Do you have to know?"

"No, sir, not at all. They told us—"

"Well, you'd better ask them then."

"Any particular number you can be reached at? If you're
out?"

"I won't be out," he said. "I'll be in my room or the bar
there, one or the other."

The doctor went to his room and sat on the side of the
bed looking at nothing in particular for five minutes. Then
he took off his clothes and lay on the bed. After a while
he picked up the telephone book and turned its pages
slowly.

"St. Vincent's Hospital 210 E Palace Ave 3-3366," he
read aloud. He put the book down, pulled his legs up,
each in turn, and rubbed a finger between his toes.

> *"They get 'em when they're young*
> *and they get 'em when they're sick,*
> *Oh, the holy Roman Catholics,*
> *they never miss a trick,"*

he chanted. He lay on the bed a few minutes longer. Then
he got up and opened his bag. He did not take a shower
and he did not shave, but he managed to occupy half an
hour doing what would normally take him five minutes.
Afterward he put back on the rumpled suit he had taken
off, and stood in front of the room's window staring out
of it. The window looked across the inner roof that half
covered the hotel's central patio, but the body of the hotel
rose a story above this roof, and against the polished late-
afternoon sky all he could see were the flat tops of the
towers of St. Francis Cathedral a block away. He stood
there looking out, listening to the murmur of voices from
the patio below, until the phone rang.

"Pederson," he said as he went to the phone. "Yes?" he said into it in the same tone of voice.

"Yes," he said again after a moment, "it was all right if you don't mind sitting all day in a C-47 that should have been junked two years ago. It was all right."

"Sure, I know," he said after a moment.

"I see," he said finally. "Well, I'll meet you in the barroom. Make it when you can."

Beale left his room and went directly to the bar. It was nearly six but the room had not yet begun to fill. He sat down at a large table in one corner, a table big enough for eight, with upholstered wall-benches half enclosing it. A waitress came up to him; she had on a long black skirt with four bands of brilliant color around it; Beale stared at her skirt long enough to embarrass her, then looked up slowly and crudely, letting his eyes rest briefly on her breasts before he looked at her face.

"I'd like a bourbon and soda," he said.

"Will you be having dinner here?" the waitress asked him.

"I don't know. Probably."

"How many of you will there be?"

"One more."

"Oh, just two of you? I wonder if you'd mind taking a smaller table, sir? We'll need this table for a larger party."

"Let's say there'll be six of us, some of whom may not show up. Can I have that bourbon and soda, please?"

Beale had one drink, then another, and then a third. The room filled. The waitress came over twice to ask if he wouldn't move to a smaller table. With his third drink he ordered dinner. With his coffee he ordered another drink. It was nearly seven-thirty. He was drumming quietly on the table, holding his glass halfway to his lips, studying an ornate Mexican tin light fixture that hung above the big table, when Pederson appeared.

Pederson, obviously tired, obviously out of sorts, spoke with no fluency; he fumbled with his words and repeated himself. But he moved from approximately one point to approximately another, and from the fumbled words, Beale learned at last more than Pederson could bring himself to say.

"The serum phosphorus and the serum sodium don't jibe at all," Pederson said carefully near the end of his recital. "As I've said, I don't know what this means and I can't get anyone to tell me what it means, but it must mean something. His temperature hasn't showed any signs of going up. I told you that too. Well, the over-all picture isn't good, of course, not with that abdominal erythema, and the marrow, but— Well, I guess I've said all this."

Beale had met Pederson at the time of Nolan's death, but only for a moment, and he had, in any event, forgotten him. Swishing the liquor in his glass, listening to Pederson now, Beale wondered how old he was; not more than twenty-eight, maybe twenty-seven, not more than a couple of years removed from his internship. Theoretically, Beale thought, I am old enough to be his father; in the hot countries I could easily be his father; I don't look that much older, he thought, I simply do not look it, and I don't know how much older I feel. Louis Saxl would be thirty or thirty-one; in a very hot country I could even be his father.

"You're the pathologist," Pederson was saying. "Do you— you haven't been saying much—what conclusions are you getting to?"

From the vent of an air duct in the wall a little way from their table a deep, beating sound was coming in a rapid, monotonous rhythm. Beale had been listening to it off and on, with annoyance to begin with, then with interest as it seemed to combine in his ear with the voice sounds of the room, giving their randomness a bass beat that throbbed through the voices of the women and the voices of the men like the drum for a tribal dance. Dola-rum, dola-rum, dola-rum, Beale said to himself; dola-rum, dola-rum, dola-rum.

"I don't understand you," he said to Pederson, "you don't make sense to me."

"No? Where don't I make sense?"

"You talk like you wish he had a chance and so you've got yourself thinking he has a chance. But he hasn't got a chance. Wish it, we all wish it, but don't clutter up the picture."

Pederson looked down at the floor, then back at Beale. He started to raise his glass, then stopped. He relaxed the pressure of his fingers on the glass, slowly, and it slipped down, and fell to the floor. Beale sat straight up in his chair, heads turned, the waitress started over toward them. Pederson, his arm still half raised, spoke to Beale.

"All right. That's the opinion of the visiting pathologist. Don't you clutter up the picture with what you came out here to do. Louis hasn't written himself off. Maybe you should talk to him—" Pederson stopped, stood up, stared down at the puddle of glass and liquor on the floor, and then went on, quietly.

"No, you can't do that. Of course, you mustn't do that. No, you stay right here. Most of them feel like you do. I don't."

Beale had slumped back on the cushioned bench again, had turned his head to watch the waitress cleaning up the mess right beside them. He said nothing for a moment after Pederson stopped talking.

"Sit down, you damned fool," he said then. "This isn't your first case. No, I'm sorry, I'm sorry, sit down. I know how you feel. I've known Louis Saxl for fourteen years. I—sit down."

Beale ran his hand over his face and squeezed his eyes with his fingers. He stared at Pederson, sitting in self-conscious quiet, and squeezed his eyes again. The succession of drinks was beginning to affect him. And about time, he thought.

"No, really," he said, "let's get off this. I'm sorry. Opinions are possible, of course. Say, tell me, how well do you know Louis?"

"The trouble is," Colonel Hough had said in the car, "if he knows we've brought you out here he'll know we've given up hope. And yet the doctors tell me they want you here—they seem quite in the dark as to when it might happen. I understand that even a thirty-minute delay cuts down what you learn from the tissues after death. Just what happens to cause that, doctor?"

"Fourteen years," Beale was saying to Pederson. "I had him in a class I was teaching in Chicago first year he came there. I was all over the place then. *Quelle confusion*! I instructed physicists in biology, so naturally I'm a pathologist and wish I were a physicist. What more natural? Half the physicists I know are going into biology now. We'll all be one in the end, I suppose. I haven't had anything to do with your project out here, but I was in at the beginning of it. 1932 to 1934. That's when we got down to cases. Lot of dumb bastards in the science business before that."

"It couldn't have been as pat as all that," Pederson said glumly.

"Of course not. Who says it was. I'm being impressionistic. More or less, roughly speaking, by and large, so forth and so forth. Anyway, it happened."

"The difference between the twenties and the thirties must have had a good deal to do with it," Pederson said. "You got a more serious—"

"By the time the bright ones came along, there I was, teaching them," Beale went on. "A joke on them. Oh, yes, the twenties and the thirties. But that's not what accounts for it. You had revolutions in the early thirties, when I'm talking about. Colossal discoveries. Like when they came on X rays and radioactivity in the 1890s, and then the electron, and radium, all in three or four years. That leak of energy from the middle of nowhere. Hah! There's a friend of mine writes doggerel, wrote the history of science in a hundred and thirty-two stanzas. There's a stanza in it:

> *"Oh, off with the shiny, anointed coat*
> *of the Nineteenth Century atom.*
> *It leaks! It seeps! It's a thing of*
> *parts—a very significant datum.*
> *The king is dead! Long live the king!*
> *Hail the radiant subatom."*

Beale delivered these lines in a sing-song voice, rocking his glass to mark the beats, matching the beats to the dola-rum, dola-rum coming from the air vent. He had slumped even farther back against the cushions. Pederson watched him uncertainly. And a little girl had stopped to watch him too. She was at the tag end of a procession of half a dozen people being led past Pederson and Beale from a table in the barroom to a table in the dining room beyond. At the head of this procession was an elegant lady who was lame; she supported herself on the arm of a younger woman and in one hand she held high a glass; her features were small and birdlike, and she moved in shuffling steps that set the pace for all her family. The family resemblance ran like a banner from rank to rank in the procession, to a son behind her, a daughter behind him, two adolescent boys, and a little girl. The little girl had detached herself and was staring gravely at Beale, who was staring back, still rocking his glass. He leaned out over the table toward her.

"It leaks! It seeps! It's a thing of parts!" he intoned.

Contempt came into her expression. With dignity, she turned and walked on.

"Well, anyway," Beale said, slumping back again, "it was the same in the early thirties. They'd probed around in the bowels of the atom for forty years and they were getting a little uneasy—didn't really know where or how to go next. Come 1932, things were at a pause. Then came the neutron—positron—heavy hydrogen—all in a year. More besides. Then artificial radioactivity. All this made for excitement—that's what brought the bright ones in. Whether they knew it or not—that's the way it works."

Pederson was looking gloomily into his glass, glancing at Beale from time to time. Pederson was feeling sorry for himself. He wanted to be at the hospital, where there was nothing for him to do except to represent the cause of hope. He most especially did not want to be sitting here in the bar listening to Beale telling him more than he wanted to know about things that he did not know but considered to be probably elementary and hence uninteresting. Moreover, he was shocked at what he considered Beale's gross insensitiveness to the assignment that had brought him here from St. Louis. Pederson did not like the very sight of Beale, sitting slouched against the cushions, drinking, drinking, running on.

They had explained the arrangement to him; he had agreed to come into the hotel, to keep Beale informed, to talk.

"Now you take Louis," Beale was saying.

Please, oh, please, Pederson said to himself.

"Wasn't this excitement that brought him up to Chicago," Beale went on, "don't know what it was, maybe he had a good teacher somewhere along the line—unlikely though, high schools being what they are—maybe his parents, anyway he didn't know anything. The things he didn't know! But he had this curiosity, he had that. Maybe Jews have more of it, that's what they tell me, only I never saw it. I've known some awful dull Jews. Dull or bright, they always seemed to me ninety-seven per cent like everybody else. What people make out of the other three per cent! Goddammit, everybody's ninety-seven per cent like everybody else. Don't look so glum, cousin. Call the cousin *señorita* and we'll have us a drink. Drink, drink, doctor wants a drink."

But nobody said I had to wetnurse this character, Pederson thought; I don't know why I just sit here. Why doesn't he get sleepy, after all day on that plane? I'll stick through one more. I'm not going to put him to bed, he can take care of himself if he passes out.

"Although the Jews do have a curious kind of religion," Beale was saying, "It's as full of nonsense as any, still it does seem to come a little closer to real life now and then. That set of rules for how to behave in the sickroom, right out of the Talmud, very intelligent rules too—you take that one, be careful to sit so your eyes aren't too far above the sick person's eye level. Good sense. Well, Louis had this curiosity, *sine qua non*. Maybe you aren't interested in things like this. The high schools pour out a lot of these boys that don't know anything, just enough to know they'd like to know something. I'm not counting the home-work-shop boys either—they've got some curiosity, but they satisfy it awful easy. Well, in 1932 the kids that really had it, they ran into this excitement, like Louis did. Of course, some of them never got beyond the excitement. It was all big doings, new frontiers, ain't it great to be alive with all this going on—they just made pap out of something real. The excitement was the sugar, but the pill was plain hard work, just like always. Only there was more to work on. Just the neutron, all by itself— Your project started there, and Louis—"

The waitress had brought new drinks and Beale was well into his. But he was sitting up straighter and some of the cynicism had gone out of his voice. Pederson contemplated his glass more steadily than ever. He was sober and Beale was not. He was young and Beale was not. He was—diffident?—and Beale was not. He was unknown and Beale was not. He was trying to save Louis Saxl and Beale was— He could not look at Beale.

The change in Beale's voice came to him like a change in temperature, invisibly affecting the climate in which they sat. And it seemed to move the center of the table from Beale's side a little toward himself. He found himself wondering, for the first time since he had asked Beale his medical opinion, what Beale would say next.

"Well, so," Beale said at last, "it's been a long day. When did it happen? Tuesday, this is Thursday. So."

Pederson waited.

"It's the counter attractions that usually get them. Marrying, begetting, settling down. If it doesn't drain off their curiosity, it surer than hell drains off their capacity for work. Even so, some live through it. Then a company comes along with a cushy offer. That does it for so-and-so and so-and-so. Does it give you pause that virtually all the science that went into this project came out of Europe? Not just most of it—vir-tu-al-ly all of it? I pause. I yield to no man in my admiration for the tool-users, but all hands and no head makes somebody a dull boy. Poor Louis. He was a little island of something we need more of. Oh, well, who said we had to talk this way?"

Poor Louis, he was— Pederson noticed it. The words washed out the promise he had sensed in Beale's voice a few minutes before; and his earlier anger, which had run shallow under the stirring of his interest, flooded back into him.

"How well do you really know Louis?" he asked Beale, sitting up and leaning across the table for almost the first time. "You make him out a precious kind of person that doesn't mean anything to me and I doubt would to him. We need more of him, all right, but not because he's the superior double-dome you make him out. What's wrong with tools? Louis's a first-rate tool-user, and that's one reason everyone respects him. They do *not* respect him because he sits all day mooning over his lost opportunities in science spelled with a capital S. I daresay you know a great deal about these things. I don't pretend to. Maybe you've forgotten science is meant to serve people and not the other way round."

"God bless us!" said Beale, staring at his revitalized companion. "And so you've been serving people out here with your bombs? Well, to be sure, so you have—relax. You've been serving some people at the expense of others. God *bless* us! Don't turn me in yet. I'm right up among those who can justify this on grounds of necessity—my

friend Robert Hutchins spoke of it at the beginning. We
will achieve no victory, he said, but we can stave off defeat
from one spectacular direction. Well, we done it—spec-
tacularly. God bless us all—all on our side. But forgive
me if I vomit at the mention of science serving *people*. You
haven't been practicing science out here anyway. Been in
the manufacturing business, turning out a new product."

"You're a cold fish," Pederson said, "You're about the
coldest fish I ever saw. You talk about your friend Louis,
and you sit here and talk, talk, talk about him as if he were
a specimen. Is that all a friend means to you? Do you have
feelings when you think of him lying thirty miles from
here in the shape he's in?"

Beale passed his hand over his face, one side and then
the other, and squeezed his eyes as he had done earlier.
He looked at Pederson, and smiled; and let his gaze travel
around the room as the smile retreated before a frowning,
puzzled expression.

"A terrible thing not to feel," he said, still looking around.
"Curse of modern man, ain't it? But is it because he can't
feel or, confronted by problems beyond him, doesn't know
what to feel? If he can't any longer feel, he's doomed to
the jungle, where this isn't required so much. But if he
can't keep his problems in range of his feelings, he's doomed
too, to jungles of decisions that don't decide anything,
while his doom is decided for him. And then still a third
doom occurs to me, you know, because just in a project
like this one out here, there come times when feelings
have to be put aside, they'd make a hand tremble—divert
the mind. Maybe it's best not to be able to feel at such
times, but then what of all the other times? Or say you
know how to feel and what to feel, why, then, what a
terrible discipline is required at those particular times.
Feelings—bad things in a physicist, most particularly a
physicist making bombs. But then you take a physicist who
doesn't know how to feel and he's making bombs—well,
I don't know, would the other be as bad as this? An im-

passe! You pose a big question when you get on feelings, my friend. How did Louis come to die? I beg your pardon, how did he come to make this slip that exposed him to so much radiation? I doubt very much he knows for sure himself. Still, you've got to know before you know, I mean, before you know how you feel about it, you really do."

"You've certainly answered my question," Pederson said. "You've answered it, all right."

"Still I have feelings."

"Hurrah," said Pederson.

"Yes," Beale said. "Yes, in answer to your other question, did you know I'm old enough to be Louis's father? And yet I cannot honestly, not really honestly, say I feel worse about him than I did about all those people killed by the bombs he helped build. Which would you rather avoid seeing: a man killed by a truck or a parade of people marching? What a terrible thing a parade is! It makes you think of all people everywhere, all at once, and whether this fills you with compassion or loathing, it's too much— too much for either feeling to be endured. How lonely, yes, let me tell you, how lonely and even a sad, ridiculous thing a person is, one person in this parade, any marching parade. Not so the man killed by the truck, lying there— or the young man lying thirty miles out from here, Louis. It is sad, oh Jesus it's sad, but it's endurable. When it can't be endured, don't you understand, is when you think of him as one among others, so many tens of thousands at Hiroshima, so many tens of thousands at Nagasaki, what-ever, and worse, much worse, among the millions who never found what they were looking for, who got just to the point and then—something happened. Perhaps an ac-cident or a fear maybe, maybe some kind of refusal, or— Do you know? Do you know what makes a trained hand slip, what makes the mind fail to guide the hand for a moment, what acts on the mind?"

"Dr Beale, I can't listen to any more of this, I really can't. You said back there I didn't make sense to you, but

you've talked a great deal more than I have—you've really
talked a great deal. But the parades and all that. I can't
take any more."

Beale suddenly stood up.

"Gotta take a leak," he said. "Sit tight, don't move." He
pushed against the table to get past it, fell back onto the
cushions, got up again, carefully moved out past the table,
and started walking slowly, carefully, away. After two or
three steps he stopped and turned back. "Just felt a leak
coming on," he explained, looking at Pederson with an
intent expression. He walked on two more steps and turned
again. "Order me a drink," he said. Walking very carefuly,
he moved on out of the room.

After ten minutes Pederson went to look for him. Beale
was not in the men's room; a phone call to his room got
no answer. There was no sign of him. Pederson was angry,
annoyed, but relieved too. He went back to the barroom,
paid for his three drinks, and signed Beale's name to the
check for his drinks and dinner. He left the hotel and,
walking faster with every step, went to the parking lot
around the corner. He drove his car through the center
of town as fast as he could, pushed his speed up as he
neared the edge, and by the time he was a hundred yards
up the long hill with which the road to Los Alamos began,
his speedometer passed seventy.

From a bench in the plaza Beale saw Pederson leave the
hotel and round the corner to the parking lot. He looked
at him without interest. He sat alone on the bench, but
on other benches were other people, old men, some old
women, young men and women together, groups of boys
and girls talking in quiet voices that rose to high pitches,
broke in loud laughs, and fell to quiet again. There was a
small movement of people across the plaza in all directions
when Beale came out, but this movement fell off as he sat
there, and the autombile traffic on the four streets that
bounded the plaza quieted to an infrequent car. The leaves
of the trees rustled. Beale sat and let his eyes follow the

occasional woman who went past. Some stopped and talked
to one person or another. None spoke to Beale, whose
eyes followed each.

After an hour or so the woman from the telegraph
office came into the plaza with a slow, sauntering walk. She
stopped and looked down at Beale—everyone else had
gone—and said something to him. He made no response. Again she spoke, moving closer and leaning down
over him. As she did, his head rolled to one side; he had
fallen asleep, and he began to snore. She looked at him a
moment longer, then turned and continued her walk. Her
heels clicking on the walk made the loudest sound to be
heard in the night. The sound faded off down one street
or another, leaving the park silent, and empty save for
Beale.

2

At the guard house Charley Pederson slowed his car, held
up his pass for the soldier to see, and started on through
without stopping. But the soldier called him and came
running to the car.

"You going to the hospital, Dr Pederson?"

"Yes."

"There's a letter here, for Louis Saxl. A special. It'll
be going up in twenty minutes or so, but I thought
maybe—"

"Sure. Where is it?"

The soldier ran back into the guard house. The motor
of Pederson's car idled softly. He sat motionless, his eyes
on the small glow in the sky that came from the lights in
the Technical Area. The soldier came running back, and
Pederson took the letter, heavy with stamps. The envelope
bore the insignia of the Santa Fe Railroad and the postmark
had been put on at Chicago.

"Are things going all right, doctor?"

He turned it over. On the back flap was scribbled "Theresa Savidge," no address.

"Doctor?"

Pederson turned to the soldier and nodded absently. Then he smiled. "I'll take care of it."

Perhaps Dave Thiel could tell him what to do about this, he thought. He shifted into gear and the car pulled forward. But why shouldn't Louis get his mail?

"So I'll talk to Dave," he said aloud, doggedly.

David was not at the hospital, however. Pederson called his room but got no answer. He put the letter in his pocket then and went along the corridor of the hospital to the end farthest from the conference room, turned and went down a side corridor to the end of that. Down here, in a hospital room that had been converted the day before into a laboratory, Dr Novali had his headquarters. He stood among his microscopes, his slides, and his counters, backed by trays of needles and flanked by jars of dyes. Two autoclaves were by the window; steam connections had been made to them only that afternoon. A flame photometer stood on a wobbly table. The hospital's laboratory work was customarily handled at a very large and well-equipped laboratory just outside the Technical Area across the street, two blocks down. That arrangement had collapsed Tuesday evening.

Novali was studying the connections on the autoclaves. He looked up as Pederson came in. There were wooden boards on another table, with charts and notes attached to them. There were more charts on two walls. Pederson looked at the one closest to him. It was marked for Saxl and it contained seven short columns of figures under the heading "Urine Chemistry."

"How are things, Lou?" Pederson asked, still looking at the chart.

Novali shrugged his shoulders.

"Most interesting thing, aside from what you know, is

still this white-cell count. It's over twenty-three thousand now, and that's real high. How long can it stay up there?"

"How far will it fall when it falls is the question," Pederson said.

"It's not so rare, but it's not common either," said Novali, in a rather pettish voice. "Emotional factors, apprehension and so forth could have something to do with it, Charley. It's never true with dogs. Rabbits, but not dogs."

Pederson nodded his head. He reached out and fingered the photometer.

"Anything else?"

"What do you want, Charley? You want to go over things in general? Nothing's worse, if that's what. He looks good, considering, a lot better than even this noon. Feels pretty good."

"Who's up there?"

"Betsy was half an hour ago. Some of them went over to the Lodge to eat."

Pederson glanced along the rows of charts.

"What's with the phosphorus? I don't see anything."

"We're not keeping that any more, Charley."

Pederson studied a chart entitled "Platelets (Hundred Thousands)—Rectics (%)." He stared at it for nearly a minute while Lou Novali stared at him.

"Who dropped the phosphorus?" Pederson asked then, reaching out to finger the photometer again.

"Berrain said to, I think. Morgenstern told me, but Berrain told him, I think." After a moment, as Pederson said nothing, Novali said again: "It was Berrain. Unreliable, he says. They're using just the serum sodium for neutron measurements."

Pederson put one hand to his face and squeezed his eyes. The gesture brought to mind Beale, who had done this so many times during the evening; he started to take his hand away, and then, sighing, brought it back.

"Well, I'll see you later, Lou. I'm going upstairs. Has Louis been asking any hard questions?"

"He was pushing me some about that sternal puncture."

"What about what we told him earlier? Doesn't he believe it any more?"

"Well, what'd we tell him, Charley? A dilute version of
what we found, more or less. Sure he believes it, I guess,
including the dilution."

"So has anyone told him anything different? What's the
pitch?"

"No, no, same things, same exactly. They only get harder
to tell."

Pederson nodded. Like his slides, Novali was full of
information and noncommittal. And yet Novali didn't seem
to be withholding himself, indeed he seemed ready to
answer almost anything he might be asked, seemed even
to be waiting. Why then don't I ask him? Pederson thought,
and words did come to his mind. Then, like a schoolboy
on the verge of asking a girl for a kiss, unsure of the answer,
embarrassed in advance of his own formulation, he drew
back. And although his expression had not changed, he
blushed.

"Charley, you ought to get a few hours in the sack.
You're tired as hell."

Pederson left Novali in the cluttered room and went on
back along the corridors to the stairway, and up the stairs
to the second floor. On the way it struck him that Novali,
who knew very well where he had been for the past few
hours, had said nothing about it. He had every reason to
feel grateful for this, but instead he felt annoyed. I am
being excommunicated, he thought, with a flare of self-
dramatization.

He approached the door to Louis's room, but he stopped
short of it; it was nearly closed but not quite, and he could
hear Betsy's voice inside. He stood there listening to her—
he could not catch the sense of what she was reading—
and suddenly he remembered her standing in the conference room, saying: "I'll be glad when we get past Tuesday
the twenty-first." Well, we didn't do it, did we? he said to

himself. But the sound of her voice from the room now, reading quietly, was a nice and reassuring thing, although, as he opened the door and stepped inside, he glanced at her as indifferently as always. She stopped reading and Louis, turning his head on his pillow, spoke with a kind of self-conscious excitement.

"Who can this be, Betsy? Chance, free will, or necessity? Charley, listen—keep your needles in your pocket—sit down—you've got all my blood anyway—listen. This is fine stuff. Read that again about the loom, Betsy. 'It was a sultry afternoon—' "

Pederson could not see what the book was; Betsy had it flat on her lap, bending forward over it, leaning a little to one side so that the light from the small lamp on the table by her chair would reach the pages. She read slowly, deliberately, and her voice seemed deeper and surer than it did when she was talking.

" 'It was a cloudy, sultry afternoon,' " she read. " 'The seamen were lazily lounging about the decks, or vacantly gazing into the lead-colored waters. Queequeg and I were mildly employed weaving what is called a sword-mat, for an additional lashing to our boat. So still and subdued and yet somehow preluding was all the scene, and such an incantation of revelry lurked in the air, that each silent sailor seemed resolved into his own invisible self.

" 'I was the attendant or page of Queequeg, while busy at the mat. As I kept passing and repassing the filling or woof or marline between the long yarns of the warp, using my own hand for the shuttle, and as Queequeg, standing sideways, ever and anon slid his heavy oaken sword between the threads, and idly looking off upon the water, carelessly and unthinkingly drove home every yarn: I say so strange a dreaminess did there then reign all over the ship and all over the sea, only broken by the intermitting dull sound of the sword, that it seemed as if this were the Loom of Time, and I myself were a shuttle mechanically weaving and weaving away at the Fates. There lay the fixed

threads of the warp subject to but one single, ever returning, unchanging vibration, and that vibration merely
enough to admit of the crosswise interblending of other
threads with its own. This warp seemed necessity; and here,
thought I, with my own hand I ply my shuttle and weave
my own destiny into these unalterable threads. Meantime,
Queequeg's impulsive, indifferent sword, sometimes hitting the woof slantingly, or crookedly, or strongly, or weakly,
as the case might be; and by this difference in the con-
cluding blow producing a contrast in the final aspect of the
completed fabric; this savage's sword, thought I, which thus
finally shapes and fashions both warp and woof; this easy,
indifferent sword must be chance—aye, chance, free will,
and necessity—no wise incompatible—' "

Betsy stopped and looked up, and Louis shook his head
appreciatively.

"Isn't that wonderful?" he said, and the undercurrent of
self-conscious excitement was still in his voice. "If you'd
only leave me alone with Betsy and *Moby Dick,* I'd be all
right. Blood, always blood. Just leave me enough to listen
with. Blood and ice. We've got four hundred pages to go."

"I'm surprised you find it so wonderful," said Pederson,
who wanted to keep the mood alive and who really was
surprised as well. "I should think a physicist would think
something like that was—I don't know—kid stuff—well,
no, but romantic or mystical."

"What physicist?" Louis exclaimed. "Physicists believe
a hundred things. The most beautiful emotion we can experience is the mystical. That's what Einstein believes, or
at any rate what he said once. Well, of course Mr Melville's
Loom is mystical, but it's a creation of free imagination, as
natural laws must be. 'This indifferent sword must be
chance—' What's the dose, Charley?"

Pederson had moved to the end of the bed and was
looking at the chart there, just under the watch that Betsy
had hung. Still resolved a little by Melville into his own
invisible self, he did not at once comprehend Louis's question.

"Dose?" he asked, his eyes on the temperature reading of an hour or so before, which showed a rise of three tenths of a degree.

"The dosage of ionizing total-body radiation, with particular reference to the neutrons," said Louis.

Pederson looked up sharply. Louis's face was mocking, almost merry.

"I don't think anyone knows, least of all me," Pederson said. He looked down at the chart again. There was an instruction; two bullae, or large blisters, on the thumb and palm of the left hand had ruptured at about six o'clock; Pederson was to check them for signs of infection and have the nurse clean the area. He looked up at Louis again.

"Wisla and Dave Thiel are the authorities on that. What do they say?" He signaled to Betsy, who got up from her chair.

"They lie, naturally. That is, they say nothing, which is a lie. Nobody ever tells a patient anything. You know that, Charley."

Pederson slowly removed one of the towels from the trough that held Louis's left hand and arm.

"Well, they're lying to me then too," he said, not looking up. "How's the pain in there, Louis? Still quiet?"

"All quiet."

Betsy switched on a light, a standing photographer's light that had been brought in earlier and placed in the corner near Louis's bed; she adjusted it to keep the glare from Louis's eyes, and the edge of the yellow circle of its glow cut across the middle of the bed. Then she and Pederson, standing on opposite sides of the trough, reached out across it, moving their arms back and forth in alternation, lifting off the towels that lay crisscrossed in a dozen layers. The ice in the melted ice water below made small and regular sounds as the trough vibrated slightly; the room was otherwise silent, although through the door, from the corridors, or from other rooms, came an occasional seepage of muted talk.

The hand was tightly swollen and intensely cyanotic; the

swelling extended up along the arm and had a waxy appearance; the edges of the ruptured blisters hung loose,
and a yellow fluid had congealed around them.

Louis glanced down at the trough, and then rolled his
head away toward the window at the right side of the bed.

"You know what you are, Dr C. Pederson?" he said,
and although there was very little expression of any kind
on his face, his voice still mocked. "You are what us natural
philosophers call the single-minded layman—determined,
that is, that there's a mold from which physicists are poured,
all from the same mold, to serve some inscrutable function,
not to be confused with people. If I quote Schrödinger or
de Broglie, particularly with equations, the single-minded
layman is impressed and content that I am content. But if
I quote Melville he gets worried. Are you all right? he
says. Maybe you need a little vacation? he says. Or else he
goes off thinking I've been duping him and never should
have been a physicist to begin with."

Pederson and Betsy, intent on the blistered hand, were
nonetheless laughing.

"And yet hath not a physicist senses and passions? Fed
the same, hurt the same, healed by the same means as a
person is? If you poison us, do we not die?

"Well, not to put too fine a point on it," he went on,
turning his head back toward them and arching his neck,
then looking down the length of his body under the sheets.
"Of course, one shouldn't have his eye on Queequeg, looking out over the waters so indifferently, when one is doing
certain things. The sword, yes, but Queequeg's too distracting. He won't go away though. You rule him out and
he edges in again, careless as ever.

"What nonsense you make me talk. Betsy, throw this
boor out. He's not doing anything anyway."

Louis could feel nothing in his left hand; nor had he
looked at it since that first glance. The towels went back
on again and all was as before. One of the night nurses
came in; she whispered to Dr Pederson that some of the

doctors were waiting for him in the conference room and thought Mr Saxl should get his rest as soon as possible. Louis, overhearing, said he was tired of resting. Betsy looked at him covertly, for it was beginning to seem to her that his voice had taken on a degree of petulance like a small boy's, which would mean that he was more tired than he knew. And Louis, petulant at the prospect of no more reading, pondered whether he should press invalid's privileges in the face of the evident fact that Betsy was exhausted. He gazed at the night nurse, who spoke in a high and squeaky way. Pederson stepped outside the door and motioned Betsy to follow him; they disappeared from sight, and Louis watched gloomily as the night nurse, saying things to which he did not listen, made small changes here and there, straightened the table by which Betsy had been sitting, and closed *Moby Dick*.

Good-night, Queequeg, said Louis to himself.

In the corridor Pederson took the letter from his pocket and handed it to Betsy.

"I think it's from the girl who was visiting him here last week," he said.

Betsy turned the letter over in her hand.

"Theresa Savidge," she read. "I don't know her name. I saw them on the terrace one day. Is she—?"

"Don't ask me what the situation is. I don't know anything about his private life. I don't know what to do about the letter either. It might upset him."

Betsy looked from the letter to Pederson and back again. And Pederson stood indecisively, thinking how late it was, but thinking also how cozy the scene in Louis's room had been when he had walked in a few minutes before, and how pleasant the sound of Betsy's voice.

"You'd have to read it to him," he said finally. "I don't know. Use your own judgment, use your woman's intuition."

3

A few minutes after this the night nurse came out, with the patient's chart in her hand. Inside the room, seated again in the chair in the corner by the table, her head inclined slightly so that the light from the little lamp would catch the writing, Betsy began to read.

"It says 'Monday night' at the top."

" 'Dearest Darling—' " she looked up at Louis and smiled at him—" 'Dearest darling—it is nearly thirty minutes since the train left Lamy and you standing there in the night beginning. A man with pointed ears and a very large cigar— he does not go together—has finished his letter and yielded me his place, and I think I shall stay here across a third of the continent, thinking of us and writing to you. Writing to thee. Do you remember the man in *Pity the Tyrant*— the book by which we met (and do you remember that?)— who wondered how he could make love any more without saying thou after his year among the gentle Spanish speak- ers—thou, thou, thou, thou, a full thousand thous and love and love again. (*Lamy? why Lamy? she asked why don't the Santa Fe trains actually reach to Santa Fe and not just this brick waiting room twenty miles out and its long, long platform empty, waiting? there's the horn she said that far-off bellow of the Chicago train, my train she said.*)

" 'That man leaned over to tell me he's from Winnetka. I pretended he was you and thanked him for our wondrous three days together and he just ran away—now he's gone I'll add for you yourself that we've got some years to make up, you and me. No more little visits. We've had these three days and some other times over these past years, but how many years have there been?—I've counted them, seven—and how many times?—not a lot more than that, maybe nine times, and that's not enough, that's not nearly enough.

" 'But enough. There are so many things to be done. For instance, where will we have dinner the first night? We must make plans. (*It was not nine but ten but not nearly enough. I know. I'm sorry, I am sorrier than you can know, Theresa.*) We can go to your house in Georgetown for some of your mother's braised lamb with lentils (*and some of her cottage pudding too*) or we can go to Mr Biscanti's house to eat *zabagliones* and write poems. So many things for us to do! (*Come walk with me into the night and I must follow, this—oh, no; oh, no, Theresa!*) Once we get away from those gates and guards and those tight and ugly secret buildings we'll do things, both of us together, and there'll be an end to remorse and guilt and worry and all those things you and David and Ulanov have been half talking about along with the water shortage and the laundry problems. (*But I will this day think not of the future beyond two days from now and I will think no more of the past beyond two days ago, do I dare to eat a peach, do I dare to think—?*)

" 'I suppose there were fulfillments during the war years, even exaltations—I suppose—at least I can see the point of pride in doing something well first against the threat of others doing it with a war on. Your letters from Los Alamos then never said a word of what you were doing but still they spoke with a feeling of dedication, the way you and David and Ulanov and some of the others spoke the other night, always looking backwards. But there wasn't any looking forward except about getting away to work of your own—away from the war and away from that armored place for war—so we'll get you away.

(*Let's go to Mr Biscanti's first for dinner, then after that we can go to my mother's.*)

" 'David told me about that unpleasant letter from your university friend—no job there—a contemptible thing. You're not a self-pitier, you won't let the wound lie open. What worries me is that you just might decide to stay where you are, to expose yourself to no more hurts. You just might get yourself more involved on this Bikini trip—

damn Bikini! To hell with stupid bomb shows—I told you
about that piece in the *Times* saying this Bikini is more of
a show-off than a show—and stupid universities and stupid
prejudices. We'll do without them, and we'll do damn well
too. Just you wait and see. (*I want to tell everyone about that
letter except that even more I want to tell everyone to forget it.
There's no point discussing such things with a Jew is there,
like that man at Mr Biscanti's said that evening. People hardly
ever like dedicated men I think I heard him say. GET OUT!
Mr Biscanti told him and we all heard that.*)

  " 'In bed one night—' " Betsy stopped reading; she noticed a smile on Louis's face. She had decided several lines
back that her intuition had played her false but the smile
confused her. This was not a letter to be reading to a very
sick man who was facing the night not willing yet to sleep.
She could simply be firm and leave him with the lights out,
couldn't she? No, she told herself. Should she give him
more sedatives? Dr Berrain had told her she could. Would
he take them? His eyes had shone like a boy's when she
told him she had the letter and they still shone; he said
nothing, and so she went on reading.

  "—'one night at Mr Biscanti's house of beloved memories—that very night before the war began, the lovely
night before that awful wait at the station—that time I
asked you to tell me straight what your science meant to
you, and after a while you began to talk about challenges
and puzzles—(*The fun was what I meant. What was I working on then? Soft betas? Absorption effects? Patterns—the
isomers—whatever.*)—and the way you talked it sounded
like some kind of hideaway—maybe from things like that
university letter. (*Not hiding—the plain damn fun of it!*)
But then you said something different that I still remember—(*Yes, I told you to think of life as the whole countryside
and if you ask science to tell you about it science answers by
giving you a few roads through. The roads don't go through
all the countryside at all—Grandfather Saxl used to talk that
way—but they do take you to heights not otherwise to be reached
and—*)

" '—and it is along those roads that the minds of people everywhere can move and touch.

" 'Of course, you were twenty-four then and pale and wan from a night's love—maybe you don't believe things like that any more. Maybe Los Alamos has knocked out such thoughts—sometimes you've talked as though Los Alamos is a kind of monastery, but your armored place is no monastery. Monks really live for the object of their denial. There's no denial at Los Alamos, not a truly felt one, there's an obsession—not an excitement any more, whatever there was once, but a nervousness—not anything moving people's minds but something, maybe in themselves, moving against them.' "

Betsy stopped reading and there was silence in the room except for the faint sounds from the drip injection stand beside the bed. She assessed Louis critically and decided it was just possible that he might be asleep; the smile was gone. But he moved then, very slightly but enough to tell her he was at least half awake. She watched a moment longer, trying to assess his state of mind and feeling worries about her own. She opened her mouth to speak to him; this letter would really have to be put aside. Later on— the next day—when he was rested—she didn't know what to say—

(*The day we walked out to the edge of the mesa before that party and I started to tell her some of the problems and why it's a hard place to get away from. There's a terrible lot to be done here, I said, but she turned away abruptly and said, "We're all of us very busy," half under her breath and her bitterness surprised me. But I am busy, I told her, I'm not making it up. "So what are you busy about? Tell me that. What are you doing here? And I don't mean this or that project—not your housekeeping—I'm talking about meanings of things—" Just tell me what you want Theresa I said and I touched her hair, just tell me straight out and I'll do it if I can. "Tell you want I want! What I want has hardly anything to do with the matter. You tell me what you want! That's the question. You've driven me half crazy trying to figure out what you want*

*to do, and you know perfectly well what I want to do. I want
you in my bed at night and across the table from me in the
mornings—nights and mornings, let's start with them! The
war's over. What are you here for? Tell me that." It cannot be
answered so simply I started to say. "And so you want me to
answer for you. I'm to tell you what I want you to do—as
though you haven't known—and so carry your guilt around
on my back. You want to avoid responsibility but you can't
avoid responsibility like that. Nobody's attacking you here—
except me—and I want to know what your science has come to
mean to you here in this fenced place. What's become of those
roads through the countryside?" You're making it hard Theresa, I said. "But you're not a little boy now, you know. You
decide." This is a part of the countryside the roads don't go
through I started to say but I have hopes they pick up on the
other side of here and the answer calls for— "Much thought,"
she interrupted, "and more feeling." We were both upset when
we got to the party, but afterwards, at St. Peter's—)*

"Louis," Betsy said, standing up, "I'll read you the rest
of her letter tomorrow. You just can't stay up any more
now. It's more important than anything for you to rest."

Louis looked at her and she saw that he was wide awake,
more awake than before, more awake than sedatives would
handle. He smiled at her. "I can see the letter in your
hand—there's not much more, only a few lines more—
read me those and then I'll go to sleep, I promise you."

And so Betsy read on: " 'How long have we been dith-
ering? In letters some of which I take no pride in (they
were selfish) any more than you can take pride in some of
yours (they've been selfish and illogical too, at least for
nine months past). So we've made two patterns of life for
seven years and the patterns don't fit and we're going to
make them fit. Now you go on to your Bikini but then
you come back to me.

" 'It's very dark outside. The whole world's out there
beyond the train window, and so many places in it—to
see—to be in—places for us and for now—I might give
you a few roads through the countryside myself.

" 'Dear Louis, you were a wonderful host—afternoons of flowers and flowerings on St. Peter—and you made your guest's every wish your own. So let me remind you that in a month you are to repay this visit, this time for life, at a place to be picked—wherever roads need building.' "

Betsy read through to the end. She dared not look up, and when she finished reading her voice was so low that it was hardly more than a vibration in the room.

4

"Afternoons of flowers and flowerings," thought Louis, and a wave of pity, for Theresa and for himself too, rolled over him; he almost shook from the force of it. But it rolled away, taking on such a physical property in his mind's eye that it seemed to him he could see it recede. And then it was not the pity but himself that seemed to have receded, to some point, not too remote, not more than a few levels of awareness away, from which Theresa and Theresa's letter, together with Betsy's tortured reading of it and the actual person of himself, could all be seen as points in a pattern, somewhere below. He had had sensations like this sometimes when falling asleep, feelings of being quite disembodied and able to observe his curled-up self from a point that he recalled as being approximately at the ceiling.

Not more than ten or fifteen minutes could have elapsed since Betsy had come into the room, and standing at the foot of the bed with her hands behind her back, had told him that she had a surprise for him if he would be good and go to sleep right afterward. He could remember the joy he had felt when she held the letter forth, and the eagerness with which he had listened as she read. These feelings too, had become points in the pattern; he watched them as Betsy got up from her chair, folded the letter away, moved about the bed, and finally went out, leaving him alone.

The face of the watch on the end of the bed penetrated

his consciousness—another point in the pattern. He must have been asleep; the watch read a little after twelve-thirty, and he remembered that Pederson had left at ten-thirty. But he could swear that the sound of Betsy's voice reading had only just ended, and to test the watch he listened carefully. He could hear nothing except threshold sounds without identity and the distant, deep throbbing of generators.

Much as an old man might sit watching a playing child, Louis considered Theresa's letter again. And as an old man might become absorbed in the movements of a child's game, although without any sense of participation in it, so Louis's mind recreated that afternoon of flowerings, all of which he could remember and none of which seemed now to have touched him; those flowerings moved within his mind like shadows just out of reach.

What Theresa said about the university set up more cumbersome feelings within him. His friend's letter—full of contempt for the university's quota system, well-intentioned, full of the writer's declarations that he would speak to this one and that one, so that perhaps someday—this letter had arrived on the last day of Theresa's visit. He could not have avoided mentioning it to David since they had been planning to work together at the university; but David should not have said anything about it. Undeniably the meaning of the letter had been a hurt. Still, he had lost his sense for the smell and sound of that kind of hurt during the years on the project. Among the people he worked and lived with there was none of that, none that he had experienced at all events.

Like many Jews, Louis had long ago fashioned within himself a kind of emotional chute down which such things could go, entering the eye or ear but bypassing the channels of consciousness. He had learned, long ago, that a Jew could not react to hurts the way a non-Jew could; prejudice imposed so many that too often one reaction would not be ended before another would have to begin. The fact

was that his emotional chute had grown rusty with disuse.
It was really no matter, he thought.

Although it was, of course; it always was. He stared
straight down along the bed, beyond the watch, to the
windowsill, where the flower was. And the sight of it at
just this moment brought up again, from the depths of his
mind, his half-dream of the early morning and those searing
few minutes of so long ago on the high school lawn. He
wondered, idly, whether his subconscious thought it had
achieved a triumph by serving up that incident; he could
without difficulty think of two dozen other such, and he
had the uneasy feeling that if he were to lean back, mentally, and let his subconscious take over, it would self-
righteously serve up all of these and many more.

The trouble with a subconscious, he thought testily, was
that it drew so heavily on the values and judgments of
childhood days; and he had occasionally thought of this
vague and speculative realm of the mind as a spoiled child,
roused out of fatted torpors from time to time to point a
finger, stamp a foot, and make claims concerning which it
was sometimes right, often wrong, and always sure.

Moreover, it personalized everything and debased half
of what it pointed at, pretending to the candor of innocence
that indeed it sometimes had, but more often only ex-
ploiting the patness of its primitive judgments. Well, so
much for that. He felt an itching at one corner of his mouth
and turned his head to rub the itch against his shoulder.
But it had been so natural to raise an arm and scratch with
his hand that involuntarily the muscles of his right arm
contracted, and he felt a pure and woeful frustration at
being denied this simple measure of relief. He tensed the
muscles of both arms, but felt nothing much beyond his
shoulders. He continued to move his face against his shoulder, although the itching had stopped. The movement continued for a while, slowly, half forgotten.

"Say it," Theresa had said.

"I love you."

"Say it again."

"I love you."

"And we'll be married in a month."

"In a month."

Theresa took shape within his eyes. He saw her as she must have sat at the writing desk of the train, her head bent forward, her hair covering the sides of her face, her body tight with the intensity that it brought to tasks. Now like the old man who, watching the remote child, wants at some point to reach out and touch her, only touch her, Louis wanted suddenly to reach out before him, to hold his arm out as he would to touch Theresa if she had been there. This writing figure was Theresa to every stray hair and to every thought that he sought to see within the bent head. He lay perfectly still, deliberately still, as though waiting or watching, and abruptly, with a sense of real panic, he had the horrible feeling that Theresa, as he still could see her, was about to turn to him and would not know him when she did—would turn to say the very things she had been writing, to offer him the wholeness of her heart, to speak, to touch, and would not know him—or even, like the little playing child turning to let her eyes pass over the old man, would see nothing that held any possible interest for her.

But the figure continued to sit as he visualized her, and the panic died. If she should turn, he told himself, to search him with her eyes, why, the expression of her eyes and the movements of her lips would be—would be— Now he wanted her to turn, and closed and opened his eyes two or three times rapidly to make a picture of her looking at him. But he could not get her face; it eluded him, it wasn't there. What she was writing he remembered very well, all of it about such a variety of energetic thoughts and prospects—so busy, so distracting, so full of the details and involvements of life.

With a feeling that the remoteness that had taken hold of him earlier was feeding on and sapping his senses, he grew aware that in truth it was he who would not know Theresa, if she should turn to him, or, worse, that he would have to meet with indifference the expression of her eyes and the movements of her mouth—as the old man, called on to feel more than he can and to understand what he has forgotten, finally exhausts his capacity to watch the playing child and turns away. At the back of his head there was a chattering, faint and indecipherable. But toward that too he felt indifferent; and toward the oppression of the ice that weighed him down on both sides and across the middle; and toward all the convolutions of his recent thinking.

He heard sounds from the corridor outside his room. Something rustled, something clicked across the way. Then he heard stealthy footsteps going by. He counted them all the way to the stair leading to the first floor. And instantly, without the preparation of a thought, he decided that he would get up.

He listened again, and heard nothing, except from the outside, through the partly open window to his right, from somebody's house somewhere down the street, he heard a baby's crying. And then, without any great effort, he tensed the muscles of his abdomen and drew himself up slowly; the bags and pads of ice slid down. He watched the mound of towels over his left hand heave and disintegrate as he worked to withdraw his arms from the troughs. He reached his legs, one after the other, over the side of the bed, and stood, his hands hanging stiffly at his sides, the drip tube dragging from his ankle. He took two steps to the window, and looked out.

To the left he could see the farthest reach of the yellow glow from the light, itself invisible, that stood by the pond beyond the end of the hospital; and across the street, from rooms within the Lodge, fingers of light stretching out across the empty terrace and cutting faintly, here and there, into the otherwise black space of the big open lawn. He heard again the baby's cry. The dark beyond the window

looked soft and not unfriendly; the cold of the night air
he didn't notice; and the small sounds of the trees were
the sounds that he and Theresa had walked among only a
few evenings ago.

She'd been standing on the farthest edge of the open
lawn; she had run out ahead of him, the flame-colored skirt
that she had put on for him swirling and her long hair
flying, and he was walking toward her. She beckoned, urging him on with her arm; and then she gathered up one
edge of the flame-colored skirt and held it out, bowed,
looking at him, whirled once, and looked again, laughing.

The sense of remoteness did not sustain itself against
this picture in his mind; it seemed—and maybe just because his getting up had been an act and not a thought—
to have been routed from the smothering hold it had taken
and to have been compressed into a cold core of something.
Against the unyieldingness of this, as it seemed, his thoughts
rose to hit and, falling back, to hit again.

The chattering at the back of his head kept on, inces-
santly, too loud to be ignored, but not loud enough to do
more than register on his consciousness. He was warm and
cold, not bodily, not with any reference to his frozen hands—
he ignored them, he had not once looked down at them—
but entirely as a matter of the climate of his mind. It was
plain to him, beyond the need of analysis, that within the
cold core something was crystallizing which sooner or later
would require all of his attention, and which, just because
he recognized this, could be left for the time being to its
own devices and would leave him, so to speak, to his.

So he stood there, looking out into the night. He thought
of the flame-colored skirt again, and of the way it swirled.
But then, hardly noticing the transition, he was wondering
how the quota system operated at the university—one for
each branch of science, with perhaps two for chemistry?
From some forgotten room in the storehouse of his mind
came the recollection that in England, up to the latter part
of the Nineteenth Century, no one could get a degree

unless he subscribed to the Thirty-Nine Articles of the Anglican Church. The quota system had never touched him before; it never would, he thought.

Was science a haven to him, as Theresa had once asked. Why, yes, the answer, he supposed, was that once it had been, of a sort, always bearing in mind that the fire of Miss Oliver had preceded the ice of the high school lawn. Poor Miss Oliver! How could he explain, even to himself, what she had meant to him?

Fermi, surely one of the greats, was going back to Chicago determined to teach physics to freshmen himself. The earlier it is taught well, he had said with no false modesty, the more and better scientists there will be. I am sure he would understand, thought Louis, if I told him that Miss Oliver would have approved, although she would not have been as impressed as I am.

He shuddered slightly. If I have not done much good, I trust I have done less harm, he thought suddenly. Who said that? Didn't Pickwick? On his deathbed? Oh, Miss Oliver, I wish I could say it! We will talk about it later, he said to himself. His thoughts of Miss Oliver had been warm thoughts, but now he was cold, all in a minute, really no more than a minute or two. He listened. The baby was crying, but there was no sound from the hall, except a loud snoring that he judged to be from Tim Haeber's room. "I'm sorry I got you into this, Tim," he said, almost automatically, for he had said it several times before.

Betsy's remark of the morning came into his head. "This is the crossroads of the town—the roads don't cross here, but the people do."

"She was right," he said to himself. "That's Wisla out there. I didn't see him come, although it's not surprising. He looks like Queequeg now, come to feature an event."

5

Wisla was standing across the street, a little way back from it. The gloom of the big lawn spread behind him; a street light in front of the center of the hospital, a hundred feet or so to the right, illuminated the front of him. He was wearing a little helmet-like cloth cap, he had a heavy scarf around his neck, and he was carrying a piece of broken tree branch, which he was idly stabbing here and there at the ground.

Louis continued to look out, smiling a little. Once, two years or so before, during one of the innumerable crises of the atomic project, he had been out walking through the dark himself (when the material was beginning to arrive in quantity from Oak Ridge and Hanford and he was helping to refine the measurements of neutron constants given something more than theory to work with)—he had been going home about two or three in the morning and had recognized Wisla strolling along up ahead of him. He had stolen up quietly behind and discovered that Wisla was singing softly to himself:

> *"She got so damned nice*
> *And so goddamned high-priced*
> *She'd only go out with Jesus H. Christ—"*

"And occasionally John Jacob Astor," Louis had sung out.

Well, in general, it was a difficult thing to catch Wisla off guard. Wisla had looked at him severely and said that, as one who did not believe in the divinity of Christ, he could not appreciate the limerick. And he had looked back and said that, as a foreigner, Wisla could not possibly comprehend the significance of John Jacob Astor.

"A fulfillment?" he quoted from Theresa's letter. But the smile left as he stared at Wisla. "Are you a frightened

man, Ed?" he said to himself. "Urey says he's a frightened
man, and I know some who don't say it but they are too.
Theresa's frightened and so am I—we had a terrible wait
at the station and I've not seen her enough in nearly seven
years. That day of the wait—you do appear most oppor-
tunely! It was from seeing you that I went to see her, wasn't
it? An omen! You featured the event that got me into this
and here you've come to see me out! Queequeg to be
sure!"

Wisla was looking directly up at the window. Louis was
quite sure that he could not be seen through the blinds,
although he felt Wisla's gaze, and he felt, moreover, odd
at being here by the window at all; he could not have said
why he had decided to do such a foolish thing.

"You're a stubborn man, certainly that's a fact," he went
on. "I can't imagine how you get along with the politicians,
or they with you. 'Where's this fellow's art of compromise?'
they must say. And then of course you never met a payroll.
Scientists are fashionable these days, that helps, but they
weren't six or seven years ago. Stubborn, yes. About fear—
certainly it was fear then, of one kind, but it's fear now,
of another. Or are the fears the same? Fear then for the
fate of the world because the Germans might make a bomb,
and fear now because we did."

The baby's cry stopped abruptly, in mid-flight; Louis
could almost see the breast or the bottle being taken. Wisla
had turned his head to look in the direction of the stopped
cry, but he still stood in the same spot, still stabbing his
stick around, looking very much like a blind man rapping
his cane for attention at a street crossing.

And now that the baby cried no longer, Louis could hear
from across the lawn, very faint but clear enough here at
the window, a familiar music. It came, he supposed, from
the phonograph at the Ulanovs, which could be counted
to be going at almost any hour; the Jersilds, whose house
was in the same direction, a little farther off, might also
be making the music, but their taste ran heavily to jazz,

and this was Beethoven. It was interesting, he thought, how you could tell Beethoven just from a bar or two.

Wisla stopped stabbing his stick; his head turned in the direction of the music. Then, just at this moment, the music stopped, not in completion but as though gathering itself for a fuller reach, and it suddenly dawned on Louis that Wisla had been hearing this right along and his apparently aimless stabbing had been a rough kind of keeping time, a private conducting that he had stopped for the voices. They soared across the lawn, still faint but clearer and more penetrating in their higher pitch, carrying the Ninth Symphony out beyond the reach of instruments.

He could not hear this without catching his breath a little, and he caught his breath, although possibly a little from the night's chill too.

"A crossroads, yes. Theresa's frightened for me, but she's got the real fear too. The gates and guards and the secret buildings—a place for people to deny themselves— for what? Tell her, Edward, can you tell her? Can you tell me?"

But Wisla was walking away, back into the gloom of the big, empty lawn.

The truth is, Louis thought, there's no one of us can tell another any more. We've used up all the good explanations—all we've got left is the bad ones—the ones nobody wants to give, or mumbles. A place for denial, with guards.

Edward, he said to the retreating figure, all but lost in the dark, do you remember that blind girl in Albuquerque, who noticed a brightening in her room after the flash of the bomb at Alamogordo, more than a hundred miles away from her? "What was that?" she asked. Ed, God damn it, Ed, don't go away! What *was* that? But there's a brightness now in all the rooms, he whispered. Then he half laughed; and then he discovered he was crying too. That's all I meant this afternoon, he said to Wisla's figure.

———

Wisla had been in for a visit early in the afternoon, for half an hour or so before the drip injection had started. Concerning the accident, Wisla announced that, inasmuch as he had never done Louis's experiment or even seen it, he knew nothing whatever about it and could be of no help. Having said that, he had then asked Louis forty or fifty questions bearing on various details of the experiment; and had excoriated it, as an idiotic arrangement, and the Army, for letting it remain so, and Louis, for performing it, in approximately even measure.

Wisla, of course, knew a great deal about the experiment, although it was true that he had never actually witnessed it. All of the scientists at Los Alamos knew about it at least generally. It was one of the crucial experiments by which the great scientific triumph of a self-sustaining nuclear reaction had been channeled into the great military triumph of the fission bomb. The assembly used in this experiment was, in effect, a crude sort of bomb, although it also had come to have its uses in the calculation of neutron behavior for some peaceful applications of the endless energy. It was not encased and hence could not explode; maneuvered to a certain point, it gave measurements of amounts and configurations of fissionable material that would produce a chain reaction, and this was the experiment's function; beyond that point, it gave the chain reaction itself, in a burst of uncontrolled radioactivity. The trick and the trickiness of the experiment lay in the barely perceptible separation of its measurements from its breakdown into the burst of radioactivity.

In a sense, the experiment might be said to have had unusual elements of safety. Nothing went on in the course of it that was not the direct result of actions controlled by one person, and all of the results were foreseeable as to kind and even roughly predictable as to degree. It is dangerous to put your head in a lion's mouth because the lion, on his own initiative, might close his mouth; dangerous to do a thousand things that depend for their safety on a moving part that might break, on a collaborator who might miss a cue, on one variable or another not under direct control. It was dangerous enough just to be in Hiroshima on the sixth of August, 1945, or in Nagasaki on the ninth; since no one there had been given any warning of what was going to happen and so didn't know that it was dangerous, which made it doubly so. Louis's experiment had involved none of these dangers; indeed, it had involved but one: the danger of a slip, a barely perceptible slip.

"As you know," Louis had said to Wisla in answer to one of his excoriations, "controls and real shielding would have made it more cumbersome. It was a wartime setup—jerry-built and single-minded. It wasn't the only one."

"None so dangerous."

"But think how well it worked most of the time. So fast. So simple."

"Indeed," said Wisla, scowling at the tone of Louis's voice. "I am not certain controls would make it so cumbersome. If—"

"Installing them would have cut the experiment out for months."

"Thiel says you did not more than half try to change it."

"If it was a half try, that's because it was a whole no response."

"Idiotic arrangement," Wisla said testily, and for the seventh time.

It would have been obvious to anyone, despite Wisla's testiness and in part because of it, that he was very troubled by what had happened. It was obvious to Louis, who knew Wisla well, that he was also troubled by a particular difficulty he was having in expressing what troubled him. The difficulty was that, while he felt sorry for Louis (and had trouble enough expressing that), he felt angry too. He took it—so Louis decided—as inexplicable, hence insupportable, that the experiment, however idiotic, should have failed in Louis's hands. If there had been an accident, why, there had been an accident to a very unlikely person, hence a very unlikely accident—too unlikely for Wisla to condone.

"How many times you did this?"

"This was the sixty-fourth, so Dave tells me. I guess I did it sixty-three times."

Wisla had paced around the room, stared at the ice troughs now and again, and hinted at but did not express these troubled certainties, while Louis listened, at first somewhat amused and finally touched. For it became plain that not himself but the simple fact of the accident was the target of Wisla's feeling, and plain that Wisla found himself unable to speak his feelings out of fear that Louis would think himself the target. I wish I could help him, Louis thought; but he did not know what to say.

"Tell me about Washington."

Wisla shook his head sadly.

"You wouldn't believe it."

"But you seem to get along with Congressmen. How do you talk to them?"

"Hah! I speak to them of politics and they tell me about the atom. We entertain each other, though possibly not for long."

"I've never met a Congressman, but I've heard some strange stories. Willie Ticken told me last fall about being introduced to a Senator, and this Senator said—there were Willie and a couple of other guys from here—the Senator said: 'My fellow Americans, I want you to know I've *always* been a friend of atomic energy.' Is this real?"

"To be sure it is. Also Willie and I can tell more such stories, but more about last fall than this spring." Wisla looked at Louis rather sternly. "We have not spent all those months in that awful city for nothing."

"No," Louis said, looking at Wisla speculatively.

But the success of the scientists' lobby, as it had come to be known, was written very clearly in the Congressional defeat of the May-Johnson Bill, which would have contin-ued the Army in control of atomic energy; and in ten thousand speeches, talks, private buttonholings, pam-

phlets, leaflets, educational campaigns, conferences, even
classes in physics for Congressmen, and more besides—
all planned, undertaken, and brought off by scientists with
no experience at doing these things, no money to speak
of, and in the teeth of a wide assortment of myths, prejudices, complacencies, misinformation, refusals to believe,
and tribal dreams concerning the nature and the meaning
and the uses of the bomb.

"No," Louis said again, forgetting that his gaze was still
resting on Wisla and not noticing that Wisla was becoming
restive under it.

For the scientists who had lighted the atomic fires knew,
from all the history of their science, that no man had had
the power to hold back the lighting and no man could keep
the fires from burning; and what they knew they had intoned over and over like the *Kyrie eleison*—there are no
secrets, there is no defense, there can be no monopoly—
and then had translated and intoned again, over and over—
survival is at stake, the time is short, and the crisis is
political. Certainly this had not been for nothing. The words
had become as familiar as the daily paper.

"No," said Louis, for the third time. "But we're still
making bombs."

"So," Wisla said, impatiently. "That is a problem to be
worked out in the United Nations. But we go with cleaner
hands there than before—at least without Generals to lead
us."

"I just wonder if we're being took."

"What is 'took'?"

"Still making them," Louis repeated, ignoring Wisla's
question, "and that on the top of the way we used them—
not once but twice—no warning—after Japan started peace
overtures at that. Oh, very unclean hands! Sam Allison
says this was a great tragedy. Senators and Generals say
this is the way modern wars are fought, which is what the
Germans said when they bombed out Rotterdam. The ter-
ror isn't only in what's done but in the speed of our ad-

justment to it. What we did shortened the war and saved
lives, so we say—that's what the Germans said about Rotterdam too. But it did turn out that the invasion of Japan
was planned for November and we dropped the bombs in
August—not losing lives in August so the lives we were
saving were November lives, and at the very least why
didn't we wait with the Nagasaki bomb to see what the
effect of Hiroshima might be? Might have saved the lives
of six hundred medical students. Modern wars aren't fought
that way and when Hutchins and the Pope say our use of
the bombs lost us our moral prestige they aren't talking
to the subject except I read all the time how our possession
of the bomb is a sacred trust. Somewhere along the line
we had a choice."

The words came out of Louis's mouth with almost no
change of inflection. He looked at Wisla as he talked,
although occasionally his eyes turned toward the window.
His head did not move at all. The flow of words came to
a stop, but Wisla, his mouth partly open as though he had
started to say something and then had forgotten what, did
not speak. There was a moment of silence, of helplessness,
and the flow started again.

"If you keep on looking do you suppose you'll find the
clue that explains everything here or in Washington in the
stars or in ourselves? I was looking the other day Tuesday
I was trying to think how things were at the end of war
when Nolan died—week after the end of the war—and
chance we had then to do something about what we'd done
like the time about the time of Lucretius—probably odd
for a Jew to think of it—before the birth of Jesus and after
the old-fashioned gods were dead and there was man alone
looking out on a universe he only dimly understood with
nothing to tell him what values to use other than those of
his own devisings the gods being dead and the doctrine of
salvation by common sense and the fruitfulness of nature
made some headway—I was thinking Tuesday how if week
after the war if we had proceeded by the doctrine of com-

mon sense and fruitfulness of nature—how if we all said
as Urey and some others did say then that the future that
could have been more important than the past will be
poisoned day by day by bombs piling up all made here and
only here marked 'Made and Used by the U.S.A.'—but
we didn't. Couldn't find the clue except not enough voices
were raised—I keep remembering someone saying 'In a
time of weakness strength may be the highest morality'
but I can't remember who it was or where—perhaps it is
the clue—"

"Louis!" Wisla called. He came between the bed and
the trough, but Louis went right on. Then Wisla turned
abruptly and went out of the room; he left the door open
and even from the corridor Louis's voice, quiet and tone-
less but quite strong, could be heard.

"—except making bombs quite a difference between
what we're doing and what every other country is doing—
not a difference of course that will continue for long and
how if we talk about control while making bombs—"

Not more than ten feet down the corridor, Wisla, looking anxiously this way and that, saw Charley Pederson
come into sight from the stairway and hurried to meet him.

"He talks on and on," Wisla told Pederson. "He is not
himself."

They walked rapidly down the corridor to Louis's room.

"But he is not in the least incoherent. He is most co-
herent. The words make a sense."

"—this new law supposed to please us what is pleasing
about its embodiment of fiction we have secrets to be
guarded and if it is now treason punishable by death to
disclose the number of neutrons released in fission of plu-
tonium a discovery made possible by the work of Germans
Austrians Scandinavians Italians Hungarians among others
why then it has become treasonable to think and a prov-
ocation—"

"Dreadful," Wisla said.

Pederson put a hand on Wisla's shoulder, holding him

where he was, and leaned forward to peek around the door
frame into the room.

"—accumulating pile of the twice-used bomb refusal to
share what we found even with the British gave us all their
information to make it possible for us to do what we did
and what possible proposals for control can we build on
the premise that we go on making bombs while no one
else without our approval can—leave us be realistic and
leave us make use of a good thing when we have it and
besides who else has so much of the morality that goes
with strength in a time of weakness—single-mindedness
of war that is so rational if you grant certain premises
proceeds from an irrationality so great as to require no
premises utmost of which men are capable—hating and
fearing their fellow inhabitants of the one known popu-
lated star and soon themselves. Control of that."

The voice stopped. Pederson glanced at Wisla, then drew
him back away from the door.

"Go back in," he whispered. "Say something to him."

Wisla walked on in. "I went to the bathroom," he said.

"Did you? Just now? I had a funny feeling, dizzy, like
fainting. We were talking."

"We still are, but I think you talk too much. You should
not talk so much when you are sick."

"You forget you've had quite a shock," Pederson said
from the door. "Also," he went on, coming into the room,
"you haven't been keeping much nourishment down. So
we'll give you some nice body-building glucose, good for
what ails you. OK?"

The stand to hold the bottle and the tube for the drip
injection was in a corner of the room, and Pederson went
over to it and fussed with it; and finally caught Wisla's eye
and gave him a reassuring nod. In a moment Betsy had
come in with the bottle. Wisla had paced back and forth
a little longer, but no more was said, and then he had left.

The voices singing in the night above the woodwinds and the strings abruptly ended. Somebody called them, Louis thought, somebody said: "Listen, old friend, will you leave the night to sleep for once so I can get up in the morning and make a bomb?" Good-night, Ulanovs. Good-by, Beethoven. Good-night, blind girl of Albuquerque. That brightness in the room was the glint of an interval in man's questioning of nature, which has no beginning and has no end. But as for the present brightness, that's something else, and we are as blind as you.

He felt a vibrating pain in his left hand, and a pain that did not vibrate in his right. He discovered that he was shivering. The glow from the light around the end of the hospital disappeared. It's one o'clock, he thought; they turn it out at one.

He heard careful footsteps mounting the stairway or it seemed to him that he did. The night held nothing and nobody. The chattering at the back of his head was gone and the cold core had dissolved. He felt neither warm nor cold.

A thought fluttered across his mind like an autumn leaf—Theresa, did you get the wire?—and was gone.

In a purely scientific sense, in the sense that the profoundest laws of nature are evolved as free inventions of the imagination, he now suddenly had the conviction that he was going to die, and it was as plain as the night to him that this was going to require all his attention, and possibly for some time, because it would not be for several days.

He turned from the window; he walked stiffly; but he went directly to the bed and got into it. His hands were quite painful now, but he simply laid them in the troughs. The night nurse came in, with noisy stealth, and the day ended as it had begun, with alarms and the fixing of sheets and towels. The pain increased; two doctors were brought; sedatives were administered.

But all this seemed peripheral to Louis, as the noise and movement of a hurricane might seem to one in the quiet eye at the center. He answered when he was spoken to

and cooperated with the doctors and the nurses as they came and went. But his mind was in the quiet eye of the center, alone. That the eye was moving with the wind he knew, and would move, in a certain time, on over and through him and away. But it held him now, it contained him utterly.

The undercurrent of excitement that he had noticed earlier, which had then seemed pointless to him, seemed now to have been a preparation for this; and the indifference and the remoteness that had come over him with Theresa's letter, so full of the involvements of life.

The involvements of life were all part of the noise and movement that did not and could not touch him in this quiet center where he was alone, which nothing could enter.

6

"With his bare hands," said Colonel Hough.

"With his bare hands," Mrs Hough repeated, and wrote the words down.

"With his bare hands he—or, no make that the young scientist—the young scientist knocked apart the structure."

"The young scientist knocked apart the structure."

"And put out the fire. Read me up to there now."

Mrs Hough read and the Colonel listened.

"All right," he said. "Now going on from there. In this heroic action both of his hands were burned and he suffered bodily—"

"Not so much at once, dear," Mrs Hough interrupted. "In this heroic—"

And so they continued until the story was done. They had started at a little before eleven and, what with changes and reworkings and some discussion about the best way to say one thing and another, it was after midnight when they put the story aside.

Mrs Hough said she'd be glad to fix the Colonel a little something to eat before they went to bed, but he thought not. She suggested that he come to bed then since it was later than usual for them. He kissed her on the cheek and said he'd be up very soon. After she left he read the draft of the story once more; then he opened the front door and stepped out onto the walk leading to the empty street. He could not see the hospital from here, but he saw it in his mind with the window to Louis's room black and dominant.

God damn it, fellow, I salute you, he thought. He felt sad and respectful, looking across at the houses on the other side of the street, and he looked away only as the sound of phonograph music gradually penetrated his consciousness.

This, he decided, was coming from the Ulanov house; he thought of Ulanov and his noisy habits with irritation, and pondered whether to call and tell him to turn off his phonograph. But then, without knowing quite why, he decided he wouldn't, not tonight at least.

What a plain damn hell of a thing to have happen, just a day before you're supposed to leave, just a day after your fiancée— Colonel Hough had seen her. He had watched her from across the big lawn in front of the Lodge, dancing on the grass, in something red—pretty as anything, he'd thought, pretty and alive and warm, he could tell, even from the distance. He'd have liked a night with that one, or a weekend, and this thought pushed up now to shame him horribly—God Almighty, and Louis lying over there!

And lying over there now, or at a time like now or any late or lonely hour, if he's not asleep he's thinking what? What would I think? What would I think these next few days while this Beale sits waiting and all those other doctors wait and everybody waits and whatever goes on goes on without your being able to do anything about it—and then? What does Dave Thiel know that I don't know? Don't accidents just happen?

PART 5

Thursday night: a room by the garden

1

Not since the day the war began had Theresa been at Mr
Biscanti's house. Many times she had planned to go or had
even started to go; it was only that she had not got there.
Other things had intervened. And thus more than six years
had passed. Now, on this rather muggy Thursday evening
in May—at just about the time that Pederson was pre-
senting himself to Beale at the hotel in Santa Fe—Theresa
set forth to find out if in fact Mr Biscanti's house was still
there, if he was in it, and if he would enter into the plan
she had evolved out of emotions left over from her letter
to Louis. Her plan was no more than that she and Louis
should have dinner and spend the night at Mr Biscanti's
as they had done so many times before. This could not be
for a month but the sooner the arrangement was made the
longer it could be savored.

Although she had gone from the train straight to her apartment and had been there most of the afternoon, she was not there when the Western Union office called to read the telegram it had just received for her from Santa Fe. She was around the corner at the little cleaning shop, waiting for the proprietor to press her flame-colored skirt, which, since it was corduroy, she was afraid to press herself. She had worn it to the party at the Ulanovs' house at Louis's special behest, and she would wear it, as a private gesture, for tonight's trip.

She could have looked in the telephone book and established whether or not her trip had a destination, but it didn't occur to her to do so. In fact, she was quite prepared to find that Mr Biscanti had moved, since life was like that; but separately she was also certain that he would be there and would enter into her sentimental plan with joy, since that was what she wanted.

Mr Biscanti's house was there, as it had always been. Children were playing on the stoop, as other children had played there before. She rang the bell. Mr Biscanti came to the door, and—

"It's my little lady!" Mr Biscanti exclaimed. His voice was joyful, his whole face smiled, and he struggled to push away the door so that he could hold out both arms to Theresa.

She sat in the little dining room overlooking the garden behind the house, while Mr Biscanti was up and down, speaking to customers. But he was at the table with her when he could be, and between them they made arrangements for what would surely be a lovely night—to be added to the many lovely nights that she had spent in this house, and to the half-lovely, half-sad one, the last one, the night before the war began.

"Not seven years ago," she said. "Six and three-quarters."

"Too long."

"There'll be nobody in the garden talking about war this

time either," she said. "You won't have to throw anyone
out."

She smiled fondly at him and he looked sheepish.

Mr Biscanti's garden was a joke of a garden. The floor was
cement, an awning roofed it over, board fences enclosed
it. Still, between the top of the fencing and the bottom of
the awning, a space of a foot or so, the night was visible
along with the backs of apartment houses on all sides; and
in the light from their windows a small plane tree could
be seen, providing at least the illusion of outdoors. In
midtown Manhattan there were dozens if not hundreds of
places like this, though none with the meanings of this
one, which was, as Theresa noted with satisfaction, still as
it had been at those earlier times—the same tree providing
the same illusion—all as before, including the worn furniture and Mr Biscanti himself and doubtless some of the
patrons from that other muggy Thursday evening of August 31st, 1939, the night before the war began.

"You should know your history better—alliances like
this happen all the time—take it for what it is—just power
politics."

This or something like this had come from the tall man
in the garden that other time, and the plump man had then
said he had seen it coming, and the woman with him,
wiping her glasses with her handkerchief, she had said,
"The Russians have no morals."

"Ho, who has any more? The British? The French? Don't
make me laugh—they've all got their fingers—"

Theresa couldn't remember who had said that, but the
cynicism of the words hung in the air over the neatly arranged tables slowly filling her mind with the patrons and
the interplay of that other muggy Thursday before the war.
The talk had risen and fallen while music from the old
radio, under the talk or off to one side, became a steady
flow that broke now and again for the newest report, which
was much like the last one. The announcers had striven

desperately to hint at sharper meanings than their information contained at nine o'clock on that evening. Everyone had known from the sound and the look and the feel and the sense of things, from the reverberations that could be felt across continents and oceans, that the sharper meanings were there, awaiting only the sanction of official statement. Pending that there were time and compulsion to review, speculate, sigh, and nod one's opinion.

The music stopped, heads turned toward the little cabinet; Hitler might call a meeting of the Reichstag in the morning. There had been unconfirmed information to this effect.

"But will Hitler actually move?" the announcer concluded. "Poland is tense—"

And so the music came on again. The tall man was shaking his head.

"The question isn't that, it isn't that at all. Are we really waiting to hear whether Hitler is going to invade Poland? He will if he wants to, and it looks like he wants to. The question is whether anyone's going to do anything about it. That means England, eh? Can anyone say for sure she will?"

"She won't do anything," the young man sitting off by himself in a corner of the garden had said, "and neither will anyone else. But if anyone does do anything it won't do any good. There isn't going to be a war. But what's wrong with that?"

The young man was a newcomer to Mr Biscanti's; no one there seemed to know him. He was a perfectly ordinary-looking young man, sitting very straight in his chair; when he finished speaking, his face held no particular expression. After a moment he spoke again.

"Excuse me, I didn't mean to interrupt. I think that gentleman was about to say the same thing." He looked at the tall man. "Weren't you?"

"Well, you make it pretty out-and-out. Things are more complicated—"

"Are they? Either there will be a war or there will not.

The question, as you say, is whether England will fight."

The tall man referred to pros and cons while Mr Biscanti, standing in a French doorway between his garden and his small dining room, listened. Mr Biscanti himself did not seem to know the young man, but he spoke to him.

"I heard you to say there is nothing wrong if England does not oppose Germany. You think it is right for Hitler to do what he is doing?"

"It isn't a matter of right or wrong," the young man replied promptly, "except that it's better to avoid war than to have it. Hitler has made Germany strong. It won't do any good to oppose Germany because Germany is too strong." He gestured with his arms. "And England is weak—as is France."

"I know the argument," said Mr Biscanti, "it was the argument a year ago too. It is an argument that gives the world over to Hitler. Do you want to do that?"

"Well, really, I can't give the world to Hitler just by argument. We all form our opinions, don't we? That's mine. If Germany were weak and England were strong our opinions would have to be different."

The radio droned on, nestled between a water pitcher and a butter bowl on a serving table. Mr Biscanti shook his head vigorously.

"It is not enough to say that. You are just saying that strength must be bowed to always forever. When is a thing like Hitler stopped? A time is necessary to do the stopping, no matter what the strength is. You do not agree with that?"

Heads turned and the young man looked around before answering.

"In a time of great weakness—a time like the present—strength may be the highest morality."

Then all the talking stopped as the radio music faded out again. The newest report still dwelt on the meeting of the Reichstag, which was still unconfirmed. The talk went on again.

Mr Biscanti's dining room, smaller than the garden, held

four or five tables, each with its little cluster of oil and vinegar bottles. All of these tables were empty except the one at which Louis and Theresa sat beside a window arch opening onto the garden. Mr Biscanti walked over to their table from the doorway. He was a large man, with a heavy frame and a heavy head, and the features of his face sagged and shook as he walked. He bent forward slightly and held his hands clasped before him. He cocked his head on one side and, smiling, said: "How are you getting along?"

Theresa smiled back. "Everything's lovely." She nodded her head toward the garden. "Who's your friend?"

Mr Biscanti's smile went away and he shook his head slowly. "You heard what he was saying? How do you like that? I can't imagine— Well, I do not know him, I do not know him. But let me get you something." The smile returned.

Louis lifted his hand from Theresa's hand, which was held out flat against the edge of the table. "Why don't you get three zabagliones and we'll have a last supper, you, Therese, and I. For tomorrow—" He waved his arm.

Theresa moved her eyes away from him and patted a chair beside her, looking up at Mr Biscanti, her body leaning forward, her head tilted back, her hand still held out. Louis, watching her, suddenly put his hand back into hers.

"Come on, Mr Biscanti," she said. "It's a very special occasion—you sit here."

Mr Biscanti demurred. He would have to be getting up all the time; they preferred to be alone. But she pressed him.

His great head moved up and down. "It is a very special occasion." He bowed slightly, his hands pressed against his stomach. "With such a very pretty lady." He turned his bow toward Louis. "And our good friend—we will miss him so much." His face grew solemn. "It is too bad he must go away, too bad after so long, Mr Saxl."

"Dr Saxl," she reproached him. "You forgot already."

"So I did, so I did!" he cried. "I cannot remember. It

is a wonderful thing for our friend—very bad for us. He stays here a mister—he is made a doctor today, and tomorrow he goes."

Louis slapped the table and spoke self-consciously. "As the newest Doctor of Philosophy in all the world, but most of all the man who is waiting for—well, I will be specific—that's what's needed, I can see—Mr Biscanti, those zabagliones and the pleasure of your company?—it is later than we think."

Mr Biscanti, as he had predicted, was getting up all the time. In the intervals the talk was the talk of farewells and reminiscences, intuitive, over-eager, full of sudden silences. Mr Biscanti remembered for them how Louis had first come to his place, tired one evening from wandering around the neighborhood looking for a room.

"He had such a big book," Mr Biscanti recalled. "Eh? That was the beginning of the doctor, right there. Well, I didn't know that. But I find out this young man is looking for a place. He stays so long everybody has gone away, he talks to me at last."

"Did I tell you," continued Mr Biscanti, who had told it many times, "how only that day, that very morning, I decided to rent the little room on the top floor? What a strange thing!"

Theresa had spent much time in that little room, with its view of the backs of apartment houses. She had read to Louis lying on the bed, his legs spread out and his head thrown back, his eyes closed; and had been read to, lying on the bed herself, Louis at the little table. It was a very small room, not big enough for two unless the fit were perfect. When she brushed her hair before the mirror over the bureau he could not get past her from the bathroom to the closet. He had sometimes stood and waited, watching, as she had seen in the mirror from a corner of her eye; or had sat on the end of the bed that was the obstacle, abstractedly studying the carpet or wriggling a toe, getting up automatically when she moved to let him pass.

She remembered well the wriggling toe, and she remembered how suddenly, sometimes, he fell asleep. In the dimness of the city glow through the single window she had lain beside him, her head propped on her arm, and studied the bony modeling of his face, softened by night and sleep; she had traveled with her eyes, or sometimes delicately with her fingers, the long muscles under the smooth flesh of his legs. She remembered well the feel of the flesh, the taut wet weight and the smell of it. She remembered all this from years ago—and from Los Alamos the week before.

"I knew the rent could not be much. He looked—" Mr Biscanti had gone on to tell them how he looked.

The zabagliones were eaten; the chatter from the garden continued; Mr Biscanti got up; the drone of the radio music went on. Suddenly Louis pushed his legs hard against Theresa's; the movement had a kind of desperation in it, and she looked at him with brief surprise. But she dropped her hand to his thigh and her fingers pressed against him. A man came in from the hall and over to their table, talking as he came.

"What's this I hear? Big happenings, eh? Mr Biscanti tells me the news. So you're a doctor, and now you go away and leave us—good evening, miss."

She felt the long muscle of his leg tighten as he moved, leaning toward the window. The radio music stopped again and the talk with it.

"—still no official confirmation of the report broadcast earlier this evening over these stations that Hitler has called a meeting of the Reichstag for ten o'clock tomorrow morning, five o'clock Eastern Standard Time."

She thought of the war and the room above, of the night ahead, and of time thereafter.

"—might march, in his opinion, even without the formality of a declaration by the Reichstag, whose authority, in any event, is tied completely to the will of Hitler."

The voice would be there with them in the little room,

overwhelming the last night. There might be nothing said
of the things to say with so much to say; nothing done;
and the feelings left untouched. She closed her eyes, heard
the voice again, and was suddenly angry.

"Well," said the man standing by their table, "I don't
know, I don't know. Well, I see you later."

He nodded pleasantly and was off.

"Will he see us later?" Theresa asked after a moment.
Then she formed the words to say what she meant: "We'll
be alone this last night, won't we?" But they weren't said;
the ebb of her sudden anger washed them away. Instead
she asked, "What do you want to do, Louis?"

Still he didn't answer. In the face of her questions he
sat silent, turning his glass slowly around; she leaned back
on her seat, watching him. She reached out to put her hand
on his arm and say her question again, in more answerable
words. But she drew back, for in that moment Louis's
tightly drawn features suddenly seemed like a child's and
her gesture the gesture of a mother. She was half amused
and half angry again. Louis pushed his glass away from him
decisively.

"I—" he started, studying an indeterminate point on her
arm, "I'm afraid of last nights. I can't tell you what I want
to do, I don't know. Tonight I'm afraid of you—myself—
and what there will be in the morning—" He shook his
head and after a moment went on. "I'm acting like a fool,
I can't say anything. But I can do better when we're alone,
I promise you I can."

How hard it is for him to say a simple thing, she thought.

The young man in the garden was speaking—lecturing
rather. He had been talking about strength, morality, the
German genius, the Versailles Treaty, certain admitted
excesses of the men around Hitler and had come to the
unmistakable dedication of the latter.

"Personally, since I'm not a German, I have no feeling
toward Hitler, except I can see he's a dedicated man, and
you have to respect that, whatever else. Don't you think?"

The plump man grunted. "That's a paper point. Hitler
may be dedicated, like you say, but he's a dedicated son
of a bitch, so what's the difference?"

"The British probably said things like that about Washington."

"Oh, come on now—are you comparing Hitler to Washington?"

"It's not relevant. From a distance and in a time of stress
any leader may be wrongly pictured. That's not to say all
leaders are alike."

From the expression on the tall man's face, Theresa
guessed that he privately agreed with much of what the
young man had to say; only, she thought, he can't top the
other's words and for this reason most of all he does not
enjoy the situation. The tall man stared up at the doorway
to the dining room, and as he did so Louis glanced out
into the garden and caught his eye.

"Hey, Saxl," he called, rising from the table, "come on
out here. We've got a regular Nazi here saying a lot of
things. Come on out. You're a Jew. You tell him."

Behind him the young man spoke. "There's really no
point in discussing these things with a Jew."

For several moments there was only the radio to be
heard and only tiny movements to be seen; Theresa drew
her hands up, the plump man's bright eyes moved back
and forth, the woman with him lowered her head slightly.
Louis did not move at all. He looked at the young man—
who was looking at him—and his expression was almost
contemplative. In Mr Biscanti a wrath was rising and he
had not yet shaped and trimmed it into words.

The young man's words held no living, personal spite-
fulness, they held nothing living or personal at all. Had
anyone noticed that? Louis was thinking. Did anyone see
that this was the very distillate of the reverberations that
could be felt across continents and oceans? He wanted to
tell everyone about this, but wanted equally to tell them
to forget it. So he had told Theresa once, afterwards.

The silence ended abruptly with the crystallization of

Mr Biscanti's wrath. He stepped down the two steps into the garden and said to the young man: "Get up now! Get up from that table and please leave here!"

Mr Biscanti put out his two hands and laid hold of the young man. The young man made protests, but they were weak and ineffectual. With his great head thrust forward, Mr Biscanti marched his captive out.

Just before they reached the doorway the young man tried to free himself, not violently, really only to negotiate the steps more easily. But Mr Biscanti jumped forward, muttering, "*no,* no—*no,* no—*no,* no," like a chant; the young man bumped against the table with the radio and the butter bowl and the water pitcher on it, and the radio bounced, rasped and was silent.

Then the captive was captive again, red in the face, outraged but passive. Mr Biscanti propelled him ahead, up the two stairs, across the dining room, into the hall, and through that to the front door.

Later, lying on the bed sheet damp from their bodies in the heavy air, listening to the regular rustle of Louis's breathing, studying the body lines of them both, her head propped on her elbow to give her a little height from which to see better in the faint glow of the city light—later on, in the deepest part of the night and at the very lowest level of the threshold of hearing, a voice rose briefly out of the never wholly silent radios of the apartment houses and was instantly cut down to a murmur; all she heard were the words, "—heavy cruiser *Schleswig Holstein* . . . city of Danzig—" which meant nothing to her. Shortly after that, her elbow aching from her vigil, she had fallen asleep.

2

"I tell you what," Mr Biscanti said to Theresa now, "you go up and see for yourself."

The room on the top floor had not been rented for two years; the furnishings were not quite the same as they had been when Louis lived there; the bureau, for instance, had been given away, and the rug—Mr Biscanti could not remember what had happened to the rug.

"But you go look," he said again, nodding his head. "Then you tell me what to do. Maybe you like to look anyway?"

So Theresa went up the stairs, on up to where the little room was, silent and dark. She reached around the side of the doorway, felt for the light switch and flipped it. She had forgotten how tiny the room was, she had forgotten all kinds of things about it, and she renewed them, standing just inside the door. She went on in and sat on the edge of the bed. She felt the drapes; they were filthy. She leaned her head against the wall.

"Oh, do hurry!" she said aloud.

She stood that way for a minute or more, then looked around the room briskly, made a mental inventory of things to be done, flipped the light switch off again and went down the stairs to report.

It was after eleven o'clock when she left Mr Biscanti's house for her apartment. A Western Union messenger had filled out a telegram notice for her and stuck it in the mailbox in her absence; but children had swirled like autumn leaves in and out of the small entrance hall that evening, and by the time she got back to it the notice was crumpled on the floor, one with the little pile of litter that was always there.

It was long after midnight when she got into bed. Lying in the dark, she worried over the letter she had written on the train, thinking of what she should have said differently, what she shouldn't have said at all, and what she might have added. She dozed and woke with a start, hearing words that she knew no one had said, seeing in the dark details of Louis's old room as clearly as her own, and feeling, as she fell into sleep, his form and weight beside her.

———

Louis had come into the bookstore where she had been a clerk during the summer when she was twenty-one, newly graduated from Columbia University. The bookstore job paid her $22.50 a week, and it had been very important.

He had looked at her diffidently and asked if by any chance she had a book called *Pity the Tyrant,* written by a man named Hans Otto Storm, who was an engineer.

She had never heard of it, nor of its author either.

"Well, you may not have it yet," he told her, "it's just out. It's a novel, a kind of novel. I can't think who published it. It's got a bright yellow jacket."

She found a listing for it, and he ordered two copies. Then, remembering that he had described the book's appearance, she asked if he had already read it. He said he had, and they talked about it for ten minutes and through three interruptions by other customers. Later in the day she prevailed on the store manager to order three copies.

When the books arrived she read the publisher's blurb, which prophesied that "in a very short time all those who pride themselves on discovering new talent will add his name to their list." She felt like a discoverer, remembered Keats's "Homer," and was superior to customers who came in to order best-sellers. In stolen glances at the book she found passages that interested her, and by the end of the day she was asking customers if they had heard of the unusual new book. None of them had and none of them bought it.

A day or two later Louis came in. She was looking toward the door when he opened it, and she watched him as he walked to the desk at which she sat. He was shorter than she had remembered him, hardly taller than she was. He gave her an impression of tautness; his hair was brown, his eyes were brown, his suit was brown, and everything seemed to fit together with nothing left over. He started to smile and she noticed that his teeth were uneven. Within a few feet of her he came to a stop.

"Do you remember me?" he asked.

"Yes—yes, of course—hello. The books came in and I've already read it. It's a wonderful book."

For half an hour, and through a number of interruptions, they talked about the book and other books and other things; and each made private notes and found small details—the shape of an ear or the movement of a hand—to dwell on and return to. Neither used the other's name, and for two weeks they did not see each other.

There had been excitements in Theresa's life, and yet no one of them had given her as much as she was prepared to take from it. She had a sense of her own worth and sought in others for a better sense of their own worth than most of them had. The young men who wanted her were not up to that, not aware of the devotion it held, or perhaps frightened by what too often they couldn't sense. Her years as a liberal-arts major had failed to blunt her sensitivities, and her mind was active still. She sought to probe and to comprehend the thinking of the men she met, and this was either too much for them to bear or too demanding for them to meet. She was, in a word, more mature than the company she kept. But in that summer she was not yet mature enough to have broken with it or to have moved beyond it.

Besides, if her forcefulness caused alarms and trepidations among cautious young men, it also warmed their blood before that. They took her to dances, to sail on the Sound, walked with her at night along the river, sat with her over beer in respectable neighborhood beer parlors. She took what they offered her and wanted more, and wanted most of all to give, as strong-willed people often do. At the time she met Louis, she was turning slowly in upon herself, and she was touched with both the fact and the fancy of despair.

Her first two meetings with him disturbed this turning-in. She dwelt on what her eyes had seen and her ears heard and her spirit felt, but cause and effect down there were too raw to be accepted or clearly acknowledged in the areas of inhibition higher up. She pictured him to herself from time to time. One evening she leaned on the windowsill watching the activity of the street when she might have gone out with her friends. Her life seemed emptier than before, her friends more remote, and she even put aside despair for the more precise occupation of puzzling why these things should be so. She puzzled for a week. When Louis came into the bookstore then, she got up from where she sat and ran to meet him.

Every day they were together more, although these days did not begin for them until Theresa's work ended, and did not go far into the evenings. Most evenings he studied in his room for the degree he would receive a year hence, or worked in a laboratory on an upper floor of the physics building. He had pointed out to her which windows were his, and sometimes, at the window of her apartment five miles down the island, looking north toward where he worked, she would shape in her mind a single frame of light steadily shining in the dark, and behind it creation burning bright.

They were together when they could be, except for the nights beyond the evenings. The circumstances of their lives were not really strict enough to have kept them apart then, nor their temperaments either; yet there was enough strictness in both together to hold unless it were assaulted and time went on and it was not. She found that what she had to give—the wholeness of her heart—he was able to receive and not view warily. And so she gave it all the more. If she saw a dam she felt a pressure, and the days and nights alike were full with one thing and another.

She found he knew things she did not. She learned a little of the nature of the physical world from what he said about his work, and something, she felt, of the nature of mankind, and something of herself, from the way they talked about it. So she came to understand the nature of the Heaviside layer, why Chadwick's discovery of the neutron had been such an enormous discovery, and the difference between science and technology. They talked often of growing up, in Sandridge County, Illinois, and on Riverside Drive, of the likenesses and unlikenesses of their childhoods, of the similarity of people everywhere, of the oneness of life, and of life. But when they got to themselves, the talk was different, less free, merging into silences that held meanings less easy to discuss than the meaning of life.

She spent a night in his room, the very room she had just left, for the first time about two months after they started seeing each other. Theresa had got a raise at her bookstore, and they talked of that. For an hour the tension grew. They moved about and then sat on the daybed, got up, looked out the window, and again came to rest, this time with Theresa lying on the floor, her head on her hands, her legs stretched out. They talked of many things, each more inconsequential than the last, and it happened that Theresa recalled a poem and said a line of it. Louis told her he had once written a poem. She asked him please to say it, and he told her he couldn't. She demanded and he demurred. She asked again, and again he told her he couldn't say it. She lay silent for a while, looking up at him, her head right at his feet. Then she said, "Tell me it." And finally he did, speaking low and evenly:

> "If Death should say: 'I offer you
> A robe of earth, a crown of dew,
> Communion with the roots of things
> And friendship with the blossomings
> Of violet and meadow rue,'
> I think that I should find content
> In going to his tenement.
> But Death says this: 'It's time to go;
> I offer you the dark, the flow
> Of silence and imprisonment
> In clay.' He says: 'Life nears its close,
> Forget the blossom and the rose,
> Forget the things of sound and light,
> Come walk with me into the night.'
> And I must follow. This he knows."

As he said these words Louis leaned back more and more
on the daybed, for self-consciousness compounded his passion into breathlessness; at the end he was all the way back
and wholly out of breath. From this position he could not
see Theresa at all, could see only the ceiling in fact, but
he could feel her head and for a long time it didn't move.

"It's a lovely, lovely poem," she said then, but still no
movement.

"How did you come to write a poem like that?" she
asked after another long time. Then she got up from the
floor and sat down on the bed beside him. He lay with his
arms at his sides, with one hand waiting to be taken, and
she took it. They often walked hand in hand, or made a
point of touching each other or standing with their shoulders touching in much the way that animals nuzzle each
other.

"Everyone writes a poem about death, or thinks one
anyway. But it's not a real poem, you know, it's a trick. I
wrote it to see if I could do it. Do you see what the trick
is?"

"It's a trick to write a poem, but you don't mean that,
do you?—you mean something else."

"I just did this to see if I could do it. I wanted to write
a lyric poem, you know, an emotional poem, without using
emotional words, only nouns and verbs, no adjectives or
adverbs. So I wrote this. There aren't any adjectives or
adverbs in it. It's a trick poem."

Her fingers moved among his fingers, pairing off against
them, pressing them back, intertwining with them; but her
mind followed his words and she looked at him, both serious and amused, to learn from his face if he was telling
the truth.

"But why did you want to do that, I mean write an
emotional poem without emotional words?" Before he could
tell her she laughed. "I suppose it's perfectly clear why,"
she said, "it's the way a scientist writes a poem. But no, it
isn't that, because it's a real poem. 'If Death should say—'
Tell it to me again, Louis.

> *"If Death should say: 'I offer you*
> *A robe of earth—'*

"And what then? I want to know it."

Theresa got a pencil and paper, he said the poem, and she wrote it down.

"Now what you should do is see if it's really best for the poem to leave out adjectives and adverbs." She burst out laughing again. "What a funny way to write a poem!" But then she was serious. "It's a good poem, it's more than a trick, so you have to treat it like a poem, and if it wants an adverb—"

"It isn't the kind of poem that can have an adverb," he objected, "adverbs are for other kinds of poems."

"No sir, that's the scientist speaking, not the poet. You've made a poem and it's a living thing, don't you see?" She bent down to him and kissed him and immediately drew back. "See?" she said. It was the first time she had really kissed him; but at once she lowered her head over the paper with the poem on it, forming the words soundlessly. The kiss was warm on Louis's lips, but still he lay motionless.

"You know, this line's less good," she said, "this line about 'Life nears its close.' Maybe there— What else rhymes with rose and knows? Those—grows—pose—"

"That's true," he said, stirring, "that's true about that line. You know, I did have another line there:

> *". . . He says: 'Forget the rose*
> *And every other thing that grows. . . .'*

"But those are adjectives."

"I like that line better," she said. "I'm going to write it in."

He shook his head. "You're destroying the whole point. There's nothing to this but the discipline of the trick—if you take away the discipline you destroy the meaning. You wouldn't add an extra line to a sonnet just because you happened to think of a nice extra line, would you? You wouldn't have a sonnet if you did."

"You know," Theresa said, "I think you could have it read:

> ". . .'Forget the rose
> And every other thing that grows
> And every sound and every sight.
> Come walk with me into the night. . . .' "

She repeated this and nodded her head approvingly. "There are disciplines and disciplines," she went on. "You might have the discipline of using words with an *e* in them, or maybe words without an *e* in them. That would be a discipline too, but not a very intelligent discipline. What's more important, the poem or the trick?"

"Which is better," said Louis, "a successful experiment or a third-rate poem?"

"A first-rate poem is better than either."

"But it's not first-rate."

"Then it isn't a successful experiment."

In the end they rewrote Louis's poem, although not so very much; it came out with adjectives and adverbs in it, and Theresa gave it an official reading:

> "If Death should say: 'I offer you
> A robe of earth, a crown of dew
> Communion with the roots of things
> And knowledge of the blossomings
> Of rose or weed or meadow rue,'
> I think that I should go content
> To his enormous tenement.
> But Death says this: 'It's time to go,
> I offer you the dark, the flow
> Of silence, and imprisonment
> In endless time. Forget the rose

> *And every other thing that grows*
> *And every sound and every sight.*
> *Come walk with me into the night.'*
> *And I must follow, as he knows."*

When she finished she sat on the edge of the daybed, half facing him, and put the paper aside. "You should be proud of having written that, Louis," she said.

"But it's not mine, it's ours," he answered, and then was flooded with embarrassment. Embarrassment made him crude; he reached up and pulled her to him awkwardly, found her lips and kissed them hard. The embarrassment receded, and the crudity went with it. Theresa, lying flat on her back, her eyes closed, smiled faintly to herself, remembering her question: "What's more important, the poem or the trick?" Well, the trick, she guessed—her trick, not the word trick—but her trick was the poem. And all had been fair.

Coming awake now through the words of that poem and through the sound of some other radio on the threshold of hearing and through the faint rustle of his breathing— which, however, turned out to be her own as the room turned out to be her own and the time turned out to be the present—she remembered how, early in the morning of the day the war began, they had got up from his bed and put their robes on and walked noiselessly down the stairs through Mr Biscanti's silent house, back along the hall to the garden.

At the table by the doorway he had turned to the radio, switched its knob and stood waiting while they looked at each other with sleepy eyes; the dial glowed as the set warmed up but no voice followed. Then, suddenly re- membering, he had turned the little box around and peered into its works, took out a tube, tapped it, and put it back; peered some more, then reached for something dangling from a wire.

"The grid cap's off," he had said. "Precision upset by passion."

He had turned the set off and carefully replaced the cap atop its tube, and then again turned the set on. The glow returned and a moment later came the clear hiss of a broadcasting channel and out of it the words:

"Danzig was fired on by a German battleship an hour ago. Troops have crossed the Polish border."

Six and three-quarters years ago, she thought, and next month the war will at last be over for us. We can go down again in the morning early and turn the radio on again—to records and weather and things like that.

And today is Friday, she thought; maybe I'll hear from him today; I might if he wrote me a letter before he left for Bikini, and he said he would.

One more involvement, just that single one, and then there'll be an end to separation, yes. But the portly figure of Wisla now took shape in her mind and she remembered her worry that he might let the Bikini trip involve him more and more in the work she had come to fear. Wisla and the thought appeared in her mind together; she did not know which had led the other in. She pushed the thought aside, and failed, though she tried, to thrust out Wisla.

He peered at her out of bright, impersonal eyes, as indeed he had looked at her only a few nights before at the Ulanov house. Why did she dislike those bright, impersonal eyes and the owner of them, when Louis so admired him? Well, of course, she thought, silently addressing the portly figure, staring back at those eyes, you are my rival.

"I suppose you are a great man," she said to the figure in her mind. "Louis has great respect for you; he has told me so. I suppose you have a commitment, but I don't trust it or you."

"You are somewhat harsh," she said for him. "I have great hopes for him—even as you."

It was from seeing Wisla, she remembered suddenly, that Louis had come to her on that day of the awful wait at the railroad station, on the day the war began. And you have had him mostly ever since, you and all you stand for, she thought—you and David. But now no more, really no more. She lay looking up at the high ceiling of her room, and even up there she continued to see Wisla's portly figure, "floating above, pure and happy." The phrase came to her from something someone had told her, not Louis, not Wisla, but some figure from the University where Louis had gone to see Wisla that day. She could not bring that figure to mind; she seemed to have forgotten everything about it but this phrase. Thinking of that, half seeing Wisla now, she wished, as she had often wished before, that she could have been with Louis that day. She wished she could have heard whatever this portly, floating Wisla— her rival—had had to say to her lover all those years ago, what siren song he might have sung, what road he might have started Louis on.

Finally the figure receded, his bright, impersonal eyes upon her to the last.

PART 6

1939: a few roads
through the countryside

1

On that first day of September 1939, when the war began, Edward Wisla sat in the chair of the head of the department of physics at Columbia University, his feet on the desk in front of him, his face hidden behind a newspaper. Two or three other newspapers lay on the floor beside him. From time to time he let the paper he was reading fall to his lap, thrummed on an arm of the chair, or stared off into space. Each time he returned to the paper, reading over and over what was said there about the beginning of war. Dr Plaut, in whose chair Wisla sat and on whose desk he had his feet, hadn't come in yet.

"I don't expect him till anyway eight-thirty," his secretary had said. "He made a speech last night. Make yourself at home. Would you like some coffee?"

Wisla was an Austrian, a young man, not yet thirty-three, a little roly-poly in appearance, usually quite diffident in manner. But on other occasions he laughed and joked, clapped people on the back, tried painfully to work unfamiliar slang into his conversation, and was generally puzzling to his friends and, it sometimes seemed, to himself as well. Walter Nernst, who had been Wisla's mentor in the 1920s, would have recognized the mannerism for what it was.

Wisla had studied under Nernst for two years in Berlin, and, like most of his students, had found him the very model of what a rounded man should be. A scholar among scholars, sharp and witty besides, Nernst had done a great deal to shape the massed brilliance of German chemistry and physics for the quarter of a century that began with the Kaiser's patronage of scientific research and flickered out in the fog of the Fuehrer's racism. The Kaiser's interests were military and economic and the scientists were free to live morally within their work, paid for by the money that Emperor Wilhelm II extracted from German industrialists in return for inviting them to state breakfasts and keeping the preserves of the public interest open to them.

Fertilized by the luminous genius of Einstein—whom Nernst had helped to cajole out of Zurich in 1913—the get-togethers of the physical scientists in Berlin paced and prodded man's thinking about the world all through the twenties. German and Austrian scientists took half of the Nobel science prizes in that rich period, and their students took a good many of the rest. Many of Nernst's students went through at least a period in which they tried to model their personalities after his, which was sometimes free and easy, sometimes passionate and vain, and never simple. Wisla, although his modeling was a caricature of the original, seemed to get a grim satisfaction from the effect he produced, and in any event the means by which he produced it had long since become his own.

From Nernst, more importantly, Wisla had learned a

whole repertoire of those laboratory tricks by means of
which the observations and imaginings of inquiring minds
are tested, interpreted, and fitted together into the general
laws of the universe. And he had sharpened his scientific
instincts on Nernst's real passion for knowing the inter-
relations of nature. There were few centers of learning in
the world where he could have learned so well on either
count. At the University of Berlin in the twenties the
swelling cord from Bismarck to Hitler ran through the corridors as well as through the streets outside, and the
cool rigidities of the Prussian approach to science or anything else were there alongside the intuitive, expansive,
even liberal perceptions of many of the scientists. Just as
diffidence and sudden aggressiveness conflicted in Wisla,
so did a kind of tolerance and a kind of stiffness.

After his studies at the university Wisla did some research work for a while, went back to Austria, taught at
Vienna, and spent his hours and days exploring the glim-
mering subworld of radioactivity. In the course of his work
he wrote a dozen papers; the workers of Vienna were
massacred and he hardly heard about it. In Germany and
Italy, where the doom of Austria was being written, his
papers were read with interest and respect. In France they
came to the attention of members of the Curie Institute,
and so it happened that Wisla was invited to come there.

One night in a café a Czech scientist, surprised at Wisla's
ignorance of what had been going on in Austria, told him
a little about it and two years late Wisla burned with anger
and shame. He wanted to leave Paris at once, to go back
to Vienna and fight for freedom, build barricades, separate
Church from State, and much besides. The sophistication
of his colleagues was the rock on which his ardor foun-
dered. They whetted it, baited it, laughed at it, but in the
end, since they recognized better than Wisla the deadly
seriousness of the things that called it forth, they reasoned
and philosophized with him, and, having worked him quickly
up, they worked him slowly down. At the end of his year

Wisla was thinking instead of burning, and his work was better.

A few months after his return from Paris, Wisla made a trip to Salzburg. The day he arrived, and right at the railroad station, he saw Chancellor Schuschnigg, whom he had met once as Minister of Education. Schuschnigg had just come from a meeting with Hitler at nearby Berchtesgaden, and there he was as Wisla got off the train from Vienna. He was sitting in a car, and a dozen people, in and around the car, were talking to him. The bodyguards had quit their functions to gather around the Chancellor's car to listen in. But suddenly they turned and began to shoo the crowd away. At this moment Schuschnigg looked out directly at Wisla with an apparent effort to bring him to mind. Wisla smiled and bowed slightly. When he looked up, the Chancellor was still gazing at him, but the recognition was gone, the eyes were blank, the whole face was dead and stunned. And then a bodyguard reached Wisla and waved him on.

Schuschnigg's near-breakdown, which should have been private, had been so public that within an hour all of Salzburg knew about it, and about the meeting with Hitler that had preceded it. That evening Wisla took the train back to Vienna. Official secrecy was being maintained about everything. Wisla searched out friends and told them what he had seen; they all did a great deal of looking at each other and less talking than usual. So Wisla passed three days, pondering all the time what he would do if— As to that he wasn't sure. He wasn't a Jew, not a trade-unionist, neither a Socialist nor a Communist. He asked himself what could happen to him, and by this question saw that something had happened already.

In the next morning's papers Wisla read that Schuschnigg had turned over the key posts in his cabinet to the Nazis; by evening he had made the decision to leave Austria. From the middle of February to the middle of March, as Austria's thin props cracked one by one, Wisla heard the sounds almost with satisfaction, finding confirmation of the wisdom of his decision.

He was at the radio when the last prop cracked and the waves washed over Austria. In the tempo of a death march, the Austrian national anthem was played, and then the opening bars of the Seventh Symphony. For three hours thereafter—with only occasional interruptions for curt instructions to the people, the army, and others—voices from the days of glory sang Austria to its death: Beethoven, Schubert, Mozart, Strauss. For three hours Wisla sat listening. He was depressed and weak with sentimental feelings, then he was fearful, and then exhilarated.

Shortly before midnight the radio blared forth the *Horst Wessel* song. The Nazis were in the streets and in the Chancellory as well; Schuschnigg was a prisoner. Wisla left his room. He stopped at three apartment houses where friends of his lived; no one was at home in any one of them. He ran into a medical student who had helped him in some of his work; the student stared at him.

"I thought you were leaving."

Wisla told him he had tickets for Paris for two days later. The student continued to stare.

"Did you hear about Professor Baumgarten? He killed himself tonight, with his wife. Have you seen what they are doing to the Jews in front of the Bristol? You'd better—"

"But I'm not—" Wisla stopped himself.

"No, you're not," the student said. "I hope no mistakes are made. Also, I hope the trains are leaving two days from now."

He looked at Wisla a moment longer, then turned and walked quickly away. And Wisla turned and walked quickly away too, back to his room. He reached the South Station a little after one o'clock, and two days later he was in Paris at the Curie Institute.

His old colleagues greeted him warmly, asked him endless questions and finally remembered that a letter was

waiting for him there. It was from Dr Theodore Plaut, at
Columbia University in New York, and it invited Wisla
to join his department: "Baillie is here with us and Cardo
is too . . . we have most interesting plans . . . I am sure you
could contribute a great deal . . . I am sorry the salary cannot be more."

Wisla looked at his watch. It was a quarter to nine. His
thrumming on the chair arm took on a faster beat and he
stared angrily at the door. "Why isn't he here?" he said to
himself. "He's a fool." And then he heard Plaut's voice
outside.

"Theodore!" he shouted.

Plaut carried himself in the self-effacing way that tall
men often do. He looked younger than Wisla and was
actually seven years older; there was a tiredness in his eyes
but not a line on his face. He had on a tweed suit and in
all had a rather tweedy air about him, which he had borrowed from the British, whom he admired. Moreover,
tweeds made him look even younger, and from this he
drew an innocent and increasing pleasure.

"Where have you been?" Wisla demanded. "Haven't you
read the papers? We haven't a day to lose."

Plaut smiled, crossed the room, and sat down in the
chair Wisla had just left.

"Oh, come on. It isn't as bad as all that."

Wisla looked at him coldly. "There are all kinds of scientists," he said, "including even heads of departments.
Humble researchers such as I cannot do everything, but
are we not expected to? You vass not there, Charlie. Shall
I tell you about it?"

Wisla was walking back and forth, striking poses.

"Einstein wrote a letter to the President three weeks
ago. But Hitler stopped the sale of Czechoslovakian uranium two months ago. What is Weizsaecker doing? What
are Heisenberg and Hahn doing? Have you seen a German
physics journal lately? What do the papers say to those

who can read? Mr Hitler shouts from housetops that projects for the fission of uranium are well under way. Close
quotation marks. When will the Einstein letter be delivered? Who has it now?"

"A man who knows the President," said Plaut.

"A man who knows the President. How often does this
man see the President, and also does he read the papers?"

"You know him," Plaut said, "Mr Sachs. He reads the
papers."

"Can't we do things faster, Plaut? I'm most serious. There
is not now truly a minute to lose. Who knows what the
Germans have found out? Einstein himself can only guess.
What do you guess?"

Neither of them said anything for a moment, while Wisla
stood in front of Plaut's desk looking for all the world like
a student waiting for word of an examination result. Pres-
ently he continued.

"Perhaps we are all of us wrong, the Germans and all
the rest of us. It is possible. It may come to nothing. It
does not seem so. And yet it will take a terrible effort to
find out. I wonder if we can—swing it. It will take so much
money."

Again he stopped. And again he and Plaut faced each
other while surmises of the future hung between them.

"And of course people—many people," Wisla added
after a while.

2

From Theresa and the little room in Mr Biscanti's house,
that morning of the day the war began, Louis went uptown
to Columbia. He had an appointment to say good-by, to
receive some words of praise for his work and some coun-
sel on his future. Dr Plaut was a decent fellow, and—best
of all for present purposes—really worked to line up jobs
for the young men on whom he conferred his degrees.

"And what about Plaut?" Theresa had asked a few weeks before, when Louis was telling her about the remarkable minds of Wisla and Cardo and some others.

"Whatever you mean by scientist when you talk about Plaut isn't what you mean when you talk about Wisla. Plaut's up to his ears in a thousand things, Wisla's up to his ears in one. Plaut's an administrator. That's why he isn't really a scientist any more—well, a different kind. It would be interesting to know why he made the change."

"Something for the ego."

"No. I have the feeling it would be the reverse of that."

From Plaut's office Louis could hear the voices as he sat, like Wisla earlier, looking at the papers, reading the stories over and over.

"What's all the talk about in there, Lily?"

"I wouldn't know," she said. "Were you scared at your orals?"

Lily's phone rang, and Louis walked over to the window and leaned his head against it, looking out at the smooth lawn of the campus five floors down, studying the shapes into which the walks cut the lawn. A boy was going along one of the paths with a girl, their legs moving slowly in exaggerated unison. Louis watched them, then turned from the window as the office door opened and Dr Plaut came out.

"Louis, I'm sorry to keep you waiting. Come in, come in."

They talked mostly about what he might do, Plaut sitting at his desk, Louis in the straight chair beside it where he had sat many times before. Wisla walked around the room restlessly, sometimes taking part in the conversation, more often not.

"Now if you were a chemist, Louis," Plaut was saying, "we'd call up Du Pont or Eastman or Dow or somebody and have you signed up for thirty-five hundred or four thousand right away. But a nuclear physicist! The companies don't know what one is. Do you know how many chemists there are in the United States, Ed?"

Wisla grunted. "They are outnumbered only by the English sparrow."

"Well," Plaut said, "I can get you twelve hundred here, Louis—I wish you'd take it. If only there were an instructorship. I do wish you could stay on here. Of course, twelve hundred— You're not married though. Maybe you're not going to get married?"

Louis smiled. "I might."

"Yes," said Plaut. "What does a young man do, Ed? This is not an ordinary young man. This is what a Ph.D. was meant to be and seldom is. Honors at college and he did a first-rate job here, one of the best. Fought a war too. How long were you in Spain, Louis? Six months?"

Louis shrugged. "Four. That wasn't anything."

"So what can I line up for him? A research fellowship here. A teaching job in Montana—that's a western state, Ed. And a couple of odds and ends that are no better."

"The English sparrows shall inherit the earth, is it not so?" said Wisla. "Why not stay with us?"

"Mr Wisla," Louis thought of saying, "to begin with, I don't know. I haven't been home in two years, although what can that mean to you who had to leave your country for good? I want to feel a small town again, my own, to sit on my family's front porch. I must give my father the opportunity to take me into the family business, an opportunity that I shall refuse, but it can't be done by default. Maybe there, from a thousand miles away instead of an inch, I can discover why I don't marry the girl I love. I want to find out why I am leaving, and maybe I will when I have left. As for the twelve hundred dollars, it is not much but it is not the reason."

But he said only that he had not been home in two years, that he would hope for something better to come along.

Wisla listened politely, nodded his head in agreement, and walked to the window, turning his back on them.

"Excellent ideas," he said to the window. "Why do good people always have to have these good thoughts? The dullards stay for their twelve hundred dollars. If they don't become heads of departments, why, they may go on to discover new elements. How many neutrons will a certain panel of that stained-glass window in the chapel release under fission? A trivial matter, a problem for dullards."

Wisla turned away from the window and began walking back and forth.

"It is a funny thing how the real unknown always sells itself so cheaply. It does not show even its ankle for large sums of money, say, ten thousand dollars. Maybe at most up to the knee for six or seven thousand—a titillation for the rich persons, not the real thing. But for twelve hundred dollars, that very minimum of sums—oh boy, oh boy, she stands up naked and waits to be taken!"

Wisla suddenly turned on them, looking from one to the other with the utmost seriousness. Then he laughed loudly, walked over quickly, and slapped Louis on the back.

"You mustn't mind, you mustn't mind!" he shouted. "It's a funny joke!"

He laughed some more, then moved back to the window.

"All true though," he said.

Louis could think of nothing to say. He fidgeted in his chair and looked inquiringly at Plaut.

"Mr Wisla would like a few hundred thousand dollars to advance some projects dear to his heart," Plaut said. "The money not being at once available, he has taken to exalting poverty."

Wisla said nothing. Plaut got up.

"Also he's trying to win a war we aren't in yet."

Wisla stirred and muttered some indistinguishable words.

"As an old warrior, Louis, what do you think? Is this the beginning?" Plaut asked.

"I think so."

"Hah!" said Wisla.

"You think England will fight?" Plaut went on.

"Yes."

"And then what?"

Wisla turned toward them, speaking as he turned.

"What this *diseur* means to ask is whether this war will spread to include us—will the Americans get in it?"

Louis felt as though he had walked in on a private quarrel. But he said yes, he thought the United States stood a very good chance of getting in it.

"Maybe that will take care of my future," he added.

Plaut discounted this; Wisla seemed not to have heard it.

"Of course," he said, "you may get in too late. Even of course, you might be too late right now. Should we thank the complacency of some unmentioned individuals for that?"

He bowed stiffly at Plaut.

"You are very bright, Mr Saxl. Plaut tells me so himself. Also I know it. Also he says just now that you fought in Spain. That I didn't know. You went over and joined up, ha?"

Louis said it hadn't been like that. Right after he'd graduated he'd gone to a scientific conference in Barcelona—his grandfather had left him a little money for his education, he felt it necessary to explain—and he had been there when the war broke out. He had stayed, and staying meant doing something; but as for real fighting—

"Yes, I see. I see," Wisla said. "You saw Germans there, of course."

"No."

"No!" Wisla exclaimed, so indignantly that Louis laughed.

No, he hadn't seen any, but he had seen their planes; they were there all right.

"Well, it will do," Wisla said. "Mr Saxl, tell me what you think. If the Germans march through Poland and then through France and then take England—invasion, surrender, bombings, one way or another, all is possible—she will then have all Europe, yes? And suppose she then has a means for laying waste this country. She would not hesitate to use it, would she, do you think?"

It was a preposterous marshaling of assumptions, Louis reflected, to reach a point that recent history had put pretty well on record. But the question had a seriousness, almost a pathos, as Wisla said it, and Louis answered him straightforwardly.

"No, I guess she wouldn't. Nor any other country, if it stood in her way."

"Thank you very much, Mr Saxl." Wisla bowed. "Your answer is uncomplicated. Perhaps only among ourselves, it is even obvious. Do you know the President?"

"As the object of all this irony," Plaut broke in suddenly, "we thank you for the performance." He laughed with great good nature. "Come on, Ed, we all love you, relax. And Louis—as for you—don't you get obsessions about war putting an end to your work." He put an arm across Louis's shoulder; they were all standing now. "You've got a rare quality, boy, really you have, you know. Ed, you should have been at his orals. Baillie got this young fellow talking about absorption effects in counting those soft betas. Old McGregor threw in a question about end points, and had Louis taken some perfectly elementary correction factor into account. Old Mac just had to prove he was there."

Plaut chuckled benevolently; he still had his arm around Louis's shoulder and they were pacing around, pacing in unison, and Louis thought of the boy and the girl on the campus walk.

"I must say he could have answered the question in ten words and he took ten minutes. You know what orals do to people. Anyway, you were good, my boy. Sit around at home for a while, think about things—a necessity if you can afford it, very desirable if you can't. And let me do a little more work on you. There may be some things—"

Plaut took his arm away and stepped back a little.

"Well, Louis—" And he held out his hand.

Louis and Wisla left the room together. But Louis stopped to say good-by to Lily, and Wisla went right on, out into the corridor, with no word at all. And even as he started toward Lily's desk, Louis wavered; maybe he could have walked on a way with Wisla; it didn't really make any difference about this good-by. His snobbishness shamed him and to make amends he confronted Lily with such familiarity that she looked at him with surprise. He pumped her hand, blew her a kiss, and then, suddenly thinking he could catch up with Wisla, he ran out through the door. Wisla was standing there.

"I was thinking. You go to Chicago on your way home, yes? You are from Illinois?"

"Yes, I—"

"You must know Neimann."

"Well, I know who he is, of course."

Wisla nodded as though this proved his point.

"Of course," he said. "So you call him in Chicago. Tell him I said so. He might know some things better than that Montana place. So—" Wisla bowed and held out his hand "—happy days." He turned and walked rapidly down the corridor. Walking slowly, Louis followed.

From his office window, five floors up, Plaut saw Louis emerge from the building. But Plaut was thinking of Wisla and related matters; in the shoals of his mind a random driftage joined and fragmented and joined again behind the motionless plane of his unlined face:

—and no one more interested than he is about keeping this uranium business quiet; not a word, no publication, he says;

well the journals are full of it thanks to that article of Joliot-Curie's; a high school teacher could keep up with it now if he really wanted to;

what a stink Wisla raised over Joliot's publishing and not just Wisla either I have to say; of course Joliot had a right to;

I wonder if he's a better physicist than his mother-in-law was; who was it, someone was saying that Einstein said Lise Meitner is too; if that is so I've missed it;

Lise, a pretty name;

really what a childish performance; no harm done I suppose but no purpose served certainly;

the British know more than we do about this and I suppose the Germans most of all; Wisla has a point of course;

we've got men as good as Weizborn though; Ottoberger is first-rate but a conceited ass too if you ask me; he's impressive but how can you like him;

what Wisla wants is impossible; I don't think anyone's isolated more than a microgram of 235 and he's talking about pounds;

he's a very clever man; these Germans and Austrians and Hungarians, what accounts for them? but I wonder how much he's thinking as a physicist and how much as a man who had to leave his country; I don't feel quite easy around refugees;

we'd need tons of moderator too, tons of it, purified beyond anything ever just to try for a chain reaction;

I wonder if Bohr is really right and if right practical beyond microscope quantities;

the trouble with me is I never got beyond the routine mathematics of a physicist; I simply never had the taste for those creative constructions;

there wasn't any theoretical physics in this country before the World War always excepting old Gibbs of course, and the great theoretical discoveries still come from abroad;

they come with the abstractors like Wisla and they'll be picked up here by the kids like Saxl, unless we get a war to turn us all into experimenters and mechanics;

I guess Oppenheimer at Berkeley is a really first-rate theoretician though;

the theoretical case for an explosive chain reaction is impressive but the amount of plain mechanical work to be done is prodigious; it seems like a fly moving on the wall could throw things off;

Einstein says a bomb is, what is the word he used, conceivable;

I really doubt it and Wisla is nuts anyway; even Roosevelt won't hand out that kind of money for a chase like this;

millionth of a gram hell, more like a hundred-millionth—

And with the thoughts bobbing in the shoals of his mind, Plaut focused on Louis again, standing now in the middle of a grassy place looking around him. He's bright, Plaut thought, and a really nice kid too; if this uranium thing should actually go through we'd need a hundred like him; I suppose I could get him an instructorship but Lord it would take a push and there just isn't time for everything. If only he weren't a Jew—and mixed up in that Spanish business to boot.

From below Louis looked up, saw Plaut at the window and waved. Plaut waved back, smiled and nodded, and stood watching while Louis disappeared from sight.

3

Theresa had on a pink dress with a flouncy ruffle at the throat, and a wide-brimmed straw hat. She stood by herself on the street in front of the restaurant where she had arranged to meet Louis at one o'clock, and it was one o'clock. The oppressiveness was gone from the air; it was fresh and charged as it had been when they had gone to the World's Fair a few days before. The street was a busy one, only two or three blocks from the terminal. She should have gone inside; instead she stood watching and feeling happy with the activity of the street. She did not notice Louis until he was at her elbow, whereupon she caught his head between her hands and kissed him, and laughed at his self-consciousness.

Because the day was special they had a split of champagne with their lunch, and drank to each other, each relieved that the other did not try to fit words to the

gesture. They wondered together what the situation might
have been that Louis had interrupted; and so they talked
as their gaiety subsided and slowly sifted out of them.

After an hour there was no one else in the restaurant
except three men at the bar near the front door. From the
back Louis and Theresa could hear the drone of their talk,
about baseball and the war and all in familiar words strung
like beads on a single inflection. Theresa grew panicky as
they sat there silent, with only this dull trickle from the
other end of the long room.

They went out into the street; inconsequential talk that
cost no effort came back to them; they scrutinized shop
windows and watched a man opening oysters in the window
of a seafood bar; they shouted aloud together when an
elevated train roared over them, and all the time they held
each other closer; each felt the movement of the other's
legs, regularly, insistently at every step.

They walked the streets near the terminal for half an
hour, and it was nearly three-thirty. They had planned
things the worst possible way, for an hour and a half remained until Louis's train left. Still they walked, stopping
at windows, studying automobiles and wristwatches and
lingerie and books, saying words that now came hard again
and meant nothing at all. At a crossing Theresa stepped
forward into the street and Louis, his eyes on a car coming,
drew her back and half swung her around. Her lips parted
as she brought her face up to his and they kissed, clinging
to each other. A dozen people watched. Nobody knew
quite what to make of it; plainly their passion was too
advanced to be smiled at easily.

They should have gone to a hotel, but neither of them
was accomplished at things like that. At a quarter after four
they were in the station, close to irritability, each seeking
desperately for a word or an action to keep things from
ending this way. They opened their ears to the chatter of
the station crowd, searching for something out of an unknown mouth to help them refocus their feelings. But they

had gone too far within themselves for a random word to reach them, or to serve that purpose if it should.

At four-thirty, travelers began to assemble around the gates to Louis's train. He had two bags and he carried both of them, while Theresa carried newspapers and magazines and a big box of candy corn she had bought him as a joke. They attached themselves to the crowd and after a while the gates opened, sucking them all out of the great vaulted concourse through the narrow passageway into the dark, low-roofed court of the ramps and the quietly waiting trains. Theresa wasn't supposed to go beyond the gates, but she asked if she might so charmingly that the gateman, with an understanding smile for Louis, told her to go ahead. This little play, simple but at least complete, loosened their tensions; and the excitement that always gathers with a moving crowd began to catch them up.

They found his car and put his things in his seat, then walked back onto the ramp, inspected the other passengers, and talked quietly. She patted his tie and he touched her hair under the wide-brimmed hat. He kissed her then, holding her tightly against him, while people brushed past them onto the train.

And so they left each other.

4

For a hundred and twenty-five miles from New York's Grand Central Terminal the trains to the midwest run due north, or used to, along the flat edge of the Hudson River. The western windows look out across the water, first on the stately Palisades and then on the softer Catskills (where once roamed the light and bulky wolves that Darwin wrote about); they unroll a river traffic of barges and sailboats and freighters, and clusters of towns, an occasional castle, and numerous estates. This is the prettiest part of the trip, but the midwesterner returning home by train hardly considers his journey begun until this part is over and the train turns west across the river to begin its penetration of the continent.

The fast trains leave New York (or once they did) on a schedule that brings them to the turn at just about dusk of a late summer day. They pause a moment before crossing the bridge, and then roll slowly over it, from day into night, and out of the arm of the northeast into the whole great body of the land. They stop again at once, for the Albany station, and the traveler may get out to put his feet on this firm ground, or he may lean against the train window looking at the lights sharpening in the city. It is here for the traveler long away that the sights and sounds and smells of home begin to fill his mind again.

In Georgetown, nine hundred miles away, Mr Benjamin Saxl locked the door of his office at his lumberyard, stood a moment gazing about from the top of the three steps leading to the street, and then started off to his home eight blocks away. His mind turned on lumber, on his son's imminent homecoming, on the news of war, and on what there would be for dinner. He greeted and was greeted by numerous friends, themselves coming home from work, or sitting on their porches, or watering their lawns. They congratulated him on his son's success, for they had all seen the little item that his wife had phoned in to the town paper. They changed their expressions to say a few words about the war, citing the prevailing opinion here that it would be over before the United States could be drawn in; the reverberations that could be felt across continents and oceans moved more thinly in the prairie air. One spoke to another, watching him go down the street:

"You know, he never says a word about what's happening to his people in Germany."

"No, I've never heard him."

"It must be a burden to him."

"They don't make them any better than Ben Saxl. I don't mean just for a Jew either."

It wasn't a burden to him though. Precisely because it was a terrible thing to think about, he didn't think about it. His wife did. He knew she sent money to organizations in New York, to funds and appeals, but he seldom discussed these things with her. He thought Hitler a monster, as who did not, and felt sorry for the Jews of Europe and the Czechs, and now the Poles. But the virus and the tissue of these far-off happenings were invisible to him, and the Jews were as remote as the Poles.

A block before his house he came upon his daughter, a dramatic little figure pumping furiously on her bicycle to meet him. Her hair was black, her arms and legs were golden-brown, and she had on brilliant white shorts and an orange sweater. She was fourteen, but she looked a year or two older, and she was capable of acting much more than that depending on the needs of an imagination that the circumstances of her life fell short of satisfying. Today she was playing sister to her brother, and in the privacy of her room, before the mirror that knew her well, this role had produced overtones of his mistress.

But in the street she showed only a child's excitement together with an extra measure of devotion to her father, whose virtues were enlarged by the occasion. She called out that Louis's wire had just come, that her mother had only that moment received it over the phone, and that she herself had computed Louis's arrival as twenty-one hours away. Wheeling her bicycle, dancing ahead of him, she led him down the street and across the lawn to their house.

That evening, after the dinner dishes had been washed and put away, the Saxl family gathered on the porch that ran across the front of the house and part way around one side. At the corner a swing hung by chains; three or four wicker chairs, a little wicker table, and two flower stands were grouped nearby. There was nothing else on the porch except Libby's bicycle, a broken rocker waiting for a day of repair, and some garden tools around at the side.

Mr Saxl came out first, adjusted the largest chair imperceptibly, gazed along the street, hitched his trousers

up, and sat down. In a few minutes Libby appeared; she
had a kitten in her arms, and she stroked it gently and
murmured to it. She sat in one corner of the swing and
fixed her eyes on the ceiling. It was nearly dark. A screen
door banged on another porch and a murmur of voices
rose and fell away. Mrs Saxl appeared, stood by the door
for a moment, then walked quickly across to the swing.
She was a large woman, taller than her husband and heav-
ier; but her figure rose from small feet and slender ankles,
which seemed too slight to support her and lent a precar-
ious, awkward grace to her movements. She leaned down
to stroke the kitten and sat, her hands in her lap.

"Will Louis go to war?" Libby asked.

"Heavens! I hope not. I don't think so. I hope none of
them have to." Mrs Saxl sighed, moved, and the swing
creaked.

"He might be dead in a year," Libby said.

"Libby! Don't say such things!"

"Well, he might—if he goes to war."

Her father made a gesture, more felt than seen. "He's
not going to war, child. It'll be over soon."

"He went once."

"A very different thing that was. He didn't really—"

"He got hurt," said Libby.

"Yes." Her father lit a match and applied it to the cigar
he had been holding. The circle of light touched Mrs Saxl's
face; her lower lip was pushed up and she was looking at
her husband. "Yes, he did," said Mr Saxl.

The cigar glowed, the swing creaked, Libby put the kitten down. "I've never seen a dead man," she said, and her
voice was infinitely remote.

"What on earth has got into you?" Mrs Saxl demanded.
"A lovely day and a nice dinner—we were all so happy
then, you particularly—and now, death and war. We won't
talk this way any more, no more now. We'll talk about
tomorrow and what we're going to do."

Libby neither moved nor spoke; and abruptly her mother
added:

"Besides, you have. You saw your grandfather."

"No, I didn't. I didn't look."

"Well, now, dear," Mr Saxl said, "you're not helping matters any."

She laughed—a rich, pleasant sound—and confessed that she was not. And they began talking of tomorrow; they might have a surprise party; what could they do?

"You feel quite sure about this war?" Mrs Saxl asked her husband later. He told her why he did but there was nothing new in it to her. "I'm terribly disappointed by the Russians," she said. "Despite everything, I thought—and now who knows what to think? I'm afraid for Louis, Ben, oh, and for all of them. They're all babies."

"I just can't figure out what he plans now, he hasn't said a word to go on," Mr Saxl remarked; he had dismissed the war. "It would be a good thing if he settled down, but I don't suppose Georgetown—"

He did not know what to say for sure. What did a Ph.D. do? Teach? Could he live by that? Might he still come into the business? They would talk one day soon. He looked at his watch, craning to see it in the glow from the lamp in the living room. "Nearly ten-thirty—well." He yawned and scratched his side, reached out and patted his wife's cheek. "Ready?" he said.

After the train left, Theresa wandered across 42nd Street, went into a theater and sat motionlessly inattentive through a mystery movie, a newsreel, and a cartoon. On the street again she thought of dinner, started into a restaurant, and suddenly lost interest. She watched the electric sign on the Times Building for a while; the letters flashing across it told of German successes in Poland, of British cabinet meetings, of baseball scores and the weather. A man spoke to her and she let him talk, but he was callow, became wary of her openness, dull before her abstractedness, and soon moved on; she hardly noticed when he left.

When she got home she sat for a long time leaning against the window, watching and listening to the life on the street. She noticed after a while that she was shaking, and she turned from the window and walked around the room in the dark. The sound of her footsteps was loud to her and so she took off her shoes, but she continued to walk, stopping and peering through the window for a moment, then walking on again, circling the room.

She stopped in front of a small table and slowly, almost without thought, pushed an ashtray onto the floor, where it broke; she kicked the pieces and trembled at the sound.

He will never come back, she said to herself. I'll see him five years from now at a convention and he will show me pictures of his wife and children.

Something had gone wrong, leaving still the core that there was no other and nothing else she wanted. What should she do? And after a while she said the words aloud, "Break the core." In the internal dialogue that followed she pondered the how of doing this and concluded that she didn't know enough. But anyone can break a core, she told herself; you break a core the way you break an ashtray, you give it a push, you smash it. She paced around the room again, testing this thought. It's true, she decided, picking up the pieces of the ashtray as she paced; you don't have to smash the core, you can remake it, add to it, build it up, give it a different shape. That's what he's been doing all this time, she decided. And if he can do it, so can I.

It was after midnight when she sat down to write him the letter she had promised to write that very night. It was nearly three when she finished the fourth draft, tore up the first three, and put her letter in an envelope. She had never written him a letter before—they had never been apart—and she wasn't wholly sure that she had written him a letter so much as a manifesto, or perhaps she had simply written a letter to herself.

In the club car of Louis's train, moving out of the Genesee Valley toward Buffalo, the radio was scratchy and its information all but lost in the loud business of the train's movement. The eleven o'clock news round-up came on, and a man set his watch by it; people playing poker at one of the tables shifted expectantly, cupped their ears, and held their glasses to stop the steady tinkle they made. Louis listened as the announcer told of German successes, of the destruction of Polish towns from the air, of the beginning of the bombardment of Warsaw.

He had told Wisla that he had never seen a German while he was in Spain, but suddenly, out of the montage of pictures the announcer's voice was making in his head, came a German face that he had seen and forgotten. This face belonged to the pilot of a light bomber that Louis and every other gunner in his sector had shot at and missed one day, had cursed and reluctantly admired. He had detached himself from a group of three flying high overhead, and had come down in a great sweep almost to the house-tops. And then he had buzzed back and forth and around for fully five minutes, slipping once in a sharp turn directly over Louis's station. He was close enough for Louis to see him, and he seemed to be rubbering out through the hood, like a sightseer.

The guns were firing, but there weren't many, and most of them were old and inefficient. The German left with a string of fancy rolls and a sharp spiraling climb and took that day's morale with him; the casualness and the control that combined to make the flaunting brilliance of the feat had left Louis feeling lumpish and inadequate, and he had a revival of the feeling, remembering.

And the recital of the German advance, in the unreal cadences of the radio voice, against the clicks and rumbles of the train, made it seem that the whole German air force was performing a kind of gigantic barrel roll over Poland, dropping bombs incidentally, killing people and destroying towns incidentally, peering out at the scene with curiosity, and making all the right turns at the right time.

At the Illinois State Fair in Springfield, years ago, he had once or twice watched barnstormers from flying cir-cuses, and had automatically searched within himself for the resources to perform such tricks; he had left these exhibitions with the lumpish feeling too, as though he had been tried and found wanting. Even the exploits of characters in novels and heroes in movies sometimes made him feel that way. As a boy he had been ecstatic on discovering from his grandfather's encyclopedia that Shelley, the greatest poet in the history of the world, had also been a chemist; he, Louis Saxl, had written poems, and he was going to be a scientist of one kind or another too, and he had felt uneasily that the fact and the intention were flaws in each other. But Shelley! The discovery had sanctified him for a moment, and then had taken away all hope.

The news went off and conversation started in little islands here and there within the car, but none of it included Louis, who held a book before him although he was not reading. His thoughts moved in slow cycles from Wisla in New York to Neimann in Chicago, from Theresa in New York to his family in Georgetown, from his past to his unknown future, from Spain to Poland, and from night to morning. Midnight in America, he suddenly said to himself—dawn in Europe, he added, if only by the clock. The face of the German pilot came back to him, and hung in his mind vividly. He got up and moved out into the narrow, shaking corridors of the cars, and walked through three of them to reach his own.

He found himself puzzling again over what Wisla and Plaut had been bickering about. It had had something to do with the excitement over uranium fission, he could be sure of that. You can be sure, he thought, that any time you see two physicists together these days they're not far from that; it's the glamour theme of 1939, all right. He turned out the little light in his cubicle, raised the shade, and stared out into the darkness. It was perfectly possible, he reflected, that an awful lot more was going on in the fission business than was dreamt of by him; the fact was that his work of the last year toward a doctorate was not designed to keep anyone much in touch with anything but that. The nuclear isomers—now, if anyone wanted to know about isomers he would be happy to tell them. He smiled suddenly from the recollection of a silly fight he had had with Theresa months before, on an evening when he had been full of nuclear isomers and she had tired of them.

"Sometimes I think Ortega may have a point," she had said abruptly.

"Ortega?" he had inquired warily, sensing attack, too doubtful of his own knowledge of the Spanish philosopher to trust Theresa's.

"When he said the modern scientist runs the risk of becoming the modern barbarian," she had informed him with every evidence of objective interest in a concept above and beyond them both.

But they were talking politics more than physics, he thought, returning to Wisla and Plaut. Had someone heard something new about the German work on fission? Maybe it was that. There were all kinds of theoretical prospects, of course; there had been theoretical prospects for years, and certainly the theories were more sophisticated now than once they were; but my God! did they think, did somebody really think, had somebody really done something—for *now*?

At the ____ Center, one of several camps maintained by the French for those Spaniards who fled across the border at the end of the Spanish war, a man came out of a long, low, weather-beaten building—almost black in the faint light of dawn—and walked slowly across to a little outcropping of scrub vegetation. He opened his trousers and urinated; he watched himself for a moment, then looked up at the streaks of light emerging in the east and over the bushes to the mingled weeds and rocks and sand that stretched out of sight to the Mediterranean. He listened to the soft surf, though the sea itself was not visible.

A second figure emerged from the building and walked over toward the first. "Gustavito? Is that you?"

"Yes."

The newcomer, a smaller man, said nothing, but continued on until the two stood together within a few feet of a straggly wire fence. The fence was intended to contain them and two thousand or so compatriots, but it had been allowed to fall into disrepair. The men here had no papers, no money, no hopes.

"What you were saying about the war news yesterday. You're wrong, Gustavito."

"I said nothing has happened. Or, if so, not enough. In any event, what?"

"Everybody—"

"Don't bother. I believe there is a pact. I believe the Soviets signed. I even believe the Nazis have invaded Poland. This is not nothing, to be sure. Thousands will die. Well, if they are going to die, then there should be a war— not for people to die in, but to stop the killers. How else? Will they never get around to it?"

"You might ask it of your Russians."

"Ah, 'my Russians.' I am brokenhearted at that. Not at what they did, but that they had to do it."

"Gustavo, you said nothing was going to happen. That is what you said. Which is to say that the English and the French will do nothing, nor the United States. But you—"

"The United States? Well, what do you expect them to do?"

"I—well, sooner or later, if it goes far enough, they will wake up."

Gustavo looked at his companion with contempt.

"Do you really mean to say a thing like that?" He paused, staring at his friend. "I guess you do, despite everything. It beats me, but I guess you do." He sighed. "Oh, Jesus. Do you think they have been asleep that they will wake up? God Jesus, must you have it rammed inside you, twisted, turned and broken off before you feel it? When do you wake up? Who shot your friends? With whose bullets? Bought with whose money? Oh, Christ!"

The other man, plainly, had endured such tirades before from his friend. He picked up a little stone and tossed it in his hand, looking covertly at Gustavo from time to time, saying nothing. And Gustavo looked steadfastly away.

"Despite your talk," the smaller man said finally, "I know these things as well as you. Who doesn't? Still, you have to forget the Americans who helped us, several thousand of them. There was a young fellow I came across right at the beginning. He was an American. I don't think you met him. His name was Saxl. He didn't come for any purpose except to take part in a convention of some people, scientific people, including Professor Narvaez. Certainly you know Narvaez, he's a great man, or was. I used to see him often, although I didn't know him. His left arm was shorter than his right."

"Who didn't know Narvaez?"

"Well, when the bastards started, this convention was going on. This young fellow Saxl—he was a student, of no standing, but it was an important convention—doctors and professors and so forth from France and England too. Well, you know, most of them left. But this Saxl I'm telling you about, an American, an innocent too, didn't go away. He was about twenty, maybe nineteen, a nice-looking fellow. It's sometimes hard to tell how old Americans are. Well, he could have left, but he stayed."

Gustavo had sat down on a little outcropping of rock. His legs were spread apart, his fly was still open, and a patch of underwear showed through. He seemed wholly listless and was still looking away across the fence and the sand leading out to the sea.

"Well," the smaller man went on, "he became an anti-aircraft gunner. Just imagine that. You must understand this, like you used to understand such things. This young Saxl was not a very good anti-aircraft gunner as it turned out. Still, he made one or two hits, or may have. Some of us thought he shouldn't be doing this, I don't mean because he didn't hit many—most of us had to learn—but because he was trained for being a scholar, and this was not the best way to use scholars even at the time. Well, he said an interesting thing, because this was discussed from time to time, he said, and this is just the way he said it, he said: 'Not so, I've got a stake in this laboratory too.' "

"Laboratory? What laboratory?" Gustavo said.

"Why, the laboratory at the university. Didn't I tell you? The convention was held there. It's gone now, Gustavito."

"What was this fellow?"

"Well, I told you, didn't I? A scientist. An American—"

"Yes, well, what's so special about what he said?"

"For a young American not more than twenty-two at most? You—"

"Well, what became of him?" Gustavo interrupted, still looking away.

"They dropped one nearby and he was hit by a piece of it. He was in the hospital and then they made him go home."

"Who made him go home?"

"The Ministry of War, at the suggestion of the Anti-Aircraft Command, University Sector, at the suggestion of Professor Narvaez and four or five others."

"Why? Couldn't he fight any more?"

"Well, not for a while, but that wasn't the reason. The reason was he didn't belong here. He should be doing his work, Professor Narvaez said so himself. Also, he might be able to tell them in the United States—"

"Did he?"

"Well, I don't know as to that. But that isn't the point. You knew Americans like this too."

"Yes, I knew some," said Gustavo. "I've seen bombs that didn't explode and bees that didn't sting. I am pleased every time these things happen, but Spain is rotting there—" he waved his arm— "and idealistic young scientists aren't stopping the bastards. No, nor their countries that trade with them either. That's for us to do, you and me, rotting here at the water's edge." He got up, but abruptly sat down again. "Let me be here, let me be, I'll see you later on."

Still holding a stone in his hand, shaking it around, the smaller man moved off, walking slowly, toward the building from which they had come, a dirty gray now under the morning sun. And the other one sat quietly, looking out across the fence and the sand stretching away, as one sits in contemplation of mysteries. Then he reached in through his open fly and began to move his hand in a methodical fashion.

Down from Buffalo Louis's train rolled on, along the curve of the shores of Erie, out across the flatland of the little one-street towns, all wrapped in darkness, all silent except for the crossing bells. In New York Theresa slept; the fingers of one hand, palm down on the unused pillow, gently moved from time to time. In New York Plaut slept and Biscanti slept, but Wisla was awake, reading quietly under the lighted lamp in his hotel room with shared bath. In Georgetown the Saxls slept, and in the French camp the Spaniards came forth as the sun rose higher. In the darkness of his berth Louis slept and was awake by turns.

5

Three days after Louis reached Georgetown from New York a letter came from Neimann:

> Dear Mr Saxl—I have pleasure in writing to you. You know about the plans for the University cyclotron—this will be quite important. There can be an opening for you for $1500, I am sorry no more. Mr Wisla tells me you plan to go to Montana. I believe this will be more important. I trust you will join us and am sending forms for that purpose. Our term starts October 1.
> Sincerely,
>
> Conrad Neimann

So Wisla had got in touch with Neimann. As to why, no explanation would fit. The cryptic talk in Plaut's office the day he had left came back to him, but still it meant nothing. And anyway it couldn't have had anything to do with him, he concluded, feeling sure that it had. But what arrogance; Wisla hardly knew him, Neimann knew him not at all, and his own department head hadn't been able to line up much of a job for him. How could there possibly be any hidden meanings to a $1500-a-year research job?

For his first week at home he did virtually nothing. The broken rocker on the porch offended his sense of order, so he fixed it. His mother was reminded that a pair of her reading glasses needed fixing too. The frame was loose at one hinge; it was a more complicated job than the rocker, and Louis worked at it one afternoon, sitting on the porch with his mother.

"This very beautiful science," he murmured, testing the strength of the hinge delicately with a cumbersome pair of old pliers.

"What is that, Louis?"

"It is the flower of the whole of philosophy, and only through it can the other sciences be known."

"What are you talking about?"

"I'm speaking of optics, Mr Bacon's beautiful science. That's what he said. A rough epitome; behold." He held the glasses up.

His mother looked at him fondly.

"My boy has really learned a great deal, hasn't he?" she said. She wanted him to go on and tell her of beautiful sciences, and she would have paid as little attention as possible to his words, the better to concentrate on his expressions, to study the shape of his head, to watch the movement of his hands, to remember as she watched, and to bring him back again to the things she remembered. But he was not yet at ease enough with himself to cope with such remarks; he fell silent in the face of them, or looked at her exasperatedly, or at best made a joke of them and then fell silent anyway.

In the evenings, on the porch, the talking was easier. To the creaking of the swing and the soft blend of leaf sounds and other voices on other porches, Louis's rapt audience learned, in bits and pieces, enough to give them the impression of a picture of Theresa and Wisla and Mr Biscanti, of university life and life in what they understood to be Greenwich Village, of the study of the physical sciences as they were taught near the end of the fourth decade of the Twentieth Century, and of the immense distance to which circumstance and inclination had removed a member of their family.

"But you're still my baby," said Mrs Saxl. And in the evening light Louis could answer, gently enough, and go on.

"Are you very fond of her?" she asked.

"Yes," said Louis.

"I suppose you've thought of marrying?"

"I know I have."

"Are you sure it would work?"

"You mean because she's not Jewish? She has no feeling about that and neither do I."

"Yes," his mother said, "but that's not all there is to it."

"You and father wouldn't object, would you? It's not as though we're any of us very religious."

"Well, I for one can't answer that," she said. "I've not met her, you know."

"You know what I mean—I mean in principle."

"I've known marriages like that to be bitterly unhappy. Still, some work out, some do. It depends on—oh, I don't know—many things."

"But if he loves her?" Libby inquired.

"Oh, dear, we shouldn't be talking like this in front of Libby. Go somewhere, Libby."

And once when Mr Saxl and Libby were not on the porch with them:

"Louis, tell me, you've lived with this girl, haven't you?"

Louis sat silent for a moment, and then smiled across at her.

"I'm sure you aren't shocked by that, and I guess you know it."

"You've never told me, how should I know it? You've really told me very little about this. Louis, are you being fair to the girl?" He made no answer; his mother studied him a bit, sighed and went on. "Besides, I am shocked, at least it's nothing I've ever run up against before, and I can think of some people here in town—heavens, if they knew!"

The talk was never satisfactory on the subject of the lumber company either. From time to time, in the guise of reporting on events of his day, Mr Saxl raised questions about the business and asked Louis for his opinions, or told a story to illuminate some aspect of the business. Up to seven or eight years before Mr Saxl had assumed without question that his son would one day, in proper time, come into his business with him. He had doubted it progressively through Louis's college years, had known it would never be at least since the last of those years, had never said a word about it in all this time, and yet even to this moment had not once thought that it wouldn't have to be gone into, formally and officially, sometime. In the first days after Louis's return home the subject was shyly and tentatively laid on the table where it could be seen and perhaps picked up, until it might grow more familiar to both of them.

One afternoon Louis went downtown and ran into Chuck Braley, the high school friend with whom he'd once made pushmobiles. They went into a bar, looked each other up and down, and marveled at the predictableness of life.

"Set 'em up, Henry, bourbon for me!" Chuck slapped Louis on the arm. "Well, boy, tell me all about it. What's the dope on this war? Where do we all go from here? You're set, aren't you, boy? A Ph.D. and all?"

Louis mentioned Neimann's letter and the salary.

"Fifteen hundred lousy bucks!" Chuck exclaimed, horror in his voice. "Why, so help me, you could beat that right here in the high school, I'll bet. You sure could with a company. Tell 'em to stick it up, Louis. Why, hell, you've got enough savvy to get three times that with a company. That's what Skip Seago did."

"Tell me about Skip. We used to figure out life together."

"He's doing OK for himself now, I'll say. Haven't you seen him? You used to be pals."

"I don't think I've seen Skip in five years. Is he still with the gauge company?"

"The gauge company! Why, Jesus, boy, haven't you even heard what he's doing? Say, you really gotta pay him a visit. How about it, boy, right now?"

Chuck went to the telephone and was back in a moment to announce that Mr Seago would be delighted to see them. They rode in Chuck's car out past the edge of town, where they would find—but as to that Chuck made only mysterious hints.

Where they would find, Louis thought—while Chuck gossiped about everyone in town, demanding no answers—the authoritative idol of his childhood, who, on quiet nights of sitting on the boulevard or just beyond the spread of an old cottonwood tree on the Seago lawn, had expounded many mysteries. But in the week or so that he had been home he had not thought to ask about him. He was puzzling over this when Chuck poked him.

"Look up, my boy, look up. We are here."

"What is it?"

"Read the sign."

Louis saw no sign. He saw an island of wondrously neat and landscaped lawn carved out of the cornfields that lined the road here, and far back at the end of the island an immaculate structure of white brick. It was low, blocky and unbroken except for a single smooth line of windows that went around its walls in a belt of glass and steel, and was so white that it shimmered in the sun. Dark green shrubs were set against the lighter green of the grass. No door was visible. But as the car moved slowly past this incongruous clearing, a group of cars parked behind the building came into view, and Louis noticed a white gravel road leading away from the highway; it ran alongside the far edge of the lawn unobtrusively, as though the planners of the temple had resented and hence obscured this means of access. At one side of the roadway stood a small sign; white letters on dark green said: CABOT CHEMICALS.

"Cabot Chemicals," said Louis.

"Cabot Chemicals," said Chuck, "put half a million bucks into this little setup."

He swung the car across the highway onto the white road, and the wheels crunched the gravel crisply. "They don't tell you on the billboard, but this here is a division of Lowe & Waterson, which makes everything and more besides. It's an experimental laboratory. And do you know who the executive assistant to the guy who heads it up is? Mr Vernon Seago, your friend and mine."

"I'll be damned," said Louis, while Chuck nodded approvingly. "What do they experiment on?"

"Skip'll tell you," said Chuck; and, turning the car in a graceful circle, he brought it to a stop beside the others against a neat white rail.

From the rear the experimental laboratory of Cabot Chemicals, division of the great Lowe & Waterson, Inc. and Ltd., disclosed some ties to the working world—a loading platform, two trucks, and a railroad spur stretching away through the fields on a manicured roadbed. Chuck and Louis walked over to a simple, handsome, dark-green door that was obviously the official entrance because there was no other. It opened into a little room that held only cleanness, and that room opened into a large room furnished with blond wood chairs and a blond young woman who smiled at them at once.

"I remember you. You're a friend of Mr Seago's. Does he expect you?"

Louis thought it would have been fitting if a page boy had come forth to transfer them from the lesser presence to the greater, but the young woman led them herself down a clean white corridor paved with dark-green linoleum, and at an open door they stopped. She spoke into the room. "Francy, the two gentlemen to see Mr Seago."

But Mr Seago himself came forth. He took their arms and walked them into his own office, which was blond and white and green and provided a view of the smooth sweep of the lawn and of the corn that stretched away in strong, straight lines beyond the highway. Seago had grown into a thin, poised but nervous young man with lines forming deep around his mouth (a doctor could have predicted imminent ulcers at a glance); he was plainly proud of the cornfield temple and unduly modest under Chuck Braley's admiring prods.

"Say, is that the truth," Chuck asked, staring through the windows, "it's gonna cost five thousand smackers just to keep the lawn mowed?"

The question seemed to annoy Seago. "Oh, hell, I don't know," he said. "It's a kind of advertising, so what?"

A small, framed card hung alone in a corner and Louis leaned over to read it: "Never say a thing can't be done. You may be interrupted by someone saying, 'I have done it.'" The words were printed; in ink beneath them was the name "Keith Jessup." Louis found Seago looking at him with an expression so compounded of cynicism and sheepishness that Louis laughed. "Who's Jessup?"

"The boss," said Seago. "Forgive him his sins, he's really a bright guy, wonderful to work for. Engineers are a curious breed, particularly when they have to be executives. Is it the same with scientists, Louis? Platitudes and prejudices for one world, the world they don't really live in, and the most painstaking analyses for the other. Jessup—" But Seago stopped with that and there was silence for a moment.

"Yes, I suppose so," Louis said. "What's the analysis for putting all this way out here in the prairies?"

Seago smiled and shrugged his shoulders. "There's a lot

of little plants like this in the east. I don't know—a company like this can afford to play heavy on hunches; the big outfits can get things done. We're interested in some extractions from silage, some possibilities for synthetics. They might work out, might not. Well, so Lowe gambles."

Seago teetered on his chair, stared at the pencil that he was turning slowly in his hand, and then without looking up addressed himself to Chuck.

"I told Eddie Brinckerhoff you were coming out, Chuck. He said he wanted to see you."

"OK, I'll give him a look."

Seago gave Chuck a friendly little push as he left, and then went over to the window.

"Chuck told me over the phone about your looking for a job. I don't know what you think about it, Louis, but I think a guy who plugs for a Ph.D., a real one like yours, not a thesis on ways to save steps in the kitchen—I think he deserves more than fifteen hundred a year and it's one of the tragedies of the century that he doesn't get it. I thought for a while I'd plug for one myself, and I know that's one of the reasons I didn't. I'll always regret it, but I'm going to regret it in comfort. Maybe you don't mind. On the other hand, maybe you do. And I'm saying all this because first of all I want to find out if you do. Do you?"

Seago spoke perfectly easily, even smoothly, and with the last words he turned around and faced Louis. The shadings of nervousness were wholly gone; it seemed to Louis that Skip had begun to speak as though from a score, which called for a turn at just that point, and Louis felt lumpish again, almost as he had on the train.

"Well, yes, I do, of course. None of the universities pays much, as you know. I'll never get rich, and if you mean do I mind that, why probably not so long—so long—"

"How does one explain what he means, particularly to an old friend with whom he used to ponder the mysteries of life?" Seago stopped and smiled—he had a warm, friendly smile—and then began walking slowly around the room. "You embarrass me a little, Louis, you know. I respect what you've been doing and what you are, perhaps I envy you some too. I've heard about you from time to time— people think very well of you here, you know. Sometime I'd like to hear what happened in Spain, but— You're not mixed up in any Red stuff, are you, Louis? Some people got that notion. I told them—"

"Because I went to Spain?"

"Because you stayed there. But it's not important, you're not the only one who doesn't think so much of Franco. How old were you anyway—twenty-one—twenty—?"

"Twenty-two," said Louis, abruptly enough to attract Seago's notice, "but don't justify me on that count. I stayed because it was hard to get out, but once I stayed I was glad I did. And it wasn't Franco nearly so much as it was the Germans, the same Germans as now."

Seago looked at him with something like compassion, or so Louis thought, and the thought irritated him. I know what that expression means, he said to himself, I have seen it many times; it means I am being listened to as a Jew— and it means right now that I am being "understood" about Spain.

"Which isn't to say," he said aloud, "that Franco isn't bad enough."

"I know how you feel," Seago said. "I don't blame you." He resumed his pacing. "But it's not the important thing, Louis, not for anyone like yourself. You've just come through one of the best science departments in the world, kid. I used to know Plaut; he was at Urbana before he went east, and what he gives you you can sell. Don't give it away, don't sidetrack it, and don't bury it in a lousy fifteen-hundred-a-year trap that you'll never get out of." Seago smiled down at Louis. "Words of wisdom from Uncle Vernon," he said, and then suddenly swung himself into a chair directly facing Louis. "There's one thing. Can I talk to you frankly about this one thing?"

Louis smiled to Seago's smile and nodded. Let us talk frankly, he said to himself, but let us keep our powder dry.

"I don't really know too much about you now," Seago went on, "but I know you're a bright boy. I'd like to get you here. I've talked to Jessup about it already, a little bit, and he's interested, as he damn well ought to be. This place is his baby and he's on the make. So am I, for that matter, and I don't mind saying it. We've got to build up a staff and bright boys don't grow on trees."

Seago was up again. "I'm putting it to you straight, Louis, and it don't sound so glamorous this way, but it could be, it could be. This is a hell of a big company and this little piece of it is a good place to get a toehold—if it pays off."

Louis felt cramped; he shifted in his chair and noticed the slight crackle of paper in his coat pocket as he moved—Neimann's letter. He couldn't have said why he was carrying it, but the fact that it was there struck him as funny and made him feel fond toward the letter. He shifted again and looked inquiringly at Seago.

"Louis, if you want to make your work count, this is where the future is. I can only propose, of course; Jessup disposes. But he sees how young guys like you can fit in. There's one thing. Now, take this the right way, kid—"

Seago stopped by his desk, and ran a finger around the outline of a picture pressed beneath the glass. "Jessup's a—well, he's an engineer—practical, a little limited on some things, a little— I'll give it to you straight, Louis. Jessup shoots his face off about Jews. He doesn't know what he's talking about in things like this. And he doesn't really mean anything by it. He'll like you a lot, I know. And you'll like him, when you get to know him for what he is. But can you—handle that sort of thing, Louis?"

Louis reached into his pocket for his package of cigarettes, but when he drew it out he felt, without looking, that his hand was trembling, and so he put it back.

"Louis?"

"I understand, Skip. I know how it is."

Seago reached across and patted Louis on the shoulder. "That's the spirit, kid, first things first."

Louis's eyes moved around the room, across Seago's face, to the window, to the door.

"—tomorrow, next day at the latest—" Seago was saying.

"That'll be fine, Skip."

In the car going back to town Chuck probed to find out what their talk had led to. From answers that he judged evasive and from the quietness of Louis's manner, he concluded that Seago had decided not to press the question of a job. He felt sorry about this, but not for long. He drove Louis right to his house, chatting and gossiping, and they ended the afternoon as they had begun it, for by then the warmth of recollection was coming back to Louis too.

6

The next day was a beautiful day, just touched with the crispness of the fall to come, but warm and glowing and with the smell of earth and maturing corn in the breeze. At breakfast Louis borrowed the family car and invited Libby to drive over to the University of Illinois with him. It was not much more than an hour's drive on one of the smooth roads that stretch across this part of the state for miles with hardly a curve or bend. He knew half a dozen people at the university; he might find out something about what was going on at Chicago.

The road to the university was bounded on both sides by rows of corn, on which the cobs were beginning to stand out from the stalks and the tassels were silvery; and widely separated houses and barns, regularly white and red; and occasional farmers standing or working among the assorted paraphernalia of their yard, with chickens running and pecking at their feet and the cows off behind them. There were only three or four little towns along all this road, each of which announced itself with a white sign: White Hall 1800, Pleasant Plains 900, Menard 2200. The road ran straight through them all, under an arch of trees for a few blocks, past old houses behind wide lawns, past shiny store fronts and dusty cars, and then out through the pastures and fields of corn again.

Libby, familiar with all this, tucked her legs up on the seat and fixed her eyes on her brother. She was as gossipy as Chuck Braley, twice as curious, and full of excitement at the prospect of seeing the university with such a distinguished guide. She sang a lurid song that she had learned at school, told stories about her teachers and schoolmates, tried to find out more about Theresa, and shocked Louis with a broadness of understanding of which he had detected no hint the last time he had seen her.

From a drugstore just inside the town Louis called Eugene Voss, a Hungarian two or three years older than himself who had left Europe as many others had since 1934, had worked in England for a year, and then had come to the United States to take his degree. They had seen a good deal of each other in New York, although their opportunities had been circumscribed by Voss's boredom with movies, plays, social gatherings, or anything at all that enforced silence or diluted conversation; besides, he never had a penny and was enabled to do his work only by virtue of a particularly liberal scholarship, one of a number provided by a notably realistic board of trustees to tap the glittering vein of talent flowing out of Europe.

Voss advanced improbable hypotheses with the utmost seriousness, argued them with skill, and cheerfully abandoned them when they came to nothing, moving ahead at once into others. He was a tall, gangling individual, sparse of hair, long of nose, and sharp of eyes. He was delighted to hear Louis's voice and immediately wanted to know if Louis had seen the Bohr-Wheeler paper in the *Physical Review*. Louis had not. Voss said he'd bring it—"a milestone," he added. Furthermore, he would bring along a friend, a magnificent fellow, David Thiel. They would like each other no end.

The three young scientists and Libby sat jammed together at a tiny table in the corner of a crowded room that was a drugstore in front, an eat shoppe in back, and a meeting-place all over. Voices, dishes, and a juke box jangled and clashed in a deafening din. Libby was disappointed. She had expected they would eat in a hushed, high-ceilinged room with sweeping drapes at windows that would overlook tennis courts and young men and women studying with their heads together under oak trees. She ordered chicken salad, which, at fifty cents, was the most expensive item on the mimeographed menu.

Voss quickly bored her. He greeted her very politely, shook hands with her as though she were a woman of thirty, and at once put her out of mind. It hardly occurred to her, since she sensed his difficulty as soon as he did, that he was anyone to be spoken to or would say anything to be listened to. David Thiel was a different proposition.

His lameness, his stick, the slender frame in the loose clothes—each of these things was novel to her, each therefore interesting. She shook hands with him and smiled in response to his smile. It was not a greeting smile at all, but warmth itself; his eyes confirmed it, and even, it seemed to her, the inclination of his head, a beautifully formed head, cocked slightly toward her as he leaned on the cane and held her hand.

He said to her: "You're wearing the colors of the university. That's a nice thought."

She estimated that he was very old, probably even older than her brother. Still, she was quite as tall as he was, which at least confused things. She waited for his withdrawal into the caste that held adults, releasing them only for introductions and for occasional diversions, but the withdrawal did not come about; at the table he talked with her from time to time and even included her in some of the things he said to the others.

Halfway through the meal she got around to a consideration of what it would be like to be married to him. Usually her considerations of marriage were routine and fleeting. Now she sat quietly, nibbled at her chicken salad, stole looks at her companions, and spoke when she was spoken to, while in her mind she tested the sound of "Mr and Mrs David Thiel," tried to check off the letters of their names, wondered what he liked to do, and whether their children would be lame.

"It irritates me no end how long we all took to find out what it was we were doing," Voss was saying. "I remember those papers of Fermi's four and five years ago when he was in Rome."

"Who could have foreseen then—" Louis began.

"Why, anyone might have foreseen. It just remained for someone to put aside his preconceptions and take a good look. So what's going on in Germany? Believe me, that's the important thing now."

"You sound a little bit like Wisla," Louis said.

"He is a little bit like Wisla," said Thiel, "except he's a Hungarian and hence like nobody except other Hungarians. One theory is that Mars, a dying planet, wanted to keep tabs on what Earth might be up to. So they sent agents into Hungary a few millennia ago. That accounts for the strange language, unlike any other, and the strange and brilliant people who come out of Hungary all the time, like Voss here."

Voss smiled, but he was impatient. He wanted to hear from Louis what people in New York were thinking, doing, and getting ready to think and do. Had this possibility been thought of, had that one?

"The thing that has to be confirmed at once," he said, "is the extent to which the heavy isotope will interfere with the fission process in the lighter one. Who's doing what about that?"

"Dunning was getting together a sample enriched with 235—using a mass-spectrograph—but it was still in the works when I left," Louis told him.

"Do you drive?" David asked Libby.

She looked at him to see whether his interest in the subject was real and decided it might be.

"I'm not supposed to, but I have. I didn't today," she said.

"Did Wisla say that?" asked Voss in great excitement. "Try to remember just what he said, Louis. Can you remember?"

David and Libby began to talk about her science teacher, Mr Harriman. "He said when he was young he lived on a farm and used to have to drive a horse and buggy over to where Mrs Harriman lived, that was before she was Mrs Harriman. He said it got awful cold and so he put a newspaper under his shirt to keep him warm while he was driving, and he told us this to explain insulation. I like science but I don't like geometry—that's boring."

"Look," said David, "I'll show you some geometry that's not boring." He took a piece of paper from his pocket and tore a thin strip from it. "This strip of paper has two sides and two edges, like a good strip of paper ought to have," he said, and then he creased and crimped the ends together after turning the paper once upon itself. "But run your finger along either edge or either side now and see where you come out." And she began to do this.

"But, my God, Gene," Louis was saying, "you're talking about getting an explosive reaction with fast neutrons, and nobody knows for sure we could even sustain a heat reaction with slow neutrons. Aren't you getting ahead of yourself?"

"The question is whether the Germans are getting ahead of ourselves. I should think that you, coming from New York, where so much of this work——"

Libby discovered that the strip of paper had come to have but one side and one edge, and she smiled her appreciation of the trick.

"It's called a Moebius strip," David said. "You don't happen to have a pair of scissors with you, do you?"

"What—" Libby started, shaking her head, but Voss's voice, raised and resonant, interrupted her.

"David," he said, "you are a very intelligent man, I keep telling you. Why is our friend, likewise an intelligent man, so blind? I don't like the quiet way he sits when I tell him the facts of life."

David took the strip of paper back from Libby and, with his table knife, laboriously began to cut it around through the center.

"Gene is trying to explain to me," Louis said, "that this fission process is not a little problem for the laboratory like the classification of isotopes—"

"I beg your pardon, that is noble work, and I said no such thing. Work like that is pure work and we've come to something impure. I only say the Germans have made it necessary for us to find out these other things."

David was on the last inch of the strip. The other three all watched him.

"All you seem to be asking," David said, "is for someone to agree with you that the work on uranium may have military possibilities. Well, it might. I agree with that." He finished his cutting, the strip separated, and fell into a single loop. Libby smiled delightedly and reached for it.

"But you're really asking for a lot more than that," David went on. "Nothing so important as that the Nazis be stopped, nothing so fearful as that their work on uranium may lead to discoveries that will make it impossible to stop them. And so nothing so important as that we beat them to such discoveries. You want science put on a war footing for a war that hasn't yet touched us. You don't want to say it that way. But that's what you mean, isn't it?"

"You can put it any way you want. But if the Germans move on from Poland to France, and if—"

His assumptions were so much like Wisla's had been in Plaut's office that the words sounded in Louis's ears like an echo; or, rather, like the reality to which Wisla's words had been an echo beforehand. For what Wisla had postulated in enigmas Voss said plainly.

"—really nothing in theory to preclude the possibility. And if the Germans achieve it they'll use it. Do you doubt that when we ourselves sit here talking of it?" He paused and sighed. "We have created these enormous energies in the laboratory, in miniature, many times. Suppose it could be done with—what? a pound? an ounce? a gram?"

It's a heavy point for a summer afternoon on a quiet campus, Louis thought. He wondered in how many places the point was being made.

"The difficulties would be enormous," David said softly, shaking his head a little.

"That is not the point. The point is to find out."

"Yes, and if your argument prevails—"

"Ah! It will prevail at the cost of science, huh? That's it, isn't it? The man of science, born and bred to probe unknown things at lonely outposts of the mind—right?—should not let himself be found leading the way to prevent a spectacular threat to civilized life! Have I quoted whoever I am quoting correctly, David?"

There was no doubting his earnestness. Voss's eyes had narrowed, his hands held the edges of the little table over which he leaned, and his expression reminded Louis of something he couldn't quite bring to mind; something of a wholly different setting and from quite some time ago. Louis glanced at Libby, who looked at him and smiled as if to say, "It's all right, I'll be patient."

"There is almost always the threat of war, and many of the threats are spectacular," David said at last. "You are quoting me, all right, also a great many other people you know, even yourself, or at least some of the thoughts you have. But if you can be romantic with your lonely outposts, I'll be romantic too. We're seeing light on a drive that's been going on for half a century. I hate to see it sidetracked or put into the hands of people who don't care."

He looked suddenly at Louis. "Of course, this war may be different. As to that, Voss speaks with more authority than I do, and we have to listen although I hate to hear what he says."

There was a pause. Voss looked swiftly at Louis and then down at the tabletop, glanced up at Louis again, and again looked down.

"You know," David went on, as if the thought had just occurred to him, "everything we find at Voss's lonely outposts will turn up in a gadget someday too. Let me resolve my views in a text, for which I shall quote, since everything has been said before. Mr Voss will join me: 'And the cries of jubilation will resound from all the craftsmen, for science will become the Diana of the craftsmen—' "

Louis interrupted him. " '—and will be turned into the wages of workers and the wealth of capitalists—' "

"And the glory of the military men," David added, "if you'll let me round out what Mr Huxley said."

He and Louis smiled at each other. They're giving a regular sermon, Libby thought, but what a pretty phrase— Diana of the craftsmen.

Voss shook his head impatiently. David turned the subject: what was Louis going to do?

He told them about Neimann's letter; and he told them about Wisla's intervention, but he only mentioned this because he was impressed by it and afraid they might see he was impressed by it. Did they know of anything special going on at Chicago?

"Their department isn't so hot these days," Voss said, "except for Neimann. Now they're building their new cyclotron they need cheap labor."

For the past two years in New York, where his work had been mainly with nuclear isomers, Louis had required a variety of isotopes, which he got from the cyclotron there. In the process he had spent some dazzlingly happy hours tracking down the inevitable and endless leaks in the cyclotron's vacuum system and in general lending a hand.

"Voss says you're an expert at fixing sick cyclotrons," said David.

Diana and a cyclotron, Diana on a cyclotron, Diana anna cyclotron, said Libby to herself.

"But the truth is," said Voss, "Wisla's probably started recruiting for his big project. I imagine he wants to keep you on tap."

"What big project?"

"Why, to get a nuclear explosive—what we were talking about. You know about Einstein's letter to Roosevelt, don't you?"

"No."

"My God, and you just came from the center of everything!"

So Louis learned about that and more about the fears concerning German activities than he had any inkling of. For a moment the enormous irony of the situation dominated his feelings, and he listened to Voss with a slight smile that he could not control. Against all the elaborate assumptions—if this, if that, if so-and-so—if this ruthless Nazi war machine rolls over great countries and they fall and if its masters realize this dreadful possibility—why, against all this, the detached Einstein, late a resident of Caputh, near Potsdam, with an apartment in Berlin, and not so long ago dispossessed of both, sits down at his writing desk in his plain frame house in Princeton, adjusts his glasses, takes a sheet of paper and begins: Dear Mr President—

But it was not the simple irony of Einstein's letter that touched him. It was the other irony—

"Did he actually mention a bomb? Did he use that word?"

"Of course. He knows the possibility."

—that irony, which was not irony but tragedy, which made him turn to look at David, in whose eyes he saw either his own feeling or an understanding of it. "We're seeing light on a drive that's been going on for half a century"—and in bits and pieces, in stops and starts, in endless links, for centuries longer than that and to a possible end that all the generations of history could not have dreamed of. But uranium, of course, Becquerel's uranium had been the birthstone of the Twentieth Century, and the atoms of uranium were the sick atoms—born unstable and doomed to decay.

Libby was fidgeting. They left the drugstore. Voss had to prepare a class; except, he discovered, staring at his watch, he didn't have time to prepare it, he barely had time to get to it, and so he left them, half running down the street. David Thiel offered to show them around, and a few minutes later they were standing in a large and dingy room at one end of which was a complex of metal masses and tubes and meters.

"What hath God wrought!" Louis exclaimed. He clapped his hands together and smiled from the simplest pleasure. He looked at David, laughed delightedly, and then, suddenly all intense interest, went over to the machine and began to examine it.

"What is it?" Libby asked.

"It's called a cyclotron. It busts up atoms," David said. "It's sort of like a microscope for things you can't see with a microscope. This one's an old one."

"This one's a museum piece," Louis called, "a noble museum piece."

It was, to be precise, about four years old. It was the third cyclotron that man had built to measure the particles that had no dimensions, to weigh what had no weight, and to see what was invisible. Not more than a thousand dollars had been spent on its whole construction. Two graduate students and a professor, with the intermittent help of three or four machinists, had put it together in about a year's time, working nights and weekends with brass sheet and meters and Bakelite surreptitiously acquired from the stockroom of the chemistry laboratories, well stocked in those days as the laboratory cabinets of the nuclear physicists were not.

The troubles that had beset the physicists in acquiring the tools without which their work could not proceed had come from the inability of anyone in those days to assign a practical value to what he was doing. Even after the great particle discoveries of the early thirties, no one had been able really to foresee anything more than an increase in man's knowledge of the universe. For nuclear physicists that prospect had generated waves of excitement that touched them all around the world; but it had had relatively little effect on boards of trustees, state legislatures, and the research divisions of the country's corporations.

Watching Louis's loving and respectful examination of this small monument to the importance of non-useful questions, David Thiel found himself remembering a morning he had spent almost exactly one year earlier, only ninety days before the discovery of nuclear fission, in an office of one of the largest electrical companies in the nation. With three hopeful colleagues, he had gone to try to interest the company in spending thirty thousand dollars on the construction of a very promising new type of cyclotron. The company executive had listened to them amiably, but had shaken his head almost at once.

"There's so little practical promise in that kind of physics, nothing to justify—"

David had been struck by the phrase "that kind of physics"; he suspected that the executive would have felt ill at ease, perhaps a little precious, if he had said "nuclear physics."

"I see you use acetone paint for leak-hunting," Louis said to David. "Any better than alcohol?"

They talked about such details for a while, and Louis's mind turned on the need for cheap labor at Chicago. They left the building, and David handed Libby into the Saxl family car for the drive back.

"What do you really think about this Chicago project business?" Louis asked him.

David touched a hubcap of the car with the tip of his cane, and followed the circle of it around and around.

"I don't know," he said finally. "Normally, of course, you wouldn't expect to see a practical result from a discovery like Hahn's for fifty years. But everybody's up to his ears with this. I don't know. I've got great respect for Roosevelt. He seems to like people. So if you like people, what do you decide to do about making a bomb that might wipe out a city at one crack?"

"Shall we say science is important enough to the President so that he shouldn't be the first to divert it?" Louis said, trying to imitate Voss's voice.

David laughed. "Voss is easy to argue down halfway but not the whole way," he said. "Or I guess I mean just the reverse of that."

"Well, but what about the possibility itself?" Louis asked.

"I know a guy here who can prove it won't work," David said. "Like you and me, he was born and brought up in the United States. But Fermi and Szilard and Wisla and Wigner and Weisskopf and Teller and some others, all here by virtue of travel more or less enforced, seem to think it will work. Well, you know—nature always gives the same answers to the same questions. But a guy running from a concentration camp—maybe he asks the questions harder, or maybe just listens harder for the answers."

David straightened up, looked both ways along the street, and seemed about to walk away.

"Yes, I think it will work," he said. "And if it does, the Nazis will try it, and that being the case, we'll have to try it. In short, I agree with Voss, and may God have mercy on our souls. There's one real hope—it may not work in time. Cling to that."

On the way home Louis figured out what it was that Voss's intense expression at the lunch table reminded him of. It was the Spaniards, and other men from other countries who had come to Spain to fight; the same drive and hardness and understanding beyond his own that he had seen in their faces had been in Voss's face. There was nothing in the expressions, and nothing in his feeling, that his intellect could not bring to order for him; but his emotions could not do as well. The hate that he had seen in the

Spanish faces had eluded him; he could not find it in himself.

But why could he not feel it? Why had he not felt it even in Spain? Was it because one hated what one feared, and he could not think of anything he absolutely feared? Was this arrogant, a sin of pride? He had feared bombs and bullets in Spain, hadn't he? Yes, but not enough to hate the ones who dropped them and shot them.

Indeed, he asked himself with some irritation, why then did I shoot at them? Why, to stop them. Did he recall that Voss's sister had been murdered by the Nazis? A Jew, like himself—a sister, like Libby sitting here beside him? Does hate mean anything to you? he said, addressing himself quite formally. Why, yes, it is something that, like an alloy, can be ruinous unless it's very carefully controlled. But it is something with which controls fail. It is the thing that reason least can deal with. It is of all things the thing to fear.

He stared down at the smooth, straight road. Libby had fallen asleep; dreaming of bicycles and marriage. The car moved steadily through some of the richest farmland in North America, through Menard 2200—Pleasant Plains 900—White Hall 1800. Hedges of Osage orange at intervals came rushing in toward them from the segmented fields of the basking crops. Cows looked; chickens scurried; farmers driving up to the highway on little country roads stopped a mile away to let them pass. He felt uneasy.

He switched on the car radio, softly so it wouldn't waken Libby. For a few miles he listened to the music. The news came on. Warsaw was crumbling; the Germans were roaming the country at will.

He reflected on the fact that, so far as he knew, no one had ever seen more than a few grams of uranium as a metal all in one place. Its very limited uses, principally in the manufacture of ceramics and glass, involved quantities that were trifling. But sooner or later it would be necessary to process tons of pitchblende—tons—to get the metal in sufficient quantities and pure enough; and then, on top of that, to separate out the light isotope that was the promising one—an enormous, absolutely unprecedented job, and perhaps it would be better to stick with the ordinary mixture.

As to that, though, it would be necessary to process tons of some moderator—carbon, oxygen, maybe deuterium, it would take a lot of experimental work—and to what degree of purity? Perhaps one part in a million? Was it possible?

And of course all this assumed the success of a very great many laboratory validations of some very audacious theory that, among other things, would probably fill in a couple of places on the periodic table of elements. Was all this really possible?

It will be interesting to hear what Neimann has to say about all this, he thought.

Thinking of Neimann, he thought of the new cyclotron, and for the first time since this trip home had started, his face relaxed. He smiled to himself, and then he punched Libby and woke her up. For the rest of the way home they talked of many things.

7

That night Louis filled out the forms that Neimann had sent down from Chicago. The next day he wrote to Theresa. His letter was full of the excitement of his afternoon with Voss and David Thiel, and it showed his love for her too. He meant both and when she got the letter she felt both. But he did not know which he felt most, and she felt that as well. She mailed on the letter she had written to Louis the night of his leaving, rewritten again.

She was giving up her job in the bookstore, he read. She had bothered friends to get a job as a teaching assistant in the English department at Columbia. The job paid very little, but it would allow her to read papers, even teach in some lowlier classes, and it was a beginning. To what end? Well, she couldn't say, or at least she didn't.

And she wanted to ask if he'd ever read a book called *The Redemption of Tycho Brahe* by Max Brod, who, she had just learned, was a close friend of Kafka's. He'd know that, of course. But a very friendly young man at the University library who told her about this book said that the character of Kepler in it was supposed to have been modeled on Einstein. Did he know that? Brod referred to Kepler's "tranquility" and wrote that there was something not quite understandable in his lack of emotion—"like a breath from a distant region of ice," Brod had put it, and he'd gone on to tell of poor Tycho's awed reaction to this and his lamentation that he, Tycho, "must love and err, flung hither and thither" while Kepler "floated above, pure and happy." Had Louis ever met Einstein, and was Einstein, who was known to love the quartets of Beethoven—so this friendly young man, her friend at the library, told her—really like that?

The young man at the library, she wrote, reminded her a little of Louis; his hair curled at the nape of his neck like Louis's did, and he was something of a poet too. He was in the philosophy department; Louis was sure to like him.

He told her, this same young man, something Bertrand Russell had written; she supposed Louis would know it, and it troubled her: "Whatever knowledge is attainable must be obtained by scientific methods, and what science cannot discover mankind cannot know." If this was so, what was one to make of poets or of Brod, for instance, who had discovered something about a scientist that a scientist might well not have discovered? What was a scientist to make of a nonscientist, who, by such a definition, couldn't discover anything? Could this mean that someone like herself had nothing of value to offer someone like Louis?

She wrote that the days were very hot in New York— the papers said sales of dress shields and ice-cream were soaring—and the nights were so hot that she had to drape herself in wet sheets.

Louis read Theresa's letter carefully; that very night he had a dream about her and himself. He wrote a letter to her, read it over and tore it up. Around his house he was preoccupied, saying nothing, but by sudden turns was garrulous with bits of impersonal information.

His mother decided that Theresa's letter must have said something to hurt him, but she couldn't bring herself to ask. As for Benjamin Saxl, he waited for an opportunity to discuss the family business, and only gradually learned of his son's plan to go to Chicago and something of what the work there might be. It made little sense to him, but he did not respect it any the less for that; it was one of the things a Ph.D. did. In the end, Mr Saxl came to believe that the business had been discussed, although it had not.

Louis wrote Theresa another letter. It was, like the earlier one, full of love for her, and, like that one, it was full of the excitement of going to Chicago. As before, he meant both, and as before she felt both. But he knew no better which he meant most, and she felt this more strongly now than she had earlier. She began to see more of the friendly young man at the University library and of other young men as well; and she wrote to tell him, when she got a raise, how important her job had become to her. For a time thereafter there were no letters.

She wrote Louis then because her mother died, and the next day he appeared in New York. He had not been with her an hour before she saw that he had hardly been aware of the months of silence. It was a strange visit, shadowed by the happening that brought them together and dappled by doubts and by certainties that at first seemed unbelievable, the most certain of which was that he loved her as much as ever in his fashion.

His letters continued to be as full as ever of the love and the excitement intermingled, although less and less could she tell what the excitement was about. He said nothing directly concerning his work; what she got was the sure knowledge that it engrossed him to the exclusion of everything outside it, save herself. As to that, the testimony of the letters and her experiences of being with him during this time were absolute; his attempts to dissemble were not often successful, and with her (as opposed to himself) he very seldom tried.

And then for three years they saw each other not at all.

Louis gave her a new address to write to—Box 1663, Santa Fe, New Mexico—but no explanation of it. She followed the war news in the papers and on the radio, began to teach regularly, saw more and more people, and wrote articles for journals. The first of these she fashioned out of her letters to Louis, which had turned into small treatises on varieties of curiosity. As time went by her letters served as covering notes for copies of articles. She came to think of Louis as some kind of soldier and formed theories about what kind, all of which collapsed with the awful news of August 1945.

"I get to pondering those two questions of Hillel's," he wrote her after that, "—'If I am not for myself, who will be? But if I am for myself alone, what do I amount to?' It is hard to figure out sometimes which you are being. I am afraid a most terrible thing has been done. Maybe not really meant, maybe just not thought about all the way through—perhaps a kind of accident, not a real design. But one is as bad as the other, now even our accidents take on the quality of design."

"So why don't you leave that place?" she wrote him. "Why do you stay?"

"—some things I have to finish, or get started, I'm not sure. It's hard to draw lines out here. But—"

"But Hillel asked a third question: 'If not now, when?' "

"—the universities, most of them, are running on military funds now, and I don't want that. There's one research program nobody can see a single military use for— I've applied there, so has David."

"Have you heard?"

"Very soon now."

And so, although the war was over, months passed; 1945 became 1946, and then it was May, a beautiful month in New Mexico.

PART 7

Friday and thereafter: those roads are ghastly silent now

1

"He's got a good hand, Louis has," Dombrowski was saying. "Very neat and careful. Quick too. I've watched him, mostly at Chicago, specially when they were putting up the cyclotron there."

Jerry Dombrowski and David Thiel stood facing each other in a corner of the machine shop that served the Los Alamos cyclotron. The reading machine Dombrowski had put together for Louis stood on a bench between them. It was finished, ready to be sent over to the hospital, but Dombrowski really did not want to let it go. He would have liked to keep it around a little while, to fool with it and perhaps to refine it here and there; or just to look at it and work it a few more times, and explain it to others who might come by and who would not have seen a contraption like this. It had been David's idea, and half a dozen others had contributed to it, but the workmanship was Dombrowski's.

"What I mean to say though," Dombrowski went on, "is that he had the feel. He could kind of walk right up to what was wrong and know what to do with it. I take it best generally if the theory people stay away. They don't generally have the feel." He chuckled. "Like once with the Chicago job some of them decided to do a little fixing on their own, so they use soft solder to set the ion probe. So help me! It sprays all over the insides, and the beam— well, it went crazy, of course."

Dombrowski reached out a hand and very delicately touched the foot pedal that operated the reading machine; jogging it through the small amount of play that he had allowed, he continued talking to David.

"But of course no one knows what threw the beam off. So they had a bad beam and they sit around scratching their heads something fierce. Well, Louis, he comes in and sniffs around and pretty soon he says, 'Someone didn't by any chance use some soft solder on that probe, did they?' That's what I mean. I had to take the whole business down and clean it. A mess."

Dombrowski was a good deal older than David, somewhere in his fifties, and he was in charge of this machine shop, one among a dozen or more specialized shops distributed throughout the Technical Area of Los Alamos. In size, in amount of equipment, and in number of operators, all of these shops together barely equaled still another, general machine shop set in the very center of the Area. That one did the routine, repetitive jobs; the construction, shaping, and finishing of basic bomb parts, the repairing of standard equipment, and a steady run of other chores, most of which called for a high degree of mechanical skill and few of which called for craftsmanship.

The craftsmen were in the specialized shops, meeting unique problems that could only be prepared for by having the craftsmen present; blowing glass tubes and vessels and hand-fashioning metal links for high-vacuum systems; shaping parts of machines that had to be understood to be worked with. The best of the craftsmen worked in the shop attached to the cyclotron building. Jerry Dombrowski had worked with cyclotrons since Ernest Lawrence put together the first one sixteen years before, and he kept his tools, passed on to him by his father, in a polished mahogany chest that his grandfather had made in Poland fifty years before that.

"Takes all kinds," Dombrowski said. "Excepting for him and maybe you a little bit—" he winked at David— "and a few others— God, that's a bad thing about Louis, a bad thing." He stood, still fingering the pedal, and let his eyes rove around the shop, over and among the lathes and drills, the saws, the milling-machines, the clutter and the men who were working, seven or eight of them. "Excepting for a few—" he said again, and then seemed to force his eyes back to David. "That Bohr fellow was down here once or twice. I was given to understand he's very important. You could see he didn't know a shaper from a punch press, but that's all right. He didn't make like he did. He looked on while I did a little piece for the big job." Dombrowski nodded his head toward the large room beyond; through a wide doorway the curving side of the cyclotron was visible.

He pressed his hand against the foot pedal that started the small electric motor of the reading machine. At once his eyes and David's turned to the book rack at the other end of the machine's frame; a gear turned, the linkage moved, and a rubber-faced fin slid across and up the right half of the book in the rack, slipping one page to the left.

"Uh-huh," Dombrowski said. "Well, you want to get from here. You tell Louis I'm awful sorry. I worked with him near three years at Chicago, right into the project, and all out here. It's a bad thing. Davey, what's the real odds?"

David lifted his cane and with the tip of it nudged the

projecting handle of a small wrench back over the edge of the bench. Then he shook his head and looked at Dombrowski.

"Not good," he said.

"I'm awful sorry. I watched him do that experiment once, four-five months ago. He made it look easy, but it was a crime." Dombrowski leaned a little across the reading machine and peered intently at David. "I'd say he knew it was too. Why'd he do it that way, Davey? That setup down there was wartime pure and simple, everybody knew it. Why wasn't it changed over?"

David gave a little snort. "He tried to get it changed over, Mr Dombrowski. Quite a few of us tried. You'll be happy to know it's going to be set up right now."

"Oh, that's good, ain't it?" Dombrowski said, straightening up. "That's good. You don't mind me saying I don't believe it—about the trying, that's to say? Leastwise, from what I know of Louis Saxl, I got doubts he tried. Like I told you, I watched him at it just the once. But back at Chicago—here too, in the early days—I was in on a lot of jobs with him—pressure jobs—where the setups wasn't so good but you had to make do. There's pressure on you, but then there's like a pressure in you too, so it works out. Many's the job I done with a handsaw that called for a do-all—but not if it wasn't a case of being necessary. That there's where Louis worked different. If it was necessary to do that job that way, you wouldn't of tried to get it changed over at all, would you?"

"That's one way to put it," David commented; he was a little irritated at this development in the talk, or possibly just at its continuing.

"Yes, sir," said Dombrowski, a little irritated himself by David's words. "That's a way to put it, and so's the other half—that's to say if it wasn't necessary, somebody could of got it changed over if they'd really tried, and don't tell me different. I wouldn't of done it the way it was, I tell you that. I got too much respect for tools to use them

wrong—people too, myself included, if it comes to that.
What's he doing a pressure job for when he don't see the
pressure no more—can't feel it anyhow? But he went on
doing it. Besides which, it's my suspicion he knew there'd
be a slip someday. He'd have to know."

"You're saying quite a lot."

"You can make a lot out of it, but that ain't to say you
necessarily got my meaning."

Dombrowski ran the fingers of one hand up the side of
his nose and into his eyebrows, which were very bushy.
He looked at David with the beginning of a scowl, but it
went away at once and his whole face softened; and meanwhile David looked down at the floor.

"Well, then, what's your meaning?" he said in a low
voice.

"Davey, this ain't the time and I ain't sure. I guess I
don't mean a thing more'n he's just full of zip about what
a fellow can do if the fellow's hisself. Or I could mean he
let hisself get the blues about things and got hisself into a
kind of what-the-hell—I don't rightly know, Davey. I
shouldn't be going on this way. I just got to thinking a
fellow with Louis's training don't get hisself in a spot like
this. Who does that is a fellow without the training or a
fellow acting on something else. I'll send the machine over.
Go on. Go on."

Dombrowski turned and walked back to his shop.

2

From the machine shop David went out across a small yard
at the far side of which was one of the gates in the high
steel fence around the Technical Area. At the gate he was
checked out. He walked along the outside of the fence for
a block or so, which brought him to a street leading into
the business center of the town. He stopped in front of a
drugstore window to look at a display of water fins—a

bright and profitable idea of the manager's to cash in on
the Bikini tests. It was close to noon, and since this was
Friday, shoppers were out in force for the weekend. David
proceeded past them to the military headquarters of the
Los Alamos post—a one-story, double-H structure, painted
ghastly green; a flagpole stood before it in a small patch
of excellent lawn; a dozen official cars were lined up on
either side. He went in, turning at once beyond the door
into the outer room of the office of the commanding officer. The WAC secretary said hello and picked up her
telephone.

As the commanding officer, Colonel Hough had a rug
on the floor of his office, a stiff brown leather sofa, and a
globe in a walnut stand. Aside from these perquisites of
office, the room contained little to distinguish it; it was not
large, and the desk was an ordinary green steel desk.

Contemplating his globe in the moment between the
WAC's call and David's entrance, Colonel Hough was
thinking how profoundly true it was, as he had often said,
that this project had two heads. He had no illusions about
the relative importance of the heads; and the existence of
the other, civilian head stirred up no prejudice, pride, or
competitiveness that amounted to anything in him. In the
great days, indeed, when the war was on and Oppenheimer
was driving everyone to distraction and achievement, he
as readily as anyone had recognized that there were two
heads only on paper and in fact but one. He had heard
someone say once that the laws of physics were the decrees
of fate; lacking a knowledge of the laws, he had simply
taken Oppenheimer's decrees as a reasonable substitute
for them. But Oppenheimer was gone and times had
changed.

Of course, now as before, there was only one official
head, he being General Meacham; but General Meacham
was not often on hand to be seen, and he wasn't now. If
you looked at things another way, there were heads without number, one of whom was coming in the door.

In the ordinary course of events, Colonel Hough would discuss with the civilian director such matters as that of holding up a prepaid telegram, of dealing with an erratic Congressman, or of preparing a release for the nation's newspapers. He had been telling himself that he had not consulted the present civilian director because that person was in Washington attending conferences related to Bikini, but it was time to recognize that this was an evasion—besides, the civilian director would be back the next day.

"Hello, Dave," Colonel Hough said, getting up from his desk and coming around it. "Anything new?" The question was routine, almost automatic, but even as he asked it he had a sudden feeling of self-consciousness; he had overslept this morning; he had not called the hospital; suppose there *was* something new.

"*Is* there anything new?" he asked anxiously.

"No," David said. He lowered himself onto the stiff sofa. He had been to the hospital before he had gone down to see Dombrowski, and before that he had had a talk with Wisla, and before that a talk with Berrain and Pederson. There were answers to Hough's question, but not simple ones.

"No," he said again, and after a moment, "I heard about this Congressman."

"I suppose Ulanov told you."

"No, not Ulanov. Anyway, is there any remotely conceivable shadow of a possibility—"

"He isn't even here anymore. He's gone back to Washington."

"Good. I also heard you're holding up telegrams. I thought the censors were called off last December."

The Colonel studied his globe; he felt quite unsure of his ground in the matter of the telegram; he decided on camaraderie.

"Dave, look, I had to do that. I know what you think, but we just couldn't let anything at all out on this. After all, this is still an Army post. Try to see it our way a little, Dave."

David smiled; he seemed to be studying the globe now too.

"I know. Live and let live. This is a very fine doctrine, and I only wish the Army understood it. However—" His cane was lying on the floor beside him; he spread his hands slightly. "Since you stopped the wire two days ago, will you at least please keep it stopped? Can you see to it that it's not rushed through now, out of some sudden contrition on the part of the Army?"

"Certainly, Dave. I understand."

"No snafu?"

"No snafu."

"You know Louis's family will be notified today? Berrain and Morgenstern thought you were the one to do that."

"I have no objection to doing it. Can't say I'll enjoy it."

"You understand the situation, you say?"

Colonel Hough smiled a resigned smile.

"Dave, I wrote out a draft of a release myself last night. Public relations has it. I gave it to them this morning to touch up. Somebody will be bringing it back here any minute. Do you want to wait to see it?"

"Yes," David said. "I'll wait for that."

For a minute or so they said nothing.

Then the Colonel said, oh, by the way, he'd only just heard that David had been offered a very good place at one of the best of the universities, and congratulations, he'd been expecting this, and he'd miss Dave a lot, but he wanted to wish him all the best. David nodded, but said nothing.

Then the Colonel walked across the room, turned and walked back and sat on the edge of his desk.

"Dave," he said. "What *did* happen? Can you tell me what went wrong—what you've found out?"

David was looking at the globe again. He said he wasn't sure just how much the Colonel knew about how the setup worked. The Colonel said he wasn't sure either, he supposed he didn't really know too well.

"Yes, I should imagine so," David said in a mild voice, nodding his head.

Of course, he went on, Hough would know that many laboratory experiments released nuclear radiation, and consequently set up a hazard to people around. But the intensity of radiation given off as a rule was fairly slight; with a cyclotron, for example, there was always some leakage but not enough to harm a person walking by. On the other hand, a person working regularly with a cyclotron might accumulate enough to hurt himself; so he wore a radiation register, a film badge that would fog or some sort of pocket ionization chamber.

In short, David observed, in such situations intensity is slight, time is long and the product of these is relative safety. Reverse that formula, turn it exactly around, and you have the formula for the setup in the canyon.

To be sure, warning signals of a sort were given as the danger point was approached. If the operator was listening very intently, using his eyes ingeniously, and had all his wits about him—since the human control called for was really too much for a man except at his very most vigilant— why, then he could manage.

In this connection, David wondered, had Hough ever noticed how, in the rituals of primitive societies, things were commonly thought of as persons—as in some of the rituals performed right around Los Alamos in the pueblos? Well, again, if you simply reversed this approach you got the situation that prevailed in the canyon. The Indians, David said, would probably be fascinated with this experiment.

Dropping the bombs on Hiroshima and Nagasaki, he went on, was somewhat like getting this experiment under way—many, many people killed or maimed in various ways, just as with this experiment when the first piece of fissionable material is introduced, many, many fissions result.

But except for these catastrophes to people and to nuclei, nothing wholly irrevocable has taken place either in the world or in the pile; one might stop there; the real dangers still lay ahead.

Well, said David, it wasn't necessary to itemize. As you built bombs you increased the intensity of an arms race, since other countries would have to make bombs too, or would think they had to. Similarly, with this experiment, as you increased the fissionable material you increased the intensity of the nuclear disintegration. In both cases you finally reached a stage just below critical.

But the almost eternal nervousness of uranium sometimes, David said, seemed to mesmerize people and throw them off the main point. Colonel Hough could see that the proper fear of this force was not whether men would lose control of it but whether they would lose control of themselves in handling it.

"I don't know whether you know," David went on, picking up his cane and whacking it lightly against one shoe, "that this experiment had some peaceful uses. But those uses were not what it was set up for. When you look at it closely you have to think of the single-mindedness that goes with war and ends with war for most of us. But it doesn't end for that setup in the canyon. All through the war there was a balance: the single-mindedness of the man offset the single-mindedness of the setup.

"Then," David went on, whacking his shoe again, "the war ends for the man and he goes down there and does again what he did before; the balance has shifted though. That's as single-minded as ever. He isn't. His mind has opened to different thoughts of a different kind, to everything his life is made of, every irrationality, every odd notion, what hurts, what excites, what he loves. Peace lacks the built-in control of wartime's single-mindedness. There's not enough margin for just one moment's movement of the mind to something that was mean or might be wonderful—to something private. For that you have to provide controls. But of course it's a peacetime thought to expect any controls when we don't even seem to know enough about controls to stop making bombs."

David gave his shoe a harder whack and dropped his cane again; he glanced at Colonel Hough, who was looking steadfastly out the window, and went on.

"That's what went wrong. Not a complete answer, but complete enough for the time and place. Some warning signals were missed. Intensity was built up a little too much. I can tell you one thing flat. No screwdrivers were dropped."

The Colonel's phone rang. He reached for it with an automatic motion, without taking his eyes from the window. He said, "Yes," and then almost at once, "Yes," again, and put the receiver back in its cradle. The door opened and his secretary came in with copies of the Colonel's release.

"Give Mr Thiel one," said the Colonel.

For thirty seconds there was silence in the room.

"Oh, Jesus," David said then. *"Oh, Jesus!"* he cried. Looking angrily at the paper, he groped for his cane, got it and struggled to his feet.

"If this is what you're going to do, you know what I'm going to do."

"If you mean what you said about going into Albuquerque and seeing the wire services, I refuse to take that seriously, Dave." The Colonel came up to him. "Will you sit down? Will you tell me what I've said that's so terrible?"

David shook his head.

"No, I won't, I can't talk to you any more." But he continued anyway. "There's not a word of truth in this, although it won't do you any good—I meant entirely what I said—I'll do it if I go to jail and I'll do it if I hang for it! If you're not going to tell what happened, I'm going to—one way or the other."

He started for the door of the office; the Colonel stepped in front of him.

"And you get the hell out of my way."

"I will not get the hell out of your way. And I insist you tell me what the fight's about."

David said nothing.

"Dave, I simply do not understand what gets you this way. I know the story has errors in it, deliberate errors. It's not the kind of publicity we like to get out, God knows, and I don't mean that to be undignified—but they'll turn it into publicity, whatever our ideas. Louis's action was a real heroic one in any practical meaning of the word. It just was. I think that should be said and the story says it. Will you tell me what's so wrong with that?"

For a moment David looked at the Colonel, then he turned away and walked to the window, which looked out on the patch of well-kept lawn from which the flagpole rose. He stood there silently; the Colonel watched him warily; at last he turned around, shrugged his shoulders, and laughed.

"Did you see that piece in *The New Yorker*, last year sometime? About the flag designed for the United Nations? It's supposed to be displayed under a nation's own flag. As *The New Yorker* said, if you believe in world government apparently you stand on your head to salute it. Some things are clearer if you stand on your head. If you stand on your head it turns out that the biggest fear now is just the same all around—our bombs. They terrify us, for what they'll drive the Russians to do, quite as much as they terrify the Russians for what we might do. Not all things are clearer if you stand on your head though. You can also get dizzy."

David moved over right beside the globe and stared at it.

"Neil, to the best of my knowledge there's no project work of any consequence being done even now on peaceful uses. Louis has been doing some. He wangled some and he pushed some through and he invented some. If we mean anything at all by some of our fancier official pronouncements, this is the germ of what we mean. It's modest work, not much honored here. But your story dishonors it.

"A few people have been trying to push work on a fusion bomb—the super—you know about that. Some of them argue that this is going to be vital for when we get the fission arms race all knotted up and need a new entry. OK, I won't argue. But my present point is that mankind has good reason to fear what they're doing and good reason to love what Louis has been doing. Your story neglects to tell mankind this or anything.

"My objection to your fascination with the heroism idea is simply that it isn't true and mistakes one thing for another. He would have been a hero if he'd had time. But he did what he did, he knows what it was, and can't nonsense be left out of one of the last words to be said about him? Can't such a man be treated with some respect?"

The question was not answered. David reached out one hand and gave the globe a little spin; the gesture was quick and almost surreptitious, as though he had been thinking of doing this for some time and had been holding back for fear of being caught. He watched it turn until it stopped and then abruptly he went out of the office.

3

Sometime during this Friday afternoon the computing, calculating, analyzing, reconstructing, measuring, estimating, and sheer guessing that had been going on for three days toward the end of determining the amount and quality of radiation released by the pile at the moment of the accident, and received by each of the seven differently positioned persons there, reached a kind of recess. Present at the time were Wisla, David, Ulanov, and two or three others. The recess was not announced; rather the considerable talking that had been going on gradually over a period of half an hour or so died out.

In that half hour the last of the possibilities, protected and cared for and force-fed from the first, expired, and the probabilities that no one had been able to ignore took over.

From the work of the three days it could now be said that
there had been only one chance in ten that any of the six
other victims of the accident would have died from it; and
only one chance in a hundred that Louis Saxl would live.
The radiation dose that Louis had received could not be
stated with any exactness. But there could no longer be
any doubt that, whatever it was or might someday be determined to be, its order of magnitude had to be about
twice that of the dosage radiologists and radiobiologists
referred to as "lethal." These men could not speak with
exactness either; also, they could err; but not by anything
remotely approaching one hundred per cent.

"I'm not surprised," one of the hematologists from Chicago was saying to the other a little later that afternoon.
"I'd have guessed about that."

"His family has been notified, haven't they?" Dr Berrain
said, turning to Dr Morgenstern, standing beside him in
the lower corridor.

"Oh, yes," Dr Morgenstern said. "The Army's sending
a plane down from Chicago to pick them up. They'll be
here tomorow. It's all arranged."

"I wonder if there's anybody else," Berrain said.

"No, that's his family," said the Colonel. "Of course—
well, let me talk to Thiel."

"Yes, there's someone else," David said. "I've been trying
to get her. I'll take care of it."

"A reading machine?" Dr Morgenstern inquired, staring
at the two men from the cyclotron shop who had found
him near the doctors' conference room. "I know nothing
about it. Mr Thiel? I haven't seen him in some minutes.
Perhaps Dr Berrain—"

"I see," Berrain said to the men with the machine. "I'm
afraid you'll have to take it back. It was a very nice thought
of somebody's, but I think it's not advisable—not now."

"Charley," said Berrain at the end of the afternoon, "may
I tell you something—will you listen to me? I can say it
two ways. I can tell you that your agonized expressions

make you more trouble than you're worth. Or I can say
that what you've come to is the end of your hope, which
still leaves Louis Saxl a few days to go before he comes to
the end of his life. God help us if we get bad hemorrhages,
but maybe Briggle's dyes can help God a little if we do—
help Louis too. There's just no telling what all we'll run
into when the white count begins to fall off—which, incidentally, it hasn't yet. He's still got a few thousand. Do
you want to lend a hand with some chores that won't accomplish all you or any one of us would like?"

"For Christ's sake," Pederson said to Betsy at the beginning of the evening. "Will you try to look not quite so
desolate? You can't go in there looking like that."

David tried eleven times without success to reach Theresa,
but on the twelfth he reached her. It was a little after seven
o'clock at Los Alamos; in New York it was a little after
nine. Theresa had found a Western Union notice in her
mailbox, had called and heard David's message. She had
hardly put the phone down when it rang again. She said,
"David!" and she said, "Yes, just now, just this minute";
and then she listened to what David had to say.

She put the phone down again. She called the air terminal; there were no seats to be had. She pleaded and
cajoled; hung up in despair, and began automatically to
pack. The suitcase she had yesterday put away she took
out again, and some of the clothes she had yesterday put
away she took out again. And for the third time the telephone rang. It was Western Union; there was a wire for
her; a voice read it to her.

"But you just called me with that! Just a few minutes
ago!"

"This is not the same message, miss. This one came in
yesterday. We left a notice, but you didn't call."

"I didn't get a notice. It's the same telegram."

"Those messages originated in different offices. Yesterday's was sent from Santa Fe, New Mexico. The one we

left the notice on today originated in Los Alamos, New Mexico.

"But they're the same! Will you please read them again?"

The words were identical, concealing with almost complete success the worry David told her not to feel. For just an instant as she listened she was held by the thought that there must have been another message intended for the second one, that by some terrible mistake this other message, saying something worse or better, had been mislaid or lay somewhere now unread by anyone. But of course the only thing that counted she had just heard straight from David.

Again she called the air terminal. "Well, miss, I can do better by you this time," the voice of the terminal said. "I just got a cancellation. You're in luck tonight."

4

" 'There is a scuffle of feet, a scraping of chairs,' " David read. " 'The angry one aims a haymaker at the party who aroused him. But just in time an alert MP grasps the arm of the pugnacious character firmly, and hostilities are narrowly averted.

"Here in the Service Club are the medals of two hundred nationalities, minted as one coin and stamped with the American eagle, jangled together in a common exchequer—' "

"Block that metaphor," Louis said.

David lowered the paper; it was a copy of the *Los Alamos Times* that Betsy had brought into the room.

"But don't stop," Louis added. His head was back high against the top of the bed, which had been cranked up. He was looking away from David toward the window; he'd hardly moved since David had come in just after seven, and it was nearly eight. At eight o'clock the last blood sample of the day would be taken, some examinations made, and preparations for the night begun.

"Are you sure you want to hear more of this?" David asked.

"Very sure."

" 'Old America, in the persons of swarthy, hair-braided, stolid-gazing Indians,' " David continued, " 'brash young recruits of the Army . . . plainly dressed, mildly borne men of science. . . . At various tables young couples go through the harmless primary stages of love-making, the prerogative of youth from Los Alamos to Nagasaki. . . . This is your Service Club, the hub of the Hill people's neighborly communion with each other.'

"End of story," David said.

Louis said nothing.

David turned the paper; his eyes moved quickly over the page; he was a very fast reader.

" 'The latest Army reorganization plan calls for the continental United States to be divided into six Army areas.' That sounds ominous.

" 'Community planners are figuring on a bathtub for every permanent unit, it was learned from the office of Colonel Cornelius Hough this week.'

"That could be ominous too. I don't think anyone knows where the bathtub originated. Didn't Mencken say President Fillmore put the first one in the White House? With the Romans bathing was a public diversion."

"We could make a public bath of the pond perhaps," Louis said after a pause. His voice was polite and uninterested, and the words gave David an uneasy feeling.

"That's a fine idea," he said.

He noticed that Louis was looking at him, head lowered a little—not so much looking as contemplating. Then he shook his head, or seemed to—the motion was barely perceptible—and turned to face the window again.

"Dave," he said after another pause, and in a voice a little less formal, although not much so. "I was thinking

of that day we met. Gene Voss was there. I had my sister
Libby with me."

"That's right. You were wondering about going up to
Chicago."

"I've been thinking about Voss."

He turned his head toward the door. Betsy was there,
looking in on them with professional cheerfulness.

"Time for a little donation," she said. "Last today. May
I have a wee drop, sir?"

She took the blood and as soon as she had finished Louis
turned back to face the window again.

"You were talking about—" David began.

"Yes," Louis interrupted. "Would you read me that poem
again, Dave?"

"Betsy read you one. Is that the one you want?"

"Didn't you read it?"

"Betsy said—I'm damned if I remember, Louis. I think
maybe you're right."

"It doesn't matter. Frost is a very economical man."

David knew well enough which poem it was; he found
it in the anthology he had brought over and, speaking
slowly and softly, he read it:

> *"Some say the world will end in fire,*
>   *Some say in ice.*
> *From what I've tasted of desire*
> *I hold with those who favor fire.*
>   *But if it had to perish twice,*
> *I think I know enough of hate*
>   *To know that for destruction ice*
> *Is also great,*
>   *And would suffice."*

"Have you seen Voss lately, Dave?" Louis asked, turning
his head back once more to look at David.

David continued to look at the book. In 1942 Voss had
thrown over all his work to enlist; he had been dead three
years.

"No," David said.

"It doesn't matter," Louis said, turning once again to the window.

In the lower corridor near the foot of the stairs, Dr Briggle, talking with Mr Herzog, watched Betsy come down the stairs from Louis's room and walked after her along the corridor that ran back to Dr Novali's laboratory. Four doctors came forward from there, including Berrain and Pederson. They side-stepped to let her pass, and they all looked at what she had; then they all turned back.

In the laboratory room Novali put the blood in a chamber. He bent over it and the others bent over with him. By the time David reached the room all he could see was the backs of people. Then Briggle turned away. He looked at David, spread his hands, and walked out. Betsy turned so suddenly that she bumped squarely into him, but she said not a word either. Looking straight ahead, she walked out too.

"What's the count?" David asked.

"Down to nine hundred, Dave. Maybe a little more."

5

The small charge of excitement that had been generated in the hospital on Thursday morning, when Dr Berrain had gone to work, died Friday afternoon. It left a vacuum in which, after the blood count of Friday evening, the doctors and nurses seemed to move aimlessly. Throughout that night the vacuum was filled first by a resignation that at least permitted everyone to function and finally by a determination with which they functioned very well. Louis was left alone no more, not even for a minute. He slept and was awake by turns, grew steadily weaker, and continued to take a detached interest in everything.

About one o'clock in the morning he woke after a brief sleep and turned his head to see Dr Morgenstern sitting over in a corner. The light on the little table there was off, but the door to the room was more than half open and dim light from the corridor just caught Morgenstern's face.

"Hello, Major," Louis said.

Dr Morgenstern did indeed have a commission, but hardly anyone ever thought of it, even when he wore his uniform; something in his nature or his manner was too unmilitary for the title, except as an occasional friendly nickname.

"You go right back to sleep," Dr Morgenstern said. "You were doing fine."

"Sleep, sleep," Louis said. "What time is it?"

"Can't see my watch here. I'll tell you in the morning."

For quite a long time Louis said nothing; Morgenstern sat motionless, holding his hand to his head and peeping through slightly separated fingers.

"There used to be a flower on the window ledge. I'm sorry it's gone."

"It isn't gone. The nurse put it down on the floor for the night. Do you want it back up? Will you sleep then?"

Again there was a long silence.

"No, put it back in its cranny."

"What are you going to do after the war, Julian?" he asked after another silence. "Do you enjoy Army doctoring?"

"Doctoring's pretty much the same one place as another," Morgenstern said; he got up from his chair. "How about a little codeine? You must get more sleep."

"Just a minute, Julian," Louis said, speaking faster and in a louder voice. "Time enough for that, just a minute."

Morgenstern stood beside his chair.

"Something moved then, something's moving," Louis said, quietly again. "Julian, my nose itches. Will you rub my nose for me?"

Morgenstern came over to the bed and did this. "Does that get it?" he asked.

"More to the right—wonderful," Louis said. "Why are you here so late?"

"I work here," Morgenstern said, smiling down at him. "No, really, I just dropped by. You were a little fidgety. You need sleep."

"You probably need sleep more than I. Are there any secrets between us, Major?"

"No, Louis."

"Secrets are the terrible thing, particularly when there aren't any. They lead to such illusions—how you come to fear and hate whoever breaks them, or tries to. Do you hate anyone?"

"I don't think so, not really."

"Fear anyone?"

"I suppose—I suppose I can think of some I fear."

"Do you know what I fear, Julian, almost most of all? That it might happen without any real meaning on anyone's part. That it might just be somebody's mistake."

Louis moved his head slowly from side to side two or three times.

"Good night, Julian. I'll sleep. I promise you, I'll sleep."

On Saturday morning Louis's white blood count was down further to approximately three hundred cells per cubic millimeter; his body was defenseless against any infection, although there were no signs that any had yet taken hold. To make sure that none did, Dr Berrain ordered that the penicillin injections be given every three hours. For some mixture of reasons he could not have explained even to himself, Louis had said nothing about the soreness of his tongue across from the gold-capped tooth; but this morning, soon after he woke, while he was getting a blood transfusion, he called attention to it. A small, whitish, ulcerated lesion was found, and the tooth was promptly covered with gold foil to contain its radioactivity. The swelling of the left arm had reached to the shoulder, but nothing could be done about that. The freezing kept the pain in control; underneath the ice both hands were bluish-gray.

The front of Louis's body, from the forehead to the feet, over the tanned and untanned parts alike, was slowly turning a deep red. The photographer recorded changes; Betsy took her post again and talked or kept silence in accordance with such assessments as she could make of Louis's preferences. He was for the most part silent; there was very little strength in him; there seemed less interest than before. Even Berrain thought things were progressing faster than expected; but on the charts the curves for temperature, pulse, and respiration still were jagged lines of ups and downs, still not far above normal. There was no extravasation of blood at the needle punctures, no signs of spontaneous bleeding—no need, in short, for Dr Briggle's dyes.

In the corridor near the head of the stairway, toward the middle of the morning, one of the doctors mentioned the pathologist sitting and waiting in Santa Fe.

"What's his name—Bell? Should someone get in touch with him?"

"Not yet," Berrain said. "Pederson's been keeping him informed. His name is Beale."

There was really no reason any longer for Beale to stay holed up in Santa Fe; it occurred to Berrain that they had been somewhat alarmist in having him stay there at all, but at all events he might just as well be at Los Alamos, except—except that no one wanted to see him, to put it bluntly. It's easier to leave things as they are for as long as we can, Berrain reflected; much easier on Beale.

A little before noon Berrain went into the doctors' conference room. Louis was asleep; everything was under control, which meant that nothing they could deal with was out of control. Berrain had got to the hospital before eight this morning; he was tired already; it had been nearly one when he had left the night before. But he was also keyed up, as much that as the other. Wisla was in the room, standing by the window that overlooked Truchas.

"Mr Wisla," Berrain said, "would you like to go out for a small ride?"

Wisla turned from the window.

"So? Everything is quiet?"

Berrain shrugged his shoulders; Wisla nodded his head slightly.

"OK."

"I have Louis's car. Do you have any feeling about that?"

Wisla looked at him with some astonishment.

"About riding in it? No." Wisla was walking toward the door, but then he stopped and looked at Berrain again. "About Louis not riding in it, yes. But then I have many feelings like that."

On the way out they ran into Ulanov and asked if he wanted to join them. A few minutes later they were out beyond the main gate, on the road that led to the valley. Men were working on it; squat trucks were parked here and there precariously on the edge of the road or in little work spaces hacked back into the canyon walls. From time to time the whole sweep of the valley showed itself to them; then the trees and the walls closed their vision to a few feet. Wisla looked straight ahead, Ulanov looked at everything, and Berrain kept his eyes on the edge of the road.

"It would have been better to go the back way," said Wisla.

"Oh, no!" Berrain exclaimed. "This is a marvelous road, a fascinating road."

Berrain began to talk about what an incredible place Los Alamos was, what a laboratory of opposites, extremes, even cross-purposes—intellectuals and workmen, scientists and technicians, foreign scientists, American scientists, theoreticians and experimenters, all of these on the one side more or less and the military men on the other—and then one had to think of it at one and the same time as one of the biggest and best-equipped scientific laboratories in the world and the biggest arms-factory, and therefore as a kind of double symbol of the future and the nonfuture of the world.

"Perhaps the place to demonstrate whether God does or does not play dice with human beings," he said.

"It is all of these things, to be sure," Wisla said. "But

the dice-playing is with ourselves. Perhaps God looks on—
with amusement perhaps? maybe a little sad?"

"He saw a very bad roll this week, whichever," Ulanov
said.

"Didn't He?" said Berrain. "Didn't He? Tell me, is that
true about the dates of the two accidents—this Tuesday-
the-twenty-first business?"

"So I heard," said Wisla in a bored voice.

"It is much more to the point," Ulanov said bitterly,
"that he had an argument with the Army over remote
control the morning of the accident."

"It is not impossible that both might have touched the
point," Berrain said. "I am not urging the cause of superstitious explanations. Still, it sometimes takes a little mental energy to resist them—they are so simple. And then
sometimes they do cross a mind—even a very good mind—
perversely, at an inconvenient moment. However—"

The road flattened and straightened out; Berrain turned
north toward the little town of Espanola, a few miles up
the Rio Grande; Wisla drummed steadily on the car door.

"There's a chocolate bar in the glove compartment,"
Berrain said. "Would anybody like some of it?"

They crossed the bridge that spans the Rio Grande here
and drove on into the little town. The proximity of Los
Alamos's thousands had changed Espanola from a quiet
village into a semi-commercial stop. They drove through
it, turned, and started back.

"Neither of those things is to the point," Wisla said after
they had driven a mile or so in silence. "Still, this thing so
hard to explain has a relation to some sort of superstition.
What is this almost touching belief in secrecy but a superstition? Is anything less eligible to the protection of
secrecy than a law of nature—most especially one that
everyone knows? These Congressmen in Washington say
all the time: 'We must keep the secret.' I have given up
asking them: 'What secret?' The question means nothing
to them. They think because we have something that others
do not there must be a secret, forgetting where we got it.

If we made Russia a present of one of our bombs it would take them a year or two to get themselves ready to make their own. Since we won't do that, it will take them three or four. Who are we arming? Ourselves of course—but equally of course all possible enemies. Naturally, no one pays attention to such talk."

"I do," said Berrain. "I have not heard it just that way before."

"But it does no good to put the blame on even the Army," Wisla went on. "The Army is trained to make cops-and-robbers games of everything, which can ruin science, although only the scientists really object to that. But the fears and suspicions are all over, they have become a sickness, perhaps they are the symptoms. If you are sick and do not wish to know the progress of your disease, you cover it with secrecy—secret arms factories and secret piles of secret papers, in the present instance.

"But one dies anyway," he added. "Perhaps sometimes from causes that might have been treated, except for the secrecy. Is it not so, doctor?"

"One dies anyway," Berrain agreed. "What would you do against all this, by the way? Would you just give the bomb to the Russians?"

Wisla laughed.

"Einstein proposed that since the Russians don't yet have the bomb one should invite them to draw up the draft constitution for a world government. Isn't that eccentric? Absolutely impossible! Its only merit is that it deals with the central issue. No. I do not propose giving them the bomb. We would not trust each other more after such a gesture than before—not enough anyway. It would be nice, however, not to do ourselves in trying to keep it from them—especially since we can't. This secrecy, which is a superstition, is worse than that. It corrupts us."

"And like the Gadarene swine, we shall rush possessed to destruction," said Ulanov, smiling to himself, looking out of the window of the car.

"A possibility," Wisla said in a solemn voice. "Myself,

I think mostly of sleepwalkers. Whose feelings are more numbed—but mainly, whose progress is more shrouded in secrecy—than a sleepwalker's? However, sleepwalkers are sometimes very lucky." He gave a loud laugh. "Maybe we shall all be lucky, hey?"

Berrain nodded his head two or three times thoughtfully, but he said nothing. Wisla drummed the edge of the car door while Ulanov talked about the early days of the project, telling anecdotes about this person and that; he referred to Louis's "purity" in passing, and Berrain asked him what he meant.

"It is true enough," said Wisla.

"But I mean—"

"I will illustrate," Ulanov said. "During those Chicago days, in 1942 and early 1943, there were many painful moments—painful because we would find out something or accomplish something of great novelty and couldn't say anything about it. The first chain reaction of course—but there were many littler ones. I remember thinking myself in those days how nice it would be to pick up a newspaper and see a big headline—'New Mexico Site Picked for Bomb Development'—or 'President Pushes Button to Open Big Hanford Plant'—'Clinton Reactor Goes Critical'—everything would have seemed so much realer. People were frustrated, working so behind doors. Not Louis though. He seemed not to feel this need. This takes a kind of purity—not a feeling for secrecy, it would have been the same to him if there had been headlines—a kind of purity."

Berrain had taken the car again around the curves and the trucks and the men at work improving the road. He reached the flat stretch before the main gate, and just as he did an Army sedan with a soldier driving went by. Colonel Hough was in the front seat; an older man and woman and a pretty, black-haired young girl of nineteen or twenty were in the back. All of the heads turned; the girl could be seen saying something in obvious excitement.

"Do you suppose that's—" Berrain began.

"Yes," Ulanov said. "That's his family and this is his car."

6

At the hospital there was confusion. As Berrain, Wisla, and Ulanov came through the door they saw Colonel Hough standing at the foot of the stairway to the second floor. He was talking to two Military Police; his voice was controlled, but plainly he was upset.

"And just who gave that order?" they heard him say.

Mr and Mrs Saxl and Libby were standing to one side, rather huddled together and looking ill at ease. David Thiel appeared on the stairs behind the MP's, pushed down between them, paying them no attention at all, and went over to the Saxls. Wisla joined them; Ulanov started forward but drew back.

"All right," the Colonel said to the soldiers. "Now get the ones upstairs and get the hell out of here, all of you."

With David and Wisla the Saxl family passed by Berrain and Ulanov. Berrain looked at David, who shook his head.

"We are more than seventy-five hundred feet high here," Wisla was saying. "The air is a little thin but very pure." He was apparently speaking to Libby, although he was not looking at her.

They went on out of the hospital. Colonel Hough took a step after them, stopped, stood irresolutely, then turned back and walked rapidly down the corridor to the doctors' conference room.

Berrain, without a word or a glance at Ulanov, made for the stairway; and Ulanov, equally intent, walked down the corridor to the conference room where the Colonel was talking on the telephone. Ulanov stood listening. Once or twice the Colonel stared at him, as though to open his mind to the possibility that he might stand around some place else.

"It wasn't an order, was it?" the Colonel demanded.

"So it wasn't an order, was it?" he said after a moment.

"Well, then, you goddamned fool, why couldn't you have waited thirty minutes?"

When he put the telephone down he stared at Ulanov again.

"The Congressman?" said Ulanov.

"Is it really any business of yours?" the Colonel asked. Ulanov said nothing.

"What the General did was perfectly reasonable," Colonel Hough said. "The trouble was he had to deal with screwballs at both ends."

General Meacham had given ear to the Congressman's notion that if Louis were as sick as the doctors had said, guards should be placed around his room to prevent the possible disclosure of nuclear secrets to possibly uncleared visitors in possible moments of delirium. The Congressman had heard about an incident at Oak Ridge during the war when a whole private hospital wing had been constructed to house a man there who had had a nervous breakdown. The General had given a running summary of the Congressman's views to Colonel Hough's deputy in the Colonel's absence. "So this goddamned halfwit takes over," the Colonel said, "and decides to order out the MP's all on his own."

"Uniforms," said Ulanov.

"If you want to know the truth," said the Colonel, "you give me an awful pain. Uniforms or no uniforms isn't the point. There's a certain elementary respect due a person." The Colonel walked out.

Under the ministrations of David Thiel, whom they had met some years before, and of Wisla, who impressed them greatly, the Saxls crossed the street to the Lodge, where rooms were ready for them. There they assembled their thoughts and changed their clothes; then they returned to the hospital. Louis had awakened from his sleep and had been prepared for his family to the extent that preparations were possible. It was a painful reunion. The ice troughs jutted out both ways from the bed and impeded movement; Louis's father and sister did not know what to say or how to say it; his mother, who knew, fell silent as soon as she looked into his eyes. Louis tried a little joke with Libby, but his mind was so far from the words, there was so little meaning or spirit in them, that they made almost an ugly sound in the air of the room. He spoke to them, then turned his head on the pillows and gazed at one or another of them; and whatever he did, a silence followed it.

Mr Saxl walked over to the window and looked out.

"It's pretty at night," Louis said. "There's a light around at the end of the hospital—"

He did not go on. He looked back to his mother and this time his eyes and his features softened, but a second later he was looking right through her, lying with his eyes open and watching intently something deep inside them.

Charley Pederson came in and did what he could to break the hush over the room, speaking cheerfully and louder than usual. He took the Saxls out; Berrain was waiting for them. Walking slowly along the corridor, and down the stairs, choosing his words with great but unostentatious care, Berrain told them what he felt he should.

At the door of the hospital David took over from Berrain—none of this was prearranged, although it seemed so—and walked with the Saxls back to the Lodge. He stayed with them, and there, in Mrs Saxl's room, everybody cried. Words poured out, and the silences were alive with meanings and understandings. The excitement of release made Libby almost merry; she told a funny story about Louis and a girl at home in Georgetown, and started to tell another. But she stopped in the middle of it, and they all sat silent again. Then, one after another, the members of the family began the small preparations of establishing themselves for what was to come—unpacking, laying out toilet articles, hanging clothes. In the midst of this David left them. Halfway down the stairs from their rooms he heard Mr Saxl behind him.

"Is there some place I could get a bottle of whiskey, David?" he said. "Is that possible? Would it be a trouble?"

7

Theresa came up to Santa Fe from Albuquerque, where she had got off the plane, by bus. The plane ride had been an ordeal—the weather not good, a long wait in Chicago, and no place to bury her head, no place to be alone. In her seat by the window she had had to be conscious of the person next to her—who had reminded her for a shocked moment of Wisla—and to think the thoughts she could not escape, looking out into the enormous sky. She had been grateful only for the roar of the engines. Soon the sun would be going down—it was already nearly five— and what the night would bring she did not know.

The road was straight and flat; the countryside was barer on this side of Santa Fe than it was on the other; the bus was half full. No one sat next to her. Since she had not slept she felt tired and drained and dirty. One thought moved round and round the rim of her mind, exhibiting itself in many aspects; it had started while she had been listening to David on the phone the night before, and it had not stopped moving since: she had written her letter on the train before this terrible thing had happened to Louis and it had happened even before the letter could have been given to him. The thought moved and faded and flared and was like a tiny light, too dim to reveal anything, too bright to let her have peace.

She sat quietly, hardly looking at the land and the sky that had cushioned and crowned their plans of less than a week ago. And so at last she came to Santa Fe.

The bus stopped just down the street from the sprawling pink hotel in the center of town. Theresa took her one

bag and set off. The bag bumped against her legs at almost
every step, but she paid no attention to it, although it made
her progress uneven and made it seem almost rakish. The
bus driver, standing on the sidewalk, turned to watch her.
A little Mexican boy ran out of a doorway and collided
with her. The sidewalk was full; she moved among and
between people, going faster than any of them.

A week ago she had been driven through Santa Fe,
coming and going; she had had a taste of its flavor; she
knew little of its streets. She had come by train and Louis
had met her at the Lamy station (where, only five days ago,
she had seen him fade into the night). On the way up to
Los Alamos he had taken her through some of the narrow
and winding roads of the town, along the river, around the
Cathedral, and past a long, low wooden building with a
wooden arcade in front. Back in there, he had said, there
was a patio and on the patio was the Santa Fe office for
the Los Alamos project. A very nice woman ran it; it was
the second oldest building in Santa Fe; some funny things
had happened there in the early days of the project; it was
where he had gone when he had first come out from Chicago; once—

"Your eyelashes have grown, I think," she had said then.

The building was only a block and a half from the hotel.
It housed a series of shops and offices, and she walked
more slowly under the arcade looking at the signs; there
was a bookshop, a law office, an art gallery, a Woman's
Exchange; and then a doorway leading back into the patio.
By the doorway, so inconspicuous that at first she didn't
notice it, a sign said, "Los Alamos Scientific Laboratory."

On the patio were more shops and offices; the one she
sought was on the far side. She entered it, and a woman
with gray hair and a young face looked up at her; two men
sitting on a bench in a half-separated room looked up too.
She walked over to the woman, still carrying her bag.

"My name is Theresa Savidge," she said. "I came to see
a friend at Los Alamos. How can I get out most quickly?"

"Has your clearance been arranged?"

"I don't know."

"Well, does your friend know you're coming?"

"I don't—yes, he does."

"You don't know whether he's arranged a visitor's pass for you?"

"No. He's had an accident. What's the quickest way to get out?"

"What is your friend's name?"

"Louis Saxl."

"Oh," the woman said. "I see."

"What is the quickest way to get out?"

"If you'll just put your bag down, and have a chair, I'll call out right—"

"*What is the quickest way to get out?*"

"Please, I'll—"

"What is the quickest way to get out?"

The woman jumped from her chair and the men from their bench. Theresa put her bag down and leaned up against the woman's desk; she raised one hand and caught her hair, and then tossed her head back.

"I'm sorry," she said. "Please forgive me. I'm terribly anxious to get there as soon as I can. I only heard last night."

The woman came from behind the desk, put an arm around Theresa, and guided her to a chair. She patted her on the leg and automatically tried to smooth out some of the wrinkles the long journey had worked into Theresa's suit. One of the men brought a cup of water; the woman watched approvingly as Theresa sipped it.

It turned out that a pass for Theresa had been been put through by David Thiel; it was waiting at the gate.

"Someone might have let us know," the woman said coldly into the phone. "Not necessarily you. Just somebody," she added, hanging up.

A staff car, only just back from a trip to Los Alamos, would take Theresa there right away. The woman went over to a small chart stuck up on the wall behind her desk, a trip record for the staff cars. The last name on the list was "Dr Galen Beale." Under this she wrote "Miss Theresa Savidge."

In the staff car, Theresa smoked a cigarette, took off her shoes and wriggled her toes, straightened her stockings, and studied the wrinkles in her suit. For the first few miles the soldier tried conversation; Theresa opened her handbag and took out a comb. For the next few miles, while the soldier watched through the rear-vision mirror, she attended to her appearance.

After the road crossed the Rio Grande and began its climb up toward the mesa, they talked a little. The soldier had taken some famous people back and forth and he mentioned some; Oppenheimer had impressed him most; his eyes got into you like bayonets, the soldier said, and he scared your pants off you just by looking at you, but you could see at once what a brain he had, and still he was a nice guy, everybody said so, and the soldier certainly couldn't say different.

"I wouldn't want to be him though," the soldier added.

"Why not?"

"Because I like to get my sleep nights. I wouldn't want to be any of them."

"Were you in the war?"

"Yes'm. Some of it."

"I suppose you get your sleep nights after doing whatever you had to do."

"Yes'm, I know about that. But it's some different between one at a time or even a thousand at a time and a hundred thousand at a time."

Theresa rearranged herself on the seat so that she was half facing the side of the car; she had lost some of the tautness and bleakness that she had had all night and all day, but now with night coming on again she felt them coming back.

"Maybe you should talk to some of them, maybe you

should find out better what you're talking about," she said, feeling this was as stupid as it sounded but not caring.

"Oh, I've talked to lots of them. But then I was reading in the paper just the other day about one of them saying there wasn't more than one chance in God-knows-what, a trillion maybe, that these Bikini bombs could blow up the world. I said to myself, this seems pretty safe odds. But then I said to myself, hey! how come any odds at all? Who's running this show anyway?"

The soldier spoke blandly, but in a nagging, insinuating voice that Theresa seemed to hear with her teeth rather than her ears; the soldier was having fun. Of all the ways he had devised to relieve the boredom of these interminable trips, baiting the visitors along these lines was much the best.

"Like that school story about the guy who discovered fire, and then the gods tied him to a rock and the vultures been pecking at his liver ever since. Could be some things aren't meant to be discovered. Could be—"

"Oh, will you stop talking!" Theresa cried. "Won't you please leave me alone!"

This was the most astonishing reply the soldier had ever got to his baiting, and he said nothing for the rest of the trip.

At the gate Theresa's pass was ready for her. There was a note for her too, from David; it told her that she should go straight to the Lodge, where a room was waiting for her, and that if she wanted to see the Saxls they were there, and that he would be there as soon as he could.

At the Lodge she ran into Libby Saxl just inside the door. Without a word they took hold of each other, and embraced, clinging together for a long time; when they started upstairs Theresa felt, for the first time since she had left New York, that she didn't want to be alone.

8

"You have told me everything except one thing," said the man sitting at the table. "Maybe no one can ever tell that, my son least of all perhaps. I've known it to happen when a thing goes wrong, a sudden thing like this, why, the person hurt sometimes can't tell you as much as someone else, who maybe didn't even see it. I wonder if you haven't a feeling about it, more than that, a suspicion even. It would do no good, of course, except to know is better than not."

In the fading light that came through the bank of windows across one end of the room, the man who spoke was hardly distinguishable, nor the table at which he sat, one of many dim bulks in the near-dark. He let his wonder hang from his words, testing the willingness of the young man at the window to answer without being asked, but there was no answer.

"Was it really unavoidable?" he said finally.

There was only enough light coming through the window to show the outline of the young man's head, like a cutout of black paper held against the window rather low, for the body that held it there was small and fatigue made it smaller.

"I'm not sure it's better to know, Mr Saxl, not always." David's voice vibrated, not with badly controlled emotion, but with tiredness uncontrolled; the words, for this distant and opposite reason, seemed to carry a charge that was not in them. "If one could be sure or use the knowledge one way or another— But just to know for the sake of knowing—in some things, anyway, things like this—"

"Louis used to say that's the way the very biggest secrets are discovered. I remember once a man in our town, Brinckerhoff—he's a builder, a contractor—he asked Louis, he said what's all this study going to get you, you know, the practical value of it? Louis said it might not have any practical value, at least not as far as he could speak to, and Brinckerhoff couldn't make head or tail of that. Just to find out, just to know for the sake of knowing, Louis used to say, just like you said now. He has great respect for you, David. He always spoke about you when he came home."

The light had gone almost entirely. Mr Saxl, peering through heavy glasses, could not even make out David's form as he left the window and picked his way across the room, moving slowly but with familiarity around and between the numerous objects in it, his cane hitting the concrete floor unevenly. By the door David stopped; even in the dark he could see the panel of switches, four in a row. He lifted his cane and sought with the tip of it for one of them, found it and pushed, as he had many times before, coming into this room.

Mr Saxl glanced up automatically as the light came on, then down at his watch, after which he sat as he had been sitting—quietly, even a little stiffly, his hands on the table. His neat, mild appearance brought to mind the sound of the sprinkler on the lawn before dinner, the smell of the cigar on the front porch afterward, and all the patterns of circumspection. Circumspection, which had preserved him, looked through his glasses and spoke his words. The light made him silent; he wished David had not turned it on; still, it was almost time to go. He cleared his throat to speak again.

"Tell me, David, do you think it was really unavoidable?"

David studied the tip of his cane, holding it before him, turning it this way and that. He looked quickly at the older man, who was watching him patiently, and in the same movement turned his eyes to the structure at the far end of the room; he moved toward it as Mr Saxl waited.

"I spent nearly four years working with Louis," David said, and his voice was stronger. "Three of them here at Los Alamos and half that time right in this room—days, evenings, some whole nights. What he did the last time he had done many times before, time and time again. I've done it too, several of us have done it. But no one as well as Louis, as skillfully—so carefully."

David looked back across his shoulder at Mr Saxl, and then moved on again toward the structure.

"I've sat in that chair you're sitting in or stood here, right here or over at that side, and watched him do this thing over and over. I never saw the beginning of a slip. Still, we all knew something could go wrong. It was a risky thing, there was always this element of risk."

Just in front of the structure David stopped again. He was close enough to touch it, but he did not. He leaned on his cane and he put one hand to his head, and for a moment the exhaustion that had gone out of his voice seemed to come back in his body. Mr Saxl from his chair noticed this with something like annoyance. He was very tired himself, and the tired are not often moved by the tired. Moreover, David's gesture was made with a kind of grace—an overflow perhaps from the disciplining of his lameness—which Mr Saxl associated with temperament. He shifted his eyes to the structure, and tried to visualize what it was that had happened when his boy had stood where this one now stood, before they took him to the hospital room.

"But the answer to your question isn't what happened. I came down here that same night, after I heard. I read the records and I did the experiment over again the way Louis had done it. I know what happened. They won't let me tell you, for reasons known only to God and the Generals. But please believe me it means nothing, it was only that element of risk, a technical matter. As to why it happened—well, that's a hard thing to explain, except— No, it was really unavoidable, Mr Saxl, things being what they were."

"Except, you said. Except what, David?"

"Except—I really meant nothing, Mr Saxl. I was just

thinking of that element of risk again—in a different way."

"It might be no one can ever tell, although I think you have a feeling on it. Do you mind if I say I think you would be hard to know? Please don't misunderstand. My own son is hard to know in many ways. Perhaps the things that make it hard are what you respect. The others like him too, you said?"

Mr Saxl could make nothing of the cube-shaped pile that he understood to be the machine that had gone wrong in his son's hands. In the office of his lumberyard back in Georgetown he himself had put together a work table not unlike this framework table that supported the pile. There were familiar objects on the table too—pencils and tools and the rest. But with the gray brick pile he could find nothing from which to start a thought; it had no front, or else it was all front and so equally all sides; he could barely make out some of the lines of the edges of the bricks; his eyes reported the unbroken smoothness of the surfaces; and this made his mind uneasy more than anything.

"Where did he stand, when you stood here as you said a while ago?"

David had not heard the older man come up behind him; the words startled him.

"I think it would be better—" he started to say.

"No, it's better to know something at least. Will you show me where he stood?"

David moved right against the front face of the structure; he leaned over the table top slightly and shifted his feet into position.

"About like this," he said.

"And what did he do then? What went on?"

"Mr Saxl—" David began. But Mr Saxl took a step forward and spoke again.

"What did he do? Tell me, David."

There was a very long pause.

"It's not going to be done any more, not the way it was," David said. "I don't think the Colonel told you, Mr Saxl, or if he did I didn't hear it—you should know that nobody will ever do just this thing again."

David moved away from the structure.

"That last time for Louis was the last time for anyone. It should have been stopped earlier, of course. There'd been enough talk about it."

"I don't understand," Mr Saxl said. "I've got the hint of this before, but I don't understand. Why did Louis do it that last time if it wasn't necessary?"

"Mr Dombrowski was using that word just yesterday," David said, looking at Mr Saxl carefully. "I don't know what to say to it—I didn't then and I don't now. It would be easier if you knew more about this—" he waved an arm rather generally, whether at the structure or at the whole room or at all of Los Alamos or beyond it was not possible to tell— "or if I could tell you things I can't. Still Mr Dombrowski knows, he knows a great deal—you'd like him, Mr Saxl, you'd like each other."

The sound of an automobile penetrated the room, and David looked around him, and then at Mr Saxl, with something close to desperation.

"But you mustn't think it was just a meaningless accident that could have been prevented if someone had only thought to prevent it," he went on. "Maybe if a great many people had thought harder—then this, and not only this— It was unnecessary like war is unnecessary, Mr Saxl—like war, which solves nothing—like that."

The sound of the automobile was louder now and growing. Mr Saxl, who had been looking at David steadily, glanced around him; David lowered his head, but raised it at once and went on.

"And just the way a soldier is hurt, in a war, Louis was hurt, in a war. That's the only way you can think of it, Mr Saxl—it doesn't make sense, it makes a nonsense, but a familiar one—the sense isn't familiar enough." He lifted his cane and pointed at the structure. "There is a moment when you're working that, just before an accident can happen— Or let me say that that is very impersonal, but Louis is a very personal person, he knows the delicate network the mind has made around the world, he might have—he has helped to make it. And he—" David stopped. Mr Saxl looked at his watch.

The lights from the automobile glowed for a moment through the windows; the rays swept the room as the car turned into the clearing outside; the engine sound pitched up and then fell off to nothing; a car door slammed.

"It took this thing that happened to get you in this room," David said. "But just this once, for an hour, and by dispensation of the very highest brass. They sent a plane for you and Mrs Saxl and Libby, but next week they'd stop you at the gate. The war isn't over out here. When it is, there won't be any place like this."

Mr Saxl had found his overcoat and was putting it on, struggling with the sleeves.

"They've been very good," he said. "They've done everything for us, that plane and all. Still, the war—you know, it does seem closer here than I ever knew it, even when it was going on, reading about it in the papers. That Colonel Hough, he's a nice fellow though." Mr Saxl straightened up.

"And so are you, David. I think I know what you're saying, some anyway. It's too bad, isn't it?—too bad."

The door to the room opened and a soldier's head appeared.

"Are you ready, doctor? Colonel Hough is here."

Colonel Hough came into the room, nodded to David, went straight over to Mr Saxl, and did not try to avoid the subject.

"I've just come from the hospital, Mr Saxl," he said. "There is no change. You do understand that's all we can expect for a while? It is really hopeful."

Mr Saxl nodded, but not as though he understood. "The doctors still think that Mrs Saxl and I—"

"Yes," said the Colonel. "Please believe me, I know

how hard it is on you. But it would be harder if you went
in. He is comfortable, there is no pain. Dr Berrain told
you the absolute truth this afternoon."

Mr Saxl nodded again, this time as though he did understand. He sighed slightly, looked from the Colonel to
David and back again. He was smaller than the Colonel
and, standing so close to him, looked almost shabby, for
the Colonel was very trim and straight; his uniform was
neither new nor too well pressed, but it fitted him well.
The skin around his eyes was crinkled with his obvious
eagerness to assume any burden Mr Saxl might put upon
him.

"Well," Mr Saxl said after a moment, "I suppose we'd
better get back to the—Lodge?"

"Fuller Lodge," said the Colonel. "If you're ready." He
looked at David, and they all began to move toward the
door. "We inherited the Lodge and its name too when we
built the site here. Did you know this used to be a school
for boys? boys from the east principally, wealthy boys. The
people who had it didn't want to give it up, told the Army
it wasn't for sale. Well—" they went through the door; the
soldier was standing there; Colonel Hough gave him a little
punch as they walked past him, and the soldier grinned—
"we bought it anyway."

They stood outside on the porch. It was quiet, and cool
and wild. On both sides of the clearing in front of the
building jagged boulders cropped out from the sides of
canyon walls that rose sloping up into the night. Above
the boulders trees took over, yellow and ponderosa pine,
covering the walls with massed green going off into black;
and high above the heads of the men standing there the
trees reached the rim of the canyon and made a fringed
edge faintly visible in the dark. A vague, sourceless throbbing could be heard, and the soft random chirping of the
birds settling themselves for the night in the trees around.

They stood for a moment, finishing the buttoning of
their coats. Part of the prehistory of the continent lay

brooding all around them, in this and other nearby canyons and ravines and arroyos. What they saw from where they stood had not changed much, or had changed only to renew itself, for thousands of years. Up on the mesa to which they were now going a town had been built, with sidewalks and streets and many buildings and the beginnings of gardens. The building down here in the canyon was a part of it; the road connected it; a clearing had been made and in the clearing stood the Colonel's jeep with its headlights glowing against the boulders and the trees, and with the sound of its idling engine running back and forth between the canyon walls. But the town seemed a long way off, and the darkness was more impressive than the light, and the quiet more noticeable than the sound.

"We bought it," said the Colonel, "and inside of a year we'd built a city. There isn't anything like it in the world."

They got into the jeep and the driver swung off onto the road, which curved out of the clearing and began a steep curving ascent up through the trees and among the boulders out of the canyon. The Colonel said something to the driver, and he looked back; as he did, the jeep was jolted by a small ridge of rock in the road.

"Watch it," said the Colonel, "you've got to keep your eyes open down here."

David grunted. "The sheer cussedness of nature, eh, Colonel?"

"The what? Oh, by God, that's right. That's one of our famous phrases, Mr Saxl. One of the scientists was tearing his hair one day over some ticklish problems and that's what he said—'the sheer cussedness of nature.'" He chuckled. "Pretty good."

The Colonel turned himself around and leaned back over the edge of the front seat. "You know, you've got a very fine boy, Mr Saxl. Everybody here thinks the world of him."

"He was always a fine boy," Mr Saxl began, and then stopped as the high, tight whining of an airplane came to them through the trees. No one spoke as it passed over and faded off, and then Mr Saxl continued. "There was a mail plane used to fly over Georgetown every morning. They've changed the route now, but it used to, and I used to take Louis down to the front porch with me years ago about that time. That's a funny thing to remember, isn't it? I had a little song I used to sing to him, sitting on the porch. He was just a little boy then. He'd laugh and clap his hands when I'd sing him that song, and the plane went over."

The Colonel said nothing, but David turned his head and looked at the older man, and after a moment spoke to him.

"What was the song, Mr Saxl?"

"Oh, a silly song. I made it up. Just a silly song."

"There's a little song I've heard Louis sing once in a while. He said you used to sing it to him. About a wagon."

"He still remembers it? That was years ago."

"Won't you sing it?"

"Yes," said Colonel Hough, also turning to look at Mr. Saxl. "I'd like to hear it too."

Mr Saxl did not answer. The jeep jolted, the engine sound beat against the canyon walls. And then he began to move his head from side to side rhythmically; and in time with this movement, looking at David, smiling a little with embarrassment, he sang:

"Here comes the wegetable wagon, the wegetable wagon,
the wegetable wagon,
Here comes the wegetable wagon, to bring little Louis a—"

"Right then," he said, turning to include Colonel Hough in this explanation, "I'd wait a little and Louis would guess. He'd say watermelon, or cauliflower, or tomato, or something. But whatever he'd say, I'd shake my head and then say something else, like parsnip or cantaloupe. I must have sung it a thousand times, those mornings and other times."

He chuckled, and turned away to look at the trees banked
solidly.

"Here comes the wegetable wagon," he sang softly, "to
bring little Louis a—"

9

In consultation with each other, Berrain, Morgenstern and
some of the other doctors had decided to call Dr Beale
out during the afternoon. There were still no signs of spontaneous hemorrhages, and there was no evidence of the
liver breakdown and the jaundice that the doctors feared
almost as much. The blood counts were taken, checked,
and recorded, but in fact no one paid more than passing
attention to their testimony. They were down about as low
as they could be, and they were beyond anyone's intervention. By the end of the afternoon—at about the time
Theresa arrived from Santa Fe—things were at a lull, as
they had been when Berrain had gone for his drive.

But for this very reason the doctors and nurses were,
one and all, more dispirited than they had yet been. The
things they could prevent or treat were almost all past; the
things still to come were things for which they could only
wait. If jaundice developed, it would be terminal jaundice:
they could relieve it a little, but they could not affect that
deterioration of the liver that would lead to it. If spontaneous hemorrhages began, perhaps Briggle's dyes would
work, perhaps not; in any event, what then? A time lag
had followed the establishment of the dosage and the pre-
cipitous fall of the white blood count, but the lag ended
on Saturday evening, the twenty-fifth of May, when Louis's
temperature began, at last, its slow, inexorable rise.

Theresa had been at the Lodge no more than a few
minutes when David came up from the canyon with Mr
Saxl and Colonel Hough. The word from the hospital—
from Charley Pederson, specifically, standing by himself

at the foot of the stoop in front, smoking a cigarette as the
jeep drew up—was that Louis could not be seen just then,
possibly not at all during the evening. The Colonel walked
across to the Lodge with Mr Saxl. David stared at Pederson.

"You know, she should be here by now," David said.
"I'll have to get over to the Lodge. She'll want to see him."

Pederson dropped his cigarette. David poked at it with
his cane and ground it out.

"They were going to be married in a month."

Pederson said nothing. David continued to grind the
cigarette.

"What do the doctors propose? That he die unat-
tended?"

Pederson said nothing.

"How long, Charley?" David asked. He peered up at
Pederson.

"Maybe two or three days."

For about an hour after he found Theresa and took her
away from the Saxls, David kept her from the hospital,
quoting doctors over and over as she protested. They went
to his small room and sat there; they walked; they stopped
in the drugstore and had sandwiches in place of the dinner
neither had eaten; then they walked some more. At the
end of this time Theresa knew everything important, including Charley Pederson's last estimate.

She insisted on going to the hospital. If she could not
see Louis, she could at least be in the same building; if she
could not stay there, she could stand outside; if she could
not see him at once, possibly she could see him later.
Theresa was reasonable and insistent and did not raise her
voice. David thought that she was hoping against hope, as
indeed all of them had. He thought this was the best state
of mind for her to have; he couldn't have it any more, but
there was the slightest tinge of reassurance, the smallest
turn away from finality, in Theresa's having it. And because
his illusion served his need, it took him longer than it
should have taken to discover that his assessment of Ther-

esa was in fact an illusion, that she had no more hope than
he had. He used an "if." And she turned on him bitterly.

"Don't talk that way! Don't make it happen twice!"

She did not press him, as Mr Saxl had, about the accident
itself. Her thoughts and feelings centered on Louis in his
hospital room. She wanted to know about the doctors and
the nurses, what David and Louis talked about during David's visits to his room, what David had read to him and
what Louis had said. With what seemed to David almost
clinical curiosity, she asked about the effects of the radiation sickness, and listened silently to as much as he would
tell her. If he tried to cut something short, or turn away
from it, or soften it with phrases that said nothing, she
spoke at once.

"David! You're not telling me! What happened then?"
Even so, he held some things back.

Sleeplessness, grief, too little food, and whatever it was
that was served by this fixed determination to learn all the
details of Louis's dying had combined to give Theresa's
face the appearance of a mask. The expressions that moved
her face, coming and fading, shaded only slightly the complicated intensity of expression that came from the drawn
flesh over the bones. Her hair seemed darker, her eyebrows stronger, her eyes larger and deeper.

David stole looks at her and was seized by the oddest
notions. He wanted to touch her softly, to trace and soften
the outline of her eyes, or to touch the edges of her mouth.
She walked and sat usually with her head held forward,
and her long hair sometimes curved around her face; he
wanted to reach out and bring it back. He did none of
these things. They walked and talked, and at about eight-
thirty they finally got to the hospital.

Theresa agreed to wait downstairs while David went up
to see the doctors. He took her to the conference room,
but the door was closed and he could hear voices inside.
Then he took her to the little cubicle where he and Wisla
had sat on Thursday working out their estimations of the

radiation dosage. She sat there and he went on upstairs.
In two minutes he was back.

"They say no. They say, please not tonight. I think it
would be better, Theresa."

She stood up.

"No, I have to see him, if I only just see him, but I have
to see him."

David looked at her silently.

"Will you take me up there?"

"Theresa, I can't take you past the doctors."

"Will you take me to the doctors?"

He walked ahead of her up the stairs, and at the top of
the stairs he motioned to Pederson, who was talking to
Betsy down the corridor the other way from Louis's room.
A night nurse was sitting outside the door there.

Pederson came over, and Betsy followed him.

"She wants to know if she can't just look in on him. I'm
sorry. This is Theresa Savidge. She—"

"I know," Pederson said. "But it's not a good idea tonight."

Betsy was staring at Theresa, but she shook her head,
more or less automatically.

"If he's asleep, I'll not disturb him," Theresa said. "If
he's awake, I'll only let him know I'm here. Surely that
wouldn't hurt—if you're afraid for him. If you're afraid for
me, please don't be."

Betsy considered this an effective statement; it proved
Theresa had her emotions under control at least at the
moment. Theresa was standing very straight, and quite
involuntarily Betsy stood straighter herself. Her first sight
of Theresa in the corridor had hardened her; she knew
who Theresa was without being told, but she shouldn't
have come upstairs; besides, she was dressed inappro-
priately, she had too much color in her skirt. But as Betsy
looked now at Theresa's face she saw there much the same
as David had been seeing, and she reacted much the same
way; she began to remember the letter, which had moved

her, and just the thought of it, now in the presence of its
writer, moved her again. Oh, she thought, let her in!

Pederson looked at David as though for a signal. But
Theresa's face really told him more, and in fact enough.
For the briefest moment the thought occurred to him that
he might just refer this to Berrain or Morgenstern, but he
spoke even before that thought quite formed.

He said, all right, she could go to the door of the room;
Louis almost certainly would be asleep; if not, he might
not recognize her; generally he lay looking away from the
door and she was not to do anything to attract his attention;
did she understand the situation?

"Yes," she said.

"Come along after me," he said, and walked toward the
room.

He stopped where the night nurse was sitting, and bent
over, whispering something to her. Then he took two light
steps to the door; it was open an inch or two. He pushed
it back a little way and looked in. After that he stepped
back and motioned to Theresa, and as she came forward
he walked on past her and down the corridor to where
David and Betsy were standing.

They saw her move slowly and very quietly to the doorway, and stop just outside it. She stood motionless for
what seemed a long time, looking into the room, and then
she leaned forward a little. They were standing perhaps
twenty feet away from her, and her face was in profile from
where they stood; it was difficult to tell when the smile on
her face had come there; but each of them saw that it was
there, although it was so gentle a smile that it affected the
planes of her face from the side hardly at all. She continued
to look into the room, and then she raised her fingers to
her lips and blew a kiss. She turned quite quickly then and
came back along the corridor. Her eyes were glistening,
but she walked steadily; a trace of the smile remained on
her face, perfectly distinct in just the way that a voice heard
from a long way off in the open air is distinct, but too faint

to carry its meaning, and by the time she got to where they stood the smile had gone.

She nodded her head and said, "Thank you," in a low voice to Pederson and Betsy; she went directly down the stairs, and David followed her.

From the front of the hospital they walked around to the pond, under the yellow-glowing light, and by the pond to the street that ran along the high steel fence of the Technical Area. Floodlights illuminated everything there; the guards stood by the gates; windows shone in the buildings, mechanical sounds rose and fell and mingled, figures could be seen crossing the spaces between buildings. Theresa and David walked along the opposite side of the street—sheer randomness had put them there. Finally Theresa stopped just before a barracks-like structure with a porch across the front of it; the sound of a juke box came from inside.

"What's this?" she asked David.

"The Service Club," David told her, pointing with his cane to a sign on the side of the building. "The local night club."

"Can we go in?"

"We can, but it's a noisy place Saturday nights. Do you want to?"

Theresa said she thought she did, and they went inside. They couldn't find an empty table, so they stood at one side of the room; David went over to a counter by an enormous refrigerator and came back with two bottles of beer. The juke box played steadily, but a group of a dozen people, sitting together at one end of the room, broke into song, drowning out the instrument. The place was getting fuller all the time, and after they finished the beer they left.

10

Sunday's air was the softest of air and the day was a day
of sunny glory. Spring was in full flood that day, across the
mesas, up and down the canyon walls, in the calls of birds
and the mists of flowers in the sheltered fields; the sky was
a limitless glow of light and the snow made a dainty fringe
on Truchas. The children were out, as they always were,
but their games seemed bigger and their voices clearer.
By nine o'clock all of the horses had been taken from the
riding stable. By ten o'clock the soldiers at the main guard
house had recorded the heaviest outbound traffic of the
year.

But before the riders and the fishermen and the pic-
nickers started, Theresa left her room at the Lodge and
walked quickly across to the hospital. She went up to the
second floor without attracting any attention. She recognized Betsy as she walked down the corridor to Louis's
room, but no one seemed even aware of her until she was
almost there. Then Betsy looked at her, looked away, and
quickly looked up again, shaking her head. A doctor whom
Theresa didn't know stepped out of the group by the door
and pointed out a chair beside a desk a few feet back along
the corridor; the others were talking in low tones; and in
this setting she was afraid to speak.

For fifteen minutes Theresa sat. She heard and saw nothing that meant anything to her. Doctors came and went.
Betsy went by, tight-faced; but a few feet past Theresa she
turned and came back. Theresa got up from her chair;
Betsy only backed off a little and continued to look. She
was moving her head, neither nodding nor shaking it but
just moving it, or letting it move in small erratic motions;
her mouth was drawn tight and her face was a confusion
of expressions. She did not seem about to cry and she did
not seem about to speak, and she only stood there, her

head moving in this strange way. Then she turned and walked away; and Theresa, trembling from that look, sat down again. She gripped the chair arms and sat looking straight forward. And thus she was sitting when Louis's voice, loud and sharp, broke from the room.

"Harry! Nine o'clock, Harry!"

This was the beginning of a delirium that went on, in fits and starts, for most of Sunday. The eye of the hurricane had passed beyond him and left him to the storm, heightened by the stresses of his body and the end of all controls. He talked coherently for minutes, then incoherently for an hour; lapsed into silences, then droned, then called. As soon as it began Theresa jumped from where she sat and ran to the room. Nobody stopped her. She went to the bed and looked down at him, listening. She put her hand on the covers over his legs and spoke to him softly, but there was no sign that he heard her. She leaned forward and rested her hand against his breast, bare and red, and spoke again; he gave no sign that he heard her. His eyes stared at her, moved away, returned, and turned away again. Berrain took Theresa gently by the arm, but she shook him off. As she stood there, stroking the shape of Louis's legs, he quieted and looked up at her.

"Those roads are ghastly silent now."

But before she could say a word he was off on something else. Some of what he had said to Wisla two days before he said again, coherently and incoherently; and much more that went along with that. But he spoke at almost equal length, and with apparent pleasure, of some things of which no one present knew a thing—of an old cottonwood tree, of the moons of Jupiter and Descartes's vortices.

"That's good, Skip, you get a lot out of that," he said earnestly.

His parents came over, and his sister. Wisla came, stood and listened gravely, left, and came back again. David came and went and came and went.

There are sounds that come in across the great inter-

stellar spaces, hisses and crackles from remote and sometimes not even detectable bodies. It is quite certain that
they are nothing more than a kind of radio signal generated
by matter in turmoil, a cosmic gibbering, sounds coming
in from a long way off, puzzling, not to be answered. Most
of what Louis said during this Sunday was like that.

Sometime during the afternoon he fell very quiet, and
out of this quiet he asked for Theresa. At that moment
she was lying on a bed in an unused room nearby. She
went in and stood by the bed again, as she had been doing
most of the day. He looked at her, and shook his head
slightly. She spoke to him, over and over, but he said
nothing. She looked at Betsy and the doctors to see if it
was all right for her to sit on the side of the bed, and they
signified that it was, meaning that it made no difference.

In the wreckage of things, whirling like the driftage of
a river trapped and twisted in an eddy after the storm has
passed—so they were together for about an hour. After
that he slipped into a deep coma. His temperature had
passed a hundred and five degrees; all other signs were
consistent with what the doctors knew.

The coma lasted through Sunday night and all of Monday and most of Monday night. Early on that night Dr
Beale moved over from the room in which he had been
staying to a small room that had been put in readiness for
him down on the first floor of the hospital, not far from
the room that had been converted into Dr Novali's laboratory. Early Tuesday morning Louis died. It was still dark.
The sun had not yet risen even beyond the great plains to
the east, and Truchas was invisible. In all the night around
there was only the brightness that came from the floodlights in the Technical Area, where, behind the high steel
fence, the silent, secret work continued as before.

11

Going south from Santa Fe one road slants off west to Albuquerque and another road, slanting east through a desert land, sends an offshoot out to Lamy, twenty miles from the town it serves. Lamy is a few houses, a few sheds, one or two stores, and the Santa Fe Railroad station. The station platform is wide and smooth and long, and is indeed the noblest work in Lamy, except when the muttering Diesels roll in, as they do (or used to do) three times a day, pulling long trains of polished cars behind them. From the platform the trains are visible for a long way west; going east they lose themselves quickly in the abrupt hills that bring the Sangre de Cristro range, falling off from Truchas, to its southern end.

At a little before noon on Wednesday morning an Army ambulance came slowly along the road into Lamy; it passed the houses and sheds and stores, and just before the station it stopped. Three soldiers got out. One walked out onto the platform and looked along the tracks. The other two lit cigarettes and together walked back to the stores and houses. Under the hot sun the roof of the ambulance gave off a radiant shimmer of heat; and so half an hour passed in quiet, heat, and motionlessness.

Then an Army staff car came into the parking area. The two soldiers came running back. The staff car drew up beside the ambulance, and Colonel Hough and an Army Captain got out of it. Another car, an ordinary passenger car, entered the area and come to a stop nearby. From a great distance away came the faint bellow of the horn of the Chicago train.

Colonel Hough went over to the passenger car, and the soldier driver jumped out. He opened the rear door, took Mrs Saxl by the arm, and passed her on to the Colonel. He did the same with Libby and with Theresa. Mr Saxl

stepped out and stood blinking in the sun. David joined
him.

The horn bellowed again. The soldiers extracted luggage
from the sedan, took it to the platform, and assembled it
there. For a third time the horn bellowed and the nervous
muttering of the Diesel, slowing for its stop, was distinct;
everyone looked west; the train gleamed and glinted; nobody spoke. Except for the soldiers there was a general
movement out across the platform toward the tracks.

It had been Colonel Hough's idea that, if things were
planned properly, he might be able to get the coffin on
the train after "the family" and thus avoid griefs that, he
felt, would otherwise be unavoidable. The Santa Fe Railroad had been consulted by officers of the United States
Army, and the soldiers had been coached. Pursuant to the
plan, the soldiers by the ambulance made no move when
the train stopped. Pursuant to the plan—which, however,
not everyone was aware of—Colonel Hough began to exercise tactics of voice and body designed to get his charges
on the train. But Mr and Mrs Saxl, and Libby, and Theresa,
and David, and then the Army Captain, and then several
other people standing near, and finally Colonel Hough
himself, simply turned to face the ambulance, and stood,
and waited.

The soldiers, coached for what they had to do and trained
not to do otherwise, waited too. And the train waited.
Under the burning sun again there were only quiet, heat,
and motionlessness. Who could have foreseen such a perversity?

At last, quietly and with military bearing, Colonel Hough
walked across the platform to the ambulance and said
something to the soldiers. They opened the ambulance
doors immediately. There was a baggage truck near the
ambulance and one of the soldiers started to move it into
position. But Colonel Hough shook his head. Counting
the soldiers from the ambulance and the two soldier drivers, there were five; Colonel Hough made himself the

sixth. Together they got the coffin out of the ambulance. Walking very slowly, they carried it out onto the platform, and along the platform beside the train to the baggage car.

When the Colonel got back the Saxls and Theresa had boarded the train. The Army Captain had taken over the Colonel's shepherding functions. David stood by himself, looking out across the empty platform, as the Colonel joined him. They stood there together, watching, as the train began to move, gathered speed, and so began the long curve that would take it through the last of the mountain barrier out to the great plains stretching eastward.

"Will you drive back with me, Dave?" the Colonel asked at last.

"I think I'll take the fancy limousine, if you don't mind," David said.

The Colonel nodded.

"OK, fellow," he said. He gripped David's arm, then patted him two or three times on the back.

"I don't suppose you'd like to see the paper, doctor?" the soldier driving David's car asked after a few miles.

"Sure," said David, "let's see it."

David looked at it abstractedly. It had been folded to the sports page, and he read some of that. He put it down and looked out of the window for a while. Then he picked it up again and opened it to the front page.

The story of the accident had a prominent position under the heading, "Atom Bomb Scientist Dies; Six Saved." The accident had involved an experiment in which radiation was released in a brief flash; the experiment had been an important one in the development of the atomic bomb, although details concerning it could not, of course, be released. Most of the story concerned itself with the heroism of the young scientist who—at the cost of his own life—"tore the experimental structure apart and so saved the lives of his colleagues."

Again David put the paper down and looked out of the window. By this time the car had passed through Santa Fe, taken the long hill with which the road north from there begins, and was out on the floor of the valley. There was hardly a sign of life to be seen, except for a few roadrunners and the stunted tree-shrubs, brown with the faintest cast of green in them. The mountain ranges ran parallel to each other now on either side of the road, and the feeling began to grow on David, as it often did when he took this road, that something was bearing down on him, that something grooved and channeled a person when he took this road through the ancient land.